CATS OF SHADOW,
CLAWS OF DARKNESS

CATS OF SHADOW, CLAWS OF DARKNESS

Stories of Were-Cats, Ghost Cats, and other Supernatural Felines

CHAD ARMENT, EDITOR

COACHWHIP PUBLICATIONS

Landisville, Pennsylvania

CONTENTS

1780

THE KING OF THE CATS
THOMAS LYTTELTON

CREDULA TURBA SUMUS—We are a credulous race of beings; and the most steady professors of skepticism are deceived by others, and deceive themselves, every hour of the day. Religion, which commands, among its evident truths, the belief of matters which we cannot entirely comprehend, will sometimes so habituate the mind of its submissive disciple to acts of faith, that he does not know how to withhold his assent to the most improbable fictions of human fancy; and the *Credo quia impossibile est* of *Tertullian* is readily adopted by his yielding piety. I shall confirm the truth of this observation by a story which I have heard related, and is not more extraordinary in its nature than the tone, look, and language of belief which accompanied the relation. A traveller, benighted in a wild and mountainous country, (if my recollection does not fail me, in the Highlands of Scotland,) at length beholds the welcome light of a neighbouring habitation. He urges his horse towards it; when, instead of an house, he approached a kind of illuminated chapel, from whence issued the most alarming sounds he had ever heard. Though greatly surprised and terrified, he ventured to look through a window of the building, when he was amazed to see a large assembly of cats, who, arranged in solemn order, were lamenting over the corpse of one of their own species, which lay in state, and was surrounded with the various emblems of sovereignty.—Alarmed and terrified at this extraordinary spectacle, he hastened from the place with greater eagerness than he approached it; and arriving, some time after, at the house of a gentleman who

7

never turned the wanderer from his gate, the impressions of what he had seen were so visible on his countenance, that his friendly host enquired into the cause of his anxiety. He accordingly told his story, and, having finished it, a large family cat, who had lain, during the narrative, before the fire, immediately started up, and very articulately exclaimed, *"Then I am King of the Cats!"* and, having thus announced its new dignity, the animal darted up the chimney and was seen no more.

MURTOUGH MURPHY'S STORY
BEING YE MARVELLOUS LEGEND OF TOM CONNOR'S CAT
SAMUEL LOVER

"THERE WAS A MAN in these parts, sir, you must know, called Tom Connor, and he had a cat that was equal to any dozen of rat-traps, and he was proud of the baste, and with rayson; for she was worth her weight in goold to him in saving his sacks of meal from the thievery of the rats and mice; for Tom was an extensive dealer in corn, and influenced the rise and fall of that article in the market, to the extent of a full dozen of sacks at a time, which he either kept or sold, as the spirit of free trade or monopoly came over him. Indeed, at one time, Tom had serious thoughts of applying to the government for a military force to protect his granary when there was a threatened famine in the county."

"Pooh! pooh! sir," said the matter-of-fact little man: "as if a dozen sacks could be of the smallest consequence in a whole county—pooh! pooh!"

"Well, sir," said Murphy, "I can't help if you don't believe; but it's truth what I am telling you, and pray don't interrupt me, though you may not believe; by the time the story's done you'll have heard more wonderful things than *that*,—and besides, remember you're a stranger in these parts, and have no notion of the extraordinary things, physical, metaphysical, and magical, which constitute the idiosyncrasy of rural destiny."

The little man did not know the meaning of Murphy's last sentence—nor Murphy either; but, having stopped the little man's throat with big words, he proceeded—

9

"This cat, sir, you must know, was a great pet, and was so up to everything, that Tom swore she was a'most like a Christian, only she couldn't speak, and had so sensible a look in her eyes, that he was sartin sure the cat knew every word that was said to her. Well, she used to sit by him at breakfast every morning, and the eloquent cock of her tail, as she used to rub against his leg, said, 'Give me some milk, Tom Connor,' as plain as print, and the plenitude of her purr afterwards spoke a gratitude beyond language. Well, one morning, Tom was going to the neighbouring town to market, and he had promised the wife to bring home shoes to the childre' out o' the price of the corn; and sure enough, before he sat down to breakfast, there was Tom taking the measure of the children's feet, by cutting notches on a bit of stick; and the wife gave him so many cautions about getting a 'nate fit' for 'Billy's purty feet,' that Tom, in his anxiety to nick the closest possible measure, cut off the child's toe.

"That disturbed the harmony of the party, and Tom was obliged to breakfast alone, while the mother was endeavouring to cure Billy; in short, trying to make a *heal* of his *toe*. Well, sir, all the time Tom was taking measure for the shoes, the cat was observing him with that luminous peculiarity of eye for which her tribe is remarkable; and when Tom sat down to breakfast the cat rubbed up against him more vigorously than usual; but Tom, being bewildered between his expected gain in corn and the positive loss of his child's toe, kept never minding her, until the cat, with a sort of caterwauling growl, gave Tom a dab of her claws, that went clean through his leathers, and a little further. 'Wow!' says Tom, with a jump, clapping his hand on the part, and rubbing it, 'by this and that, you drew the blood out o' me,' says Tom; 'you wicked divil—tish!—go along!' says he, making a kick at her. With that the cat gave a reproachful look at him, and her eyes glared just like a pair of mail-coach lamps in a fog. With that, sir, the cat, with a mysterious 'mi-ow' fixed a most penetrating glance on Tom, and distinctly uttered his name.

"Tom felt every hair on his head as stiff as a pump-handle; and scarcely crediting his ears, he returned a searching look at the cat, who very quietly proceeded in a sort of nasal twang—

"'Tom Connor,' says she.

"'The Lord be good to me!' says Tom, 'if it isn't spakin' she is!'

"'Tom Connor,' says she again.

"'Yes, ma'am,' says Tom.

"'Come here,' says she; 'whisper—I want to talk to you, Tom,' says she, 'the laste taste in private,' says she—rising on her hams, and beckoning him with her paw out o' the door, with a wink and a toss o' the head aiqual to a milliner.

"Well, as you may suppose, Tom didn't know whether he was on his head or his heels, but he followed the cat, and off she went and squatted herself under the edge of a little paddock at the back of Tom's house; and as he came round the corner, she held up her paw again, and laid it on her mouth, as much as to say, 'Be cautious, Tom.' Well, divil a word Tom could say at all, with the fright, so up he goes to the cat, and says she—

"'Tom,' says she, 'I have a great respect for you, and there's something I must tell you, becase you're losing character with your neighbours,' says she, 'by your goin's on,' says she, 'and it's out o' the respect that I have for you, that I must tell you,' says she.

"'Thank you, ma'am,' says Tom.

"'You're goin' off to the town,' says she, 'to buy shoes for the childre',' says she, 'and never thought o' gettin' me a pair.'

"'You!' says Tom.

"'Yis, me, Tom Connor,' says she; 'and the neighbours wondhers that a respectable man like you allows your cat to go about the counthry barefutted,' says she.

"'Is it a cat to ware shoes?' says Tom.

"'Why not?' says she; 'doesn't horses ware shoes?—and I have a prettier foot than a horse, I hope,' says she, with a toss of her head.

"'Faix, she spakes like a woman; so proud of her feet,' says Tom to himself, astonished, as you may suppose, but pretending never to think it remarkable all the time; and so he went on discoursin'; and says he, 'It's thrue for you, ma'am,' says he, 'that horses wares shoes—but that stands to rayson, ma'am, you see—seeing the hardship their feet has to go through on the hard roads.'

"'And how do you know what hardship my feet has to go through?' says the cat, mighty sharp.

"'But, ma'am,' says Tom, 'I don't well see how you could fasten a shoe on you,' says he.

"'Lave that to me,' says the cat.

"'Did any one ever stick walnut shells on you, pussy?' says Tom, with a grin.

"'Don't be disrespectful, Tom Connor,' says the cat, with a frown.

"'I ax your pard'n, ma'am,' says he, 'but as for the horses you wor spakin' about wearin' shoes, you know their shoes is fastened on with nails, and how would your shoes be fastened on?'

"'Ah, you stupid thief!' says she, 'haven't I illigant nails o' my own?' and with that she gave him a dab of her claw, that made him roar.

"'Ow! murdher!' says he.

"'Now, no more of your palaver, Misther Connor,' says the cat; 'just be off and get me the shoes.'

"'Tare an' ouns!' says Tom, 'what'll become o' me if I'm to get shoes for my cats?' says he, 'for you increase your family four times a year, and you have six or seven every time,' says he; 'and then you must all have two pair a piece—wirra! wirra!—I'll be ruined in shoe-leather,' says Tom.

"'No more o' your stuff,' says the cat; 'don't be stand in' here undher the hedge talkin', or we'll lose our karacthers—for I've re-marked your wife is jealous, Tom.'

"''Pon my sowl, that's thrue,' says Tom, with a smirk.

"'More fool she,' says the cat, 'for, 'pon my conscience, Tom, you're as ugly as if you wor bespoke.'

"Off ran the cat with these words, leaving Tom in amazement. He said nothing to the family, for fear of fright'ning them, and off he went to the *town* as he *pretended*—for he saw the cat watching him through a hole in the hedge; but when he came to a turn at the end of the road, the dickings a mind he minded the market, good or bad, but went off to Squire Botherum's, the magisthrit, to sware examinations agen the cat."

"Pooh! pooh!—nonsense!!" broke in the little man, who had lis-tened thus far to Murtough with an expression of mingled wonder and contempt, while the rest of the party willingly gave up the reins to nonsense, and enjoyed Murtough's Legend and their companion's more absurd common sense.

"Don't interrupt him, Goggins," said Mister Wiggins.

"How can you listen to such nonsense?" returned Goggins. "Swear examinations against a cat, indeed! pooh! pooh!"

"My dear sir," said Murtough, "remember this is a fair story, and that the country all around here is full of enchantment. As I was telling you, Tom went off to swear examinations."

"Ay, ay!" shouted all but Goggins; "go on with the story."

"And when Tom was asked to relate the events of the morning, which brought him before Squire Botherum, his brain was so bewildered between his corn, and his cat, and his child's toe, that he made a very confused account of it.

"'Begin your story from the beginning,' said the magistrate to Tom.

"'Well, your honour,' says Tom, 'I was goin' to market this mornin', to sell the child's corn—I beg your pard'n—my own toes, I mane, sir.'

"'Sell your toes!' said the Squire.

"'No, sir, takin' the cat to market, I mane—'

"'Take a cat to market!' said the Squire. 'You're drunk, man.'

"'No, your honour, only confused a little; for when the toes began to spake to me—the cat, I mane—I was bothered clane—'

"'The cat speak to you!' said the Squire. 'Phew! worse than before—you're drunk, Tom.'

"'No, your honour; it's on the strength of the cat I come to spake to you—'

"'I think it's on the strength of a pint of whisky, Tom—'

"'By the vartue o' my oath, your honour, it's nothin' but the cat.' And so Tom then told him all about the affair, and the Squire was regularly astonished. Just then the bishop of the diocese and the priest of the parish happened to call in, and heard the story; and the bishop and the priest had a tough argument for two hours on the subject; the former swearing she must be a witch; but the priest denying *that*, and maintaining she was *only* enchanted; and that part of the argument was afterwards referred to the primate, and subsequently to the conclave at Rome; but the Pope declined interfering about cats, saying he had quite enough to do minding his own bulls.

"'In the meantime, what are we to do with the cat?' says Botherum.

"'Burn her,' says the bishop, 'she's a witch.'

"'*Only* enchanted,' said the priest— 'and the ecclesiastical court maintains that—'

"'Bother the ecclesiastical court!' said the magistrate; 'I can only proceed on the statutes;' and with that he pulled down all the law-books in his library, and hunted the laws from Queen Elizabeth down, and he found that they made laws against everything in Ireland, *except a cat*. The devil a thing escaped them but a cat, which did *not* come within the meaning of any act of parliament:—*the cats only had escaped*.

"'There's the alien act, to be sure,' said the magistrate, 'and perhaps she's a French spy, in disguise.'

"'She spakes like a French spy, sure enough,' says Tom; 'and she was missin', I remember, all last Spy-Wednesday.'

"'That's suspicious,' says the squire— 'but conviction might be difficult; and I have a fresh idea,' says Botherum.

"'Faith, it won't keep fresh long, this hot weather,' says Tom; 'so your honour had betther make use of it at wanst.'

"'Right,' says Botherum,— 'we'll make her subject to the game laws; we'll hunt her,' says he.

"'Ow!—elegant!' says Tom;— 'we'll have a brave run out of her.'

"'Meet me at the cross roads,' says the Squire, 'in the morning, and I'll have the hounds ready.'

"'Well, off Tom went home; and he was racking his brain what excuse he could make to the cat for not bringing the shoes; and at last he hit one off, just as he saw her cantering up to him, half-a-mile before he got home.

"'Where's the shoes, Tom?' says she.

"'I have not got them to-day, ma'am,' says he.

"'Is that the way you keep your promise, Tom?' says she;— 'I'll tell you what it is, Tom—I'll tare the eyes out o' the childre' if you don't get me shoes.'

"'Whisht! whisht!' says Tom, frightened out of his life for his children's eyes. 'Don't be in a passion, pussy. The shoemaker said he had not a shoe in his shop, nor a last that would make one to fit you; and he says, I must bring you into the town for him to take your measure.'

"'And when am I to go?' says the cat, looking savage.

"'To-morrow,' says Tom.

"'It's well you said that, Tom,' said the cat, 'or the devil an eye I'd leave in your family this night'—and off she hopped.

"Tom thrimbled at the wicked look she gave.

"'Remember!' says she, over the hedge, with a bitter caterwaul.

"'Never fear,' says Tom. Well, sure enough, the next mornin' there was the cat at cock-crow, licking herself as nate as a new pin, to go into the town, and out came Tom with a bag undher his arm, and the cat afther him.

"'Now git into this, and I'll carry you into the town,' says Tom, opening the bag.

"'Sure I can walk with you,' says the cat.

"'Oh, that wouldn't do,' says Tom; 'the people in the town is curious and slandherous people, and sure it would rise ugly remarks if I was seen with a cat afther me:—a dog is a man's companion by nature, but cats does not stand to rayson.'

"Well, the cat, seeing there was no use in argument, got into the bag, and off Tom set to the cross roads with the bag over his shoulder, and he came up, *quite innocent-like*, to the corner, where the Squire, and his huntsman, and the hounds, and a pack o' people were waitin'. Out came the Squire on a sudden, just as if it was all by accident.

"'God save you, Tom,' says he.

"'God save you kindly, sir,' says Tom.

"'What's that bag you have at your back?' says the Squire.

"'Oh, nothin' at all, sir,' says Tom—makin' a face all the time, as much as to say, I have her safe.

"'Oh, there's something in that bag, I think,' says the Squire; 'and you must let me see it.'

"'If you bethray me, Tom Connor,' says the cat in a low voice, 'by this and that I'll never spake to you again!'

"'Pon my honour, sir,' said Tom, with a wink and a twitch of his thumb towards the bag, 'I haven't anything in it.'

"'I have been missing my praties of late,' says the Squire; 'and I'd just like to examine that bag,' says he.

"'Is it doubting my charackther you'd be, sir?' says Tom, pretending to be in a passion.

"'Tom, your sowl!' says the voice in the sack, '*if you let the cat out of the bag*, I'll murther you.'

"'An honest man would make no objection to be sarched,' said the Squire; 'and I insist on it,' says he, laying hold o' the bag, and Tom purtending to fight all the time; but, my jewel! before two minutes, they shook the cat out o' the bag, sure enough, and off she went with her tail as big as a sweeping brush, and the Squire, with a thundering view halloo after her, clapt the dogs at her heels, and away they went for the bare life. Never was there seen such running as that day—the cat made for a shaking bog, the loneliest place in the whole country, and there the riders were all thrown out, barrin' the huntsman, who had a web-footed horse on purpose for soft places; and the priest, whose horse could go anywhere by reason of the priest's blessing; and, sure enough, the huntsman and his riverence stuck to the hunt like wax; and just as the cat got on the border of the bog, they saw her give a twist as the foremost dog closed with her, for he gave her a nip in the flank. Still she went on, however, and headed them well, towards an old mud cabin in the middle of the bog, and there they saw her jump in at the window, and up came the dogs the next minit, and gathered round the house with the most horrid howling ever was heard. The huntsman alighted, and went into the house to turn the cat out again, when what should he see but an old hag lying in bed in the corner?

"'Did you see a cat come in here?' says he.

"'Oh, no—o—o—o!' squealed the old hag, in a trembling voice; 'there's no cat here,' says she.

"'Yelp, yelp, yelp!' went the dogs outside.

"'Oh, keep the dogs out o' this,' says the old hag— 'oh—o—o—o!' and the huntsman saw her eyes glare under the blanket, just like a cat's.

"'Hillo!' says the huntsman, pulling down the blanket—and what should he see but the old hag's flank all in a gore of blood.

"'Ow, ow! you old divil—is it you? you ould cat!' says he, opening the door.

"In rushed the dogs—up jumped the old hag, and changing into a cat before their eyes, out she darted through the window again, and made another run for it; but she couldn't escape, and the dogs gobbled her while you could say 'Jack Robinson.' But the most remarkable part of this extraordinary story, gentlemen, is, that the pack was ruined from that day out; for after having eaten the enchanted cat, *the devil a thing they would ever hunt afterwards but mice.*"

1883

THE MAN-TIGER
H. Wellington Vrooman

IT WAS THE FIRST TIME I had succeeded in getting my old friend, Major Melville, to leave the house since his return from India. He had remained shut up indoors like a monk, and, until this particular night, had obstinately refused to accept of any of the invitations from his former friends and acquaintances in the shire, so that all of us were completely in the dark as to why, when he was winning a name and rapid promotion, being advanced from a simple Ensign to Major of the 5th Bengal Artillery, and would probably have won the epaulettes of General, in another year, or two, he had abruptly thrown up his commission and left India, to shut himself up in his dead father's house here in the town of Milton, Somersetshire.

But tonight he had surprised me by coming to take dinner, after which Jack Burrows, himself, and I sat smoking around the fire in the library. During the conversation Jack, who had never been in India, happened to speak of the Hindoo belief in transmigration—the passing after death of one's soul into the body of some animal. "You needn't laugh at it," abruptly said the major. "There are stranger things in the world than you fellows here at home dream of. Now, I believe I'll tell you a story, which is true, on my honor as a gentleman."

We both hastened to assure the major that nothing would give us greater pleasure than his story, and so after filling his narglieh again, he began, with his eyes fixed on the fire:

"What I'm about to tell happened within the last year of my stay in India, and since I'm to tell you of it, you may give it more attention and thought if you know that the strange circumstances of the affair determined me to resign my commission and return to England."

Both Jack and myself here stared at him in amazement, and then at each other for a moment or two. We were after all to learn the reason of his return.

"The beginning of it," continued the major, still gazing into the fire, "was one day in May, '69.

"I was then stationed with my regiment in Mysore. We hadn't much to do, being the garrison of the fort, and the boys used to do considerable roaming around the country about, hunting and exploring the wonderful ruins that one stumbles upon in almost every square mile of the province. On this particular day I started out with a brother officer named Phillips, up the river after the water buffaloes, which are sometimes found in the marshy jungles further up, toward the Mellajella Mountains.

"After our servants had rowed us up the river eight miles, we left some them on the bank and started out, with one Hindoo each, into the jungles that stretched ahead to the north.

"Phillips' man was a wiry old Shikarri, who had hunted everything from a Bengal tiger to a mad elephant, while mine was the son of a Buddhist priest in a little village near Mysore.

"He was a handsome, pleasant, faithful fellow of some twenty five years, but he had been in my service only a short time, and I had not taken much notice of him.

"We pushed ahead, sometimes up to our waists in water, and sometimes cutting our way through the thicket with our axes, until Phillips, who led the party, suddenly stopped at the edge of a clump of trees and cane, and motioned to us to come up noiselessly. When we reached him, he silently pointed ahead across a stretch of open water, to a small island, some two hundred yards ahead, where, his head turned the other way, stood the largest buffalo I had ever seen. He was feeding on the young shoots of cane, and evidently suspected nothing of our presence.

"Phillips motioned us to the right, and took the left himself, and we separated, each one wading noiselessly across the sheet of water, which was only up to our armpits.

"I had gotten within fifty yards of the buffalo, and was about to fire, having a good show at his side, when Phillips' rifle rang out, and the great animal pitched forward on his knees, and then fell heavily over on its side, evidently dead. I was just starting toward it, with a shout of congratulation, when directly before me, from the muddy water rose an object that made me almost give a yell of terror. There, not more than two feet from me, was an enormous crocodile, its gnarled head raised fully two feet above the surface, and he gazed at me with his dull, filmy eyes.

"Before I could recover from my surprise and terror, he began to paddle toward me, his upper jaw lifting until his great mouthful of jagged teeth were yawning before my face.

"This acted as a reviver, and raising my rifle, I fired almost point blank down his throat, but to my horror, the monster only shut his jaws with a snap, as if tasting the bullet, and then opening them again, started ahead.

"I hadn't time to load again, so I pitched my rifle into the yawning chasm, and turned toward the shore. But I had not gone a dozen feet when I looked around, and saw the crocodile within an arm's length of me.

"He bent over a little to one side to seize me around the waist, and in another instant there would have been two pieces of me, when the dark form of my servant, Byndar, dashed forward from somewhere, I didn't see where, and threw himself between us.

"As I stared at him he thrust his hand, in which he grasped his long, thick knife, which he used for cutting our way through the jungle, down the very throat of the reptile.

"Its jaws shut with terrible force, and I expected to see the faithful fellow's arm cut off at the shoulder. But, instead, the knife, which he had held firmly upright, the hilt actually resting on the lower jaw of the crocodile, pierced the upper jaw, and such was the force with which the monster had closed it, that the point of the weapon went clear through the roof of his mouth and came out through the scales on top, the blade sticking up like the horn of a rhinoceros.

"This was a mouthful the brute couldn't swallow, and he turned completely over, lashing the water to a foam with his tail, then came up gnashing his jaws, but only driving the knife more firmly into its place.

"We both threw ourselves up in the water and struck out for shore, which we reached without pursuit from the reptile, who was alternately standing on his head, and then on his tail, and then turning hand springs and circles with the fury and rapidity of a wounded anaconda.

"Finally it sank and we saw it no more.

"Phillips appeared on the island where his buffalo lay just in time to witness the last struggles of the wounded monster, and immediately left for the shore without waiting for anything, which was lucky for him, for the pool was evidently a regular crocodiles' nest, half a dozen of the brutes appearing where their wounded comrade had sunk, evidently bent on making a meal off him.

"From that day Byndar was appointed my body guard and companion everywhere that a native could go. I felt the deepest gratitude toward the faithful fellow, and soon learned to care for him as if he were almost a brother, while he in turn fairly worshiped the ground I walked on.

"This ends the first part of my story.

"Things went on as usual for some six months, my time being taken up either with drills, inspections, and garrison work generally, or in hunting expeditions, on which Byndar always accompanied me, and more than once proved himself a man of rare courage and sagacity.

"During this time his older brother, Merinjel, came to Mysore and entered the service of Phillips upon my warmly recommending him, which I did on the idea that the brother of such a treasure as Byndar must be at least of more than usual worth.

"Besides, he was a fellow of great plausibility, and completely deceived me, as I know now.

"Now Byndar, although always victor in the chase, had himself fallen a victim to a beautiful Hindoo girl, the maid of our colonel's

wife. I say she was beautiful, because I never saw such a face and
figure, either in Europe or India, as that girl possessed. She was
almost white in color, with lustrous black eyes, perfect features,
and a lithe, graceful form Diana herself could not have excelled.

"Byndar, being a fellow of no small physical attractions, and
withal a man of unusual education, being the son of a priest, evidently soon won the heart of the beautiful maid, and the colonel
and I were resigning ourselves to the inevitable marriage of the
two, and the consequent loss of such valuable attendants, when
one morning, Byndar was found near the colonel's house dead—
stabbed through the heart. No cause could be assigned for the
crime, he being a universal favorite, and deep was the mourning
in the garrison, and none so loud or frantic in his lamentations as
his brother, who vowed to devote his life to finding the murderer.
In fact, he was so loud in his grief that he aroused my suspicions,
and as far as I could see, he devoted his entire time, when Phillips
didn't need him, to hanging around the colonel's house and making
desperate love to the disconsolate Avesta, who at last seemed to
accept him in place of his murdered brother.

"We all laughed at the old story of woman's inconstancy, yet
thought that after all it was the best thing that could happen if the
brother could take poor Byndar's place. The affair went on, and I
believe they were to be married in a month, when I started one day
on a visit to some new ruins that had been discovered in the jungle
about fifteen miles from the city.

"Phillips insisted on going with me, since I had no body servant, and so with him and half a dozen others, I started forth, and
reached the ruins about five o'clock, without any adventure of any
sort on the way there.

"I found them to be the remains of what had once been a great
city, but probably nothing but ruins for thousands of years back.
In the center of the apparently endless waste of tumble down walls
and broken cellars, we came upon what had evidently been the
central temple of Brahma, still in tolerable preservation. Leaving
all but one man outside, to eat their dinners, I went into the great
hall accompanied by a single Shikarri, carrying my rifle. We found

nothing of special interest, and were sitting on the steps of the altar, resting, when the man uttered an exclamation of horror, and stared into the gloom in one corner of the hall.

"As I followed his gaze, I saw two fiery eyes gleaming through the darkness, and, before either one of us could move, an enormous tiger walked out into the dim light which came through the door and stood before us a moment, looking at me.

"I was utterly paralyzed, and made no effort to defend myself, while the Shikarri fell on his face and covered his head with his cotton cloak, expecting, as I did, to be crunched between the great jaws of the beast the next instant.

"To my dumb amazement, the tiger, however, began to purr like a cat, and, crouching down at my feet, began to lick my hand and then to gambol about me as if greatly delighted with me. At last I sat still, hardly believing my senses, but I could not deny but that the great animal was most amicably inclined, and was doing his best to show it.

"Was it a tame animal? I looked more carefully at its face, and, to my surprise, it seemed familiar. Where had I seen the brute before? Its eyes were almost human in their affectionate, intelligent expression, and, besides—

"'Why, they are Byndar's eyes!' I muttered, stupidly gazing in surprise at them. As the tiger heard this name, he showed the most extravagant light of joy, rubbing his head against my knees and purring louder than ever. Finally, it stuck its nose under my legs and fairly lifted me to my feet and pushed me toward the door, as if wanting me to go out with him. I walked on, as if in a dream, followed by the Shikarri, who was in abject terror. The tiger, when he had started us, trotted ahead and appeared on the platform first, looking around and purring as he went. But the moment he caught sight of my attendants, sitting on the blocks of stone outside, his whole being seemed to change. He uttered an angry roar, his tail swayed back and forth until it lashed his sides, and, crouching down, he glared at the party before him.

"I looked at them and noticed that one was affected in a remarkable way by the sudden appearance of the brute. Instead of grasping his gun like the rest, he uttered one word, 'Byndar!' and fell on his knees, with hands outstretched as if praying for mercy. The next moment, as I recovered suddenly from the strange spell the brute had cast upon me and had raised my rifle to my shoulder, the great animal sprang from the platform and landed upon the miserable Merinjel, whom he felled with one terrible blow.

"At the same moment I fired, and the brute rolled over, shot through the back of the head.

"When I hastened down to the victim I found him dead, his skull being crushed in by the blow. Turning to the tiger, I bent over him to cut his throat, thinking him also dead, when he raised up a little, looked up at me with eyes that again made me stupefied by their strange resemblance to those of dead Byndar, and with a last effort licked my hand."

"And you don't mean to say that you believe the soul of the murdered Byndar was inhabiting that tiger, do you?" ejaculated the minister, after a pause of several minutes, during which the major sat staring into the fire.

"You can judge for yourself—who knows!" said the major, in a low soft tone, and, rising, he left us without a single word, and went out into the storm.

1896

THE MAN AT THE NEXT TABLE
Robert W. Chambers

I

IT WAS HIGH NOON in the city of Antwerp. From slender steeples
floated the mellow music of the Flemish bells, and in the spire of
the great cathedral across the square the cracked chimes clashed
discords until my ears ached.

When the fiend in the cathedral had jerked the last tuneless
clang from the chimes, I removed my fingers from my ears and sat
down at one of the iron tables in the court. A waiter with his face
shaved blue, brought me a bottle of Rhine wine, a tumbler of
cracked ice, and a siphon.

"Does Monsieur desire anything else?" he inquired.

"Yes—the head of the cathedral bell-ringer; bring it with vinegar
and potatoes," I said, bitterly. Then I began to ponder on my great-
aunt and the Crimson Diamond.

The white walls of the Hotel St. Antoine rose in a rectangle
around the sunny court, casting long shadows across the basin of
the fountain. The strip of blue overhead was cloudless. Sparrows
twittered under the eaves; the yellow awnings fluttered, the flowers
swayed in the summer breeze, and the jet of the fountain splashed
among the water plants. On the sunny side of the *piazza* the tables
were vacant; on the shady side, I was lazily aware that the tables
behind me were occupied, but I was indifferent as to their occu-
pants, partly because I shunned all tourists, partly because I was
thinking of my great-aunt.

Most old ladies are eccentric, but there is a limit, and my great-aunt had overstepped it. I had believed her to be wealthy;—she died bankrupt. Still, I knew there was one thing she did possess, and that was the famous "Crimson Diamond." Now, of course, you know who my great-aunt was.

Excepting the Koh-i-noor, and the Regent, this enormous and unique stone was, as everybody knows, the most valuable gem in existence. Any ordinary person would have placed that diamond in a safe-deposit. My great-aunt did nothing of the kind. She kept it in a small velvet bag, which she carried about her neck. She never took it off, but wore it dangling openly on her heavy silk gown.

In this same bag she also carried dried catnip leaves of which she was inordinately fond. Nobody but myself, her only living relative, knew that the Crimson Diamond lay among the sprigs of catnip in the little velvet bag.

"Harold," she would say, "do you think I'm a fool? If I place the Crimson Diamond in any safe-deposit vault in New York, somebody would steal it sooner or later." Then she would nibble a sprig of catnip and peer cunningly at me. I loathed the odour of catnip and she knew it. I also loathed cats. This also she knew and of course surrounded herself with a dozen. Poor old lady! On the 1st day of March, 1896, she was found dead in her bed in her apartments at the Waldorf. The doctor said she died from natural causes. The only other occupant of her sleeping room was a cat. The cat fled when we broke open the door, and I heard that she was received and cherished by some people in a neighboring apartment.

Now, although my great-aunt's death was due to purely natural causes, there was one very startling and disagreeable feature of the case. The velvet bag, containing the Crimson Diamond, had disappeared. Every inch of the apartment was searched, the floors torn up, the walls dismantled, but the Crimson Diamond had vanished. Chief of Police Conlin detailed four of his best men on the case, and as I had nothing better to do, I enrolled myself as a volunteer. I also offered $25,000 reward for the recovery of the gem. All New York was agog.

The case seemed hopeless enough, although there were five of us after the thief. McFarlane was in London, and had been for a month, but Scotland Yard could give him no help, and the last I heard of him he was roaming through Surrey after a man with a white spot in his hair. Harrison had gone to Paris. He kept writing me that clues were plenty and the scent hot, but as Dennet, in Berlin, and Clancy, in Vienna, wrote me the same thing, I began to doubt these gentlemen's ability.

"You say," I answered Harrison, "that the fellow is a Frenchman, and that he is now concealed in Paris; but Dennet writes me by the same mail that the thief is undoubtedly a German, and was seen yesterday in Berlin. To-day I received a letter from Clancy, assuring me that Vienna holds the culprit, and that he is an Austrian from Trieste. Now for Heaven's sake," I ended, "let me alone and stop writing me letters until you have something to write about."

The night clerk of the Waldorf had furnished us with our first clue. On the night of my aunt's death he had seen a tall, grave-faced man, hurriedly leave the hotel. As the man passed the desk, he removed his hat and mopped his forehead, and the night clerk noticed that in the middle of his head there was a patch of hair, as white as snow.

We worked this clue for all it was worth, and, a month later, I received a cable dispatch from Paris, saying that a man, answering to the description of the Waldorf suspect, had offered an enormous crimson diamond for sale to a jeweller in the Palais Royal. Unfortunately the fellow took fright and disappeared before the jeweller could send for the police, and since that time, McFarlane in London, Harrison in Paris, Dennet in Berlin, and Clancy in Vienna, had been chasing men with white patches on their hair until no gray-headed patriarch in Europe was free from suspicion. I myself had sleuthed it through England, France, Holland and Belgium, and now I found myself in Antwerp at the Hotel St. Antoine without a clue that promised anything except another outrage on some respectable white-haired citizen. The case seemed hopeless enough, unless the thief tried again to sell the gem. Here was our only hope, for, unless he cut the stone into smaller ones, he had no more chance of selling it than he would have had if he had stolen the Venus of Milo and peddled her about the rue de Seine. Even were he to cut up the stone, no respectable gem collector or jeweller would buy a crimson diamond without first notifying me; for although a few red stones are known to collectors, the colour of the Crimson Diamond was absolutely unique, and there was little probability of an honest mistake.

Thinking of all these things I sat sipping my Rhine wine in the shadow of the yellow awnings. A large white cat came sauntering by and stopped in front of me to perform her toilet until I wished she would go away. After a while she sat up, licked her whiskers, yawned once or twice, and was about to stroll on, when, catching sight of me, she stopped short and looked me squarely in the face. I returned the attention with a scowl because I wished to discourage any advances towards social intercourse which she might contemplate; but after a while her steady gaze disconcerted me, and I turned to my Rhine wine. A few minutes later I looked up again. The cat was still eyeing me.

"Now what the devil is the matter with the animal," I muttered, "does she recognize in me a relative?"

"Perhaps," observed a man at the next table.

"What do you mean by that?" I demanded.

"What I say," replied the man at the next table.

I looked him full in the face. He was old and bald and appeared weak-minded. His age protected his impudence. I turned my back on him. Then my eyes fell on the cat again. She was still gazing earnestly at me.

Disgusted that she should take such pointed public notice of me, I wondered whether other people saw it; I wondered whether there was anything peculiar in my own personal appearance. How hard the creature stared. It was most embarrassing.

"What has got into that cat?" I thought. "It's sheer impudence. It's an intrusion, and I won't stand it!" The cat did not move. I tried to stare her out of countenance. It was useless. There was aggressive inquiry in her yellow eyes. A sensation of uneasiness began to steal over me—a sensation of embarrassment not unmixed with awe. All cats looked alike to me, and yet there was something about this one that bothered me—something that I could not explain to myself, but which began to occupy me.

She looked familiar—this Antwerp cat. An odd sense of having seen her before—of having been well acquainted with her in former years slowly settled in my mind, and, although I could never remember the time when I had not detested cats, I was almost convinced that my relations with this Antwerp tabby had once been intimate if not cordial. I looked more closely at the animal. Then an idea struck me,—an idea which persisted and took definite shape in spite of me. I strove to escape from it, to evade it, to stifle and smother it; an inward struggle ensued which brought the perspiration in beads upon my cheeks,—a struggle short, sharp, decisive. It was useless—useless to try to put it from me,—this idea so wretchedly bizarre, so grotesque and fantastic, so utterly inane,— it was useless to deny that the cat bore a distinct resemblance to my great-aunt!

I gazed at her in horror. What enormous eyes the creature had!

"Blood is thicker than water," said the man at the next table.

"What does he mean by that?" I muttered, angrily swallowing a tumbler of Rhine wine and seltzer. But I did not turn. What was the use?

"Chattering old imbecile," I added to myself, and struck a match, for my cigar was out; but as I raised the match to relight it, I encountered the cat's eyes again. I could not enjoy my cigar with the animal staring at me, but I was justly indignant, and I did not intend to be routed. "The idea! forced to leave for a cat!" I sneered, "we will see who will be the one to go!" I tried to give her a jet of seltzer from the siphon, but the bottle was too nearly empty to carry far. Then I attempted to lure her nearer, calling her in French, German, and English, but she did not stir. I did not know the Flemish for "cat."

"She's got a name, and won't come," I thought. "Now, what under the sun can I call her?"

"Aunty," suggested the man at the next table.

I sat perfectly still. Could that man have answered my thoughts?
—for I had not spoken aloud. Of course not—it was a coincidence,—
but a very disgusting one.

"Aunty," I repeated mechanically, "aunty, aunty—good gracious, how horribly human that cat looks!" Then somehow or other,
Shakespeare's words crept into my head and I found myself repeating: "the soul of his grandam might happily inhabit a bird; the
soul of his grandam might happily inhabit a bird; the soul of—nonsense!" I growled— "it isn't printed correctly! One might possibly
say, speaking in poetical metaphor, that the soul of a bird might
happily inhabit one's grandam—" I stopped short, flushing painfully. "What awful rot!" I murmured, and lighted another cigar.
The cat was still staring; the cigar went out. I grew more and more
nervous. "What rot!" I repeated. "Pythagoras must have been an
ass, but I do believe that there are plenty of asses alive to-day who
swallow that sort of thing."

"Who knows," sighed the man at the next table, and I sprang to
my feet and wheeled about. But I only caught a glimpse of a pair of
frayed coat-tails and a bald head vanishing into the dining-room.
I sat down again, thoroughly indignant. A moment later the cat
got up and went away.

II

DAYLIGHT WAS FADING in the city of Antwerp. Down into the sea sank
the sun, tinting the vast horizon with flakes of crimson, and touching with rich deep undertones the tossing waters of the Scheldt.
Its glow fell like a rosy mantle over red-tiled roofs and meadows;
and through the haze the spires of twenty churches pierced the air
like sharp, gilded flames. To the west and south the green plains,
over which the Spanish armies tramped so long ago, stretched away
until they met the sky; the enchantment of the afterglow had turned
old Antwerp into fairyland; and sea and sky and plain were beautiful and vague as the night mists floating in the moats below.

Along the sea-wall from the Rubens Gate, all Antwerp strolled,
and chattered, and flirted and sipped their Flemish wines from
slender Flemish glasses or gossiped over krugs of foaming beer.

From the Scheldt came the cries of sailors, the creaking of cordage, and the puff! puff! of the ferry-boats. On the bastions of the fortress opposite a bugler was standing. Twice the mellow notes of the bugle came faintly over the water, then a great gun thundered from the ramparts, and the Belgian flag fluttered along the lanyards to the ground.

I leaned listlessly on the sea-wall and looked down at the Scheldt below. A battery of artillery was embarking for the fortress. The tublike transport lay hissing and whistling in the slip, and the stamping of horses, the rumbling of gun and caisson, and the sharp cries of the officers came plainly to the ear.

When the last caisson was aboard and stowed, and the last trooper had sprung jingling to the deck, the transport puffed out into the Scheldt, and I turned away through the throng of promenaders, and found a little table on the terrace, just outside of the pretty café. And as I sat down, I became aware of a girl at the next table—a girl all in white—the most ravishingly and distractingly pretty girl that I had ever seen. In the agitation of the moment I forgot that I was a woman-hater, I forgot my name, my fortune, my aunt, and the Crimson Diamond—all these I forgot in a purely human impulse to see clearly; and to that end I removed my monocle from my left eye. Some moments later I came to myself and feebly replaced it. It was too late; the mischief was done. I was not aware at first of the exact state of my feelings,—for I had never before been in love—but I did know that at her request I would have been proud to stand on my head, or turn a flip-flap into the Scheldt.

I did not stare at her, but I managed to see her most of the time when her eyes were in another direction. I found myself drinking something which a waiter brought presumably upon an order which I did not remember having given. Later I noticed that it was a loathsome drink which the Belgians call "American Grog," but I swallowed it and lighted a cigarette. As the fragrant cloud rose in the air, a voice, which I recognized with a chill, broke into my dream of enchantment. Could *he* have been there all the while,—there sitting beside that vision in white? His hat was off, and the ocean breezes whispered about his bald head. His frayed coat-tails were folded carefully over his knees, and between the thumb and fore-finger of his left hand he balanced a bad cigar. He looked at me in a mildly cheerful way, and said, "I know now."

"Know what?" I asked, thinking it better to humour him, for I was convinced that he was mad.

"I know why cats bite."

This was startling. I hadn't the vaguest idea what to say.

"I know why," he repeated; "can you guess why?" There was a covert tone of triumph in his voice and he smiled encouragement. "Come, try and guess," he urged.

I was uneasy, but I told him with stiff civility that I was un-equal to problems.

"Listen, young man," he continued, folding his coat-tails closely about his legs— "try to reason it out; why should cats bite? Don't you know? I do."

He looked at me anxiously.

"You take no interest in this problem?" he demanded.

"Oh, yes."

"Then why do you not ask me why?" he said, looking vaguely disappointed.

"Well," I said in desperation, "why do cats bite?—hang it all!" I thought, "it's like a burnt-cork show, and I'm Mr. Bones and he's Tambo!"

Then he smiled gently. "Young man," he said, "cats bite because they feed on cat-nip. I have reasoned it out."

I stared at him in blank astonishment. Was this benevolent looking old party poking fun at me? Was he paying me up for the morning's snub? Was he a malignant and revengeful old party, or was he merely feeble-minded? Who might he be? What was he doing here in Antwerp—what was he doing now!—for the bald one had turned familiarly to the beautiful girl in white.

"Elsie," he said, "do you feel chilly?"

The girl shook her head.

"Not in the least, papa."

"Good Lord!" I thought— "her father!"

"I have been to the Zoo to-day," announced the bald one, turning toward me.

"Ah, indeed," I observed,— "er—I trust you enjoyed it."

"I have been contemplating the apes," he continued, dreamily. "Yes, contemplating the apes."

I said nothing, but tried to look interested.

"Yes, the apes," he murmured, fixing his mild eyes on me. Then he leaned toward me confidentially and whispered; "can you tell me what a monkey thinks?"

"I can not," I replied, sharply.

"Ah," he sighed, sinking back in his chair, and patting the slender hand of the girl beside him, "ah, who can tell what a monkey thinks?" His gentle face lulled my suspicions, and I replied very gravely; "who can tell whether they think at all?"

"True, true! Who can tell whether they think at all; and if they do think, ah! who can tell what they think?"

"But," I began, "if you can't tell whether they think at all, what's the use of trying to conjecture what they *would* think if they *did* think?"

He raised his hand in deprecation. "Ah, it is exactly that which is of such absorbing interest, exactly that! It is the abstruseness of the proposition which stimulates research—which stirs profoundly the brain of the thinking world. The question is of vital and instant importance. Possibly you have already formed an opinion."

I admitted that I had thought but little on the subject.

"I doubt," he continued, swathing his knees in his coat-tails,— "I doubt whether you have given much attention to the subject lately discussed by the Boston Dodo Society of Pythagorean Research."

"I am not sure," I said politely, "that I recall that particular discussion. May I ask what was the question brought up?"

"The Felis Domesticus question."

"Ah, that must indeed be interesting! And—er—what may be the Felis Do—do—"

"Domesticus—not Dodo. Felis Domesticus, the common or garden cat."

"Indeed," I murmured.

"You are not listening," he said.

I only half heard him; I could not turn my eyes from her face.

"Cat!" shouted the bald one, and I almost leaped from my chair. "Are you deaf?" he inquired, sympathetically.

"No—oh no!" I replied, colouring with confusion; "you were— pardon me—you were—er—speaking of the Dodo. Extraordinary bird that—"

"I was not discussing the Dodo," he sighed— "I was speaking of cats."

"Of course," I said.

"The question is," he continued, twisting his frayed coat-tails into a sort of rope— "the question is, how are we to ameliorate the present condition and social status of our domestic cats—"

"Feed 'em," I suggested.

He raised both hands. They were eloquent with patient expostulation. "I mean their spiritual condition," he said.

I nodded, but my eyes reverted to that exquisite face. She sat silent, her eyes fixed on the waning flecks of colour in the western sky.

"Yes," repeated the bald one, "the spiritual welfare of our domestic cats—"

"Toms and Tabbies?" I murmured.

"Exactly," he said, tying a large knot in his coat-tails.

"You will ruin your coat," I observed.

"Papa!" exclaimed the girl, turning in dismay, as that gentleman gave a guilty start, "stop it at once!"

He smiled apologetically and made a feeble attempt to conceal his coat-tails.

"My dear," he said, with gentle deprecation, "I am so absent-minded—I always do it in the heat of argument."

The girl rose, and, bending over her untidy parent, deftly untied the knot in his flapping coat. When he was disentangled, she sat down and said, with a ghost of a smile; "he is so very absent-minded."

"Your father is evidently a great student," I said, pleasantly. How I pitied her, tied to this lunatic!

"Yes, he is a great student," she said, quietly.

"I am," he murmured, "that's what makes me so absent-minded. I often go to bed and forget to sleep." Then looking at me he asked me my name, adding, with a bow, that his name was P. Royal Wyeth, Professor of Pythagorean Research and Abstruse Paradox.

"My first name is Penny—named after Professor Penny of Harvard," he said, "but I seldom use my first name in connection with my second, as the combination suggests a household remedy of penetrating odour."

"My name is Kensett," I said, "Harold Kensett of New York."

"Student?"

"Er—a little—"

"Student of diamonds?"

I smiled. "Oh, I see you know who my great-aunt was," I said.

"I know her," he said.

"Ah,—perhaps you are unaware that my great-aunt is not now living—"

"I know her," he repeated, obstinately.

I bowed. What a crank he was!

"What do you study? You don't fiddle away all your time, do you?" he asked.

Now that was just what I did, but I was not pleased to have Miss Wyeth know it. Although my time was chiefly spent in shooting and fishing, I had once, in a fit of energy, succeeded in stuffing and mounting a woodcock, so I evaded a humiliating confession by saying that I had done a little work in ornithology.

"Good!" cried the Professor, beaming all over. "I knew you were a fellow scientist. Possibly you are a brother member of the Boston Dodo Society of Pythagorean Research. Are you a Dodo?"

I shook my head. "No, I am not a Dodo."

"Only a jay?"

"A—what?" I said, angrily.

"A jay. We call the members of the Junior Ornithological Jay Society of New York, jays, just as we refer to ourselves as Dodos. Are you not even a jay?"

"I am not," I said, watching him suspiciously.

"I must convert you, I see," said the Professor, smiling.

"I'm afraid I do not approve of Pythagorean research," I began, but the beautiful Miss Wyeth turned to me very seriously, and looking me frankly in the eyes, said:

"I trust you will be open to conviction."

"Good Lord!" I thought, "can she be another crank." I looked at her steadily. What a little beauty she was. She also then belonged to the Pythagoreans—a sect I despised. Everybody knows all about the Pythagorean craze, its rise in Boston, its rapid spread, and its subsequent consolidation with Theosophy, Hypnotism, the Salvation Army, the Shakers, the Dunkards, and the Mind Cure Cult, upon a business basis. I had hitherto regarded all Pythagoreans with the same scornful indifference which I accorded to the Faith Curists; being a member of the Catholic Church I was scarcely prepared to take any of them seriously. Least of all did I approve of the "business basis," and I looked very much askance indeed at the "Scientific and Religious Trust Company," duly incorporated and generally known as the Pythagorean Trust, which, consolidating with Mind Curists, Faith Curists, and other flourishing Salvation Syndicates, actually claimed a place among ordinary Trusts, and at the same time pretended to a control over man's future life. No, I could never listen—I was ashamed of even entertaining the notion, and I shook my head.

"No, Miss Wyeth, I am afraid I do not care to listen to any reasoning on this subject."

"Don't you believe in Pythagoras?" demanded the Professor, subduing his excitement with difficulty, and adding another knot to his coat-tails.

"No," I said, "I do not."

"How do you know you don't?" enquired the Professor.

"Because," I said, firmly, "it is nonsense to say that the soul of a human being can inhabit a hen!"

"Put it in a more simplified form!" insisted the Professor; "do you believe that the soul of a hen can inhabit a human being?"

"No, I don't!"

"Did you ever hear of a hen-pecked man?" cried the Professor, his voice ending in a shout.

I nodded, intensely annoyed.

"Will you listen to reason, then?" he continued, eagerly.

"No," I began, but I caught Miss Wyeth's blue eyes fixed on mine with an expression so sad, so sweetly appealing, that I faltered.

"Yes, I will listen," I said, faintly.

"Will you become my pupil?" insisted the Professor.

I was shocked to find myself wavering, but my eyes were looking into hers, and I could not disobey what I read there. The longer I looked the greater inclination I felt to waver. I saw that I was going to give in, and, strangest of all, my conscience did not trouble me. I felt it coming—a sort of mild exhilaration took possession of me. For the first time in my life I became reckless—I even gloried in my recklessness.

"Yes, yes," I cried, leaning eagerly across the table, "I shall be glad—delighted! Will you take me as your pupil?" My single eye-glass fell from its position unheeded. "Take me! Oh, will you take me?" I cried. Instead of answering, the Professor blinked rapidly at me for a moment. I imagined his eyes had grown bigger, and were assuming a greenish tinge. The corners of his mouth began to quiver, emitting queer, caressing little noises, and he rapidly added knot after knot to his twitching coat-tails. Suddenly he bent forward across the table until his nose almost touched mine. The pupils of his eyes expanded, the iris assuming a beautiful changing golden-green tinge, and his coat-tails switched violently. Then he began to mew.

I strove to rouse myself from my paralysis—I tried to shrink back, for I felt the end of his cold nose touch mine. I could not move. The cry of terror died in my straining throat, my hands tightened convulsively; I was incapable of speech or motion. At the same time my brain became wonderfully clear. I began to remember everything that had ever happened to me—everything that I had ever done or said. I even remembered things that I had neither done nor said, I recalled distinctly much that had never happened. How fresh and strong my memory! The past was like a mirror, crystal clear, and there, in glorious tints and hues, the scenes of my childhood grew and glowed and faded, and gave place to newer and more splendid scenes. For a moment the episode of the cat at the Hotel St. Antoine flashed across my mind. When it vanished, a chilly stupor slowly clouded my brain; the scenes, the memories, the brilliant colours, faded, leaving me enveloped in a grey vapour, through which the two great eyes of the Professor twinkled with a murky light. A peculiar longing stirred me,—a strange yearning for something—I knew not what—but, oh! how I longed and yearned for it! Slowly this indefinite, incomprehensible longing became a living pain. Ah, how I suffered!—and how the vapours seemed to crowd around me. Then, as at a great distance, I heard her voice, sweet, imperative:

"Mew!" she said.

For a moment I seemed to see the interior of my own skull, lighted as by a flash of fire; the rolling eye-balls, veined in scarlet, the glistening muscles quivering along the jaw, the humid masses of the convoluted brain,—then awful darkness—a darkness almost tangible—an utter blackness, through which now seemed to creep a thin silver thread, like a river crawling across a world—like a thought gliding to the brain—like a song, a thin, sharp song which some distant voice was singing—which I was singing.

And I knew that I was mewing!

I threw myself back in my chair and mewed with all my heart. Oh, that heavy load which was lifted from my breast! How good, how satisfying it was to mew! And how I did mew!

I gave myself up to it, heart and soul; my whole being thrilled with the passionate outpourings of a spirit freed. My voice trembled in the upper bars of a feline love song, quavered, descended, swelling again into an intimation that I brooked no rival, and ended with a magnificent crescendo.

I finished, somewhat abashed, and glanced askance at the Professor and his daughter, but the one sat nonchalantly disentangling his coattails, and the other was apparently absorbed in the distant landscape. Evidently they did not consider me ridiculous. Flushing painfully, I turned in my chair to see how my gruesome solo had affected the people on the terrace. Nobody even looked at me. This, however, gave me little comfort, for, as I began to realize what I had done, my mortification and rage knew no bounds. I was ready to die of shame. What on earth had induced me to mew? I looked wildly about for escape—I would leap up—rush home to bury my burning face in my pillows, and later in the friendly cabin of a homeward-bound steamer. I would fly—fly at once! Woe to the man who blocked my way! I started to my feet, but at that moment I caught Miss Wyeth's eyes fixed on mine.

"Don't go," she said.

What in Heaven's name lay in those blue eyes! I slowly sank back into my chair.

Then the Professor spoke. "Elsie, I have just received a dispatch."

"Where from, Papa?"

"From India. I'm going at once."

She nodded her head, without turning her eyes from the sea. "Is it important, papa?"

"I should say so. The cashier of the Trust has eloped with an Astral body, and has taken all our funds, including a lot of first mortgages on Nirvana. I suppose he's been dabbling in futures, and was short in his accounts. I shan't be gone long."

"Then good-night, papa," she said, kissing him, "try to be back by eleven."

I sat stupidly staring at them.

"Oh, it's only to Bombay—I shan't go to Thibet to-night,—good-night, my dear," said the Professor.

Then a singular thing occurred. The Professor had at last succeeded in disentangling his coat tails, and now, jamming his hat over his ears, and waving his arms with a bat-like motion, he climbed upon the seat of his chair, and ejaculated the word "Presto!" Then I found my voice.

"Stop him!" I cried, in terror.

"Presto! Presto!" shouted the Professor, balancing himself on the edge of his chair and waving his arms majestically, as if preparing for a sudden flight across the Scheldt; and, firmly convinced that he not only meditated it but was perfectly capable of attempting it, I covered my eyes with my hands.

"Are you ill, Mr. Kensett?" said the girl, quietly.

I raised my head indignantly. "Not at all, Miss Wyeth, only I'll bid you good-evening, for this is the 19th century, and I'm a Christian."

"So am I," she said. "So is my father."

"The devil he is," I thought. Her next words made me jump. "Please do not be profane, Mr. Kensett." How did she know I was profane? I had not spoken a word! Could it be possible she was able to read my thoughts? This was too much, and I rose and bowed stiffly.

"I have the honour to bid you good-evening," I began, and reluctantly turned to include the Professor, expecting to see that gentleman balancing himself on his chair. The Professor's chair was empty.

"Oh," said the girl, faintly, "my father has gone."

"Gone! Where?"

"To—to India, I believe."

I sank helplessly into my own chair.

"I do not think he will stay very long—he promised to return by eleven," she said, timidly.

I tried to realize the purport of it all. "Gone to India? Gone! How? On a broomstick? Good Heavens!" I murmured, "am I sane?"

"Perfectly," she said, "and I am tired; you may take me back to the hotel."

I scarcely heard her; I was feebly attempting to gather up my numbed wits. Slowly I began to comprehend the situation, to review the startling and humiliating events of the day. At noon, in the court of the Hotel St. Antoine, I had been annoyed by a man and a cat. I had retired to my own room and had slept until dinner. In the evening I met two tourists on the sea-wall promenade. I had been beguiled into conversation—yes, into intimacy with these two tourists! I had had the intention of embracing the faith of Pythagoras! Then I had mewed like a cat with all the strength of my lungs. Then the male tourist vanishes—and leaves me in charge of the female tourist, alone and at night in a strange city! And now the female tourist proposes that I take her home!

With a remnant of self-possession I groped for my eye-glass, seized it, screwed it firmly into my eye, and looked long and earnestly at the girl. As I looked, my eyes softened, my monocle dropped, and I forgot everything in the beauty and purity of the face before me. My heart began to beat against my stiff white waistcoat. Had I dared—yes, dared to think of this wondrous little beauty, as a female tourist? Her pale sweet face, turned toward the sea, seemed to cast a spell upon the night. How loud my heart was beating. The yellow moon floated, half dipping in the sea, flooding land and water with enchanted lights. Wind and wave seemed to feel the spell of her eyes, for the breeze died away, the heaving Scheldt tossed noiselessly, and the dark Dutch luggers swung idly on the tide with every sail adroop.

A sudden hush fell over land and water, the voices on the promenade were stilled; little by little the shadowy throng, the terrace, the sea itself vanished, and I only saw her face, shadowed against the moon.

It seemed as if I had drifted miles above the earth, through all space and eternity, and there was nought between me and high Heaven but that white face. Ah, how I loved her! I knew it—I never doubted it. Could years of passionate adoration touch her heart— her little heart, now beating so calmly with no thought of love to startle it from its quiet and send it fluttering against the gentle breast? In her lap her clasped hands tightened,—her eyelids drooped as though some pleasant thought was passing. I saw the colour dye her temples, I saw the blue eyes turn, half-frightened to my own, I saw—and I knew she had read my thoughts. Then we both rose, side by side, and she was weeping softly, yet for my life I dared not speak. She turned away, touching her eyes with a bit of lace, and I sprang to her side and offered her my arm.

"You cannot go back alone," I said.

She did not take my arm.

"Do you hate me, Miss Wyeth?"

"I am very tired," she said, "I must go home."

"You cannot go alone."

"I do not care to accept your escort."

"Then—you send me away?"

"No," she said, in a hard voice. "You can come if you like."

So I humbly attended her to the Hotel St. Antoine.

III

As we reached the Place Verte and turned into the court of the hotel, the sound of the midnight bells swept over the city, and a horse-car jingled slowly by on its last trip to the railroad station.

We passed the fountain, bubbling and splashing in the moonlit court, and, crossing the square, entered the southern wing of the hotel. At the foot of the stairway she leaned for an instant against the banisters.

"I am afraid we have walked too fast," I said.

She turned to me coldly. "No,—conventionalities must be observed. You were quite right in escaping as soon as possible."

"But," I protested, "I assure you—"

She gave a little movement of impatience. "Don't," she said, "you tire me—conventionalities tire me. Be satisfied,—nobody has seen you."

"You are cruel," I said, in a low voice— "what do you think I care for conventionalities?"

"You care everything,—you care what people think, and you try to do what they say is good form. You never did such an original thing in your life as you have just done."

"You read my thoughts," I exclaimed, bitterly— "it is not fair"

"Fair or not, I know what you consider me,—ill-bred, common, pleased with any sort of attention. Oh! Why should I waste one word—one thought on you!"

"Miss Wyeth,—" I began, but she interrupted me.

"Would you dare tell me what you think of me?—Would you dare tell me what you think of my father?"

I was silent. She turned and mounted two steps of the stairway, then faced me again.

"Do you think it was for my own pleasure that I permitted myself to be left alone with you? Do you imagine that I am flattered by your attention—do you venture to think I ever could be? How dared you think what you did think there on the sea-wall?"

"I cannot help my thoughts!" I replied.

"You turned on me like a tiger when you awoke from your trance. Do you really suppose that you mewed? Are you not aware that my father hypnotized you?"

"No—I did not know it," I said. The hot blood tingled in my finger tips, and I looked angrily at her.

"Why do you imagine that I waste my time on you?" she said. "Your vanity has answered that question,—now let your intelligence answer it. I am a Pythagorean; I have been chosen to bring in a convert, and you were the convert selected for me by the Mahatmas of the Consolidated Trust Company. I have followed you from New York to Antwerp, as I was bidden, but now my courage fails, and I shrink from fulfilling my mission, knowing you to be the type of man you are. If I could give it up—if I could only go away,—never, never again to see you! Ah, I fear they will not permit it!—until my mission is accomplished. Why was I chosen,—I, with a woman's heart and a woman's pride. I—I hate you!"

"I love you," I said, slowly.

She paled and looked away.

"Answer me," I said.

Her wide blue eyes turned back again, and I held them with mine. At last she slowly drew a long-stemmed rose from the bunch at her belt, turned, and mounted the shadowy staircase. For a moment I thought I saw her pause on the landing above, but the moonlight was uncertain. After waiting for a long time in vain, I moved away, and in going raised my hand to my face, but I stopped short, and my heart stopped too, for a moment. In my hand I held a long-stemmed rose.

With my brain in a whirl I crept across the court and mounted the stairs to my room. Hour after hour I walked the floor, slowly at first, then more rapidly, but it brought no calm to the fierce tumult of my thoughts, and at last I dropped into a chair before the empty fireplace, burying my head in my hands.

Uncertain, shocked, and deadly weary, I tried to think,—I strove to bring order out of the chaos in my brain, but I only sat staring at the long-stemmed rose. Slowly I began to take a vague pleasure in its heavy perfume, and once I crushed a leaf between my palms, and, bending over, drank in the fragrance.

Twice my lamp flickered and went out, and twice, treading softly, I crossed the room to relight it. Twice I threw open the door, thinking that I heard some sound without. How close the air was,—how heavy and hot! And what was that strange, subtle odour which had insensibly filled the room? It grew stronger and more penetrating, and I began to dislike it, and to escape it I buried my nose in the half-opened rose. Horror! The odour came from the rose,—and the rose itself was no longer a rose—not even a flower now,—it was only a bunch of catnip; and I dashed it to the floor and ground it under my heel.

"Mountebank!" I cried in a rage. My anger grew cold—and I shivered, drawn perforce to the curtained window. Something was there—outside. I could not hear it, for it made no sound, but I knew it was there, watching me. What was it? The damp hair stirred on my head. I touched the heavy curtains. Whatever was outside them sprang up, tore at the window, and then rushed away.

Feeling very shaky, I crept to the window, opened it, and leaned out. The night was calm. I heard the fountain splashing in the moonlight and the sea winds soughing through the palms. Then I closed the window and turned back into the room; and as I stood there a sudden breeze, which could not have come from without, blew sharply in my face, extinguishing the candle and sending the long curtains bellying out into the room. The lamp on the table flashed and smoked and sputtered; the room was littered with flying papers and catnip leaves. Then the strange wind died away, and somewhere in the night a cat snarled.

I turned desperately to my trunk and flung it open. Into it I threw everything I owned, pell-mell, closed the lid, locked it, and seizing my mackintosh and travelling bag, ran down the stairs, crossed the court and entered the night office of the hotel. There I called up the sleepy clerk, settled my reckoning, and sent a porter for a cab.

"Now," I said, "what time does the next train leave?"

"The next train for where?"

"Anywhere!"

The clerk locked the safe, and carefully keeping the desk between himself and me, motioned the office boy to look at the time-tables.

"Next train, 2.10. Brussels—Paris," read the boy.

At that moment the cab rattled up by the curbstone, and I sprang in while the porter tossed my traps on top. Away we bumped over the stony pavement, past street after street lighted dimly by tall gas-lamps, and alley after alley brilliant with the glare of villainous all-night café-concerts, and then, turning, we rumbled past the Circus and the Eldorado, and at last stopped with a jolt before the Brussels Station.

I had not a moment to lose. "Paris!" I cried,— "first-class!" and, pocketing the book of coupons, hurried across the platform to where the Brussels train lay. A guard came running up, flung open the door of a first-class carriage, slammed and locked it, after I had jumped in, and the long train glided from the arched station out into the starlit morning.

I was all alone in the compartment. The wretched lamp in the roof flickered dimly, scarcely lighting the stuffy box. I could not see to read my time-table, so I wrapped my legs in the travelling rug and lay back, staring out into the misty morning. Trees, walls, telegraph poles, flashed past, and the cinders drove in showers against the rattling windows. I slept at times, fitfully, and once, springing up, peered sharply at the opposite seat, possessed with the idea that somebody was there.

When the train reached Brussels, I was sound asleep, and the guard awoke me with difficulty.

"Breakfast, sir?" he asked.

"Anything," I sighed, and stepped out to the platform, rubbing my legs and shivering. The other passengers were already breakfasting in the station café, and I joined them and managed to swallow a cup of coffee and a roll.

The morning broke, grey and cloudy, and I bundled myself into my mackintosh for a tramp along the platform. Up and down I stamped, puffing a cigar, and digging my hands deep in my pockets, while the other passengers huddled into the warmer compartments of the train or stood watching the luggage being lifted into the forward mail carriage. The wait was very long; the hands of the great clock pointed to six, and still the train lay motionless along the platform. I approached a guard, and asked him whether anything was wrong.

"Accident on the line," he replied; "Monsieur had better go to his compartment and try to sleep, for we may be delayed until noon."

I followed the guard's advice, and crawling into my corner, wrapped myself in the rug and lay back watching the rain-drops spattering along the window-sill. At noon, the train had not moved, and I lunched in the compartment. At four o'clock in the afternoon the station-master came hurrying along the platform, crying "montez! montez! Messieurs—Dames, s'il vous plait,"—and the train steamed out of the station and whirled away through the flat, treeless Belgian plains. At times I dozed, but the shaking of the car always awoke me, and I would sit blinking out at the endless stretch of plain, until a sudden flurry of rain blotted the landscape from my eyes. At last, a long, shrill whistle from the engine, a jolt, a series of bumps, and an apparition of red trousers and bayonets warned me that we had arrived at the French frontier. I turned out with the others, and opened my valise for inspection, but the customs officials merely chalked it without examination, and I hurried back to my compartment amid the shouting of guards and the clanging of station bells. Again I found that I was alone in the compartment, so I smoked a cigarette, thanked Heaven, and fell into a dreamless sleep.

How long I slept I do not know, but when I awoke, the train was roaring through a tunnel. When again it flashed out into the open country, I peered through the grimy rain-stained window and saw that the storm had ceased and stars were twinkling in the sky. I stretched my legs, yawned, pushed my travelling cap back from my forehead, and stumbling to my feet, walked up and down the compartment until my cramped muscles were relieved. Then I sat down again, and, lighting a cigar, puffed great rings and clouds of fragrant smoke across the aisle.

The train was flying; the cars lurched and shook, and the windows rattled accompaniment to the creaking panels. The smoke from my cigar dimmed the lamp in the ceiling and hid the opposite seat from view. How it curled and writhed in the corners, now eddying upward, now floating across the aisle like a veil. I lounged back in my cushioned seat watching it with interest. What queer shapes it took. How thick it was becoming—how strangely luminous! Now it had filled the whole compartment, puff after puff crowding upward, waving, wavering, clouding the windows, and blotting the lamp from sight. It was most interesting. I had never before smoked such a cigar. What an extraordinary brand! I examined the end, flicking the ashes away. The cigar was out. Fumbling for a match to relight it, my eyes fell on the drifting smoke curtain, which swayed across the corner opposite. It seemed almost tangible. How like a real curtain it hung, grey, impenetrable. A man might hide behind it. Then an idea came into my head, and it persisted until my uneasiness amounted to a vague terror. I tried to fight it off—I strove to resist—but the conviction slowly settled upon me that something was behind that smoke veil,—something which had entered the compartment while I slept.

"It can't be," I muttered, my eyes fixed on the misty drapery, "the train has not stopped."

The car creaked and trembled. I sprang to my feet, and swept my arm through the veil of smoke. Then my hair slowly rose on my head. For my hand touched another hand, and my eyes had met two other eyes.

My senses reeled. I heard a voice in the gloom, low and sweet, calling me by name; I saw the eyes again, tender and blue; soft fingers touched my own.

"Are you afraid?" she said.

My heart began to beat again, and my face warmed with returning blood.

"It is only I," she said, gently.

I seemed to hear my own voice speaking as if at a great distance; "you here—alone?"

"How cruel of you," she faltered, "I am not alone." At the same instant my eyes fell upon the Professor, calmly seated by the further window. His hands were thrust into the folds of a corded and tasselled dressing-gown, from beneath which peeped two enormous feet encased in carpet slippers. Upon his head towered a yellow night cap. He did not pay the slightest attention to either me or his daughter, and, except for the lighted cigar which he kept shifting between his lips, he might have been taken for a wax dummy.

Then I began to speak, feebly, hesitating like a child.

"How did you come into this compartment? You—you do not possess wings, I suppose. You could not have been here all the time. Will you explain—explain to me? See, I ask you very humbly, for I do not understand. This is the 19th century, and these things don't fit in. I'm wearing a Dunlap hat—I've got a copy of the *New York Herald* in my bag,—President Cleveland is alive and everything is so very commonplace in the world! Is this real magic? Perhaps I'm filled with hallucinations. Perhaps I'm asleep and dreaming. Perhaps you are not really here—nor I—nor anybody, nor anything!"—

The train plunged into a tunnel, and when again it dashed out from the other end, the cold wind blew furiously in my face from the further window. It was wide open; the Professor was gone.

"Papa has changed to another compartment," she said, quietly; "I think perhaps you were beginning to bore him."

Her eyes met mine and she smiled faintly.

"Are you very much bewildered?"

I looked at her in silence. She sat very quietly, her white hands clasped above her knee, her curly hair glittering to her girdle. A long robe, almost silvery in the twilight, clung to her young figure; her bare feet were thrust deep into a pair of shimmering eastern slippers.

"When you fled," she sighed, "I was asleep and there was no time to lose. I barely had a moment to go to Bombay, to find Papa, and return in time to join you. This is an East Indian costume."

Still I was silent.

"Are you shocked?" she asked simply.

"No," I replied in a dull voice, "I'm past that."

"You are very rude," she said, with the tears starting to her eyes.

"I do not mean to be. I only wish to go away—away somewhere and find out what my name is."

"Your name is Harold Kensett."

"Are you sure?" I asked, eagerly.

"Yes,—what troubles you?"

"Is everything plain to you? Are you a sort of prophet and second sight medium? Is nothing hidden from you?" I asked.

"Nothing,"—she faltered. My head ached and I clasped it in my hand.

A sudden change came over her. "I am human,—believe me!"—she said with piteous eagerness; "indeed I do not seem strange to those who understand. You wonder, because you left me at midnight in Antwerp and you wake to find me here. If, because I find myself reincarnated, endowed with senses and capabilities which few at present possess;—if I am so made, why should it seem strange? It is all so natural to me. If I appear to you—"

"Appear!!!"

"Yes—"

"Elsie!" I cried, "can you vanish?"

"Yes," she murmured,— "does it seem to you unwomanly?"

"Great Heaven!" I groaned.

"Don't," she cried, with tears in her voice,— "oh, please don't! Help me to bear it! If you only knew how awful it is to be different from other girls,—how mortifying it is to me to be able to vanish,—oh, how I hate and detest it all!"

"Don't cry," I said, looking at her pityingly.

"Oh dear me!" she sobbed. "You shudder at the sight of me because I can vanish."

"I don't!" I cried.

"Yes you do! You abhor me,—you shrink away! Oh why did I ever see you,—why did you ever come into my life,—what have I done in ages past, that now, reborn, I suffer cruelly—cruelly!"

"What do you mean!" I whispered. My voice trembled with happiness.

"I?—nothing—but you think me a fabled monster."

"Elsie,—my sweet Elsie," I said, "I don't think you a fabled monster;—I love you,—see—see—I am at your feet,—listen to me, my darling,"—

She turned her blue eyes to mine. I saw tears sparkling on the curved lashes.

"Elsie, I love you," I said again.

Slowly she raised her white hands to my head and held it a moment, looking at me strangely. Then her face grew nearer to my own, her glittering hair fell over my shoulders, her lips rested on

In that long sweet kiss, the beating of her heart answered mine, and I learned a thousand truths, wonderful, mysterious, splendid,—but when our lips fell apart,—the memory of what I learned departed also.

"It was so very simple and beautiful," she sighed, "and I—I never saw it. But the Mahatmas knew—ah, they knew that my mission could only be accomplished through love."

"And it is," I whispered, "for you shall teach me,—me your husband."

"And—and you will not be impatient? You will try to believe?"

"I will believe what you tell me, my sweetheart."

"Even about—cats?"

Before I could reply the further window opened and a yellow nightcap, followed by the Professor, entered from somewhere without. Elsie sank back on her sofa, but the Professor needed not to be told, and we both knew he was already busily reading our thoughts.

For a moment there was dead silence,—long enough for the Professor to grasp the full significance of what had passed. Then he uttered a single exclamation; "Oh!"

After a while, however, he looked at me for the first time that evening, saying; "Congratulate you, Mr. Kensett, I'm sure;"—tied several knots in the cord of his dressing-gown, lighted a cigar, and paid no further attention to either of us. Some moments later he opened the window again and disappeared. I looked across the aisle at Elsie.

"You may come over beside me," she said, shyly.

IV

IT WAS NEARLY ten o'clock and our train was rapidly approaching Paris. We passed village after village wrapped in mist, station after station hung with twinkling red and blue and yellow lanterns, then sped on again with the echo of the switch bells ringing in our ears.

When at length the train slowed up and stopped, I opened the window and looked out upon a long wet platform, shining under the electric lights.

A guard came running by, throwing open the doors of each compartment, and crying, "Paris next! Tickets, if you please."

I handed him my book of coupons from which he tore several and handed it back. Then he lifted his lantern and peered into the compartment saying: "Is Monsieur alone?"

I turned to Elsie.

"He wants your ticket—give it to me."

"What's that?" demanded the guard.

I looked anxiously at Elsie.

"If your father has the tickets—" I began, but was interrupted by the guard who snapped, "Monsieur will give himself the trouble to remember that I do not understand English."

"Keep quiet!" I said sharply in French, "I am not speaking to you."

The guard stared stupidly at me, then at my luggage, and finally, entering the car, knelt down and peered under the seats. Presently he got up, very red in the face, and went out slamming the door. He had not paid the slightest attention to Elsie, but I distinctly heard him say, "only Englishmen and idiots talk to themselves!"

"Elsie," I faltered, "do you mean to say that guard could not see you?"

She began to look so serious again that I merely added, "never mind, I don't care whether you are invisible or not, dearest."

"I am not invisible to you," she said; "why should you care?"

A great noise of bells and whistles drowned our voices, and amid the whirring of switch bells, the hissing of steam, and the cries of "Paris! All out!" our train glided into the station.

It was the Professor who opened the door of our carriage. There he stood, calmly adjusting his yellow nightcap and drawing his dressing-gown closer with the corded tassels.

"Where have you been?" I asked.

"On the engine."

"*In* the engine I suppose you mean," I said.

"No I don't; I mean *on* the engine,—on the pilot. It was very refreshing. Where are we going now?"

"Do you know Paris?" asked Elsie, turning to me.

"Yes. I think your father had better take you to the Hotel Normandie on the rue de l'Echelle—"

"But you must stay there too!"

"Of course—if you wish—"

She laughed nervously.

"Don't you see that my father and I could not take rooms—now? You must engage three rooms for yourself."

"Why?" I asked stupidly.

"Oh dear—why because we are invisible."

I tried to repress a shudder. The Professor gave Elsie his arm and, as I studied his ensemble, I thanked Heaven that he was invisible.

At the gate of the station I hailed a four-seated cab, and we rattled away through the stony streets, brilliant with gas jets, and in a few moments rolled smoothly across the Avenue de l'Opera, turned into the rue de l'Echelle, and stopped. A bright little page, all over buttons, came out, took my luggage, and preceded us into the hallway.

I, with Elsie on my arm and the Professor shuffling along beside me, walked over to the desk.

"Room?" said the clerk, "we have a very desirable room on the second fronting the rue St. Honoré—"

"But we—that is I want three rooms—three separate rooms!" I said.

The clerk scratched his chin. "Monsieur is expecting friends?"

"Say yes," whispered Elsie, with a suspicion of laughter in her voice.

"Yes," I repeated feebly.

"Gentlemen of course?" said the clerk looking at me narrowly.

"One lady."

"Married, of course?"

"What's that to you?" I said sharply, "what do you mean by speaking to us—"

"Us!"

"I mean to me," I said, badly rattled; "give me the rooms and let me get to bed, will you?"

"Monsieur will remember," said the clerk coldly, "that this is an old and respectable hotel."

"I know it," I said, smothering my rage.

The clerk eyed me suspiciously.

"Front!" he called with irritating deliberation, "show this gentleman to apartment ten."

"How many rooms are there!" I demanded.

"Three sleeping rooms and a parlor."

"I will take it," I said with composure.

"On probation," muttered the clerk insolently.

Swallowing the insult I followed the bell-boy up the stairs, keeping between him and Elsie, for I dreaded to see him walk through her as if she were thin air. A trim maid rose to meet us and conducted us through a hallway into a large apartment. She threw open all the bed-room doors and said, "Will Monsieur have the goodness to choose?"

"Which will you take," I began, turning to Elsie.

"I! Monsieur!" cried the startled maid.

That completely upset me. "Here," I muttered, slipping some silver into her hand, "now for the love of Heaven run away!"

When she had vanished with a doubtful "Merci, Monsieur," I handed the Professor the keys and asked him to settle the thing with Elsie.

Elsie took the corner room, the Professor rambled into the next one, and I said good night and crept wearily into my own chamber. I sat down and tried to think. A great feeling of fatigue weighted my spirits.

"I can think better with my clothes off," I said, and slipped the coat from my shoulders. How tired I was. "I can think better in bed," I muttered, flinging my cravat on the dresser and tossing my shirt studs after it. I was certainly very tired. "Now," I yawned, grasping the pillow and drawing it under my head, "now, I can think a bit," but before my head fell on the pillow, sleep closed my eyes.

I began to dream at once. It seemed as though my eyes were wide open and the Professor was standing beside my bed.

"Young man," he said, "you've won my daughter and you must pay the piper!"

"What piper?" I said.

"The pied piper of Hamlin, I don't think," replied the Professor vulgarly, and before I could realize what he was doing he had drawn a reed pipe from his dressing-gown and was playing a strangely annoying air. Then an awful thing occurred. Cats began to troop into the room, cats by the hundred, toms and tabbys, grey, yellow, Maltese, Persian, Manx, all purring and all marching round and round, rubbing against the furniture, the Professor, and even against me. I struggled with the nightmare.

"Take them away!" I tried to gasp.

"Nonsense," he said, "here is an old friend."

I saw the white tabby cat of the Hotel St. Antoine.

"An old friend," he repeated, and played a dismal melody on his reed.

I saw Elsie enter the room, lift the white tabby in her arms and bring her to my side.

"Shake hands with him," she commanded.

To my horror the tabby deliberately extended a paw and tapped me on the knuckles.

"Oh!" I cried in agony, "this is a horrible dream! Why, oh, why can't I wake!"

"Yes," she said, dropping the cat, "it is partly a dream but some of it is real. Remember what I say, my darling; you are to go to-morrow morning and meet the twelve o'clock train from Antwerp at the Gare du Nord. Papa and I are coming to Paris on that train. Don't you know that we are not really here now, you silly boy? Good night then. I shall be very glad to see you."

I saw her glide from the room, followed by the Professor, playing a gay quick-step, to which the cats danced two and two.

"Good night sir," said each cat, as it passed my bed; and I dreamed no more.

When I awoke, the room, the bed had vanished; I was in the street, walking rapidly; the sun shone down on the broad white pavements of Paris, and the streams of busy life flowed past me on either side. How swiftly I was walking! Where the devil was I going? Surely I had business somewhere that needed immediate attention. I tried to remember when I had awakened, but I could not. I wondered where I had dressed myself; I had apparently taken great pains with my toilet, for I was immaculate, monocle and all, even down to a long-stemmed rose nestling in my button-hole. I knew Paris and recognized the streets through which I was hurrying. Where could I be going? What was my hurry? I glanced at my watch and found I had not a moment to lose. Then as the bells of the city rang out mid-day, I hastened into the railroad station on the Rue Lafayette and walked out to the platform. And as I looked down the glittering track, around the distant curve shot a locomotive followed by a long line of cars. Nearer and nearer it came while the station gongs sounded and the switch-bells began ringing all along the track.

"Antwerp express!" cried the Sous-Chef de Gare, and as the train slipped along the tiled platform I sprang upon the steps of a first-class carriage and threw open the door.

"How do you do, Mr. Kensett," said Elsie Wyeth, springing lightly to the platform. "Really it is very nice of you to come to the train." At the same moment a bald, mild-eyed gentleman emerged from the depths of the same compartment carrying a large covered basket.

"How are you, Kensett?" he said. "Glad to see you again. Rather warm in that compartment—no I will not trust this basket to an expressman; give Miss Wyeth your arm and I'll follow. We go to the 'Normandie' I believe?"

All the morning I had Elsie to myself, and at dinner I sat beside her with the Professor opposite. The latter was cheerful enough, but he nearly ruined my dinner for he smelled strongly of catnip. After dinner he became restless and fidgeted about in his chair until coffee was brought, and we went up to the parlour of our apartment. Here his restlessness increased to such an extent that I ventured to ask him if he was in good health.

"It's that basket—the covered basket which I have in the next room," he said.

"What's the trouble with the basket?" I asked.

"The basket's all right—but the contents worry me."

"May I inquire what the contents are?" I ventured. The Professor rose.

"Yes," he said, "you may inquire of my daughter." He left the room but reappeared shortly, carrying a saucer of milk.

I watched him enter the next room—which was mine.

"What on earth is he taking that into my room for?" I asked Elsie. "I don't keep cats."

"But you will," she said.

"I? never!"

"You will if I ask you to."

"But—but you won't ask me."

"But I do."

"Elsie!"

"Harold!"

"I detest cats."

"You must not."

"I can't help it."

"You will when I ask it. Have I not given myself to you? Will you not make a little sacrifice for me?"

"I don't understand—"

"Would you refuse my first request?"

"No," I said miserably, "I will keep dozens of cats—"

"I do not ask that; I only wish you to keep one."

"Was that what your father had in that basket?" I asked suspiciously.

"Yes, the basket came from Antwerp."

"What! The white Antwerp cat!" I cried.

"Yes."

"And you ask me to keep that cat? Oh Elsie!"

"Listen!" she said, "I have a long story to tell you; come nearer, close to me. You say you love me?"

I bent and kissed her.

"Then I shall put you to the proof," she murmured.

"Prove me!"

"Listen. That cat is the same cat that ran out of the apartment in the Waldorf when your great-aunt ceased to exist—in human shape. My father and myself, having received word from the Mahatmas of the Trust Company, sheltered and cherished the cat. We were ordered by the Mahatmas to convert you. The task was appalling—but there is no such thing as refusing a command, and we laid our plans. That man with a white spot in his hair was my father—"

"What! Your father is bald."

"He wore a wig then. The white spot came from dropping chemicals on the wig while experimenting with a substance which you could not comprehend."

"Then—then that clue was useless; but who could have taken the Crimson Diamond? And who was the man with the white spot on his head who tried to sell the stone in Paris?

"That was my father."

"He—he—st—took the Crimson Diamond?!" I cried aghast.

"Yes and no. That was only a paste stone that he had in Paris. It was to draw you over here. He had the real Crimson Diamond also."

"Your father?"

"Yes. He has it in the next room now. Can you not see how it disappeared, Harold? Why, the cat swallowed it!"

"Do you mean to say that the white tabby swallowed the Crimson Diamond?"

"By mistake. She tried to get it out of the velvet bag, and, as the bag was also full of catnip, she could not resist a mouthful, and unfortunately just then you broke in the door and so startled the cat that she swallowed the Crimson Diamond."

There was a painful pause. At last I said:

"Elsie, as you are able to vanish, I suppose you also are able to converse with cats."

"I am," she replied, trying to keep back the tears of mortification.

"And that cat told you this?"

"She did."

"And my Crimson Diamond is inside that cat?"

"It is."

"Then," said I firmly, "I am going to chloroform the cat."

"Harold!" she cried in terror, "that cat is your great-aunt!"

I don't know to this day how I stood the shock of that announcement, or how I managed to listen, while Elsie tried to explain the transmigration theory, but it was all Chinese to me. I only knew that I was a blood relation of a cat, and the thought nearly drove me mad.

"Try, my darling, try to love her," whispered Elsie, "she must be very precious to you—"

"Yes, with my diamond inside her," I replied faintly.

"You must not neglect her," said Elsie.

"Oh no, I'll always have my eye on her—I mean I will surround her with luxury—er, milk and bones and catnip and books—er—does she read?"

"Not the books that human beings read. Now go and speak to your aunt, Harold."

"Eh! How the deuce—"

"Go, for my sake try to be cordial."

She rose and led me unresistingly to the door of my room.

"Good Heavens!" I groaned, "this is awful."

"Courage, my darling!" she whispered, "be brave for love of me."

I drew her to me and kissed her. Beads of cold perspiration started in the roots of my hair, but I clenched my teeth and entered the room alone. The room was dark and I stood silent, not knowing where to turn, fearful lest I step on the cat, my aunt! Then through the dreary silence I called; "Aunty!"

A faint noise broke upon my ear, and my heart grew sick, but I strode into the darkness calling hoarsely:—

"Aunt Tabby! it is your nephew!"

Again the faint sound. Something was stirring there among the shadows,—a shape moving softly along the wall, a shade which glided by me, paused, wavered, and darted under the bed. Then I threw myself on the floor, profoundly moved, begging, imploring my aunt to come to me.

"Aunty! Aunty!" I murmured, "your nephew is waiting to take you to his heart!"

And at last I saw my great-aunt's eyes, shining in the dark.

CLOSE THE DOOR. That meeting is not for the eyes of the world! Close the door upon that sacred scene where great-aunt and nephew are united at last.

1897

THE EYES OF THE PANTHER
Ambrose Bierce

I

One Does Not Always Marry When Insane

A MAN AND a woman—nature had done the grouping—sat on a rustic seat, in the late afternoon. The man was middle-aged, slender, swarthy, with the expression of a poet and the complexion of a pirate—a man at whom one would look again. The woman was young, blonde, graceful, with something in her figure and movements suggesting the word "lithe." She was habited in a gray gown with odd brown markings in the texture. She may have been beautiful; one could not readily say, for her eyes denied attention to all else. They were gray-green, long and narrow, with an expression defying analysis. One could only know that they were disquieting. Cleopatra may have had such eyes.

The man and the woman talked.

"Yes," said the woman, "I love you, God knows! But marry you, no. I cannot, will not."

"Irene, you have said that many times, yet always have denied me a reason. I've a right to know, to understand, to feel and prove my fortitude if I have it. Give me a reason."

"For loving you?"

The woman was smiling through her tears and her pallor. That did not stir any sense of humor in the man.

"No; there is no reason for that. A reason for not marrying me. I've a right to know. I must know. I will know!"

60

He had risen and was standing before her with clenched hands, on his face a frown—it might have been called a scowl. He looked as if he might attempt to learn by strangling her. She smiled no more—merely sat looking up into his face with a fixed, set regard that was utterly without emotion or sentiment. Yet it had something in it that tamed his resentment and made him shiver.

"You are determined to have my reason?" she asked in a tone that was entirely mechanical—a tone that might have been her look made audible.

"If you please—if I'm not asking too much."

Apparently this lord of creation was yielding some part of his dominion over his co-creature.

"Very well, you shall know: I am insane."

The man started, then looked incredulous and was conscious that he ought to be amused. But, again, the sense of humor failed him in his need and despite his disbelief he was profoundly disturbed by that which he did not believe. Between our convictions and our feelings there is no good understanding.

"That is what the physicians would say," the woman continued—"if they knew. I might myself prefer to call it a case of 'possession.' Sit down and hear what I have to say."

The man silently resumed his seat beside her on the rustic bench by the wayside. Over-against them on the eastern side of the valley the hills were already sunset-flushed and the stillness all about was of that peculiar quality that foretells the twilight. Something of its mysterious and significant solemnity had imparted itself to the man's mood. In the spiritual, as in the material world, are signs and presages of night. Rarely meeting her look, and whenever he did so conscious of the indefinable dread with which, despite their feline beauty, her eyes always affected him, Jenner Brading listened in silence to the story told by Irene Marlowe. In deference to the reader's possible prejudice against the artless method of an unpractised historian the author ventures to substitute his own version for hers.

II

A Room May Be Too Narrow for Three,
Though One is Outside

IN A LITTLE log house containing a single room sparely and rudely furnished, crouching on the floor against one of the walls, was a woman, clasping to her breast a child. Outside, a dense unbroken forest extended for many miles in every direction. This was at night and the room was black dark: no human eye could have discerned the woman and the child. Yet they were observed, narrowly, vigilantly, with never even a momentary slackening of attention; and that is the pivotal fact upon which this narrative turns.

Charles Marlowe was of the class, now extinct in this country, of woodmen pioneers—men who found their most acceptable surroundings in sylvan solitudes that stretched along the eastern slope of the Mississippi Valley, from the Great Lakes to the Gulf of Mexico. For more than a hundred years these men pushed ever westward, generation after generation, with rifle and ax, reclaiming from Nature and her savage children here and there an isolated acreage for the plow, no sooner reclaimed than surrendered to their less venturesome but more thrifty successors. At last they burst through the edge of the forest into the open country and vanished as if they had fallen over a cliff. The woodman pioneer is no more; the pioneer of the plains—he whose easy task it was to subdue for occupancy two-thirds of the country in a single generation—is another and inferior creation. With Charles Marlowe in the wilderness, sharing the dangers, hardships and privations of that strange, unprofitable life, were his wife and child, to whom, in the manner of his class, in which the domestic virtues were a religion, he was passionately attached. The woman was still young enough to be comely, new enough to the awful isolation of her lot to be cheerful. By withholding the large capacity for happiness which the simple satisfactions of the forest life could not have filled, Heaven had dealt honorably with her. In her light household tasks, her child, her husband and her few foolish books, she found abundant provision for her needs.

One morning in midsummer Marlowe took down his rifle from the wooden hooks on the wall and signified his intention of getting game.

"We've meat enough," said the wife; "please don't go out to-day. I dreamed last night, O, such a dreadful thing! I cannot recollect it, but I'm almost sure that it will come to pass if you go out."

It is painful to confess that Marlowe received this solemn statement with less of gravity than was due to the mysterious nature of the calamity foreshadowed. In truth, he laughed.

"Try to remember," he said. "Maybe you dreamed that Baby had lost the power of speech."

The conjecture was obviously suggested by the fact that Baby, clinging to the fringe of his hunting-coat with all her ten pudgy thumbs was at that moment uttering her sense of the situation in a series of exultant goo-goos inspired by sight of her father's raccoon-skin cap.

The woman yielded: lacking the gift of humor she could not hold out against his kindly badinage. So, with a kiss for the mother and a kiss for the child, he left the house and closed the door upon his happiness forever.

At nightfall he had not returned. The woman prepared supper and waited. Then she put Baby to bed and sang softly to her until she slept. By this time the fire on the hearth, at which she had cooked supper, had burned out and the room was lighted by a single candle. This she afterward placed in the open window as a sign and welcome to the hunter if he should approach from that side. She had thoughtfully closed and barred the door against such wild animals as might prefer it to an open window—of the habits of beasts of prey in entering a house uninvited she was not advised, though with true female prevision she may have considered the possibility of their entrance by way of the chimney. As the night wore on she became not less anxious, but more drowsy, and at last rested her arms upon the bed by the child and her head upon the arms. The candle in the window burned down to the socket, sputtered and flared a moment and went out unobserved; for the woman slept and dreamed.

In her dreams she sat beside the cradle of a second child. The first one was dead. The father was dead. The home in the forest was lost and the dwelling in which she lived was unfamiliar. There were heavy oaken doors, always closed, and outside the windows, fastened into the thick stone walls, were iron bars, obviously (so she thought) a provision against Indians. All this she noted with an infinite self-pity, but without surprise—an emotion unknown in dreams. The child in the cradle was invisible under its coverlet which something impelled her to remove. She did so, disclosing the face of a wild animal! In the shock of this dreadful revelation the dreamer awoke, trembling in the darkness of her cabin in the wood.

As a sense of her actual surroundings came slowly back to her she felt for the child that was not a dream, and assured herself by its breathing that all was well with it; nor could she forbear to pass a hand lightly across its face. Then, moved by some impulse for which she probably could not have accounted, she rose and took the sleeping babe in her arms, holding it close against her breast. The head of the child's cot was against the wall to which the woman now turned her back as she stood. Lifting her eyes she saw two bright objects starring the darkness with a reddish-green glow. She took them to be two coals on the hearth, but with her returning sense of direction came the disquieting consciousness that they were not in that quarter of the room, moreover were too high, being nearly at the level of the eyes—of her own eyes. For these were the eyes of a panther.

The beast was at the open window directly opposite and not five paces away. Nothing but those terrible eyes was visible, but in the dreadful tumult of her feelings as the situation disclosed itself to her understanding she somehow knew that the animal was standing on its hinder feet, supporting itself with its paws on the window-ledge. That signified a malign interest—not the mere gratification of an indolent curiosity. The consciousness of the attitude was an added horror, accentuating the menace of those awful eyes, in whose steadfast fire her strength and courage were alike consumed. Under their silent questioning she shuddered and turned sick. Her knees failed her, and by degrees, instinctively striving to avoid a sudden movement that might bring the beast upon her, she sank to the floor, crouched against the wall and tried to shield the babe with her trembling body without withdrawing her gaze from the luminous orbs that were killing her. No thought of her husband came to her in her agony—no hope nor suggestion of rescue or escape. Her capacity for thought and feeling had narrowed to the dimensions of a single emotion—fear of the animal's spring, of the impact of its body, the buffeting of its great arms, the feel of its teeth in her throat, the mangling of her babe. Motionless now and in absolute silence, she awaited her doom, the moments growing to hours, to years, to ages; and still those devilish eyes maintained their watch.

Returning to his cabin late at night with a deer on his shoulders Charles Marlowe tried the door. It did not yield. He knocked; there was no answer. He laid down his deer and went round to the window. As he turned the angle of the building he fancied he heard a sound as of stealthy footfalls and a rustling in the undergrowth of the forest, but they were too slight for certainty, even to his practised ear. Approaching the window, and to his surprise finding it open, he threw his leg over the sill and entered. All was darkness and silence. He groped his way to the fire-place, struck a match and lit a candle.

Then he looked about. Cowering on the floor against a wall was his wife, clasping his child. As he sprang toward her she rose and broke into laughter, long, loud, and mechanical, devoid of gladness and devoid of sense—the laughter that is not out of keeping with the clanking of a chain. Hardly knowing what he did he extended his arms. She laid the babe in them. It was dead—pressed to death in its mother's embrace.

III

The Theory of the Defense

THAT IS WHAT occurred during a night in a forest, but not all of it did Irene Marlowe relate to Jenner Brading; not all of it was known to her. When she had concluded the sun was below the horizon and the long summer twilight had begun to deepen in the hollows of the land. For some moments Brading was silent, expecting the narrative to be carried forward to some definite connection with the conversation introducing it; but the narrator was as silent as he, her face averted, her hands clasping and unclasping themselves as they lay in her lap, with a singular suggestion of an activity independent of her will.

"It is a sad, a terrible story," said Brading at last, "but I do not understand. You call Charles Marlowe father; that I know. That he is old before his time, broken by some great sorrow, I have seen, or thought I saw. But, pardon me, you said that you—that you—"

"That I am insane," said the girl, without a movement of head or body.

"But, Irene, you say—please, dear, do not look away from me— you say that the child was dead, not demented."

"Yes, that one—I am the second. I was born three months after that night, my mother being mercifully permitted to lay down her life in giving me mine."

Brading was again silent; he was a trifle dazed and could not at once think of the right thing to say. Her face was still turned away. In his embarrassment he reached impulsively toward the hands that lay closing and unclosing in her lap, but something—he could not have said what—restrained him. He then remembered, vaguely, that he had never altogether cared to take her hand.

"Is it likely," she resumed, "that a person born under such cir-cumstances is like others—is what you call sane?"

Brading did not reply; he was preoccupied with a new thought that was taking shape in his mind—what a scientist would have called an hypothesis; a detective, a theory. It might throw an added light, albeit a lurid one, upon such doubt of her sanity as her own assertion had not dispelled.

The country was still new and, outside the villages, sparsely populated. The professional hunter was still a familiar figure, and among his trophies were heads and pelts of the larger kinds of game. Tales variously credible of nocturnal meetings with savage animals in lonely roads were sometimes current, passed through the customary stages of growth and decay, and were forgotten. A recent addition to these popular apocrypha, originating, apparently, by spontaneous generation in several households, was of a panther which had frightened some of their members by looking in at windows by night. The yarn had caused its little ripple of excitement—had even attained to the distinction of a place in the local newspaper; but Brading had given it no attention. Its likeness to the story to which he had just listened now impressed him as perhaps more than accidental. Was it not possible that the one story had suggested the other—that finding congenial conditions in a morbid mind and a fertile fancy, it had grown to the tragic tale that he had heard?

Brading recalled certain circumstances of the girl's history and disposition, of which, with love's incuriosity, he had hitherto been heedless—such as her solitary life with her father, at whose house no one, apparently, was an acceptable visitor and her strange fear of the night, by which those who knew her best accounted for her never being seen after dark. Surely in such a mind imagination once kindled might burn with a lawless flame, penetrating and enveloping the entire structure. That she was mad, though the conviction gave him the acutest pain, he could no longer doubt; she had only mistaken an effect of her mental disorder for its cause, bringing into imaginary relation with her own personality the vagaries of the local myth-makers. With some vague intention of testing his new "theory," and no very definite notion of how to set about it he said, gravely, but with hesitation:

"Irene, dear, tell me—I beg you will not take offence, but tell me—"

"I have told you," she interrupted, speaking with a passionate earnestness that he had not known her to show—"I have already told you that we cannot marry; is anything else worth saying?"

Before he could stop her she had sprung from her seat and without another word or look was gliding away among the trees toward her father's house. Brading had risen to detain her; he stood watching her in silence until she had vanished in the gloom. Suddenly he started as if he had been shot; his face took on an expression of amazement and alarm: in one of the black shadows into which she had disappeared he had caught a quick, brief glimpse of shining eyes! For an instant he was dazed and irresolute; then he dashed into the wood after her, shouting: "Irene, Irene, look out! The panther! The panther!"

In a moment he had passed through the fringe of forest into open ground and saw the girl's gray skirt vanishing into her father's door. No panther was visible.

IV

An Appeal to the Conscience of God

JENNER BRADING, attorney-at-law, lived in a cottage at the edge of the town. Directly behind the dwelling was the forest. Being a bachelor, and therefore, by the Draconian moral code of the time and place denied the services of the only species of domestic servant known thereabout, the "hired girl," he boarded at the village hotel, where also was his office. The woodside cottage was merely a lodging maintained—at no great cost, to be sure—as an evidence of prosperity and respectability. It would hardly do for one to whom the local newspaper had pointed with pride as "the foremost jurist of his time" to be "homeless," albeit he may sometimes have suspected that the words "home" and "house" were not strictly synonymous. Indeed, his consciousness of the disparity and his will to harmonize it were matters of logical inference, for it was generally reported that soon after the cottage was built its owner had made a futile venture in the direction of marriage—had, in truth, gone so far as to be rejected by the beautiful but eccentric daughter of Old Man Marlowe, the recluse. This was publicly believed because he had told it himself and she had not—a reversal of the usual order of things which could hardly fail to carry conviction.

Brading's bedroom was at the rear of the house, with a single window facing the forest.

One night he was awakened by a noise at that window; he could hardly have said what it was like. With a little thrill of the nerves he sat up in bed and laid hold of the revolver which, with a fore-thought most commendable in one addicted to the habit of sleeping on the ground floor with an open window, he had put under his pillow. The room was in absolute darkness, but being unterrified he knew where to direct his eyes, and there he held them, awaiting in silence what further might occur. He could now dimly discern the aperture—a square of lighter black. Presently there appeared at its lower edge two gleaming eyes that burned with a malignant lustre inexpressibly terrible! Brading's heart gave a great jump, then seemed to stand still. A chill passed along his spine and through his hair; he felt the blood forsake his cheeks. He could not have cried out—not to save his life; but being a man of courage he would not, to save his life, have done so if he had been able. Some trepidation his coward body might feel, but his spirit was of sterner stuff. Slowly the shining eyes rose with a steady motion that seemed an approach, and slowly rose Brading's right hand, holding the pistol. He fired!

Blinded by the flash and stunned by the report, Brading nevertheless heard, or fancied that he heard, the wild, high scream of the panther, so human in sound, so devilish in suggestion. Leaping from the bed he hastily clothed himself and, pistol in hand, sprang from the door, meeting two or three men who came running up from the road. A brief explanation was followed by a cautious search of the house. The grass was wet with dew; beneath the window it had been trodden and partly leveled for a wide space, from which a devious trail, visible in the light of a lantern, led away into the bushes. One of the men stumbled and fell upon his hands, which as he rose and rubbed them together were slippery. On examination they were seen to be red with blood.

An encounter, unarmed, with a wounded panther was not agreeable to their taste; all but Brading turned back. He, with lantern and pistol, pushed courageously forward into the wood. Passing through a difficult undergrowth he came into a small opening, and there his courage had its reward, for there he found the body of his victim. But it was no panther. What it was is told, even to this day, upon a weather-worn headstone in the village churchyard, and

for many years was attested daily at the graveside by the bent figure and sorrow-seamed face of Old Man Marlowe, to whose soul,
and to the soul of his strange, unhappy child, peace. Peace and
reparation.

1897

THE WERE-TIGER
Sir Hugh Charles Clifford

IF YOU ASK that excellent body of *savants* the Society for Psychical
Research, for an opinion on the subject, they will tell you that the
belief in ghosts, magic, witchcraft, and the like having existed in
all ages, and in every land, is in itself a fact sufficient to warrant a
faith in these things, and to establish a strong probability of their
reality. It is not for me, or such as I am, to question the opinion of
these wise men of the West, but if ghosts, and phantoms, and witchcraft and hag-ridings are to be accepted on such grounds, I must
be allowed to put in a plea, for similar reasons, in favour of the
Loup Garou, the Were-Tiger, and all their gruesome family. Wher-
ever there are wild beasts to prey upon the sons of men, there also
is found the belief that the worst and most rapacious of the man-
eaters are themselves human beings, who have been driven to temporarily assume the form of an animal, by the aid of the Black Art,
in order to satisfy their overpowering lust for blood. This belief,
which seeks to account for the extraordinary rapacity of an animal
by tracing its origin to a human being, would seem to be based
upon an extremely cynical appreciation of the blood-thirsty character of our race. The white man and the brown, the yellow and
the black, independently, and without receiving the idea from one
another, have all found the same explanation for the like phenomena, all apparently recognising the truth of the Malay proverb, that
we are like unto the *tôman* fish that preys upon its own kind. This
general opinion, which seems the more worthy of acceptance in
that it is the reverse of flattering to the very races that have formed

71

this curious estimate of their own unlovely character, might by the ignorant and vulgar be supposed to be the real basis of the belief of which I speak, were it not for that dictum of the Society for Psychical Research to which I have above referred. But bowing to this authority, we must accept the Loup Garou and all its kith and kin as stern realities, and not attribute it, as we might perhaps have been inclined to do, to a deadly fear of wild beasts, coupled to a thorough knowledge of the unpleasant qualities of primitive human nature.

Educated Europeans, who live in a land where even

Nature, when she can be seen for the houses, has had man's hall-mark scarred deep into her face, are apt to think that the Age of Superstition has gone to fill the lumber-room of the past. Occasionally they are awakened from this belief by the torturing of a witch in a cabin by an Irish-bog; but even an event so near home as that is powerless to altogether disabuse their minds of their preconceived opinion. The difficulty really is, that they cannot get completely rid of the notion that the world is peopled by educated Europeans like themselves, and by a few other unimportant persons, who do not matter. They know that, numerically, they are as but a drop in the ocean of mankind, but it is possible to know a thing very thoroughly and to realise it not at all. Thus they come by their false opinion; for, in truth, the Age of Superstition lives as lustily to-day, as when, in past years, witches blazed at Smithfield, or died with rending gulps and bursting lungs, lashed fast to an English ducking stool.

In the remote portions of the Malay Peninsula we live in the Middle Ages, with all the appropriate accessories of the dark centuries. Magic and evil spirits, witchcraft and sorcery, spells and love-potions, charms and incantations are, to the mind of the native, as real and as much a matter of everyday life as are the miracle of the growing rice, and the mysteries of the reproduction of species. This must be not only known but realised, not only accepted as a theory, but acknowledged as a fact, if the native view of life is to be understood and appreciated. Tales of the marvellous and the supernatural excite interest and fear in a Malay audience, but they occasion no surprise. Every Malay knows that strange things have happened in the past, and are daily occurring to them and to their fellows. Some are struck by lightning, while others go unscathed; and similarly some have strange experiences, which are not wholly of this world, while others live and die untouched by the supernatural. The two cases, to the Malay mind, are completely parallel; and though both furnish matter for discussion, and excite fear and awe, neither are unheard of phenomena calculated to awaken wonder and surprise.

Thus the existence of the Malayan Loup Garou to the native mind is a fact and not a mere belief. The Malay *knows* that it is true. Evidence, if it be needed, may be had in plenty; the evidence, too, of sober-minded men, whose words, in a Court of Justice, would bring conviction to the mind of the most obstinate jurymen, and be more than sufficient to hang the most innocent of prisoners. The Malays know well how Haji Äbdallah, the native of the little state of Korinchi in Sumatra, was caught naked in a tiger trap, and thereafter purchased his liberty at the price of the buffaloes he had slain, while he marauded in the likeness of a beast. They know of the countless Korinchi men who have vomited feathers, after feasting upon fowls, when for the nonce they had assumed the forms of tigers; and of those other men of the same race who have left their garments and their trading packs in thickets, whence presently a tiger has emerged. All these things the Malays know have happened, and are happening to-day, in the land in which they live, and with these plain evidences before their eyes, the empty assurances of the enlightened European that Were-Tigers do not, and never did exist, excite derision not unmingled with contempt.

The Slim Valley lies across the hills which divide Pahang from Pêrak. It is peopled by Malays of various races. Râwas and Menangkâbaus from Sumatra, men with high-sounding titles and vain boasts, wherewith to carry off their squalid, dirty poverty; Pêrak men from the fair Kinta valley, prospecting for tin, or trading skilfully; fugitives from Pahang, long settled in the district; and the sweepings of Sumatra, Java, and the Peninsula. It was in this place that I heard the following story of a Were-Tiger, from Penghûlu Mat Saleh, who was, and perhaps is still, the Headman of this miscellaneous crew.

Into the Slim Valley, some years ago, there came a Korinchi trader named Haji Äli, and his two sons, Äbdulrahman and Äbas. They came, as is the manner of their people, laden with heavy packs of *sârongs*,—the native skirts or waist-cloths,—trudging in single file through the forests and through the villages, hawking their goods to the natives of the place, with much cunning haggling or hard bargaining. But though they came to trade, they stayed long after the contents of their packs had been disposed of, for Haji Äli took a fancy to the place. Therefore he presently purchased a compound, and with his two sons set to work upon planting cocoa nuts, and cultivating a rice-swamp. They were quiet, well-behaved people; they were regular in their attendance at the mosque for the Friday congregational prayers, and as they were wealthy and prosperous they found favour in the eyes of their poorer neighbours. Thus it happened that when Haji Äli let it be known that he desired to find a wife, there was a bustle in the villages among the parents with marriageable daughters, and, though he was a man well past middle life, Haji Äli found a wide range of choice offered to him.

The girl he selected was Patîmah, the daughter of poor parents, peasants living on their land in one of the neighbouring villages. She was a comely maiden, plump and round, and light of colour, with a merry face to cheer, and willing fingers wherewith to serve a husband. The wedding portion was paid, a feast proportionate to Haji Äli's wealth was held to celebrate the occasion, and the bride was carried oft, after a decent interval, to her husband's home among the fruit groves and the palm-trees. This was not the general custom of the land, for among Malays the husband usually shares his father-in-law's house for a long period after his marriage. But Haji Äli had a fine new house of his own, brave with wattled walls stained cunningly in black and white, and with a luxuriant covering of thatch. Moreover, he had taken the daughter of a poor man to wife, and could dictate his own terms to her and to her parents. The girl went willingly enough, for she was exchanging poverty for wealth, a miserable hovel for a handsome home, and parents who knew exactly how to get out of her the last fraction of work of which she was capable, for a husband who seemed ever kind, generous, and indulgent. None the less, three days later she was found beating on the door of her parents' house, at the hour when dawn was breaking, trembling in every limb, with her hair disordered, her garments drenched with dew from the brushwood through which she had forced her way, with her eyes wild with horror, and mad with a great fear. Her story—the first act in the drama of the Were-Tiger of Slim—ran in this wise, though I shall not attempt to reproduce the words or the manner in which she told it, brokenly, with shuddering sobs, to her awe-stricken parents.

She had gone home with Haji Äli to the house where he dwelt with his two sons, Äbdulrahman and Äbas, and all had treated her kindly and with courtesy. The first day she cooked the rice ill, but though the young men grumbled, Haji Äli said never a word of blame, when she had expected blows, such as would have fallen to the lot of most wives under similar circumstances. She had no complaint to make of her husband's kindness, but none the less she had fled his dwelling, and her parents might "hang her on high, sell her in a far land, scorch her with the sun's rays, immerse her in water, burn her with fire," but never again would she return to one who hunted by night as a Were-Tiger.

Every evening after the Ïsa (the hour of evening prayer) Haji Äli had left the house on one pretext or another, and had not returned until an hour before the dawn. Twice she had not been aware of his return until she found him lying on the sleeping-mat by her side; but, on the third evening, she had remained awake until a noise without told her that her husband was at hand. Then she had hastened to unbar the door, which she had fastened after Äbas and Äbdulrahman had fallen asleep. The moon was behind a cloud, and the light she cast was dim, but Patîmah saw clearly enough the sight which had driven her mad with terror.

On the topmost rung of the ladder, which in this, as in all Malay houses, led from the ground to the threshold of the door, there

rested the head of a full-grown tiger. Patîmah could see the bold,
black stripes which marked his hide, the bristling wires of whis-
ker, the long cruel teeth, and the fierce green light in the beast's
eyes. A round pad, with long curved claws partially concealed, lay
on the ladder rung, one on each side of the monster's head, and
the lower portion of its body reaching to the ground was so fore-
shortened that to the girl it looked like the body of a man. Patîmah
gazed at the tiger, from the distance of only a foot or two, for she
was too paralysed with fear to move or cry out, and as she looked a
gradual transformation took place in the creature at her feet.
Slowly, as one sees a ripple of wind pass over the surface of still
water, the tiger's features palpitated and were changed, until the
horrified girl saw the face of her husband come up through that of
the beast, much as the face of a diver comes up to the surface of a
pool. In another moment Patîmah saw that it was Haji Äli who was
ascending the ladder of his house, and the spell that had hitherto
bound her was snapped. The first use she made of her regained
power of motion was to leap through the doorway past her husband, and to plunge into the jungle which edged the compound.

Malays do not love to travel singly through the jungle even when
the sun is high, and under ordinary circumstances no woman could
by any means be prevailed upon to do such a thing. But Patîmah
was wild with fear of what she had left behind her, and though she
was alone, though the moonlight was dim, and the dawn had not
yet come, she preferred the dismal depths of the forest to the home
of her Were-Tiger husband. Thus she pushed her way through the
underwood, tearing her garments and her flesh with thorns, catching her feet in creepers and trailing vines, stumbling over unseen
logs, and drenching herself to the skin with the dew from the leaves
and grasses against which she brushed. A little before daybreak
she made her way, as I have described, to her father's house, there
to tell the tale of her strange adventure.

The story of what had occurred was speedily noised through
the villages, and the parents with marriageable daughters, who had
been disappointed by Haji Äli's choice of a wife, rejoiced exceedingly, and did not forget to tell Patîmah's papa and mamma that

they had always anticipated something of the sort. Haji Äli made no effort to regain possession of his wife, and his neighbours drawing a natural inference from his actions, avoided him and his sons until they were forced to live in almost complete isolation.

But the drama of the Were-Tiger of Slim was to have a final act.

One night a fine young water-buffalo, the property of the Headman, Penghûlu Mat Saleh, was killed by a tiger, and its owner, saying no word to any man upon the subject, constructed a cunningly arranged spring-gun over the carcass. The tiger-lines were so set that should the tiger return to finish the meal, which he had begun by tearing a couple of hurried mouthfuls from the rump of his kill, he must infallibly be wounded or slain by the bolts and slugs with which the gun was charged.

Next night a loud report, breaking in clanging echoes through the stillness, an hour or two before the dawn was due, apprised Penghûlu Mat Saleh that some animal had fouled the tiger-lines. In all probability it was the tiger, and if he was wounded he would not be a pleasant creature to meet on a dark night. Accordingly Penghûlu Mat Saleh lay still until morning.

In a Malay village all are astir very shortly after daybreak. As soon as it is light enough to see to walk the doors of the houses open one by one, and the people of the village come forth singly huddled to the chin in their *sârongs* or bed coverlets. Each man makes his way down to the river to perform his morning ablutions, or stands on the bank of the stream, staring sleepily at nothing in particular, a black figure silhouetted against the broad ruddiness of a Malayan dawn. Presently the women of the village come out of the houses, in little knots of three or four, with the children pattering at their heels. They carry clusters of gourds in either hand, for it is their duty to fill them from the running stream with the water which will be needed during the day. It is not until the sun begins to rise, when morning ablutions have been carefully performed, and the first sleepiness of the waking hour has departed from heavy eyes, that the people of the village begin to set about the avocations of the day.

Penghûlu Mat Saleh arose that morning and performed his usual daily routine before he collected a party of Malays to aid him in his search for the wounded tiger. He had no difficulty in finding men who were willing to share the excitement of the adventure, and presently he set off with a ragged following of near a dozen at his heels, the party having two guns and many spears and *kris*. They reached the spot where the spring-gun had been set, and they found that beyond a doubt the tiger had returned to his kill. The tracks left by the great pads were fresh, and the tearing up of the earth on one side of the dead buffalo, in a spot where the grass was thickly flecked with blood, showed that the shot had taken effect.

Penghûlu Mat Saleh and his people then set down steadily to follow the trail of the wounded tiger. This was an easy matter, for the beast had gone heavily on three legs, the off-hind leg dragging uselessly. In places, too, a clot of blood showed red among the dew-drenched leaves and grasses. None the less the Penghûlu and his party followed slowly and with caution. They knew that a wounded tiger is never in a mood in which a child may play with him, and also that, even when he has only three legs with which to spring upon his enemies, he can on occasion arrange for a large escort of human beings to accompany him into the land of shadows.

The trail led through the brushwood, in which the dead buffalo lay, and thence into a belt of jungle which edged the river bank a few hundred yards above Penghûlu Mat Saleh's village, and extended up-stream to Kaala Chin Lama, a distance of half a dozen miles. The tiger turned up-stream when this jungle was reached, and half a mile higher up he came out upon a slender wood-path.

When Penghûlu Mat Saleh had followed thus far, he halted and looked at his people.

"Know ye whither this track leads, my brothers?" he asked in a whisper.

The men nodded, but said never a word. A glance at them would have shown you that they were anxious and uneasy.

"What say ye?" continued the Penghûlu. "Do we still follow this trail?"

"It is as thou wilt, O Penghûlu," said the oldest man of the party, answering for his fellows, "we follow thee whithersoever thou goest."

"It is well!" said the Penghûlu. "Come let us go." No more was said, when this whispered colloquy was ended, and the party set down to the trail again silently and with redoubled caution.

The narrow track, which the wounded tiger had followed, led on towards the river bank, and presently the high wattled bamboo fence of a native compound became visible through the trees. Penghûlu Mat Saleh pointed at it. "Behold!" was all he said. Then the party moved on again, still following the tracks of the tiger, and the flecks of red blood on the grass. These led them to the gate of the compound, and through it to the 'lâman or open space before the house. Here they were lost at a spot where the rank spear-blades of the lâlang grass had been beaten down by the falling of some heavy body. A veritable pool of blood marked the place. To it the trail of the limping tiger led. Away from it there was no tracks, save those of the human beings who come and go through the rank growths which cloak the earth in a Malay compound.

"Behold!" said Penghûlu Mat Saleh once more. "Come, let us ascend into the house." And so saying he led the way up the stair-ladder of the dwelling where Haji Äli lived with his two sons Äbas and Äbdulrahman, and whence a month or two before Patîmah had fled during the night-time with a deadly fear in her eyes, and the tale of a strange experience faltering on her lips.

Penghûlu Mat Saleh and his people found Äbas sitting cross-legged in the outer apartment preparing a quid of betel-nut with elaborate care. The visitors squatted on the mats, and the usual customary salutations over, Penghûlu Mat Saleh said:

"I have come in order that I may see thy father. Is he within the house?"

"He is," said Äbas laconically.

"Then make known to him that I would have speech with him."

"My father is sick," said Äbas in a surly tone, and at the word a tremor of excitement ran through Penghûlu Mat Saleh's followers.

"What is that patch of blood in the lâlang before the house?" asked the Penghûlu conversationally, after a short pause.

"We slew a goat yesternight," replied Äbas.

"Hast thou the skin, O Äbas?" asked the Penghûlu, "for I am renewing the faces of my drums, and would fain purchase it."

"The skin was mangy, and we cast it into the river," said Äbas.

"What ails thy father, Äbas?" asked the Penghûlu returning to the charge.

"He is sick," said suddenly a voice from the curtained doorway, which led to the inner apartment. It was the elder son Äbdulrahman who spoke. He held a sword in his hand, and his face wore an ugly look as his words came harshly and gratingly with the foreign accent of the Korinchi people. He went on, still standing, near the doorway, "He is sick, O Penghûlu, and the noise of your words disturbs him. He would slumber and be still. Descend out of the house, he cannot see thee, Penghûlu. Listen to these my words!"

Äbdulrahman's manner, and the words he spoke, were at once so rough and defiant that the Penghûlu saw that he must choose between a scuffle, which would mean bloodshed, and a hasty retreat. He was a mild old man, and he drew a monthly salary from the Pêrak Government. Moreover, he knew that the white men, who guided the destinies of Pêrak, were averse to bloodshed and homicide, even if the person slain was a wizard, or the son of a wizard. Therefore he decided upon retreat.

As they clambered down the steps of the door-ladder, Mat Takir, one of the Penghûlu's men, plucked him by the sleeve, and pointed to a spot beneath the house. Just below the place, in the inner apartment, where Haji Äli might be supposed to lie stretched upon the mat of sickness, the ground was stained a dim red for a space of several inches in circumference. Malay floors are made of laths of wood or of bamboo laid parallel to one another, with spaces between each one of them. This is convenient, as the whole of the ground beneath the house can thus be used as a slop-pail, wastebasket, and rubbish heap. The red stain lying where it did had the look of blood, blood moreover from some one within the house, whose wound had very recently been washed and dressed. It might also have been the red juice of the betel-nut, but its stains are but rarely seen in such large patches. Whatever it may have been the

Penghûlu and his people had no opportunity of examining it more closely, for Äbdulrahman and Äbas followed them out of the compound, and barred the door against them.

Then the Penghûlu set off to tell his tale to the District Officer, the white man under whose charge the Slim Valley had been placed. He went with many misgivings, for Europeans are sceptical concerning such tales, and when he returned, more or less dissatisfied, some five days later, he found that Haji Äli and his sons had disappeared. They had fled down river on a dark night, without a soul being made aware of their intended departure. They had neither stayed to reap their crops, which now stood ripening in the fields; to sell their house and compound, which had been bought with good money,— "dollars of the whitest," as the Malay phrase has it,—nor yet to collect their debts. This is a fact; and to one who knows the passion for wealth and for property, which is to be found in the breast of every Sumatran Malay, it is perhaps the strangest circumstance of all the weird events, which go to make up the drama of the Were-Tiger of Slim.

There is, to the European mind, only one possible explanation. Haji Äli and his sons had been the victims of foul play. They had been killed by the simple villagers of Slim, and a cock-and-bull story trumped up to account for their disappearance. This is a very good, and withal a very astute explanation, showing as it does a profound knowledge of human nature, and I should be more than half inclined to accept it as the correct one, but for the fact that Haji Äli and his sons turned up in quite another part of the Peninsula some months later. They have nothing out of the way about them to mark them from their fellows, except that Haji Äli goes lame on his right leg.

1899

A VENDETTA OF THE JUNGLE
ARTHUR APPLIN AND H. SIDNEY WARWICK

NILSON, THE TREASURER GENERAL, was stretched in a long cane chair, trying to keep his cigar alight: he was a man who used about two boxes of matches every time he smoked a cigar. The chair was only six feet long, so his legs dangled over the side and knocked the Resident on the head.

The Resident was sitting on a heap of cushions, nursing his knees and looking very wise. He was a short, angular man, with dark beard and moustache, and a yellow skin. All that was known of him was his name—Roberts. He had lived in the country all his life and expected to die there.

"I can't make out why they've let me live so long: I know it makes the Governor anxious, they'll be knocking another fifty dollars off my pay if I don't kick under soon."

Geoffrys was standing by the verandah, rolling a cigarette. Needless to say, he was an energetic man—had not been in the country long. He was popular, for until to-night his wife had been the only white woman within five hundred miles. She was neither pretty nor young, but she was a woman, and could sing English songs—after a fashion. Geoffrys was in charge of the native force, about thirty Sikhs. He was expected to keep a tract of country the size of Scotland and inhabited by several thousand natives—for the most part unfriendly—under control.

The Treasurer General was up on sick leave, the interior having the reputation of being less unhealthy than the coast.

"It's no use," Geoffrys was saying; "it's too hot for cigarette papers, they dissolve. I wonder if we shall be attacked to-night."

"Don't care if we are: I wish you'd take some interest in our visitor. You're the only fellow who should know what to do under the circumstances, and you will worry about a possible attack."

"My dear fellow," he replied, throwing himself into a chair and fanning himself after his cigarette-making exertions, "if you woke up in the morning and found a Kris sticking in your chest you'd be the first to grumble."

"If I was alive enough to complain, I'd be too grateful to do so; double your sentries."

Geoffrys was standing by the verandah, rolling a cigarette.

Nilson chuckled and lit another match.

"Sentries," grumbled Geoffrys. "A darned lot of good they are! I have to wake up five times a night and go out and look for 'em: always find 'em rolled up fast asleep. Have to wake 'em up and go to bed again, knowing they'll be asleep again before I am."

"What about Miss Langford?" And the Resident knocked out his pipe.

"Yes, what about Miss Langford?" repeated Byng, a newly-arrived cadet, who was studying jungle-fever and strong cigars.

"Better go to bed, Byng, before Mrs. Crumps comes out to feed," suggested Nilson.

"I think Miss Langford is all right," said Geoffrys. "Fetch me a cigar, Byng. You must get used to exercise."

"What on earth made the Governor send his daughter up here?" asked someone.

"Knew Geoffrys had a wife, and didn't know he'd sent her down country. What are you going to do?"

"Wonder what she is doing?"

"Gradually melting, I suppose."

"I wonder if she has any clothes?"

"Shall I go and see," suggested Byng in a meek voice.

"No," snarled Roberts. "Take the matches from the Treasurer and give them to me. Where is she going to sleep, Geoffrys?"

"My room, I suppose. I shall hunt up sentries and keep them awake."

"How many men have you got here?" asked Nilson.

"Seventeen, less three with fever."

"Um! Too many; there'll be complaints."

"You are always talking of Mrs. Crumps; who is she?" asked Byng, hiding a partially smoked cigar in his shoe. Roberts laughed.

"Mrs. Crumps is a woman who went out for a walk and got eaten by a tiger. Now—so the natives will tell you—her soul has entered the tiger's body, and she prowls about the jungle waiting to kill somebody else—her enemies for preference. She might mistake you for one, Byng. You'd better go to bed or you'll lose your way."

"I think I will." He fetched his cap. "Anyone else coming—it's rather dark."

"You'll be all right, run away."

"Good night."

"I wonder what fond mother sent her son out here to die—don't kick my head, Nilson."

Geoffrys watched Byng disappear into the darkness. Roberts shut his eyes and tried to sleep. The Treasurer-General gathered himself together and sat at, what was called by courtesy, a piano, and strummed tunes from the "Artist's Model."

The night hung hot and heavy. Now and then a big fly hurtled through the room and disappeared again; a bird shrieked in the jungle, or the weird bark of a sambur broke the stillness. Occasional flashes of lightning made the sky brilliant and cast fantastic shadows about the fringe of the jungle.

A tall, slim girl, with masses of brown hair, wrapped in a loose, white kimono, quietly entered the room. She stood beneath the lamp, uncertain what to do. Nilson continued to strum "Click, click, I'm a monkey on a stick." Roberts was already half asleep, and Geoffrys still stared towards the jungle.

At first she looked nervously from one to the other, but gradually a smile parted her lips. Then she laughed softly to herself. She wondered whom to speak to. Suddenly, Roberts yawned loudly:—

"Somebody give me a cigar." No one moved. Geoffrys was intent with his thoughts, Nilson did not hear him. The girl saw a box of cigars on the table, she quietly took one and stood over Roberts and dropped it.

It fell on his nose. "Confound you!" he cried, sleepily opening his eyes. They fell on Miss Langford. He tried to rise, but he was on his back among the cushions, and she stood above him. He had to remain as he was.

"I—I beg your pardon,—I—" Then in a hopeless aside to the figure strumming on the piano, "Nilson! I say, Nilson!"

"Hush!" she said, putting her finger to her lips, "Hush, he is playing. You must not disturb yourselves, you all look so comfortable."

"If you were to—move," he gasped, "I could rise."

"I don't want you to rise; I want you all to be as happy as if I hadn't arrived!" She looked at the Treasurer General's back, and she laughed a little louder, then she looked at Geoffrys and she was silent for a space. Roberts tried juggling feats with the cushions and cursed the piano.

"You must be awfully fond of music," she whispered presently; "shall I sing to you?"

Roberts tried to say he'd be delighted. He had kicked one of the cushions free, and was aiming it at the Treasurer's head, who was oblivious to everything. He was playing "Honey, my Honey" now, and Miss Langford began to sing the words, so softly at first that Roberts could hardly hear her, but gradually swelling into deep, contralto notes.

The Resident dropped the poised cushion and listened; Geoffrys moved uneasily; the girl sang, her eyes looked out towards the jungle now and her thoughts travelled home:—

> *Won't you wander through the grove by the pale*
> *star-light,*
> *And whisper a word to me!*
> *Where the shadows all lie deep*

Oh, so quietly we'll creep,
Not a little bird shall hear us in its nest upon
    the tree.
Oh, honey, come and listen to the music far
    away!

"What's that?" cried Geoffrys, without moving. "Do you hear?"
"Hush," cried Nilson, commencing the next bar.
"Hush," said Roberts.
The girl continued:—

Oh, come, my love,
    Oh, come, my love to me,
    Oh, come, my love,
    Oh, come, my love to me.
You shall nestle on my breast,
    And we'll dream awhile, and rest,
    While we listen to the music, to the music far away.

A big moth buzzed into the lamp and the light went out, but she sang the song to the end.

The Treasurer General ceased playing, his hands rested on the keys; he looked at nothing. All the men seemed to be waiting for something.

At last Roberts spoke:

"Gentlemen, Miss Langford."

They rose, Geoffrys took her hand and led her to his chair. "Thank you. You must forgive us for not hearing you enter."

"Awfully glad we didn't," murmured Nilson, taking himself, a cigar, and a box of matches to the long chair.

"I am sorry my wife has just gone down-country," continued Geoffrys. "You must try to be as happy as this beastly country and this awful heat will allow you—the native women I have told off to look after you will give you all you want—that is to say, all we possess."

"Which isn't much," added the Resident.

"Please don't bother about me. You must all behave as if I wasn't here. Oh, isn't it hot!"

"Thought it was cooler to-night. Got any more matches, Roberts?" Nilson spoke.

"No. You cost the Government a dollar a week for matches," replied the Resident.

"Well, then, I shall make tracks. Good-night, Miss Langford."

Roberts followed Nilson. Geoffrys began to fan Miss Langford.

They heard the Resident's voice and the tramp of a sentry gradually die away.

"I bet the beggar has gone to sleep."

"Who?"

"The sentry. They always go to sleep, the sentries."

"Have you been here long?" she asked presently.

"Long enough to want to see English faces, hear English voices. It is lonely sometimes."

"But you have your wife."

"Yes. I generally have my wife."

"Is that her photo—may I look? Why, how much older—" She stopped suddenly, confused. "Oh, I beg your pardon!"

Geoffrys smiled. "Yes, everyone says, or thinks, that. I married her when I was twenty."

She looked at the photograph and then at the man by her side. A young man, tall, with a strong face, though sad.

And she understood.

It was a well-known story, of how old Major Geoffrys, after gambling his money away on gold-mines, had committed suicide, and left his widow without a farthing in the world, their only son just expecting his commission. And then the son's marriage with a wealthy Jewess.

She met the son now for the first time—she had met his mother in England—and as she looked at him she guessed why he had married. He married her because he loved—his mother.

Three weeks passed and nothing happened; no attack was made on the Residency, Geoffrys' wife had not returned. Those were the only events expected and neither came to pass. Everything else happened with cheerful monotony—the sun blazed by day, the jungle steamed, occasional hurricanes of wind and rain tore away portions of the bungalows and frightened Miss Langford.

Roberts took two days leave, big game shooting, and the Treasurer General stuck to his cigars.

Geoffrys explained Eastern life and Eastern habits to Miss Langford.

Twenty-one days is a long time for two people to be alone—in the middle of a jungle. When a man has only the jungle, he weds himself to it—to its solitude, its strange sounds and silences. And the great jungle takes him to its heart, and teaches him its language, its life, until he loves it and becomes part of it and can never again live away from it in peace.

Geoffrys was alone in the jungle and was drawn towards it; his wife, never a part of his life, ceased to exist for him, save as a necessity or a duty, like the heat or keeping the sentries awake. Then, when she went down-country, duty claimed less of him and the jungle more—until she came. The drowsy solitude of the lonely land wove all the youth and love and passion in their lives, together. In that hot, topical country, where great creepers clambered from one tree to another, where seeds sprang to life and flowers blossomed in a night, love grew as swiftly and luxuriantly. The Treasurer General saw what was happening but took no notice, and, when he had nothing else to do, strummed on the piano, "I want yer, ma honey, yes I do!" The Resident grumbled:

"Geoffrys is going to make an ass of himself, why doesn't someone stop it?"

"My dear fellow, we're not in London; thank goodness!"

"That's the bother, it wouldn't matter in London. Why don't you stop it?"

The Treasurer General stared at Roberts and re-lit his cigar. "Why don't I stop the heat? Or why don't I cut the jungle down? You can't cut one of the seasons out of the year; summer's bound to have a look-in, even though it is a bit late now and then. Don't fool with nature, Autumn will come soon enough.

"But his wife will return, there'll be a row, the Governor will hear all about—" Roberts broke off suddenly as Geoffrys entered. He held a letter in his hand. "They've just brought the mail up. My wife ought to have arrived, she left last night—probably arrive to-night."

"Glad to see her back," said Roberts, looking uncomfortably at Nilson, who continued to strum on the piano.

Miss Langford entered and Geoffrys took her to the window, where they sat talking in whispers and watching the pathway which led through the jungle. Roberts fidgeted about the room and made remarks to Nilson which were received in silence. After a while he settled down to his thoughts and a pipe.

The sun disappeared, night came; great flies and moths buzzed through the room: wild birds and beasts cried and shrieked from the darkness.

Nilson was playing, "I want yer, ma honey, yes I do!"

"I have grown so young these last three weeks," Geoffrys said to Miss Langford, by the window.

"I am glad if I have relieved the monotony of your life, but—"

"But what?" for she had stopped abruptly. She was looking out towards the jungle—through which the other woman would come.

"I wonder if—if you will grow sad again now—more sad, more dissatisfied?"

He nodded. "But for three weeks I have been happy. I shall not forget that." His voice was not quite under his control.

"Nor I."

"It is no use saying I was wrong to see so much of you—"

"That was the jungle's fault!" she said, with a little laugh.

"Not its fault, its virtue. And I do not think it is wrong to tell you now what you know, but I have never told you—shall never again have the chance of telling—" he paused: she did not speak or move. She was twisting her little lace handkerchief between her fingers. "I want to say, to hear you say: 'I love you.'"

For a minute she was silent. Then in a low, not quite steady voice:

"After to-night perhaps you and I will never speak together alone: and I am going away soon—so—it may not be wrong to tell you—"

"Tell me."

She put her hand in his and looked into his eyes. "I love you, I shall always love you."

"Thank you."

"Won't you sing us that song again, Miss Langford?" asked the Treasurer General, swinging round his seat. "The one you sang the night you arrived, you know, and found us all asleep."

She rose and stood beneath the lamp: "You mustn't look at me," she smiled, "you must pretend you don't see me."

Nilson played the opening bars; Roberts pulled at a pipe and shut his eyes. Geoffrys looked away into the jungle and listened.

> *"Oh, Honey, my Honey, if the night would only last*
> *and never the day-light come,*
> *In a love-dream we would live, while our hearts*
> *beat fast and only our lips were dumb.*
> *All alone, my Dusky Queen,*
> *We would live and love unseen,*
> *'Mid the singing of the wood bird and the insect's*
> *drowsy hum—"*

Something was moving in the jungle, coming towards the bungalow, men running: Geoffrys watched them, probably his wife had arrived.

No, there were only native men, they ran silently and swiftly. One reached the verandah and stood before Geoffrys, "Tuan! Tuan!" he cried, "Mem suda mati oli 'riman! Adohi! Adohi!"

"My God!"

Miss Langford heard him and stopped singing; Roberts jumped up:

"What is it, old man?"

"My wife! killed—"

"Killed!" There was a terrible silence for a few moments.

"How?" The Resident spoke.

"Coming through the jungle—the tiger—" No one moved.

Outside the natives chattered and gesticulated and cried:—
"Adohi! Adohi!"

Roberts crossed to the window and sent them away: then he looked helplessly at Nilson: Nilson shook his head and quietly walked to the door. Roberts followed his example.

Geoffrys and Miss Langford were left alone: he and she and no other.

It was two years later. Captain Geoffrys and his newly-married wife were pacing the verandah of the bungalow.

"Dearest," he was saying, with a loving look at the slim figure by his side, "you must get these silly superstitions out of your head. Besides, it happened twenty-five months ago, and no one has seen Mrs. Crumps since."

"Don't jest," she replied with a shudder, her hand tightening on his arm. "It would be—*she* now. Do you remember that night twenty-five months ago? Oh, I was mad and wicked that night! You belonged to her, yet I told you I loved you—perhaps I told you at the very moment when she was being killed! And I *did* see it—not many nights ago—at the window: and I fancied I saw *her* looking at me out of the tiger's eyes, and hating me, for she loved you, Dick."

"Come to bed, dear," he said, tenderly; "you must get rid of these nervous fancies. If either has cause for self-reproach, it is I, not you, little woman. Thank goodness, we have a year's leave, and in two months you will be safe on your way to England."

Kissing her, he led her to their room. Then he returned to the balcony and continued pacing up and down.

"I wonder if this cursed country is making me superstitious?" he said, suddenly. "I wish I had shot the brute!"

For this man who had lived so long in the mysticism-steeped atmosphere of the East, until, almost unconsciously, he had assimilated into his nature some of its subtle influence, found that, in spite of himself, in spite of his reason, the horrible native belief was taking hold of him—the belief that certain man-eaters are possessed by human souls which wander in search of their enemies. And when the "thing" has killed the being it most hated in its former life, its re-incarnated soul is freed, whilst the soul of its victim, in turn, passes into the beast form, to carry on a like horrible vendetta.

So the soul of the woman they jestingly called "Mrs. Crumps," was free, but the tiger still lived. Whose soul dwelt in its great, striped body now? Whose soul now roamed through the great, trackless jungle, waiting its chance to kill the enemy it hated in mortal life? The soul of the woman who had been his wife; the soul of the woman he had never loved. And she waited to kill her enemy— the woman he did love—the woman who had taken her place.

"Bah! I am as foolish as the natives." Geoffrys threw his cigar away and tried to laugh at these fantastic thoughts. "I believe I am becoming a coward."

But his laugh could not kill his fears. With a sudden shudder, he remembered another odd fact now—an uncanny fact, that hammered tighter to his heart his growing superstitious fear. The native woman whom the tiger had killed had borne a violent prejudice—why, he did not know—against his first wife, and the latter had been the tiger's next victim!

"What a horrible business it is! I ought to have shot the brute long ago," he muttered. "Why didn't I?"

He knew why. He had advanced far into the interior one week, and had hoped to find this man-eating beast which had become a terror to the district. Though he would not confess so to himself, it was the sole reason of his expedition.

And suddenly, he had come unexpectedly upon the beast, crouching within thirty yards of him. His native servants ran shrieking away and clambered up the trees, shouting— "Riman! 'riman!—Mem 'riman!"

But as he raised his rifle and looked down the barrels, the tiger's eyes met his; he wavered, he did not fire. The man and the beast with human eyes stared at each other. He tried to feel the trigger, he tried to steady himself and fire, but he could not. A horrible thought gripped his heart—he was looking into the eyes of his wife.

The tiger disappeared and he returned to the bungalow, frightened, ashamed.

And ever since he had been haunted by the memory of those eyes, fixed cruelly on him. He tried to forget them—to laugh at them—but he could not.

Worse still, the woman he loved was haunted by the same thought, the same fear; that somewhere in the jungle, in that vast overgrown tree and flower land, a human soul in a beast's shape watched and waited—for revenge.

"Only two months," he repeated, "and I will take her away from this cursed country, where these horrible superstitions cannot follow us; where this silence and loneliness will be forgotten. God comfort her, I love her so!"

He sat on, brooding in the verandah. Only two months, but it seemed a long, long time. Two months alone with natives, fever, and the possibility! The Treasurer General had returned to the coast and his work some time ago. Byng had been sent to another district, Roberts had grown morose and taciturn of late—perhaps that had been Geoffrys' fault, he had been so wrapped up in his wife—his beloved.

It was getting late, but he thought of walking across to the Resident's bungalow now. The heat and silence were maddening. He listened to the silence—not a leaf stirring; then he started, as a human-like shriek rent the air.

"Those brutes in the jungle," he muttered. "Hang my nerves!"

The sentries were asleep, of course. He had been lax of late; keeping them awake disturbed *her*.

He rose and walked along the verandah with the intention of finding and awakening them.

As he stepped down on to the lawn and passed beneath the bed-room window he paused, surprised. For he thought he saw his wife moving about the room. Perhaps she was restless—she could not sleep; she was waiting for him, she was afraid.

"Poor little woman, I am a selfish beast!" he said aloud.

Yes, he fancied he could see the white lace of her night-gown sweeping the floor; surely she was looking out towards where he stood, her eyes were looking straight into his—strange, how clearly they shone in the darkness!

He shuddered, for at that instant they reminded him of the other woman's eyes: it was just as she used to stare at him.

"Hang the sentries! I will go to her now." He took a step forward and then paused again: her eyes fascinated and frightened him. She was looking straight at him, but yet she made no sign. And her eyes were still—the eyes of the other woman!

"God! I am going mad! Curse this folly!" he groaned, covering his face with his hands.

But when he removed them he started back and shrieked. And the sleeping sentry awoke and ran towards him—until he, also, saw what Geoffrys saw. Then he, too, shrieked at the horror of the thing, and dropped his rifle and ran away.

From the bedroom window a great tiger crept, dragging with it a woman's body—the body of his beloved.

The beast sprang from the verandah to the ground, Geoffrys heard the sickening thud. Blots of red spotted the white gown.

They were face to face—the man and the beast.

Geoffrys seized the sentry's rifle; if it was too late to save her, he could kill *it*.

It watched him, lashed his tail, and it savagely struck the woman with one of its great paws: a white hand beat the ground convulsively for a few seconds and then lay still.

His arms were steady now and he covered the tiger: it gave a long, low howl and once again its eyes met Geoffrys' along the shining barrels.

Only now they were no longer the eyes of the slayer, they were the eyes of his beloved.

The finger on the trigger grew suddenly nerveless. He could not fire between *those* eyes.

* * *

WHEN HE LOOKED up the tiger had gone.

He was alone with a dead body—only the dead body of the woman he had loved.

1901

THE GRAY CAT
Barry Pain

I HEARD THIS story from Archdeacon M —. I should imagine that it would not be very difficult, by trimming it a little and altering the facts here and there, to make it capable of some simple explanation; but I have preferred to tell it as it was told to me.

After all, there is some explanation possible, even if there is not one definite and simple explanation clearly indicated. It must rest with the reader whether he will prefer to believe that some of the so-called uncivilized races may possess occult powers transcending anything of which the so-called civilized are capable, or whether he will consider that a series of coincidences is sufficient to account for the extraordinary incidents which, in a plain brief way, I am about to relate. It does not seem to me essential to state which view I hold myself, or if I hold neither, and have reasons for not stating a third possible explanation. I must add a word or two with regard to Archdeacon M. At the time of this story he was in his fiftieth year. He was a fine scholar, a man of considerable learning. His religious views were remarkably broad; his enemies said remarkably thin. In his younger days he had been something of an athlete, but owing to age, sedentary habits, and some amount of self-indulgence, he had grown stout, and no longer took exercise in any form. He had no nervous trouble of any kind. His death, from heart disease, took place about three years ago. He told me the story twice, at my request; there was an interval of about six weeks between the two narrations; some of the details were elicited by

95

questions of my own. With this preliminary note, we may proceed to the story.

In January, 1881, Archdeacon M—, who was a great admirer of Tennyson's poetry, came up to London for a few days, chiefly in order to witness the performance of "The Cup," at the Lyceum. He was not present on the first night (Monday, January 3), but on a later night in the same week. At that time, of course, the poet had not received his peerage, nor the actor his knighthood.

On leaving the theatre, less satisfied with the play than with the magnificence of the setting, the Archdeacon found some slight difficulty in getting a cab. He walked a little way down the Strand to find one, when he encountered unexpectedly his old friend, Guy Breddon.

Breddon (that was not his real name) was a man of considerable fortune, a member of the learned societies, and devoted to Central African exploration. He was two or three years younger than the Archdeacon, and a man of tremendous physique.

Breddon was surprised to find the Archdeacon in London, and the Archdeacon was equally surprised to find Breddon in England at all. Breddon carried off the Archdeacon with him to his rooms, and sent a servant in a cab to the Langham to pay the Archdeacon's bill and fetch his luggage. The Archdeacon protested, but faintly, and Breddon would not hear of his hospitality being refused.

Breddon's rooms were an expensive suite immediately over a ruinous upholsterer's in a street off Berkeley Square. There was a private street-door, and from it a private staircase to the first and second floors.

The suite of rooms on the first floor, occupied by Breddon, was entirely shut off from the staircase by a door. The second floor suite, tenanted by an Irish M. P., was similarly shut off, and at that time was unoccupied.

Breddon and the Archdeacon passed through the street-door and up the stairs to the first landing, from whence, by the staircase-door, they entered the flat. Breddon had only recently taken the flat, and the Archdeacon had never been there before. It consisted of a broad L-shaped passage with rooms opening into it. There were many trophies on the walls. Horned heads glared at them; stealthy but stuffed beasts watched them furtively from under tables. There was a perfect arsenal of murderous weapons gleaming brightly under the shaded gaslights.

Breddon's servant prepared supper for them before leaving for the Langham, and soon the two men were discussing Mr. Tennyson, Mr. Irving, and a parody of the "Queen of the May" which had recently appeared in *Punch*, and doing justice to some oysters, a cold pheasant with an excellent salad, and a bottle of '74 Pommery. It was characteristic of the Archdeacon that he remembered exactly the items of the supper, and that Breddon rather neglected the wine.

After supper they passed into the library, where a bright fire was burning. The Archdeacon walked towards the fire, rubbing his plump hands together. As he did so, a portion of the great rug of gray fur on which he was standing seemed to rise up. It was a gray cat of enormous size, larger than any that the Archdeacon had ever seen before, and of the same colour as the rug on which it had been sleeping. It rubbed itself affectionately against the Archdeacon's leg, and purred as he bent down to stroke it.

"What an extraordinary animal!" said the Archdeacon. "I had no idea cats could grow to this size. Its head's queer, too—so much too small for the body."

"Yes," said Breddon, "and his feet are just as much too big."

The gray cat stretched himself voluptuously under the Archdeacon's caressing hand, and the feet could be seen plainly. They were very broad, and the claws, which shot out, seemed unusually powerful and well developed. The beast's coat was short, thick, and wiry.

"Most extraordinary!" the Archdeacon repeated.

He lowered himself into a comfortable chair by the fire. He was still bending over the cat and playing with it when a slight chink made him look up. Breddon was putting something down on the table behind the liquor decanters.

"Any particular breed?" the Archdeacon asked.

"Not that I know of. Freakish, I should say. We found him on board the boat when I left for home—may have come there after mice. He'd have been thrown overboard but for me. I got rather interested in him. Smoke?"

"Oh, thank you."

Outside a cold north wind screamed in quick gusts. Within came the sharp scratch of the match on the ribbed glass as the Archdeacon lit his cigar, the bubble of the rose-water in Breddon's hookah, the soft step of Breddon's man carrying the Archdeacon's luggage into the bedroom at the end of the L-shaped passage, and the constant purring of the big gray cat.

"And what's the cat's name?" the Archdeacon asked.

Breddon laughed.

"Well, if you must have the plain truth, he's called Gray Devil—or, more frequently, Devil *tout court*."

"Really, now, really, you can't expect an Archdeacon to use such abominable language. I shall call him Gray—or perhaps Mr. Gray would be more respectful, seeing the shortness of our acquaintance. Do you object to the smell of smoke, Mr. Gray? The intelligent beast does not object. Probably you've accustomed him to it."

"Well, seeing what his name is he could hardly object to smoke, could he?"

Breddon's servant entered. As the door opened and shut, one heard for a moment the crackle of the newly-lit fire in the room that awaited the Archdeacon. The servant swept up the hearth, and, under Archidiaconal direction, mixed a lengthy brandy-and-soda. He retired with the information that he would not be wanted again that night.

"Did you notice," asked the Archdeacon, "the way Mr. Gray followed your man about? I never saw a more affectionate cat."

"Think so?" said Breddon. "Watch this time."

For the first time he approached the gray cat, and stretched out his hand as if to pet him. In an instant the cat seemed to have gone mad. Its claws shot out, its back hooped, its coat bristled, its tail stood erect; it cursed and spat, and its small green eyes glared. But a close observer would have noticed that all the time it watched not only Breddon, but also that object which had chinked as Breddon had put it down behind the decanters.

The Archdeacon lay back in his chair and laughed heartily.

"What funny creatures they are, and never so funny as when they lose their tempers! Really, Mr. Gray, out of respect to my cloth, you might have refrained from swearing like that. Poor Mr. Gray! Poor puss!"

Breddon resumed his seat with a grim smile. The gray cat slowly subsided, and then thrust its head, as though demanding sympathy, into the fat palm of the Archdeacon's dependent hand.

Suddenly the Archdeacon's eye lighted on the object which the cat had been watching, visible now that the servant had displaced the decanters.

"Goodness me!" he exclaimed, "you've got a revolver there."

"That is so," said Breddon.

"Not loaded, I trust?"

"Oh yes, fully loaded."

"But isn't that very dangerous?"

"Well, no; I'm used to these things, and I'm not careless with them. I should have thought it more dangerous to have introduced Gray Devil to you without it. He's much more powerful than an ordinary cat, and I fancy there's something beside cat in his pedigree. When I bring a stranger to see him I keep the cat covered with the revolver until I see how the land lies. To do the brute justice, he has always been most friendly with everybody except myself. I'm his only antipathy. He'd have gone for me just now but that he's smart enough to be afraid of this."

He tapped the revolver.

"I see," said the Archdeacon seriously, "and can guess how it happened. You scared him one day by firing the revolver for joke; the report frightened him, and he's never forgiven you or forgotten the revolver. Wonderful memory some of these animals have!"

"Yes," said Breddon, "but that guess won't do. I have never, intentionally or by chance, given the 'Devil' any reason for his enmity. So far as I know he has never heard a firearm, and certainly he has never heard one since I made his acquaintance.

Somebody may have scared him before, and I'm inclined to think that somebody did, for there can be no doubt that the brute knows all that a cat need know about a revolver, and that he's scared of it.

"The first time we met was almost in darkness. I'd got some cases that I was particular about, and the captain had said I could go down to look after them. Well, this beast suddenly came out of a lump of black and flew at me. I didn't even recognise that it was a cat, because he's so mighty big. I fetched him a clip on the side of the head that knocked him off, and whipped out my iron. He was away in a streak. He knew. And I've had plenty of proof since that he knows. He'd bite me now if he had the chance, but he understands that he hasn't got the chance. I'm often half inclined to take him on plain—shooting barred—and to feel my own hands breaking his damned neck!"

"Really, old man, really!" said the Archdeacon in perfunctory protest, as he rose and mixed himself another drink.

"Sorry to use strong language, but I don't love that cat, you know."

The Archdeacon expressed his surprise that in that case Breddon did not get rid of the brute.

"You come across him on board ship and he flies at you. You save his life, give him board and lodging, and he still hates you so much that he won't let you touch him, and you are no fonder of him than he is of you. Why don't you part company?"

"As for his board, I've rarely known him to eat anything except his own kill. He goes out hunting every night. I keep him simply and solely because I'm afraid of him. As long as I can keep him I know my nerves are all right. If I let my funk of him make any difference—well, I shouldn't be much good in a Central African forest. At first I had some idea of taming him—and, besides, there was a queer coincidence."

He rose and opened the window, and Gray Devil slowly slunk up to it. He paused a few moments on the window-sill and then suddenly sprang and vanished.

"What was the coincidence?"

"What do you think of that?" Breddon handed the Archdeacon a figure of a cat which he had taken from the mantelpiece. It was a little thing about three inches high. In colour, in the small head, enormous feet, and curiously human eyes, it seemed an exact reproduction of Gray Devil.

"A perfect likeness. How did you get it made?"

"I got the likeness before I got the original. A little Jew dealer sold it me the night before I left for England. He thought it was Egyptian, and described it as an idol. Anyhow, it was a niceish piece of jade."

"I always thought jade was bright green."

"It may be—or white—or brown. It varies. I don't think there can be any doubt that this little figure is old, though I doubt if it's Egyptian."

Breddon put it back in its place.

"By the way, that same night the little Jew came to try and buy it back again. He offered me twice what I had given for it. I said he must have found somebody who was pretty keen on it. I asked if it was a collector. The Jew thought not; said it was a coloured gentleman. Well, that finished it. I wasn't going to do anything to oblige a nigger. The Jew pleaded that it was a particularly fine buck-nigger, with mountains of money, who'd been tracking the thing for years, and hinted at all manner of mumbo-jumbo business—to scare me, I suppose. However, I wouldn't listen, and kicked him out. Then came the coincidence. Having bought the likeness, next day I found the living original. Rum, wasn't it?"

At this moment the clock struck, and the Archdeacon recognised with horror that it was very, very much past the time when respectable Archdeacons should be in bed and asleep. He rose and said good-night, observing that he'd like to hear more about it on the morrow.

This was extremely unfortunate, for it will be seen it is just at this part of the story that one wants full details, and on the morrow it became impossible to elicit them.

Before leaving the library Breddon closed the window, and the Archdeacon asked how "Mr. Gray," as he called him, would get back.

"Very likely he's back already. He's got a special window in the kitchen, made on purpose, just big enough to let him get in and out as he likes."

"But don't other cats get in, too?"

"No," said Breddon. "Other cats avoid Gray Devil."

The Archdeacon found himself unaccountably nervous when he got to his room. He owned to me that he had to satisfy himself that there was no one concealed under the bed or in the wardrobe. However, he got into bed, and after a little while fell into a deep sleep; his fire was burning brightly, and the room was quite light.

Shortly after four he was awakened by a loud scream. Still sleepy, he did not for the moment locate the sound, thinking that it must have come from the street outside. But almost immediately afterwards he heard the report of a revolver fired twice in quick succession, and then, after a short pause, a third time.

The Archdeacon was terribly frightened. He did not know what had happened, and thought of armed burglars. For a time—he did not think it could have been more than a minute—fear held him motionless. Then with an effort he rose, lit the gas, and hurried on his clothes. As he was dressing, he heard a step down the passage and a knock at his door.

He opened it, and found Breddon's servant. The man had put on a blue overcoat over his night-things, and wore slippers. He was shivering with cold and terror.

"Oh, my God, sir!" he exclaimed, "Mr. Breddon's shot himself. Would you come, sir?"

The Archdeacon followed the man to Breddon's bedroom. The smoke still hung thickly in the room. A mirror had been smashed, and lay in fragments on the floor. On the bed, with his back to the Archdeacon, lay Breddon, dead. His right hand still grasped the revolver, and there was a blackened wound behind the right ear.

When the Archdeacon came round to look at the face he turned faint, and the servant took him out into the library and gave him brandy, the glasses and decanters still standing there. Breddon's face certainly had looked very ghastly; it had been scratched, torn and bitten; one eye was gone, and the whole face was covered with blood.

"Do you think it was that brute did it?"

"Sure of it, sir; sprang on his face while he was asleep. I knew it would happen one of these nights. He knew it too; always slept with the revolver by his side. He fired twice at the brute, but couldn't see for the blood. Then he killed himself

It seemed likely enough, with his eyesight gone, horribly mauled, in an agony of pain, possibly believing that he was saving himself from a death still more horrible, Breddon might very well have turned the weapon on himself.

"What do we do now?" the man asked.

"We must get a doctor and fetch the police at once. Come on."

As they turned the corner of the passage, they saw that the door communicating with the staircase was open.

"Did you open that door?" asked the Archdeacon.

"No," said the man, aghast.

"Then who did?"

"Don't know, sir. Looks as if we weren't at the end of this yet."

They passed down the stairs together, and found the street-door also ajar. On the pavement outside lay a policeman slowly recovering consciousness. Breddon's man took the policeman's whistle and blew it. A passing hansom, going back to the mews, slowed up; the cab was sent to fetch a doctor, and communication with the police-station rapidly followed.

The injured policeman told a curious story. He was passing the house when he heard shots fired. Almost immediately afterwards he heard the bolts of the front-door being drawn, and stepped back into the neighbouring doorway. The front-door opened, and a negro emerged clad in a gray tweed suit with a gray overcoat. The policeman jumped out, and without a second's hesitation the black man felled him. "It was all done before you could think," was the policeman's phrase.

"What kind of negro?" asked the Archdeacon.

"A big man—stood over six foot, and black as coal. He never waited to be challenged; the moment he knew that he was seen he hit out."

The policeman was not a very intelligent fellow, and there was little more to be got out of him. He had heard the shots, seen the street-door open and the man in gray appear, and had been felled by a lightning blow before he had time to do anything.

The doctor, a plain, matter-of-fact little man, had no hesitation in saying that Breddon was dead, and must have died almost immediately. After the injuries received, respiration and heart-action must have ceased at once. He was explaining something which oozed from the dead man's ear, when the Archdeacon could stand it no longer, and staggered out into the library. There he found Breddon's servant, still in the blue overcoat, explaining to a policeman with a notebook that as far as he knew nothing was missing except a jade image or idol of a cat which formerly stood on the mantelpiece.

The cat known as "Gray Devil" was also missing, and, although a description of it was circulated in the public press, nothing was ever heard of it again. But gray fur was found in the clenched left hand of the dead man.

The inquest resulted in the customary verdict, and brought to light no new facts. But it may be as well to give what the police theory of the case was. According to the police the suicide took place much as Breddon's servant had supposed. Mad with pain and unable to bear the thought of his awful mutilation, Breddon had shot himself.

The story of the jade image, as far as it was known, was told at the inquest. The police held that this image was an idol, that some uncivilized tribe was much perturbed by the theft of it, and was ready to pay an enormously high price for its recovery. The negro was assumed to be aware of this, and to have determined to obtain possession of the idol by fair means or foul. Fair means failing, it was suggested that the negro followed Breddon to England, tracked him out, and on the night in question found some means to conceal himself in Breddon's flat. There it was assumed that he fell asleep, was awakened by the screams and the sound of the firing, and, being scared, caught up the jade image and made off. Realizing that the shots would have been heard outside, and that his departure at that moment would be considered extremely suspicious, he was ready as he opened the street-door to fell the first man that he saw. The temporary unconsciousness of the policeman gave him time to get away.

The theory sounds at first sight like the only possible theory. When the Archdeacon first told me the story, I tried to find out indirectly whether he accepted it. Finding him rather disposed to fence with my hints and suggestions, I put the question to him plainly and bluntly:

"Do you believe in the police theory?"

He hesitated, and then answered with complete frankness:

"No, most emphatically not."

"Why?" I asked; and he went over the evidence with me.

"In the first place, I do not believe that Breddon in the ordinary sense, committed suicide. No amount of physical pain would have made him even think of it. He had unending pluck. He would have taken the facial disfigurement and loss of sight as the chances of war, and would have done the best that could be done by a man with such awful disabilities. One must admit that he fired the fatal shot—the medical evidence on that point is too strong to be gainsaid—but he fired it under circumstances of supernatural horror of which we, thank God! know nothing."

"I'm naturally slow to admit supernatural explanation."

"Well, let's go on. What's this mysterious tribe the police talk about? I want to know where it lives and what its name is. It's wealthy enough to offer a huge reward; it must be of some importance. The negro managed to get in and secrete himself. How? Where? I know the flat, and that theory won't do. We don't even know that it was the negro who took that little image, though I believe it was. Anyhow, how did the negro get away at that hour of the morning absolutely unobserved? Negroes are not so common in London that they can walk about without being noticed; yet not one trace of him was ever found, and equally mysterious is the disappearance of the Gray Cat. It was such an extraordinary brute, and the description of it was so widely circulated that it would have seemed almost certain we should hear of it again. Well, we've not heard."

We discussed the police theory for some little time, and something which he happened to say led me to exclaim:

"Really! Do you mean to say that the Gray Cat actually was the negro?"

"No," he replied, "not exactly that, but something near it. Cats are strange animals, anyhow. I needn't remind you of their connection with certain old religions or with that witchcraft in which even in England to-day some still believe, and not so long ago almost all believed. I have never, by the way, seen a good explanation of the fact that there are people who cannot bear to be in a room with a cat, and are aware of its presence as if by some mysterious extra sense. Let me remind you of the belief which undoubtedly exists both in China and Japan, that evil spirits may enter into certain of the lower animals, the fox and badger especially. Every student of demonology knows about these things."

"But that idea of evil spirits taking possession of cats or foxes is surely a heathen superstition which you cannot hold."

"Well, I have read of the evil spirits that entered into the swine. Think it over, and keep an open mind."

1906

A WERE-TIGER
SIR WILLIAM GEORGE MAXWELL

SOME YEARS AGO I was travelling on a somewhat delicate mission in
one of the petty sultanates of the Malay Peninsula that lie to the
north of the federated states administered under British protection. The state is a long narrow strip of land lying on the east coast,
and is traversed by a number of rivers that run parallel to one another from their source in the main range of the peninsula to the
China Sea. The area of the district watered by each of these rivers
is perhaps 500 square miles, of which at least 495 are forest. At
the mouth of every river a few hundred Malays collect and make a
living by fishing; while, scattered up and down the stream, separated from one another by distances varying from one to five miles,
are small clearings containing ten, twenty, or even fifty families,
who are dependent upon an annual crop of padi and the collection
of various forest products, such as rubber, gutta, and rattans. As
against the rest of mankind, the Malays say that the land is theirs;
but no one knows better than themselves that the real lord and
master of the country is the forest. Each clearing has been hacked
out of the primeval forest with infinite trouble; the period of its
possession is marked by one continuous fight against aggression
by forest seeds and creepers and weeds of every description, and
when, finally, it is abandoned, it is covered within a few months
by a dense and almost impenetrable scrub that will eventually grow
up to become forest. My only companion was To'Kaya, an important and influential chief of one of the districts of the state, and
our following consisted of a few Malay boatmen. To'Kaya was a

fine specimen of a Malay of the last generation. He was some fifty years old, but time had had little apparent effect upon his wiry agile frame. He was a short man, not more than five feet four inches in height, of neat trim build, with square shoulders and small hands and feet. He had little superfluous flesh, but the curves of his arms and chest showed a muscular development considerably greater than would have been expected. His head was small and well shaped, its poorest feature being a broad and somewhat flat nose. The whole of his scalp was clean shaven, and chin and cheeks were kept free of occasional hairs by the use of tweezers. The striking feature of his face was a small, fierce, closely-cropped moustache of rather coarse bristly hairs, whose almost snowy whiteness afforded a brilliant contrast to the smoothness of his face and head, and to the rich olive-brown of his complexion. His eyes were somewhat sunken, with an expression of suffering and patience, but the crow's feet at their corners often curved into unexpected lines of humour. In every expression the old man showed the quiet dignity and self-respect of the true Malay.

Round his waist he wore the national garment—a sarong, which is in shape like a somewhat wide sack with the bottom cut off. His coat was nearly as primitive, for it was innocent of buttons, and could only be put on and taken off by being pulled over the head. A big coloured handkerchief was tied round his forehead, with a fantastic peak carefully arranged in front. Sarong, coat, and handkerchief were all of Malay weaving and coloured with native dyes, and nothing could be more simple or more effective and becoming to the wearer.

We took boat at the mouth of one of the rivers, the Malays at first using their paddles in the tidal waters where the inflowing tide bore us swiftly past densely timbered banks, and afterwards exchanging their paddles for poles when at last a sandy bottom was reached. We poled slowly against a strong current until the river became so narrow and so shallow that farther progress by boat was difficult. Then we left the river, and struck inland at right angles to it. For a whole day we made our way along a narrow track through heavy forest, where the great trees afforded shade and coolness even at midday. At sunset we camped on a ridge that formed the watershed between the river we had left and the one for which we were making. An armful of leaves was thrown down to make a bed for each, and a deftly plaited screen of wild palm-leaves was placed over the beds to keep off the dew.

During the night at intervals "the spirits of the semambu" called to one another in a little ravine below us. The semambu is the Malacca cane of commerce, and the Malays imagine that each plant has a spirit. At night-time, they say, spirit calls to spirit, making inquiry as to the length of the cane between the joints: *panjang? belum?* "is it long? not yet?" cries a high resonant voice, throwing the accent of the question sharply on the second syllable of each word; then, after a pause, another voice is raised in a different key, and with the accent and falling intonation of the sad response, *panjang, belum*: "it is long, not yet."

The call is really that of an insect, but the sound is weirdly voice-like, and the vibrations of the question and reply awake a corresponding thrill in the listener.

We also heard, two or three times during the night, the trumpeting of some wild elephants that had been alarmed by meeting our tracks. The next morning we continued our journey, which lay through dense forest the whole day, and emerged at nightfall upon a little village on the bank of the river we sought. Here we requisitioned a dug-out, and the next morning started down-stream.

The pleasant easy progress of the boat, which was carried by the swift current and only required the gentlest paddling to give it steering way, was a welcome rest after the days of laborious poling and travelling. To'Kaya and I sat under a little awning made of palm-leaves sewn together, and talked the long day away, while reach after reach the bends of the river opened a gleaming way before us, and reach after reach the forest-clad banks closed in behind us. The small Malay clearings that appeared at intervals on the banks only accentuated the sense of the overpowering dominion and vastness of the all-encompassing forest. Its mastery held us, and our conversation for the most part turned upon its inhabitants, both animal and supernatural. Thus we came to the discussion of were-tigers, which are in the Malay Peninsula the counterpart of the were-wolves of Europe. That were-tigers exist no Malay doubts; and the popular belief is that the men from the district of Korinchi in Sumatra have the power of assuming the form of a tiger at will, and that in this guise they range the forest, hunting the wild game and occasionally killing mankind.

The Korinchi men, who are mostly pedlars of cloths, naturally resent the imputation, and contend that it is only some of the men of Chenaku, a subdistrict of Korinchi, who have this unholy power. But as the contention admits the existence of the power amongst certain of the suspected class, the Malays of the Peninsula are only strengthened in their opinion, and believe the charge to be true of all Korinchis. To'Kaya told me of a village where, for some months, the fowls had been harried by a tiger or panther, both of which are known to the Malays by the same generic term, and where one day a Korinchi man lying sick with fever in the house of the headman, who had had pity on him, had vomited quantities of undigested chickens' feathers. I, in my turn, told him a story that I had heard in the reaches near the source of the Slim river. There, in an iso-lated hill-padi clearing, lived a Malay, his wife, and their two chil-dren, young boys of the age when they learn to read the Koran. One night came a rap at the door of the house, which, like all Malay dwellings, was built upon posts some ten feet above the ground. In answer to a demand from the father as to who was at the door and what was wanted, a voice replied, "We ask for a light, our torches are extinguished, and we have still some distance to go to the house where we are expected." Now, it is well known that this is a common device of jins and evil spirits to obtain admission to a house, and one should always beware of opening the door to give a light to a stranger who pretends to be belated. Well, the two boys, while the father was questioning and cross-questioning the stranger, slipped out of the house by the ladder behind the kitchen. Excited by the visit of a stranger at such an hour, they moved si-lently along the ground under the bamboo flooring to peep upwards at the threshold. There, on the rung of the ladder next below the door, stood a man talking to their father; but even while he spoke a tail striped in black and yellow dropped down behind his legs, and then up and down his lower limbs ran successive ripples of change and colour. The toes became talons, the feet turned to paws, and the knee-joints, already striped with the awful black and yellow, were turning from front to back.

And all the time the human face of the creature was giving specious explanations to the questions of the master of the house. Half in fascination, half in desperation, the two boys seized the tail that dangled before them, and shouted to their father to kill the thing. But before he could reach for his spear the animal, now nearly all tiger, tore itself from the puny grasp of the youngsters and fled into the darkness of the forest. Though I did not tell the story as a true one, To'Kaya shook his head and said, "That was a narrow escape. But it is fitting that we should talk of were-tigers, for here in the village of Bentong which we are approaching, there was a were-tiger not many years ago."

This is the story: not, it will be seen, as To'Kaya told it, but as I have reconstructed it from what he told me.

A few years ago Bentong, a village of considerable importance in a sparsely-populated district, for it consisted of some fifty houses, had suffered much from the depredations of a tiger. Scarcely a month passed without a buffalo or two being taken, and the Malays were in despair. They had tied up goats with spring-guns set over them, and they had made elaborate traps, like gigantic mouse-traps, baited with dogs. But the tiger would have none of them, and the Malays were beginning to talk of abandoning the village, for they depended upon the buffaloes to plough the padi-fields, and the possible extermination of the herd meant nothing less than utter ruin.

Such was the state of things in Bentong when late one afternoon, in drenching rain and growing darkness, an old Korinchi pedlar named Haji Brahim was hastening towards the village, where he intended to spend the night. He had a regular round through the district, in which he had been known for years, and the next day would peddle cloths and silks to the women-folk, collect his small debts, and then move on to the next village. The inclement weather and slippery path had made him much later than he had expected, for, like every one else in the district, he had heard of the Bentong tiger. He was making his way somewhat nervously, therefore, hoping that every turn in the narrow forest-track would disclose the village clearing, when he was panic-stricken to hear the tiger roar within a short distance of him. Shaking with fear, he ran for his life towards the village. He had not gone far before he came on a tiger-trap built at the side of the track, ready set with its bait of village cur, and with the door wide open. Struck by the idea that the timbers which would keep a tiger in would also keep one out, he dropped on his hands and knees, crawled in, and let the heavy door fall behind him. And when the tiger roared again in still closer proximity, on one occasion within a few feet of him, and continued to roar in the vicinity at intervals throughout the night, he forgave the presence of the unclean dog that cowered beside him, and blessed the thought that had led him to seek such a refuge.

When morning broke it found him stiff and shivering from the effects of the night's rain, the exposure, and the cramped position; but it found him alive, and for that he added special thanksgiving to the morning prayer of every Muhammadan believer. He discovered that from the inside of the trap he was unable to raise the heavy falling door, but remained where he was, content with the knowledge that before long some one would certainly pass along the track. In this he was not disappointed, for soon he heard a man approaching, and shouted to him for assistance. The man looked round him on all sides, but failed to discover whence the voice came.

"Where are you?" he replied.

"Here! Here in the tiger-trap!"

The Malay came up and, peering into the darkness of the trap, cried, "Who are you? What is it?"

"It is I, Haji Brahim," was the answer. "I am in the tiger-trap."

The man peered yet closer, his somewhat dull wits puzzled by the strangeness of the situation, and then suddenly recognised the features of the captive. As suddenly a light struck him. "It is Haji Brahim, *the Korinchi*," he yelled in an access of terror. He forgot the helpless position of the inmate of the trap: he could only realise one fact, that the tiger, which for so long had been the pest of Bentong, was a were-tiger; and without another word he turned and ran down the track as though he ran for his life.

The boom of the mosque-drum soon reverberated through the village, and in answer to its summons every able-bodied Malay thronged to the house of the chief, Raja Alang. The man who had given the alarm told his story, and then, after due deliberation and consultation, the men proceeded to the tiger-trap. The raja led the way, and behind him crowded the Malays, each armed with a spear, and with a belt full of krises and daggers. As they left the cultivated area and entered the forest they strung out into single line upon the narrow track, again massing in thick array behind the raja when they reached the trap. Raja Alang stepped up to the door and demanded of the prisoner—

"What is the name of this work?"

The old man's heart sank at the tone of the stern inquiry. During the long weary vigil of the night it had not occurred to him to connect his nationality with the fact of his entering the trap: the villager's alarm had been a shock to him, but he had persuaded himself that it was the mere temporary panic of an ignorant clown. But he now saw that he was on his trial.

"Let me out," he pleaded. "Let me out, and I will explain everything."

"That cannot be," replied the raja. "First you must explain how you came to be in this trap."

"Yes," agreed the voices in the background, "for who would release a tiger when once it is caught?"

"How came you here? Was it not you whom we heard roaring last night?" demanded the raja.

"No, raja, no," answered the old pedlar; "the tiger, which is always here, roared close to me last night, and it was to save my life that I ran into this trap."

"How can any one believe such a story?" murmured the crowd.

"The sole of your foot on the crown of my head, raja; have not you and all these men known me for many years? Am I not an old man and feeble, and could I do such a thing as this that you think of me?"

"But who ever heard of an honest man in a tiger-trap?" reiterated with dull persistency the voices behind the raja.

"The tracks will prove the truth of what I say," cried the pedlar.

The justice of the contention appealed to all, and the ground was carefully examined. But the crowd had obliterated the footprints round the trap, and all that could be seen were the tiger's tracks following a wild-game path to its junction with the main forest path, and then losing themselves in the trampled ground around the trap.

The inspection was carried out thoroughly and impartially, and its result, which of course tended to confirm the suspicions of the Malays, was communicated to the trembling captive.

"But I can prove that I left the village of Siputeh yesterday afternoon to come to Bentong. Every one saw me there," wept the old man.

"That may be true," retorted some one in the crowd with relentless logic, "but it is of last night that we talk. The tiger was here last night, and you are in the tiger-trap this morning."

The pedlar, who throughout had been on his hands and knees, the only position of which the cramped space of the trap would permit, seeing the futility of argument, turned his face up to the judges who stood massed in front of the trap and tried through his tears to recognise them.

He called to the village imaum, and offered to swear on the Koran of the mosque in any form of oath that might be imposed that his story was true. But though the Malays are, as a rule, in favour of the ordeal by oath, they felt at once that there was an obvious objection to its use in this case. The question which they had to decide was whether their captive was an ordinary Malay like themselves, or that awful horror, a were-tiger. It was plain that a creature so unnatural as that they imagined their prisoner to be would not hesitate to forswear itself in order to attain its liberty: not only then would the oath fail in its effect, but their mosque and Koran would have been polluted by the presence and touch of the unclean thing. When this last resource failed him the poor old man cried to those who had known him longest and best, and begged for his life for pity's sake. He promised to do anything that was asked of him, and, if necessary, to leave the country for ever. But the Malays did not dare to let themselves be influenced by any thoughts of pity or compassion. They had to decide a question upon which their herds, their crops, and their very lives depended, and that question was put to them with Malay terseness and directness by the raja.

"If we open the trap-door," he said, turning to the men who leant upon their spears behind him, "and let this that we have here now go loose, what is our position?"

What was their position? One must realise how the little village was isolated in the midst of a vast forest, how exposed the inhabitants were to any attack from it, how powerless to retaliate upon any man-eating or cattle-eating tiger, which had such easy access and such safe retreat, and how sick with helpless misery they must have felt at the mere idea that they were at the mercy of something that was partly tiger, partly demon. It is easy to imagine their fierce exultation at the thought of having trapped so awful a creature.

The raja repeated his question.

In answer a Malay, whose chief wealth lay in his diminishing herd of buffaloes, stood forth.

"Who of us has not lost one or more of his buffaloes? Who does not know that these Korinchis can turn themselves into tigers? Did we not all hear the tiger roar last night? Have we not got his tracks here? And here, where the tracks lead up to the trap, have we not, by the grace of Allah, got the Korinchi trapped? What more?"

"WHAT MORE?" said old To'Kaya, turning to me. At a sign from the raja one of the men stepped up to the trap, and, thrusting through the open bars of the woodwork, drove his spear through the old man's side.

For a moment I was silent with horror, and then said, "Pity on an old man to die in such a manner!"

"What pity does a tiger show?" retorted To'Kaya; "and what pity can it expect? Was it not clearly proved that this man was a were-tiger? It was not that he was unjustly or unfairly tried. The men of Bentong had known Haji Brahim for many years, and against him, as a man, they had no ill-feeling. The raja—Raja Alang, whom we shall see in the village if we stop the boat and call in—is both mild and just. Could he have decided otherwise?

"If a woman is accused of sin, or a man of murder, and evidence not half so strong as that in this case is advanced against them in the justice halls of the states under British rule,— nay, even in the Great Court-House of Singapore,—does not the judge convict them?"

I made an expostulation, and was painfully aware that I was begging the question. To'Kaya politely, but firmly, pointed this out, and I then attacked the evidence, saying that it was merely circumstantial.

To'Kaya bowed and said, "That may be; but have not men been hanged on slighter evidence?"

I could not think of a suitable reply: and it must be remembered that I was on a somewhat delicate mission in a state of which To'Kaya was one of the principal chiefs. There was, therefore, silence for a space as our little boat broke the sparkle of the river. We were now passing the village: the banks were covered with green turf cropped close by buffaloes, a few of whom—animals that perhaps had often seen the tiger which poor Haji Brahim had met— raised their heads to stare at us. Farther back from the river was a grove of cocoanut-palms, whose slender heads and graceful curves were outlined against the blue sky; and at their feet, dotted at intervals, were the Malay houses, which are built of bamboo and plaited bertam palm-fronds, and whose colour is that of ripe dead leaves. A woman was pounding rice with a pestle worked by her foot, and in the river a number of children were playing and splashing; but the men were for the most part in their houses seeking a refuge from the heat of the day. Then suddenly a little dug-out shot forth from the bank to cross the river. One man poled, another steered with a paddle, and in the centre sat a fine-looking old Malay.

"It is Raja Alang," said To'Kaya.

We stopped for a while to exchange the greetings and the courtesies due to, and expected from, our various ranks. Then we parted, and at the next bend of the river the great forest swept down again to the bank on either side, shutting us off from the view of aught else, and telling us that the little village of Bentong now lay behind us.

1908

ANCIENT SORCERIES
ALGERNON BLACKWOOD

I

THERE ARE, IT would appear, certain wholly unremarkable persons, with none of the characteristics that invite adventure, who yet once or twice in the course of their smooth lives undergo an experience so strange that the world catches its breath—and looks the other way! And it was cases of this kind, perhaps, more than any other, that fell into the wide-spread net of John Silence, the psychic doctor, and, appealing to his deep humanity, to his patience, and to his great qualities of spiritual sympathy, led often to the revelation of problems of the strangest complexity, and of the profoundest possible human interest.

Matters that seemed almost too curious and fantastic for belief he loved to trace to their hidden sources. To unravel a tangle in the very soul of things—and to release a suffering human soul in the process—was with him a veritable passion. And the knots he untied were, indeed, after passing strange.

The world, of course, asks for some plausible basis to which it can attach credence—something it can, at least, pretend to explain. The adventurous type it can understand: such people carry about with them an adequate explanation of their exciting lives, and their characters obviously drive them into the circumstances which produce the adventures. It expects nothing else from them, and is satisfied. But dull, ordinary folk have no right to out-of-the-way experiences, and the world having been led to expect otherwise, is disappointed with them, not to say shocked. Its complacent judgment has been rudely disturbed.

"Such a thing happened to *that* man!" it cries— "a commonplace person like that! It is too absurd! There must be something wrong!"

Yet there could be no question that something did actually happen to little Arthur Vezin, something of the curious nature he described to Dr. Silence. Outwardly or inwardly, it happened beyond a doubt, and in spite of the jeers of his few friends who heard the tale, and observed wisely that "such a thing might perhaps have come to Iszard, that crack-brained Iszard, or to that odd fish Minski, but it could never have happened to commonplace little Vezin, who was fore-ordained to live and die according to scale."

But, whatever his method of death was, Vezin certainly did not "live according to scale" so far as this particular event in his otherwise uneventful life was concerned; and to hear him recount it, and watch his pale delicate features change, and hear his voice grow softer and more hushed as he proceeded, was to know the conviction that his halting words perhaps failed sometimes to convey. He lived the thing over again each time he told it. His whole personality became muffled in the recital. It subdued him more than ever, so that the tale became a lengthy apology for an experience that he deprecated. He appeared to excuse himself and ask your pardon for having dared to take part in so fantastic an episode. For little Vezin was a timid, gentle, sensitive soul, rarely able to assert himself, tender to man and beast, and almost constitutionally unable to say No, or to claim many things that should rightly have been his. His whole scheme of life seemed utterly remote from anything more exciting than missing a train or losing an umbrella on an omnibus. And when this curious event came upon him he was already more years beyond forty than his friends suspected or he cared to admit.

John Silence, who heard him speak of his experience more than once, said that he sometimes left out certain details and put in others; yet they were all obviously true. The whole scene was unforgettably cinematographed on to his mind. None of the details were imagined or invented. And when he told the story with them all complete, the effect was undeniable. His appealing brown eyes shone, and much of the charming personality, usually so carefully repressed, came forward and revealed itself. His modesty was always there, of course, but in the telling he forgot the present and allowed himself to appear almost vividly as he lived again in the past of his adventure.

He was on the way home when it happened, crossing northern France from some mountain trip or other where he buried himself solitary-wise every summer. He had nothing but an unregistered bag in the rack, and the train was jammed to suffocation, most of the passengers being unredeemed holiday English. He disliked them, not because they were his fellow-countrymen, but because they were noisy and obtrusive, obliterating with their big limbs and tweed clothing all the quieter tints of the day that brought him satisfaction and enabled him to melt into insignificance and forget that he was anybody. These English clashed about him like a brass band, making him feel vaguely that he ought to be more self-assertive and obstreperous, and that he did not claim insistently enough all kinds of things that he didn't want and that were really valueless, such as corner seats, windows up or down, and so forth.

So that he felt uncomfortable in the train, and wished the journey were over and he was back again living with his unmarried sister in Surbiton.

And when the train stopped for ten panting minutes at the little station in northern France, and he got out to stretch his legs on the platform, and saw to his dismay a further batch of the British Isles debouching from another train, it suddenly seemed impossible to him to continue the journey. Even his flabby soul revolted, and the idea of staying a night in the little town and going on next day by a slower, emptier train, flashed into his mind. The guard was already shouting "*en voiture*" and the corridor of his compartment was already packed when the thought came to him. And, for once, he acted with decision and rushed to snatch his bag.

Finding the corridor and steps impassable, he tapped at the window (for he had a corner seat) and begged the Frenchman who sat opposite to hand his luggage out to him, explaining in his wretched French that he intended to break the journey there. And this elderly Frenchman, he declared, gave him a look, half of warning, half of reproach, that to his dying day he could never forget; handed the bag through the window of the moving train; and at the same time poured into his ears a long sentence, spoken rapidly and low, of which he was able to comprehend only the last few words: "*à cause du sommeil et à cause des chats.*"

In reply to Dr. Silence, whose singular psychic acuteness at once seized upon this Frenchman as a vital point in the adventure, Vezin admitted that the man had impressed him favourably from the beginning, though without being able to explain why. They had sat facing one another during the four hours of the journey, and though no conversation had passed between them—Vezin was timid about his stuttering French—he confessed that his eyes were being continually drawn to his face, almost, he felt, to rudeness, and that each, by a dozen nameless little politenesses and attentions, had evinced the desire to be kind. The men liked each other and their personalities did not clash, or would not have clashed had they chanced to come to terms of acquaintance. The Frenchman, indeed, seemed to have exercised a silent protective influence over the insignificant little Englishman, and without words or gestures betrayed that he wished him well and would gladly have been of service to him.

"And this sentence that he hurled at you after the bag?" asked John Silence, smiling that peculiarly sympathetic smile that always melted the prejudices of his patient, "were you unable to follow it exactly?"

"It was so quick and low and vehement," explained Vezin, in his small voice, "that I missed practically the whole of it. I only caught the few words at the very end, because he spoke them so clearly, and his face was bent down out of the carriage window so near to mine."

"'*À cause du sommeil et à cause des chats*'?" repeated Dr. Silence, as though half speaking to himself.

"That's it exactly," said Vezin; "which, I take it, means something like 'because of sleep and because of the cats,' doesn't it?"

"Certainly, that's how I should translate it," the doctor observed shortly, evidently not wishing to interrupt more than necessary.

"And the rest of the sentence—all the first part I couldn't understand, I mean—was a warning not to do something—not to stop in the town, or at some particular place in the town, perhaps. That was the impression it made on me."

Then, of course, the train rushed off, and left Vezin standing on the platform alone and rather forlorn.

The little town climbed in straggling fashion up a sharp hill rising out of the plain at the back of the station, and was crowned by the twin towers of the ruined cathedral peeping over the summit. From the station itself it looked uninteresting and modern, but the fact was that the mediaeval position lay out of sight just beyond the crest. And once he reached the top and entered the old streets, he stepped clean out of modern life into a bygone century. The noise and bustle of the crowded train seemed days away. The spirit of this silent hill-town, remote from tourists and motor-cars, dreaming its own quiet life under the autumn sun, rose up and cast its spell upon him. Long before he recognised this spell he acted under it. He walked softly, almost on tiptoe, down the winding narrow streets where the gables all but met over his head, and he entered the doorway of the solitary inn with a deprecating and modest demeanour that was in itself an apology for intruding upon the place and disturbing its dream.

At first, however, Vezin said, he noticed very little of all this. The attempt at analysis came much later. What struck him then was only the delightful contrast of the silence and peace after the dust and noisy rattle of the train. He felt soothed and stroked like a cat.

"Like a cat, you said?" interrupted John Silence, quickly catching him up.

"Yes. At the very start I felt that." He laughed apologetically. "I felt as though the warmth and the stillness and the comfort made me purr. It seemed to be the general mood of the whole place—then."

The inn, a rambling ancient house, the atmosphere of the old coaching days still about it, apparently did not welcome him too warmly. He felt he was only tolerated, he said. But it was cheap and comfortable, and the delicious cup of afternoon tea he ordered at once made him feel really very pleased with himself for leaving the train in this bold, original way. For to him it had seemed bold and original. He felt something of a dog. His room, too, soothed him with its dark panelling and low irregular ceiling, and the long sloping passage that led to it seemed the natural pathway to a real Chamber of Sleep—a little dim cubby hole out of the world where noise could not enter. It looked upon the courtyard at the back. It was all very charming, and made him think of himself as dressed in very soft velvet somehow, and the floors seemed padded, the walls provided with cushions. The sounds of the streets could not penetrate there. It was an atmosphere of absolute rest that surrounded him.

On engaging the two-franc room he had interviewed the only person who seemed to be about that sleepy afternoon, an elderly waiter with Dundreary whiskers and a drowsy courtesy, who had ambled lazily towards him across the stone yard; but on coming downstairs again for a little promenade in the town before dinner he encountered the proprietress herself. She was a large woman whose hands, feet, and features seemed to swim towards him out of a sea of person. They emerged, so to speak. But she had great dark, vivacious eyes that counteracted the bulk of her body, and betrayed the fact that in reality she was both vigorous and alert. When he first caught sight of her she was knitting in a low chair against the sunlight of the wall, and something at once made him see her as a great tabby cat, dozing, yet awake, heavily sleepy, and yet at the same time prepared for instantaneous action. A great mouser on the watch occurred to him.

She took him in with a single comprehensive glance that was polite without being cordial. Her neck, he noticed, was extraordinarily supple in spite of its proportions, for it turned so easily to follow him, and the head it carried bowed so very flexibly.

"But when she looked at me, you know," said Vezin, with that little apologetic smile in his brown eyes, and that faintly deprecating gesture of the shoulders that was characteristic of him, "the odd notion came to me that really she had intended to make quite a different movement, and that with a single bound she could have leaped at me across the width of that stone yard and pounced upon me like some huge cat upon a mouse."

He laughed a little soft laugh, and Dr. Silence made a note in his book without interrupting, while Vezin proceeded in a tone as though he feared he had already told too much and more than we could believe.

"Very soft, yet very active she was, for all her size and mass, and I felt she knew what I was doing even after I had passed and was behind her back. She spoke to me, and her voice was smooth and running. She asked if I had my luggage, and was comfortable in my room, and then added that dinner was at seven o'clock, and that they were very early people in this little country town. Clearly, she intended to convey that late hours were not encouraged."

Evidently, she contrived by voice and manner to give him the impression that here he would be "managed," that everything would be arranged and planned for him, and that he had nothing to do but fall into the groove and obey. No decided action or sharp personal effort would be looked for from him. It was the very reverse of the train. He walked quietly out into the street feeling soothed and peaceful. He realised that he was in a *milieu* that suited him and stroked him the right way. It was so much easier to be obedient. He began to purr again, and to feel that all the town purred with him.

About the streets of that little town he meandered gently, falling deeper and deeper into the spirit of repose that characterised it. With no special aim he wandered up and down, and to and fro. The September sunshine fell slantingly over the roofs. Down winding alleyways, fringed with tumbling gables and open casements, he caught fairylike glimpses of the great plain below, and of the meadows and yellow copses lying like a dream-map in the haze. The spell of the past held very potently here, he felt.

The streets were full of picturesquely garbed men and women, all busy enough, going their respective ways; but no one took any notice of him or turned to stare at his obviously English appearance. He was even able to forget that with his tourist appearance he was a false note in a charming picture, and he melted more and more into the scene, feeling delightfully insignificant and unimportant and unselfconscious. It was like becoming part of a softly coloured dream which he did not even realise to be a dream.

On the eastern side the hill fell away more sharply, and the plain below ran off rather suddenly into a sea of gathering shadows in which the little patches of woodland looked like islands and the stubble fields like deep water. Here he strolled along the old ramparts of ancient fortifications that once had been formidable, but now were only vision-like with their charming mingling of broken grey walls and wayward vine and ivy. From the broad coping on which he sat for a moment, level with the rounded tops of clipped plane trees, he saw the esplanade far below lying in shadow. Here and there a yellow sunbeam crept in and lay upon the fallen yellow leaves, and from the height he looked down and saw that the townsfolk were walking to and fro in the cool of the evening. He could just hear the sound of their slow footfalls, and the murmur of their voices floated up to him through the gaps between the trees. The figures looked like shadows as he caught glimpses of their quiet movements far below.

He sat there for some time pondering, bathed in the waves of murmurs and half-lost echoes that rose to his ears, muffled by the leaves of the plane trees. The whole town, and the little hill out of which it grew as naturally as an ancient wood, seemed to him like a being lying there half asleep on the plain and crooning to itself as it dozed.

And, presently, as he sat lazily melting into its dream, a sound of horns and strings and wood instruments rose to his ears, and

the town band began to play at the far end of the crowded terrace
below to the accompaniment of a very soft, deep-throated drum.
Vezin was very sensitive to music, knew about it intelligently, and
had even ventured, unknown to his friends, upon the composition
of quiet melodies with low-running chords which he played to himself with the soft pedal when no one was about. And this music
floating up through the trees from an invisible and doubtless very
picturesque band of the townspeople wholly charmed him. He
recognised nothing that they played, and it sounded as though they
were simply improvising without a conductor. No definitely marked
time ran through the pieces, which ended and began oddly after
the fashion of wind through an Aeolian harp. It was part of the
place and scene, just as the dying sunlight and faintly breathing
wind were part of the scene and hour, and the mellow notes of old-
fashioned plaintive horns, pierced here and there by the sharper
strings, all half smothered by the continuous booming of the deep
drum, touched his soul with a curiously potent spell that was almost too engrossing to be quite pleasant.

There was a certain queer sense of bewitchment in it all. The
music seemed to him oddly unartificial. It made him think of trees
swept by the wind, of night breezes singing among wires and chim-
ney-stacks, or in the rigging of invisible ships; or—and the simile
leaped up in his thoughts with a sudden sharpness of suggestion—
a chorus of animals, of wild creatures, somewhere in desolate
places of the world, crying and singing as animals will, to the moon.
He could fancy he heard the wailing, half-human cries of cats upon
the tiles at night, rising and falling with weird intervals of sound,
and this music, muffled by distance and the trees, made him think
of a queer company of these creatures on some roof far away in
the sky, uttering their solemn music to one another and the moon
in chorus.

It was, he felt at the time, a singular image to occur to him, yet
it expressed his sensation pictorially better than anything else. The
instruments played such impossibly odd intervals, and the crescen-
dos and diminuendos were so very suggestive of cat-land on the
tiles at night, rising swiftly, dropping without warning to deep

notes again, and all in such strange confusion of discords and accords. But, at the same time a plaintive sweetness resulted on the whole, and the discords of these half-broken instruments were so singular that they did not distress his musical soul like fiddles out of tune.

He listened a long time, wholly surrendering himself as his character was, and then strolled homewards in the dusk as the air grew chilly.

"There was nothing to alarm?" put in Dr. Silence briefly.

"Absolutely nothing," said Vezin; "but you know it was all so fantastical and charming that my imagination was profoundly impressed. Perhaps, too," he continued, gently explanatory, "it was this stirring of my imagination that caused other impressions; for, as I walked back, the spell of the place began to steal over me in a dozen ways, though all intelligible ways. But there were other things I could not account for in the least, even then."

"Incidents, you mean?"

"Hardly incidents, I think. A lot of vivid sensations crowded themselves upon my mind and I could trace them to no causes. It was just after sunset and the tumbled old buildings traced magical outlines against an opalescent sky of gold and red. The dusk was running down the twisted streets. All round the hill the plain pressed in like a dim sea, its level rising with the darkness. The spell of this kind of scene, you know, can be very moving, and it was so that night. Yet I felt that what came to me had nothing directly to do with the mystery and wonder of the scene."

"Not merely the subtle transformations of the spirit that come with beauty," put in the doctor, noticing his hesitation.

"Exactly," Vezin went on, duly encouraged and no longer so fearful of our smiles at his expense. "The impressions came from somewhere else. For instance, down the busy main street where men and women were bustling home from work, shopping at stalls and barrows, idly gossiping in groups, and all the rest of it, I saw that I aroused no interest and that no one turned to stare at me as a foreigner and stranger. I was utterly ignored, and my presence among them excited no special interest or attention.

"And then, quite suddenly, it dawned upon me with conviction that all the time this indifference and inattention were merely feigned. Everybody as a matter of fact was watching me closely. Every movement I made was known and observed. Ignoring me was all a pretence—an elaborate pretence."

He paused a moment and looked at us to see if we were smiling, and then continued, reassured—

"It is useless to ask me how I noticed this, because I simply cannot explain it. But the discovery gave me something of a shock. Before I got back to the inn, however, another curious thing rose up strongly in my mind and forced my recognition of it as true. And this, too, I may as well say at once, was equally inexplicable to me. I mean I can only give you the fact, as fact it was to me."

The little man left his chair and stood on the mat before the fire. His diffidence lessened from now onwards, as he lost himself again in the magic of the old adventure. His eyes shone a little already as he talked.

"Well," he went on, his soft voice rising somewhat with his excitement, "I was in a shop when it came to me first—though the idea must have been at work for a long time subconsciously to appear in so complete a form all at once. I was buying socks, I think," he laughed, "and struggling with my dreadful French, when it struck me that the woman in the shop did not care two pins whether I bought anything or not. She was indifferent whether she made a sale or did not make a sale. She was only pretending to sell.

"This sounds a very small and fanciful incident to build upon what follows. But really it was not small. I mean it was the spark that lit the line of powder and ran along to the big blaze in my mind.

"For the whole town, I suddenly realised, was something other than I so far saw it. The real activities and interests of the people were elsewhere and otherwise than appeared. Their true lives lay somewhere out of sight behind the scenes. Their busy-ness was but the outward semblance that masked their actual purposes. They bought and sold, and ate and drank, and walked about the streets, yet all the while the main stream of their existence lay somewhere beyond my ken, underground, in secret places. In the shops and at the stalls they did not care whether I purchased their articles or not; at the inn, they were indifferent to my staying or going; their life lay remote from my own, springing from hidden, mysterious sources, coursing out of sight, unknown. It was all a great elaborate pretence, assumed possibly for my benefit, or possibly for purposes of their own. But the main current of their energies ran elsewhere. I almost felt as an unwelcome foreign substance might be expected to feel when it has found its way into the human system and the whole body organises itself to eject it or to absorb it. The town was doing this very thing to me.

"This bizarre notion presented itself forcibly to my mind as I walked home to the inn, and I began busily to wonder wherein the true life of this town could lie and what were the actual interests and activities of its hidden life.

"And, now that my eyes were partly opened, I noticed other things too that puzzled me, first of which, I think, was the extraordinary silence of the whole place. Positively, the town was muffled. Although the streets were paved with cobbles the people moved about silently, softly, with padded feet, like cats. Nothing made noise. All was hushed, subdued, muted. The very voices were quiet, low-pitched like purring. Nothing clamorous, vehement or emphatic seemed able to live in the drowsy atmosphere of soft dreaming that soothed this little hill-town into its sleep. It was like the woman at the inn—an outward repose screening intense inner activity and purpose.

"Yet there was no sign of lethargy or sluggishness anywhere about it. The people were active and alert. Only a magical and uncanny softness lay over them all like a spell."

Vezin passed his hand across his eyes for a moment as though the memory had become very vivid. His voice had run off into a whisper so that we heard the last part with difficulty. He was telling a true thing obviously, yet something that he both liked and hated telling.

"I went back to the inn," he continued presently in a louder voice, "and dined. I felt a new strange world about me. My old world of reality receded. Here, whether I liked it or no, was something new and incomprehensible. I regretted having left the train so impulsively. An adventure was upon me, and I loathed adventures as foreign to my nature. Moreover, this was the beginning apparently of an adventure somewhere deep within me, in a region I could not check or measure, and a feeling of alarm mingled itself with my wonder—alarm for the stability of what I had for forty years recognised as my 'personality.'

"I went upstairs to bed, my mind teeming with thoughts that were unusual to me, and of rather a haunting description. By way of relief I kept thinking of that nice, prosaic noisy train and all those wholesome, blustering passengers. I almost wished I were with them again. But my dreams took me elsewhere. I dreamed of cats, and soft-moving creatures, and the silence of life in a dim muffled world beyond the senses."

II

VEZIN STAYED ON from day to day, indefinitely, much longer than he had intended. He felt in a kind of dazed, somnolent condition. He did nothing in particular, but the place fascinated him and he could not decide to leave. Decisions were always very difficult for him and he sometimes wondered how he had ever brought himself to the point of leaving the train. It seemed as though some one else must have arranged it for him, and once or twice his thoughts ran to the swarthy Frenchman who had sat opposite. If only he could have understood that long sentence ending so strangely with "*à cause du sommeil et à cause des chats.*" He wondered what it all meant.

Meanwhile the hushed softness of the town held him prisoner and he sought in his muddling, gentle way to find out where the mystery lay, and what it was all about. But his limited French and his constitutional hatred of active investigation made it hard for him to buttonhole anybody and ask questions. He was content to observe, and watch, and remain negative.

The weather held on calm and hazy, and this just suited him. He wandered about the town till he knew every street and alley.

The people suffered him to come and go without let or hindrance, though it became clearer to him every day that he was never free himself from observation. The town watched him as a cat watches a mouse. And he got no nearer to finding out what they were all so busy with or where the main stream of their activities lay. This remained hidden. The people were as soft and mysterious as cats.

But that he was continually under observation became more evident from day to day.

For instance, when he strolled to the end of the town and entered a little green public garden beneath the ramparts and seated himself upon one of the empty benches in the sun, he was quite alone—at first. Not another seat was occupied; the little park was empty, the paths deserted. Yet, within ten minutes of his coming, there must have been fully twenty persons scattered about him, some strolling aimlessly along the gravel walks, staring at the flowers, and others seated on the wooden benches enjoying the sun like himself. None of them appeared to take any notice of him; yet he understood quite well they had all come there to watch. They kept him under close observation. In the street they had seemed busy enough, hurrying upon various errands; yet these were suddenly all forgotten and they had nothing to do but loll and laze in the sun, their duties unremembered. Five minutes after he left, the garden was again deserted, the seats vacant. But in the crowded street it was the same thing again; he was never alone. He was ever in their thoughts.

By degrees, too, he began to see how it was he was so cleverly watched, yet without the appearance of it. The people did nothing *directly*. They behaved *obliquely*. He laughed in his mind as the thought thus clothed itself in words, but the phrase exactly described it. They looked at him from angles which naturally should have led their sight in another direction altogether. Their movements were oblique, too, so far as these concerned himself. The straight, direct thing was not their way evidently. They did nothing obviously. If he entered a shop to buy, the woman walked instantly away and busied herself with something at the farther end of the counter, though answering at once when he spoke, showing that she knew he was there and that this was only her way of attending to him. It was the fashion of the cat she followed. Even in the dining-room of the inn, the be-whiskered and courteous waiter, lithe and silent in all his movements, never seemed able to come straight to his table for an order or a dish. He came by zig-zags, indirectly, vaguely, so that he appeared to be going to another table altogether, and only turned suddenly at the last moment, and was there beside him.

Vezin smiled curiously to himself as he described how he began to realize these things. Other tourists there were none in the hostel, but he recalled the figures of one or two old men, inhabitants, who took their *déjeuner* and dinner there, and remembered how fantastically they entered the room in similar fashion. First, they paused in the doorway, peering about the room, and then, after a temporary inspection, they came in, as it were, sideways, keeping close to the walls so that he wondered which table they were making for, and at the last minute making almost a little quick run to their particular seats. And again he thought of the ways and methods of cats.

Other small incidents, too, impressed him as all part of this queer, soft town with its muffled, indirect life, for the way some of the people appeared and disappeared with extraordinary swiftness puzzled him exceedingly. It may have been all perfectly natural, he knew, yet he could not make it out how the alleys swallowed them up and shot them forth in a second of time when there were no visible doorways or openings near enough to explain the phenomenon. Once he followed two elderly women who, he felt, had been particularly examining him from across the street—quite near the inn this was—and saw them turn the corner a few feet only in front of him. Yet when he sharply followed on their heels he saw nothing but an utterly deserted alley stretching in front of him with no sign of a living thing. And the only opening through which they could have escaped was a porch some fifty yards away, which not the swiftest human runner could have reached in time.

And in just such sudden fashion people appeared, when he never expected them. Once when he heard a great noise of fighting going on behind a low wall, and hurried up to see what was going

on, what should he see but a group of girls and women engaged in
vociferous conversation which instantly hushed itself to the normal whispering note of the town when his head appeared over the
wall. And even then none of them turned to look at him directly,
but slunk off with the most unaccountable rapidity into doors and
sheds across the yard. And their voices, he thought, had sounded
so like, so strangely like, the angry snarling of fighting animals,
almost of cats.

The whole spirit of the town, however, continued to evade him
as something elusive, protean, screened from the outer world, and
at the same time intensely, genuinely vital; and, since he now
formed part of its life, this concealment puzzled and irritated him;
more—it began rather to frighten him.

Out of the mists that slowly gathered about his ordinary surface thoughts, there rose again the idea that the inhabitants were
waiting for him to declare himself, to take an attitude, to do this,
or to do that; and that when he had done so they in their turn would
at length make some direct response, accepting or rejecting him.
Yet the vital matter concerning which his decision was awaited
came no nearer to him.

Once or twice he purposely followed little processions or groups
of the citizens in order to find out, if possible, on what purpose
they were bent; but they always discovered him in time and
dwindled away, each individual going his or her own way. It was
always the same: he never could learn what their main interest was.
The cathedral was ever empty, the old church of St. Martin, at the
other end of the town, deserted. They shopped because they had
to, and not because they wished to. The booths stood neglected,
the stalls unvisited, the little cafés desolate. Yet the streets were
always full, the townsfolk ever on the bustle.

"Can it be," he thought to himself, yet with a deprecating laugh
that he should have dared to think anything so odd, "can it be that
these people are people of the twilight, that they live only at night
their real life, and come out honestly only with the dusk? That
during the day they make a sham though brave pretence, and
after the sun is down their true life begins? Have they the souls of

night-things, and is the whole blessed town in the hands of the cats?"

The fancy somehow electrified him with little shocks of shrinking and dismay. Yet, though he affected to laugh, he knew that he was beginning to feel more than uneasy, and that strange forces were tugging with a thousand invisible cords at the very centre of his being. Something utterly remote from his ordinary life, something that had not waked for years, began faintly to stir in his soul, sending feelers abroad into his brain and heart, shaping queer thoughts and penetrating even into certain of his minor actions. Something exceedingly vital to himself, to his soul, hung in the balance.

And, always when he returned to the inn about the hour of sunset, he saw the figures of the townsfolk stealing through the dusk from their shop doors, moving sentry-wise to and fro at the corners of the streets, yet always vanishing silently like shadows at his near approach. And as the inn invariably closed its doors at ten o'clock he had never yet found the opportunity he rather half-heartedly sought to see for himself what account the town could give of itself at night.

"—à cause du sommeil et à cause des chats"—the words now rang in his ears more and more often, though still as yet without any definite meaning.

Moreover, something made him sleep like the dead.

III

IT WAS, I THINK, on the fifth day—though in this detail his story sometimes varied—that he made a definite discovery which increased his alarm and brought him up to a rather sharp climax. Before that he had already noticed that a change was going forward and certain subtle transformations being brought about in his character which modified several of his minor habits. And he had affected to ignore them. Here, however, was something he could no longer ignore; and it startled him.

At the best of times he was never very positive, always negative rather, compliant and acquiescent; yet, when necessity arose he was capable of reasonably vigorous action and could take a strongish decision. The discovery he now made that brought him up with such a sharp turn was that this power had positively dwindled to nothing. He found it impossible to make up his mind. For, on this fifth day, he realised that he had stayed long enough in the town and that for reasons he could only vaguely define to himself it was wiser *and safer* that he should leave.

And he found that he could not leave!

This is difficult to describe in words, and it was more by gesture and the expression of his face that he conveyed to Dr. Silence the state of impotence he had reached. All this spying and watching, he said, had as it were spun a net about his feet so that he was trapped and powerless to escape; he felt like a fly that had blundered into the intricacies of a great web; he was caught, imprisoned, and could not get away. It was a distressing sensation. A numbness had crept over his will till it had become almost incapable of decision. The mere thought of vigorous action—action towards escape—began to terrify him. All the currents of his life had turned inwards upon himself, striving to bring to the surface something that lay buried almost beyond reach, determined to force his recognition of something he had long forgotten—forgotten years upon years, centuries almost ago. It seemed as though a window deep within his being would presently open and reveal an entirely new world, yet somehow a world that was not unfamiliar. Beyond that, again, he fancied a great curtain hung; and when that too rolled up he would see still farther into this region and at last understand something of the secret life of these extraordinary people.

"Is this why they wait and watch?" he asked himself with rather a shaking heart, "for the time when I shall join them—or refuse to join them? Does the decision rest with me after all, and not with them?"

And it was at this point that the sinister character of the adventure first really declared itself, and he became genuinely alarmed. The stability of his rather fluid little personality was at stake, he felt, and something in his heart turned coward.

Why otherwise should he have suddenly taken to walking stealthily, silently, making as little sound as possible, for ever looking behind him? Why else should he have moved almost on tiptoe about the passages of the practically deserted inn, and when he was abroad have found himself deliberately taking advantage of what cover presented itself? And why, if he was not afraid, should the wisdom of staying indoors after sundown have suddenly occurred to him as eminently desirable? Why, indeed?

And, when John Silence gently pressed him for an explanation of these things, he admitted apologetically that he had none to give.

"It was simply that I feared something might happen to me unless I kept a sharp look-out. I felt afraid. It was instinctive," was all he could say. "I got the impression that the whole town was after me—wanted me for something; and that if it got me I should lose myself, or at least the Self I knew, in some unfamiliar state of consciousness. But I am not a psychologist, you know," he added meekly, "and I cannot define it better than that."

It was while lounging in the courtyard half an hour before the evening meal that Vezin made this discovery, and he at once went upstairs to his quiet room at the end of the winding passage to think it over alone. In the yard it was empty enough, true, but there was always the possibility that the big woman whom he dreaded would come out of some door, with her pretence of knitting, to sit and watch him. This had happened several times, and he could not endure the sight of her. He still remembered his original fancy, bizarre though it was, that she would spring upon him the moment his back was turned and land with one single crushing leap upon his neck. Of course it was nonsense, but then it haunted him, and once an idea begins to do that it ceases to be nonsense. It has clothed itself in reality.

He went upstairs accordingly. It was dusk, and the oil lamps had not yet been lit in the passages. He stumbled over the uneven surface of the ancient flooring, passing the dim outlines of doors along the corridor—doors that he had never once seen opened— rooms that seemed never occupied. He moved, as his habit now was, stealthily and on tiptoe.

Half-way down the last passage to his own chamber there was a sharp turn, and it was just here, while groping round the walls with outstretched hands, that his fingers touched something that was not wall—something that moved. It was soft and warm in texture, indescribably fragrant, and about the height of his shoulder; and he immediately thought of a furry, sweet-smelling kitten. The next minute he knew it was something quite different.

Instead of investigating, however,—his nerves must have been too overwrought for that, he said,—he shrank back as closely as possible against the wall on the other side. The thing, whatever it was, slipped past him with a sound of rustling and, retreating with light footsteps down the passage behind him, was gone. A breath of warm, scented air was wafted to his nostrils.

Vezin caught his breath for an instant and paused, stockstill, half leaning against the wall—and then almost ran down the remaining distance and entered his room with a rush, locking the door hurriedly behind him. Yet it was not fear that made him run: it was excitement, pleasurable excitement. His nerves were tingling, and a delicious glow made itself felt all over his body. In a flash it came to him that this was just what he had felt twenty-five years ago as a boy when he was in love for the first time. Warm currents of life ran all over him and mounted to his brain in a whirl of soft delight. His mood was suddenly become tender, melting, loving.

The room was quite dark, and he collapsed upon the sofa by the window, wondering what had happened to him and what it all meant. But the only thing he understood clearly in that instant was that something in him had swiftly, magically changed: he no longer wished to leave, or to argue with himself about leaving. The encounter in the passage-way had changed all that. The strange perfume of it still hung about him, bemusing his heart and mind. For he knew that it was a girl who had passed him, a girl's face that his fingers had brushed in the darkness, and he felt in some extra ordinary way as though he had been actually kissed by her, kissed full upon the lips.

Trembling, he sat upon the sofa by the window and struggled to collect his thoughts. He was utterly unable to understand how the mere passing of a girl in the darkness of a narrow passage-way could communicate so electric a thrill to his whole being that he still shook with the sweetness of it. Yet, there it was! And he found it as useless to deny as to attempt analysis. Some ancient fire had entered his veins, and now ran coursing through his blood; and that he was forty-five instead of twenty did not matter one little jot. Out of all the inner turmoil and confusion emerged the one salient fact that the mere atmosphere, the merest casual touch, of this girl, unseen, unknown in the darkness, had been sufficient to stir dormant fires in the centre of his heart, and rouse his whole being from a state of feeble sluggishness to one of tearing and tumultuous excitement.

After a time, however, the number of Vezin's years began to assert their cumulative power; he grew calmer, and when a knock came at length upon his door and he heard the waiter's voice suggesting that dinner was nearly over, he pulled himself together and slowly made his way downstairs into the dining-room.

Every one looked up as he entered, for he was very late, but he took his customary seat in the far corner and began to eat. The trepidation was still in his nerves, but the fact that he had passed through the courtyard and hall without catching sight of a petticoat served to calm him a little. He ate so fast that he had almost caught up with the current stage of the table d'hôte, when a slight commotion in the room drew his attention.

His chair was so placed that the door and the greater portion of the long *salle à manger* were behind him, yet it was not necessary to turn round to know that the same person he had passed in the dark passage had now come into the room. He felt the presence long before he heard or saw any one. Then he became aware that the old men, the only other guests, were rising one by one in their places, and exchanging greetings with some one who passed among them from table to table. And when at length he turned with his heart beating furiously to ascertain for himself, he saw the form of a young girl, lithe and slim, moving down the centre of the room and making straight for his own table in the corner. She moved wonderfully, with sinuous grace, like a young panther, and her approach filled him with such delicious bewilderment that he was utterly unable to tell at first what her face was like, or discover what it was about the whole presentment of the creature that filled him anew with trepidation and delight.

"Ah, Ma'mselle est de retour!" he heard the old waiter murmur at his side, and he was just able to take in that she was the daughter of the proprietress, when she was upon him, and he heard her voice. She was addressing him. Something of red lips he saw and laughing white teeth, and stray wisps of fine dark hair about the temples; but all the rest was a dream in which his own emotion rose like a thick cloud before his eyes and prevented his seeing accurately, or knowing exactly what he did. He was aware that she greeted him with a charming little bow; that her beautiful large eyes looked searchingly into his own; that the perfume he had noticed in the dark passage again assailed his nostrils, and that she was bending a little towards him and leaning with one hand on the table at this side. She was quite close to him—that was the chief thing he knew—explaining that she had been asking after the comfort of her mother's guests, and now was introducing herself to the latest arrival—himself.

"M'sieur has already been here a few days," he heard the waiter say; and then her own voice, sweet as singing, replied—

"Ah, but M'sieur is not going to leave us just yet, I hope. My mother is too old to look after the comfort of our guests properly, but now I am here I will remedy all that." She laughed deliciously. "M'sieur shall be well looked after."

Vezin, struggling with his emotion and desire to be polite, half rose to acknowledge the pretty speech, and to stammer some sort of reply, but as he did so his hand by chance touched her own that was resting upon the table, and a shock that was for all the world like a shock of electricity, passed from her skin into his body. His soul wavered and shook deep within him. He caught her eyes fixed upon his own with a look of most curious intentness, and the next moment he knew that he had sat down wordless again on his chair, that the girl was already half-way across the room, and that he was trying to eat his salad with a dessert-spoon and a knife.

Longing for her return, and yet dreading it, he gulped down the remainder of his dinner, and then went at once to his bedroom to be alone with his thoughts. This time the passages were lighted, and he suffered no exciting contretemps; yet the winding corridor was dim with shadows, and the last portion, from the bend of the walls onwards, seemed longer than he had ever known it. It ran downhill like the pathway on a mountain side, and as he tiptoed softly down it he felt that by rights it ought to have led him clean out of the house into the heart of a great forest. The world was singing with him. Strange fancies filled his brain, and once in the room, with the door securely locked, he did not light the candles, but sat by the open window thinking long, long thoughts that came unbidden in troops to his mind.

IV

THIS PART OF the story he told to Dr. Silence, without special coaxing, it is true, yet with much stammering embarrassment. He could not in the least understand, he said, how the girl had managed to affect him so profoundly, and even before he had set eyes upon her. For her mere proximity in the darkness had been sufficient to set him on fire. He knew nothing of enchantments, and for years had been a stranger to anything approaching tender relations with any member of the opposite sex, for he was encased in shyness, and realised his overwhelming defects only too well. Yet this bewitching young creature came to him deliberately. Her manner was unmistakable, and she sought him out on every possible occasion. Chaste and sweet she was undoubtedly, yet frankly inviting; and she won him utterly with the first glance of her shining eyes, even if she had not already done so in the dark merely by the magic of her invisible presence.

"You felt she was altogether wholesome and good!" queried the doctor. "You had no reaction of any sort—for instance, of alarm?"

Vezin looked up sharply with one of his inimitable little apologetic smiles. It was some time before he replied. The mere memory of the adventure had suffused his shy face with blushes, and his brown eyes sought the floor again before he answered.

"I don't think I can quite say that," he explained presently. "I acknowledged certain qualms, sitting up in my room afterwards.

A conviction grew upon me that there was something about her—how shall I express it?—well, something unholy. It is not impurity in any sense, physical or mental, that I mean, but something quite indefinable that gave me a vague sensation of the creeps. She drew me, and at the same time repelled me, more than—than—"

He hesitated, blushing furiously, and unable to finish the sentence.

"Nothing like it has ever come to me before or since," he concluded, with lame confusion. "I suppose it was, as you suggested just now, something of an enchantment. At any rate, it was strong enough to make me feel that I would stay in that awful little haunted town for years if only I could see her every day, hear her voice, watch her wonderful movements, and sometimes, perhaps, touch her hand."

"Can you explain to me what you felt was the source of her power?" John Silence asked, looking purposely anywhere but at the narrator.

"I am surprised that you should ask me such a question," answered Vezin, with the nearest approach to dignity he could manage. "I think no man can describe to another convincingly wherein lies the magic of the woman who ensnares him. I certainly cannot. I can only say this slip of a girl bewitched me, and the mere knowledge that she was living and sleeping in the same house filled me with an extraordinary sense of delight.

"But there's one thing I can tell you," he went on earnestly, his eyes aglow, "namely, that she seemed to sum up and synthesise in herself all the strange hidden forces that operated so mysteriously in the town and its inhabitants. She had the silken movements of the panther, going smoothly, silently to and fro, and the same indirect, oblique methods as the townsfolk, screening, like them, secret purposes of her own—purposes that I was sure had *me* for their objective. She kept me, to my terror and delight, ceaselessly under observation, yet so carelessly, so consummately, that another man less sensitive, if I may say so"—he made a deprecating gesture— "or less prepared by what had gone before, would never have noticed it at all. She was always still, always reposeful, yet she seemed to be everywhere at once, so that I never could escape from her. I was continually meeting the stare and laughter of her great eyes, in the corners of the rooms, in the passages, calmly looking at me through the windows, or in the busiest parts of the public streets."

Their intimacy, it seems, grew very rapidly after this first encounter which had so violently disturbed the little man's equilibrium. He was naturally very prim, and prim folk live mostly in so small a world that anything violently unusual may shake them clean out of it, and they therefore instinctively distrust originality. But Vezin began to forget his primness after awhile. The girl was always modestly behaved, and as her mother's representative she naturally had to do with the guests in the hotel. It was not out of the way that a spirit of camaraderie should spring up. Besides, she was young, she was charmingly pretty, she was French, and—she obviously liked him.

At the same time, there was something indescribable—a certain indefinable atmosphere of other places, other times—that made him try hard to remain on his guard, and sometimes made him catch his breath with a sudden start. It was all rather like a delirious dream, half delight, half dread, he confided in a whisper to Dr. Silence; and more than once he hardly knew quite what he was doing or saying, as though he were driven forward by impulses he scarcely recognised as his own.

And though the thought of leaving presented itself again and again to his mind, it was each time with less insistence, so that he stayed on from day to day, becoming more and more a part of the sleepy life of this dreamy mediaeval town, losing more and more of his recognisable personality. Soon, he felt, the Curtain within would roll up with an awful rush, and he would find himself suddenly admitted into the secret purposes of the hidden life that lay behind it all. Only, by that time, he would have become transformed into an entirely different being.

And, meanwhile, he noticed various little signs of the intention to make his stay attractive to him: flowers in his bedroom, a more comfortable arm-chair in the corner, and even special little extra dishes on his private table in the dining-room. Conversations, too, with "Mademoiselle Ilsé" became more and more frequent and pleasant, and although they seldom travelled beyond the weather, or the details of the town, the girl, he noticed, was never in a hurry to bring them to an end, and often contrived to interject little odd sentences that he never properly understood, yet felt to be significant.

And it was these stray remarks, full of a meaning that evaded him, that pointed to some hidden purpose of her own and made him feel uneasy. They all had to do, he felt sure, with reasons for his staying on in the town indefinitely.

"And has M'sieur not even yet come to a decision?" she said softly in his ear, sitting beside him in the sunny yard before *déjeuner*, the acquaintance having progressed with significant rapidity. "Because, if it's so difficult, we must all try together to help him!"

The question startled him, following upon his own thoughts. It was spoken with a pretty laugh, and a stray bit of hair across one eye, as she turned and peered at him half roguishly. Possibly he did not quite understand the French of it, for her near presence always confused his small knowledge of the language distressingly. Yet the words, and her manner, and something else that lay behind it all in her mind, frightened him. It gave such point to his feeling that the town was waiting for him to make his mind up on some important matter.

At the same time, her voice, and the fact that she was there so close beside him in her soft dark dress, thrilled him inexpressibly.

"It is true I find it difficult to leave," he stammered, losing his way deliciously in the depths of her eyes, "and especially now that Mademoiselle Ilsé has come."

He was surprised at the success of his sentence, and quite delighted with the little gallantry of it. But at the same time he could have bitten his tongue off for having said it.

"Then after all you like our little town, or you would not be pleased to stay on," she said, ignoring the compliment.

"I am enchanted with it, and enchanted with you," he cried, feeling that his tongue was somehow slipping beyond the control of his brain. And he was on the verge of saying all manner of other things of the wildest description, when the girl sprang lightly up from her chair beside him, and made to go.

"It is *soupe à l'onion* to-day!" she cried, laughing back at him through the sunlight, "and I must go and see about it. Otherwise, you know, M'sieur will not enjoy his dinner, and then, perhaps, he will leave us!"

He watched her cross the courtyard, moving with all the grace and lightness of the feline race, and her simple black dress clothed her, he thought, exactly like the fur of the same supple species. She turned once to laugh at him from the porch with the glass door, and then stopped a moment to speak to her mother, who sat knitting as usual in her corner seat just inside the hall-way.

But how was it, then, that the moment his eye fell upon this ungainly woman, the pair of them appeared suddenly as other than they were? Whence came that transforming dignity and sense of power that enveloped them both as by magic? What was it about that massive woman that made her appear instantly regal, and set her on a throne in some dark and dreadful scenery, wielding a sceptre over the red glare of some tempestuous orgy? And why did this slender stripling of a girl, graceful as a willow, lithe as a young leopard, assume suddenly an air of sinister majesty, and move with flame and smoke about her head, and the darkness of night beneath her feet?

Vezin caught his breath and sat there transfixed. Then, almost simultaneously with its appearance, the queer notion vanished again, and the sunlight of day caught them both, and he heard her laughing to her mother about the *soupe à l'onion*, and saw her glancing back at him over her dear little shoulder with a smile that made him think of a dew-kissed rose bending lightly before summer airs.

And, indeed, the onion soup was particularly excellent that day, because he saw another cover laid at his small table, and, with fluttering heart, heard the waiter murmur by way of explanation that "Ma'mselle Ilsé would honour M'sieur to-day at *déjeuner*, as her custom sometimes is with her mother's guests."

So actually she sat by him all through that delirious meal, talking quietly to him in easy French, seeing that he was well looked after, mixing the salad-dressing, and even helping him with her own hand. And, later in the afternoon, while he was smoking in the courtyard, longing for a sight of her as soon as her duties were done, she came again to his side, and when he rose to meet her, she stood facing him a moment, full of a perplexing sweet shyness before she spoke—

"My mother thinks you ought to know more of the beauties of our little town, and I think so too! Would M'sieur like me to be his guide, perhaps? I can show him everything, for our family has lived here for many generations."

She had him by the hand, indeed, before he could find a single word to express his pleasure, and led him, all unresisting, out into the street, yet in such a way that it seemed perfectly natural she should do so, and without the faintest suggestion of boldness or immodesty. Her face glowed with the pleasure and interest of it, and with her short dress and tumbled hair she looked every bit the charming child of seventeen that she was, innocent and playful, proud of her native town, and alive beyond her years to the sense of its ancient beauty.

So they went over the town together, and she showed him what she considered its chief interest: the tumble-down old house where her forebears had lived; the sombre, aristocratic-looking mansion where her mother's family dwelt for centuries, and the ancient market-place where several hundred years before the witches had been burnt by the score. She kept up a lively running stream of talk about it all, of which he understood not a fiftieth part as he trudged along by her side, cursing his forty-five years and feeling all the yearnings of his early manhood revive and jeer at him. And, as she talked, England and Surbiton seemed very far away indeed, almost in another age of the world's history. Her voice touched something immeasurably old in him, something that slept deep. It lulled the surface parts of his consciousness to sleep, allowing what was far more ancient to awaken. Like the town, with its elaborate

pretence of modern active life, the upper layers of his being became dulled, soothed, muffled, and what lay underneath began to
stir in its sleep. That big Curtain swayed a little to and fro. Presently it might lift altogether....

He began to understand a little better at last. The mood of the
town was reproducing itself in him. In proportion as his ordinary
external self became muffled, that inner secret life, that was far
more real and vital, asserted itself. And this girl was surely the
high-priestess of it all, the chief instrument of its accomplishment.
New thoughts, with new interpretations, flooded his mind as she
walked beside him through the winding streets, while the picturesque old gabled town, softly coloured in the sunset, had never
appeared to him so wholly wonderful and seductive.

And only one curious incident came to disturb and puzzle him,
slight in itself, but utterly inexplicable, bringing white terror into
the child's face and a scream to her laughing lips. He had merely
pointed to a column of blue smoke that rose from the burning
autumn leaves and made a picture against the red roofs, and had
then run to the wall and called her to his side to watch the flames
shooting here and there through the heap of rubbish. Yet, at the
sight of it, as though taken by surprise, her face had altered dreadfully, and she had turned and run like the wind, calling out wild
sentences to him as she ran, of which he had not understood a
single word, except that the fire apparently frightened her, and she
wanted to get quickly away from it, and to get him away too.

Yet five minutes later she was as calm and happy again as
though nothing had happened to alarm or waken troubled thoughts
in her, and they had both forgotten the incident.

They were leaning over the ruined ramparts together listening
to the weird music of the band as he had heard it the first day of
his arrival. It moved him again profoundly as it had done before,
and somehow he managed to find his tongue and his best French.
The girl leaned across the stones close beside him. No one was
about. Driven by some remorseless engine within he began to stammer something—he hardly knew what—of his strange admiration
for her. Almost at the first word she sprang lightly off the wall and

came up smiling in front of him, just touching his knees as he sat there. She was hatless as usual, and the sun caught her hair and one side of her cheek and throat.

"Oh, I'm so glad!" she cried, clapping her little hands softly in his face, "so very glad, because that means that if you like me you must also like what I do, and what I belong to."

Already he regretted bitterly having lost control of himself. Something in the phrasing of her sentence chilled him. He knew the fear of embarking upon an unknown and dangerous sea.

"You will take part in our real life, I mean," she added softly, with an indescribable coaxing of manner, as though she noticed his shrinking. "You will come back to us."

Already this slip of a child seemed to dominate him; he felt her power coming over him more and more; something emanated from her that stole over his senses and made him aware that her personality, for all its simple grace, held forces that were stately, imposing, august. He saw her again moving through smoke and flame amid broken and tempestuous scenery, alarmingly strong, her terrible mother by her side. Dimly this shone through her smile and appearance of charming innocence.

"You will, I know," she repeated, holding him with her eyes.

They were quite alone up there on the ramparts, and the sensation that she was overmastering him stirred a wild sensuousness in his blood. The mingled abandon and reserve in her attracted him furiously, and all of him that was man rose up and resisted the creeping influence, at the same time acclaiming it with the full delight of his forgotten youth. An irresistible desire came to him to question her, to summon what still remained to him of his own little personality in an effort to retain the right to his normal self.

The girl had grown quiet again, and was now leaning on the broad wall close beside him, gazing out across the darkening plain, her elbows on the coping, motionless as a figure carved in stone. He took his courage in both hands.

"Tell me, Ilsé," he said, unconsciously imitating her own purring softness of voice, yet aware that he was utterly in earnest, "what is the meaning of this town, and what is this real life you speak of?

And why is it that the people watch me from morning to night? Tell me what it all means? And, tell me," he added more quickly with passion in his voice, "what you really are—yourself?"

She turned her head and looked at him through half-closed eyelids, her growing inner excitement betraying itself by the faint colour that ran like a shadow across her face.

"It seems to me,"—he faltered oddly under her gaze—"that I have some right to know—"

Suddenly she opened her eyes to the full. "You love me, then?" she asked softly.

"I swear," he cried impetuously, moved as by the force of a rising tide, "I never felt before—I have never known any other girl who—"

"Then you *have* the right to know," she calmly interrupted his confused confession, "for love shares all secrets."

She paused, and a thrill like fire ran swiftly through him. Her words lifted him off the earth, and he felt a radiant happiness, followed almost the same instant in horrible contrast by the thought of death. He became aware that she had turned her eyes upon his own and was speaking again.

"The real life I speak of," she whispered, "is the old, old life within, the life of long ago, the life to which you, too, once belonged, and to which you still belong."

A faint wave of memory troubled the deeps of his soul as her low voice sank into him. What she was saying he knew instinctively to be true, even though he could not as yet understand its full purport. His present life seemed slipping from him as he listened, merging his personality in one that was far older and greater. It was this loss of his present self that brought to him the thought of death.

"You came here," she went on, "with the purpose of seeking it, and the people felt your presence and are waiting to know what you decide, whether you will leave them without having found it, or whether—"

Her eyes remained fixed upon his own, but her face began to change, growing larger and darker with an expression of age.

"It is their thoughts constantly playing about your soul that makes you feel they watch you. They do not watch you with their eyes. The purposes of their inner life are calling to you, seeking to claim you. You were all part of the same life long, long ago, and now they want you back again among them."

Vezin's timid heart sank with dread as he listened; but the girl's eyes held him with a net of joy so that he had no wish to escape. She fascinated him, as it were, clean out of his normal self.

"Alone, however, the people could never have caught and held you," she resumed. "The motive force was not strong enough; it has faded through all these years. But I"—she paused a moment and looked at him with complete confidence in her splendid eyes— "I possess the spell to conquer you and hold you: the spell of old love. I can win you back again and make you live the old life with me, for the force of the ancient tie between us, if I choose to use it, is irresistible. And I do choose to use it. I still want you. And you, dear soul of my dim past"—she pressed closer to him so that her breath passed across his eyes, and her voice positively sang— "I mean to have you, for you love me and are utterly at my mercy."

Vezin heard, and yet did not hear; understood, yet did not understand. He had passed into a condition of exaltation. The world was beneath his feet, made of music and flowers, and he was flying somewhere far above it through the sunshine of pure delight. He was breathless and giddy with the wonder of her words. They intoxicated him. And, still, the terror of it all, the dreadful thought of death, pressed ever behind her sentences. For flames shot through her voice out of black smoke and licked at his soul.

And they communicated with one another, it seemed to him, by a process of swift telepathy, for his French could never have compassed all he said to her. Yet she understood perfectly, and what she said to him was like the recital of verses long since known. And the mingled pain and sweetness of it as he listened were almost more than his little soul could hold.

"Yet I came here wholly by chance—" he heard himself saying.

"No," she cried with passion, "you came here because I called to you. I have called to you for years, and you came with the whole

force of the past behind you. You had to come, for I own you, and
I claim you."

She rose again and moved closer, looking at him with a certain
insolence in the face—the insolence of power.

The sun had set behind the towers of the old cathedral and the
darkness rose up from the plain and enveloped them. The music
of the band had ceased. The leaves of the plane trees hung motionless, but the chill of the autumn evening rose about them and made
Vezin shiver. There was no sound but the sound of their voices
and the occasional soft rustle of the girl's dress. He could hear the
blood rushing in his ears. He scarcely realised where he was or
what he was doing. Some terrible magic of the imagination drew
him deeply down into the tombs of his own being, telling him in
no unfaltering voice that her words shadowed forth the truth. And
this simple little French maid, speaking beside him with so strange
authority, he saw curiously alter into quite another being. As he
stared into her eyes, the picture in his mind grew and lived, dressing itself vividly to his inner vision with a degree of reality he was
compelled to acknowledge. As once before, he saw her tall and
stately, moving through wild and broken scenery of forests and
mountain caverns, the glare of flames behind her head and clouds
of shifting smoke about her feet. Dark leaves encircled her hair,
flying loosely in the wind, and her limbs shone through the merest
rags of clothing. Others were about her, too, and ardent eyes on all
sides cast delirious glances upon her, but her own eyes were always for One only, one whom she held by the hand. For she was
leading the dance in some tempestuous orgy to the music of chanting voices, and the dance she led circled about a great and awful
Figure on a throne, brooding over the scene through lurid vapours,
while innumerable other wild faces and forms crowded furiously
about her in the dance. But the one she held by the hand he knew
to be himself, and the monstrous shape upon the throne he knew
to be her mother.

The vision rose within him, rushing to him down the long years
of buried time, crying aloud to him with the voice of memory
reawakened.... And then the scene faded away and he saw the clear

circle of the girl's eyes gazing steadfastly into his own, and she became once more the pretty little daughter of the innkeeper, and he found his voice again.

"And you," he whispered tremblingly— "you child of visions and enchantment, how is it that you so bewitch me that I loved you even before I saw?"

She drew herself up beside him with an air of rare dignity.

"The call of the Past," she said; "and besides," she added proudly, "in the real life I am a princess—"

"A princess!" he cried.

"—and my mother is a queen!"

At this, little Vezin utterly lost his head. Delight tore at his heart and swept him into sheer ecstasy. To hear that sweet singing voice, and to see those adorable little lips utter such things, upset his balance beyond all hope of control. He took her in his arms and covered her unresisting face with kisses.

But even while he did so, and while the hot passion swept him, he felt that she was soft and loathsome, and that her answering kisses stained his very soul. . . . And when, presently, she had freed herself and vanished into the darkness, he stood there, leaning against the wall in a state of collapse, creeping with horror from the touch of her yielding body, and inwardly raging at the weakness that he already dimly realised must prove his undoing.

And from the shadows of the old buildings into which she disappeared there rose in the stillness of the night a singular, long-drawn cry, which at first he took for laughter, but which later he was sure he recognised as the almost human wailing of a cat.

V

FOR A LONG TIME Vezin leant there against the wall, alone with his surging thoughts and emotions. He understood at length that he had done the one thing necessary to call down upon him the whole force of this ancient Past. For in those passionate kisses he had acknowledged the tie of olden days, and had revived it. And the memory of that soft impalpable caress in the darkness of the inn corridor came back to him with a shudder. The girl had first mastered him, and then led him to the one act that was necessary for her purpose. He had been waylaid, after the lapse of centuries—caught, and conquered.

Dimly he realised this, and sought to make plans for his escape. But, for the moment at any rate, he was powerless to manage his thoughts or will, for the sweet, fantastic madness of the whole adventure mounted to his brain like a spell, and he gloried in the feeling that he was utterly enchanted and moving in a world so much larger and wilder than the one he had ever been accustomed to.

The moon, pale and enormous, was just rising over the sea-like plain, when at last he rose to go. Her slanting rays drew all the houses into new perspective, so that their roofs, already glistening with dew, seemed to stretch much higher into the sky than usual, and their gables and quaint old towers lay far away in its purple reaches.

The cathedral appeared unreal in a silver mist. He moved softly, keeping to the shadows; but the streets were all deserted and very silent; the doors were closed, the shutters fastened. Not a soul was astir. The hush of night lay over everything; it was like a town of the dead, a churchyard with gigantic and grotesque tombstones.

Wondering where all the busy life of the day had so utterly disappeared to, he made his way to a back door that entered the inn by means of the stables, thinking thus to reach his room unobserved. He reached the courtyard safely and crossed it by keeping close to the shadow of the wall. He sidled down it, mincing along on tiptoe, just as the old men did when they entered the *salle à manger*. He was horrified to find himself doing this instinctively. A strange impulse came to him, catching him somehow in the centre of his body—an impulse to drop upon all fours and run swiftly and silently. He glanced upwards and the idea came to him to leap up upon his window-sill overhead instead of going round by the stairs. This occurred to him as the easiest, and most natural way. It was like the beginning of some horrible transformation of himself into something else. He was fearfully strung up.

The moon was higher now, and the shadows very dark along the side of the street where he moved. He kept among the deepest of them, and reached the porch with the glass doors.

But here there was light; the inmates, unfortunately, were still about. Hoping to slip across the hall unobserved and reach the stairs, he opened the door carefully and stole in. Then he saw that the hall was not empty. A large dark thing lay against the wall on his left. At first he thought it must be household articles. Then it moved, and he thought it was an immense cat, distorted in some way by the play of light and shadow. Then it rose straight up before him and he saw that it was the proprietress.

What she had been doing in this position he could only venture a dreadful guess, but the moment she stood up and faced him he was aware of some terrible dignity clothing her about that instantly recalled the girl's strange saying that she was a queen. Huge and sinister she stood there under the little oil lamp; alone with him in the empty hall. Awe stirred in his heart, and the roots of some ancient fear. He felt that he must bow to her and make some kind of obeisance. The impulse was fierce and irresistible, as of long habit. He glanced quickly about him. There was no one there. Then he deliberately inclined his head toward her. He bowed.

"*Enfin! M'sieur s'est donc décidé. C'est bien alors. J'en suis contente.*"

Her words came to him sonorously as through a great open space.

Then the great figure came suddenly across the flagged hall at him and seized his trembling hands. Some overpowering force moved with her and caught him.

"*On pourrait faire un p'tit tour ensemble, n'est-ce pas? Nous y allons cette nuit et il faut s'exercer un peu d'avance pour cela. Ilsé, Ilsé, viens donc ici. Viens vite!*"

And she whirled him round in the opening steps of some dance that seemed oddly and horribly familiar. They made no sound on the stones, this strangely assorted couple. It was all soft and stealthy. And presently, when the air seemed to thicken like smoke, and a red glare as of flame shot through it, he was aware that some

one else had joined them and that his hand the mother had released was now tightly held by the daughter. Ilsé had come in answer to the call, and he saw her with leaves of vervain twined in
her dark hair, clothed in tattered vestiges of some curious garment,
beautiful as the night, and horribly, odiously, loathsomely seductive.

"To the Sabbath! to the Sabbath!" they cried. "On to the
Witches' Sabbath!"

Up and down that narrow hall they danced, the women on each
side of him, to the wildest measure he had ever imagined, yet which
he dimly, dreadfully remembered, till the lamp on the wall flickered and went out, and they were left in total darkness. And the
devil woke in his heart with a thousand vile suggestions and made
him afraid.

Suddenly they released his hands and he heard the voice of the
mother cry that it was time, and they must go. Which way they
went he did not pause to see. He only realised that he was free,
and he blundered through the darkness till he found the stairs and
then tore up them to his room as though all hell was at his heels.

He flung himself on the sofa, with his face in his hands, and
groaned. Swiftly reviewing a dozen ways of immediate escape, all
equally impossible, he finally decided that the only thing to do for
the moment was to sit quiet and wait. He must see what was going
to happen. At least in the privacy of his own bedroom he would be
fairly safe. The door was locked. He crossed over and softly opened
the window which gave upon the courtyard and also permitted a
partial view of the hall through the glass doors.

As he did so the hum and murmur of a great activity reached
his ears from the streets beyond—the sound of footsteps and voices
muffled by distance. He leaned out cautiously and listened. The
moonlight was clear and strong now, but his own window was in
shadow, the silver disc being still behind the house. It came to him
irresistibly that the inhabitants of the town, who a little while before had all been invisible behind closed doors, were now issuing
forth, busy upon some secret and unholy errand. He listened in-
tently.

At first everything about him was silent, but soon he became aware of movements going on in the house itself. Rustlings and cheepings came to him across that still, moonlit yard. A concourse of living beings sent the hum of their activity into the night. Things were on the move everywhere. A biting, pungent odour rose through the air, coming he knew not whence. Presently his eyes became glued to the windows of the opposite wall where the moonshine fell in a soft blaze. The roof overhead, and behind him, was reflected clearly in the panes of glass, and he saw the outlines of dark bodies moving with long footsteps over the tiles and along the coping. They passed swiftly and silently, shaped like immense cats, in an endless procession across the pictured glass, and then appeared to leap down to a lower level where he lost sight of them. He just caught the soft thudding of their leaps. Sometimes their shadows fell upon the white wall opposite, and then he could not make out whether they were the shadows of human beings or of cats. They seemed to change swiftly from one to the other. The transformation looked horribly real, for they leaped like human beings, yet changed swiftly in the air immediately afterwards, and dropped like animals.

The yard, too, beneath him, was now alive with the creeping movements of dark forms all stealthily drawing towards the porch with the glass doors. They kept so closely to the wall that he could not determine their actual shape, but when he saw that they passed on to the great congregation that was gathering in the hall, he understood that these were the creatures whose leaping shadows he had first seen reflected in the windowpanes opposite. They were coming from all parts of the town, reaching the appointed meeting-place across the roofs and tiles, and springing from level to level till they came to the yard.

Then a new sound caught his ear, and he saw that the windows all about him were being softly opened, and that to each window came a face. A moment later figures began dropping hurriedly down into the yard. And these figures, as they lowered themselves down from the windows, were human, he saw; but once safely in the yard they fell upon all fours and changed in the swiftest possible second into—cats—huge, silent cats. They ran in streams to join the main body in the hall beyond.

So, after all, the rooms in the house had not been empty and unoccupied.

Moreover, what he saw no longer filled him with amazement. For he remembered it all. It was familiar. It had all happened before just so, hundreds of times, and he himself had taken part in it and known the wild madness of it all. The outline of the old building changed, the yard grew larger, and he seemed to be staring down upon it from a much greater height through smoky vapours. And, as he looked, half remembering, the old pains of long ago, fierce and sweet, furiously assailed him, and the blood stirred horribly as he heard the Call of the Dance again in his heart and tasted the ancient magic of Ilsé whirling by his side.

Suddenly he started back. A great lithe cat had leaped softly up from the shadows below on to the sill close to his face, and was staring fixedly at him with the eyes of a human. "Come," it seemed to say, "come with us to the Dance! Change as of old! Transform yourself swiftly and come!" Only too well he understood the creature's soundless call.

It was gone again in a flash with scarcely a sound of its padded feet on the stones, and then others dropped by the score down the side of the house, past his very eyes, all changing as they fell and darting away rapidly, softly, towards the gathering point. And again he felt the dreadful desire to do likewise; to murmur the old incantation, and then drop upon hands and knees and run swiftly for the great flying leap into the air. Oh, how the passion of it rose within him like a flood, twisting his very entrails, sending his heart's desire flaming forth into the night for the old, old Dance of the Sorcerers at the Witches' Sabbath! The whirl of the stars was about him; once more he met the magic of the moon. The power of the wind, rushing from precipice and forest, leaping from cliff to cliff across the valleys, tore him away. . . . He heard the cries of the dancers and their wild laughter, and with this savage girl in his embrace he danced furiously about the dim Throne where sat the Figure with the sceptre of majesty. . . .

Then, suddenly, all became hushed and still, and the fever died down a little in his heart. The calm moonlight flooded a courtyard empty and deserted. They had started. The procession was off into the sky. And he was left behind—alone.

Vezin tiptoed softly across the room and unlocked the door. The murmur from the streets, growing momentarily as he advanced, met his ears. He made his way with the utmost caution down the corridor. At the head of the stairs he paused and listened. Below him, the hall where they had gathered was dark and still, but through opened doors and windows on the far side of the building came the sound of a great throng moving farther and farther into the distance.

He made his way down the creaking wooden stairs, dreading yet longing to meet some straggler who should point the way, but finding no one; across the dark hall, so lately thronged with living, moving things, and out through the opened front doors into the street. He could not believe that he was really left behind, really forgotten, that he had been purposely permitted to escape. It perplexed him.

Nervously he peered about him, and up and down the street; then, seeing nothing, advanced slowly down the pavement.

The whole town, as he went, showed itself empty and deserted, as though a great wind had blown everything alive out of it. The doors and windows of the houses stood open to the night; nothing stirred; moonlight and silence lay over all. The night lay about him like a cloak. The air, soft and cool, caressed his cheek like the touch of a great furry paw. He gained confidence and began to walk quickly, though still keeping to the shadowed side. Nowhere could he discover the faintest sign of the great unholy exodus he knew had just taken place. The moon sailed high over all in a sky cloudless and serene.

Hardly realising where he was going, he crossed the open market-place and so came to the ramparts, whence he knew a pathway descended to the high road and along which he could make good his escape to one of the other little towns that lay to the northward, and so to the railway.

But first he paused and gazed out over the scene at his feet where the great plain lay like a silver map of some dream country. The still beauty of it entered his heart, increasing his sense of bewilderment and unreality. No air stirred, the leaves of the plane trees stood motionless, the near details were defined with the sharpness of day against dark shadows, and in the distance the fields and woods melted away into haze and shimmering mistiness.

But the breath caught in his throat and he stood stockstill as though transfixed when his gaze passed from the horizon and fell upon the near prospect in the depth of the valley at his feet. The whole lower slopes of the hill, that lay hid from the brightness of the moon, were aglow, and through the glare he saw countless moving forms, shifting thick and fast between the openings of the trees; while overhead, like leaves driven by the wind, he discerned flying shapes that hovered darkly one moment against the sky and then settled down with cries and weird singing through the branches into the region that was aflame.

Spellbound, he stood and stared for a time that he could not measure. And then, moved by one of the terrible impulses that seemed to control the whole adventure, he climbed swiftly upon the top of the broad coping, and balanced a moment where the valley gaped at his feet. But in that very instant, as he stood hovering, a sudden movement among the shadows of the houses caught his eye, and he turned to see the outline of a large animal dart swiftly across the open space behind him, and land with a flying leap upon the top of the wall a little lower down. It ran like the wind to his feet and then rose up beside him upon the ramparts. A shiver seemed to run through the moonlight, and his sight trembled for a second. His heart pulsed fearfully. Ilsé stood beside him, peering into his face.

Some dark substance, he saw, stained the girl's face and skin, shining in the moonlight as she stretched her hands towards him; she was dressed in wretched tattered garments that yet became her mightily; rue and vervain twined about her temples; her eyes glittered with unholy light. He only just controlled the wild impulse to take her in his arms and leap with her from their giddy perch into the valley below.

"See!" she cried, pointing with an arm on which the rags fluttered in the rising wind towards the forest aglow in the distance. "See where they await us! The woods are alive! Already the Great Ones are there, and the dance will soon begin! The salve is here! Anoint yourself and come!"

Though a moment before the sky was clear and cloudless, yet even while she spoke the face of the moon grew dark and the wind began to toss in the crests of the plane trees at his feet. Stray gusts brought the sounds of hoarse singing and crying from the lower slopes of the hill, and the pungent odour he had already noticed about the courtyard of the inn rose about him in the air.

"Transform, transform!" she cried again, her voice rising like a song. "Rub well your skin before you fly. Come! Come with me to the Sabbath, to the madness of its furious delight, to the sweet abandonment of its evil worship! See! the Great Ones are there, and the terrible Sacraments prepared. The Throne is occupied. Anoint and come! Anoint and come!"

She grew to the height of a tree beside him, leaping upon the wall with flaming eyes and hair strewn upon the night. He too began to change swiftly. Her hands touched the skin of his face and neck, streaking him with the burning salve that sent the old magic into his blood with the power before which fades all that is good.

A wild roar came up to his ears from the heart of the wood, and the girl, when she heard it, leaped upon the wall in the frenzy of her wicked joy.

"Satan is there!" she screamed, rushing upon him and striving to draw him with her to the edge of the wall. "Satan has come. The Sacraments call us! Come, with your dear apostate soul, and we will worship and dance till the moon dies and the world is forgotten!"

Just saving himself from the dreadful plunge, Vezin struggled to release himself from her grasp, while the passion tore at his reins and all but mastered him. He shrieked aloud, not knowing what he said, and then he shrieked again. It was the old impulses, the old awful habits instinctively finding voice; for though it seemed to him that he merely shrieked nonsense, the words he uttered really had meaning in them, and were intelligible. It was the ancient call. And it was heard below. It was answered.

The wind whistled at the skirts of his coat as the air round him darkened with many flying forms crowding upwards out of the valley. The crying of hoarse voices smote upon his ears, coming closer. Strokes of wind buffeted him, tearing him this way and that along the crumbling top of the stone wall; and Ilsé clung to him with her long shining arms, smooth and bare, holding him fast about the neck. But not Ilsé alone, for a dozen of them surrounded him, dropping out of the air. The pungent odour of the anointed bodies stifled him, exciting him to the old madness of the Sabbath, the dance of the witches and sorcerers doing honour to the personified Evil of the world.

"Anoint and away! Anoint and away!" they cried in wild chorus about him. "To the Dance that never dies! To the sweet and fearful fantasy of evil!"

Another moment and he would have yielded and gone, for his will turned soft and the flood of passionate memory all but overwhelmed him, when—so can a small thing after the whole course of an adventure—he caught his foot upon a loose stone in the edge of the wall, and then fell with a sudden crash on to the ground below. But he fell towards the houses, in the open space of dust and cobblestones, and fortunately not into the gaping depth of the valley on the farther side.

And they, too, came in a tumbling heap about him, like flies upon a piece of food, but as they fell he was released for a moment from the power of their touch, and in that brief instant of freedom there flashed into his mind the sudden intuition that saved him. Before he could regain his feet he saw them scrabbling awkwardly back upon the wall, as though bat-like they could only fly by dropping from a height, and had no hold upon him in the open. Then, seeing them perched there in a row like cats upon a roof, all dark and singularly shapeless, their eyes like lamps, the sudden memory came back to him of Ilsé's terror at the sight of fire.

Quick as a flash he found his matches and lit the dead leaves that lay under the wall.

Dry and withered, they caught fire at once, and the wind carried the flame in a long line down the length of the wall, licking upwards as it ran; and with shrieks and wailings, the crowded row of forms upon the top melted away into the air on the other side, and were gone with a great rush and whirring of their bodies down into the heart of the haunted valley, leaving Vezin breathless and shaken in the middle of the deserted ground.

"Ilsé!" he called feebly; "Ilsé!" for his heart ached to think that she was really gone to the great Dance without him, and that he had lost the opportunity of its fearful joy. Yet at the same time his relief was so great, and he was so dazed and troubled in mind with the whole thing, that he hardly knew what he was saying, and only cried aloud in the fierce storm of his emotion. . . .

The fire under the wall ran its course, and the moonlight came out again, soft and clear, from its temporary eclipse. With one last shuddering look at the ruined ramparts, and a feeling of horrid wonder for the haunted valley beyond, where the shapes still crowded and flew, he turned his face towards the town and slowly made his way in the direction of the hotel.

And as he went, a great wailing of cries, and a sound of howling, followed him from the gleaming forest below, growing fainter and fainter with the bursts of wind as he disappeared between the houses.

VI

"It may seem rather abrupt to you, this sudden tame ending," said Arthur Vezin, glancing with flushed face and timid eyes at Dr. Silence sitting there with his notebook, "but the fact is—er—from that moment my memory seems to have failed rather. I have no distinct recollection of how I got home or what precisely I did.

"It appears I never went back to the inn at all. I only dimly recollect racing down a long white road in the moonlight, past woods and villages, still and deserted, and then the dawn came up, and I saw the towers of a biggish town and so came to a station.

"But, long before that, I remember pausing somewhere on the road and looking back to where the hill-town of my adventure stood up in the moonlight, and thinking how exactly like a great monstrous cat it lay there upon the plain, its huge front paws lying down the two main streets, and the twin and broken towers of the cathedral marking its torn ears against the sky. That picture stays in my mind with the utmost vividness to this day.

"Another thing remains in my mind from that escape—namely, the sudden sharp reminder that I had not paid my bill, and the decision I made, standing there on the dusty highroad, that the small baggage I had left behind would more than settle for my indebtedness.

"For the rest, I can only tell you that I got coffee and bread at a café on the outskirts of this town I had come to, and soon after found my way to the station and caught a train later in the day. That same evening I reached London."

"And how long altogether," asked John Silence quietly, "do you think you stayed in the town of the adventure?"

Vezin looked up sheepishly.

"I was coming to that," he resumed, with apologetic wrigglings of his body. "In London I found that I was a whole week out in my reckoning of time. I had stayed over a week in the town, and it ought to have been September 15th,—instead of which it was only September 10th!"

"So that, in reality, you had only stayed a night or two in the inn?" queried the doctor.

Vezin hesitated before replying. He shuffled upon the mat.

"I must have gained time somewhere," he said at length— "somewhere or somehow. I certainly had a week to my credit. I can't explain it. I can only give you the fact."

"And this happened to you last year, since when you have never been back to the place?"

"Last autumn, yes," murmured Vezin; "and I have never dared to go back. I think I never want to."

"And, tell me," asked Dr. Silence at length, when he saw that the little man had evidently come to the end of his words and had nothing more to say, "had you ever read up the subject of the old witchcraft practices during the Middle Ages, or been at all interested in the subject?"

"Never!" declared Vezin emphatically. "I had never given a thought to such matters so far as I know—"

"Or to the question of reincarnation, perhaps?"

"Never—before my adventure; but I have since," he replied significantly.

There was, however, something still on the man's mind that he wished to relieve himself of by confession, yet could only with difficulty bring himself to mention; and it was only after the sympathetic tactfulness of the doctor had provided numerous openings that he at length availed himself of one of them, and stammered that he would like to show him the marks he still had on his neck where, he said, the girl had touched him with her anointed hands.

He took off his collar after infinite fumbling hesitation, and lowered his shirt a little for the doctor to see. And there, on the surface of the skin, lay a faint reddish line across the shoulder and extending a little way down the back towards the spine. It certainly indicated exactly the position an arm might have taken in the act of embracing. And on the other side of the neck, slightly higher up, was a similar mark, though not quite so clearly defined.

"That was where she held me that night on the ramparts," he whispered, a strange light coming and going in his eyes.

IT WAS SOME weeks later when I again found occasion to consult John Silence concerning another extraordinary case that had come under my notice, and we fell to discussing Vezin's story. Since hearing it, the doctor had made investigations on his own account, and one of his secretaries had discovered that Vezin's ancestors had actually lived for generations in the very town where the adventure came to him. Two of them, both women, had been tried and convicted as witches, and had been burned alive at the stake. Moreover, it had not been difficult to prove that the very inn where Vezin stayed was built about 1700 upon the spot where the funeral pyres stood and the executions took place. The town was a sort of head-quarters for all the sorcerers and witches of the entire region, and after conviction they were burnt there literally by scores.

"It seems strange," continued the doctor, "that Vezin should have remained ignorant of all this; but, on the other hand, it was not the kind of history that successive generations would have been anxious to keep alive, or to repeat to their children. Therefore I am inclined to think he still knows nothing about it.

"The whole adventure seems to have been a very vivid revival of the memories of an earlier life, caused by coming directly into contact with the living forces still intense enough to hang about the place, and, by a most singular chance, too, with the very souls who had taken part with him in the events of that particular life. For the mother and daughter who impressed him so strangely must have been leading actors, with himself, in the scenes and practices of witchcraft which at that period dominated the imaginations of the whole country.

"One has only to read the histories of the times to know that these witches claimed the power of transforming themselves into various animals, both for the purposes of disguise and also to convey themselves swiftly to the scenes of their imaginary orgies. Lycanthropy, or the power to change themselves into wolves, was everywhere believed in, and the ability to transform themselves into cats by rubbing their bodies with a special salve or ointment provided by Satan himself, found equal credence. The witchcraft trials abound in evidences of such universal beliefs."

Dr. Silence quoted chapter and verse from many writers on the subject, and showed how every detail of Vezin's adventure had a basis in the practices of those dark days.

"But that the entire affair took place subjectively in the man's own consciousness, I have no doubt," he went on, in reply to my questions; "for my secretary who has been to the town to investi-gate, discovered his signature in the visitors' book, and proved by it that he had arrived on September 8th, and left suddenly without paying his bill. He left two days later, and they still were in possession of his dirty brown bag and some tourist clothes. I paid a few francs in settlement of his debt, and have sent his luggage on to him. The daughter was absent from home, but the proprietress, a large woman very much as he described her, told my secretary that he had seemed a very strange, absent-minded kind of gentleman, and after his disappearance she had feared for a long time that he had met with a violent end in the neighbouring forest where he used to roam about alone.

"I should like to have obtained a personal interview with the daughter so as to ascertain how much was subjective and how much actually took place with her as Vezin told it. For her dread of fire and the sight of burning must, of course, have been the intuitive memory of her former painful death at the stake, and have thus explained why he fancied more than once that he saw her through smoke and flame."

"And that mark on his skin, for instance?" I inquired.

"Merely the marks produced by hysterical brooding," he replied, "like the stigmata of the *religieuses*, and the bruises which appear on the bodies of hypnotised subjects who have been told to expect them. This is very common and easily explained. Only it seems curious that these marks should have remained so long in Vezin's case. Usually they disappear quickly."

"Obviously he is still thinking about it all, brooding, and living it all over again," I ventured.

"Probably. And this makes me fear that the end of his trouble is not yet. We shall hear of him again. It is a case, alas! I can do little to alleviate."

Dr. Silence spoke gravely and with sadness in his voice.

"And what do you make of the Frenchman in the train?" I asked further— "the man who warned him against the place, *à cause du sommeil et à cause des chats*? Surely a very singular incident?"

"A *very* singular incident indeed," he made answer slowly, "and one I can only explain on the basis of a highly improbable coincidence—"

"Namely?"

"That the man was one who had himself stayed in the town and undergone there a similar experience. I should like to find this man and ask him. But the crystal is useless here, for I have no slightest clue to go upon, and I can only conclude that some singular psychic affinity, some force still active in his being out of the same past life, drew him thus to the personality of Vezin, and enabled him to fear what might happen to him, and thus to warn him as he did.

"Yes," he presently continued, half talking to himself, "I suspect in this case that Vezin was swept into the vortex of forces arising out of the intense activities of a past life, and that he lived over again a scene in which he had often played a leading part centuries before. For strong actions set up forces that are so slow to exhaust themselves, they may be said in a sense never to die. In this case they were not vital enough to render the illusion complete, so that the little man found himself caught in a very distressing confusion of the present and the past; yet he was sufficiently sensitive to recognise that it was true, and to fight against the degradation of returning, even in memory, to a former and lower state of development.

"Ah yes!" he continued, crossing the floor to gaze at the darkening sky, and seemingly quite oblivious of my presence, "subliminal up-rushes of memory like this can be exceedingly painful, and sometimes exceedingly dangerous. I only trust that this gentle soul may soon escape from this obsession of a passionate and tempestuous past. But I doubt it, I doubt it."

His voice was hushed with sadness as he spoke, and when he turned back into the room again there was an expression of profound yearning upon his face, the yearning of a soul whose desire to help is sometimes greater than his power.

TOBERMORY
SAKI

IT WAS A CHILL, rain-washed afternoon of a late August day, that
indefinite season when partridges are still in security or cold stor-
age, and there is nothing to hunt—unless one is bounded on the
north by the Bristol Channel, in which case one may lawfully gal-
lop after fat red stags. Lady Blemley's house-party was not bounded
on the north by the Bristol Channel, hence there was a full gathering of her guests round the tea-table on this particular afternoon.
And, in spite of the blankness of the season and the triteness of
the occasion, there was no trace in the company of that fatigued
restlessness which means a dread of the pianola and a subdued
hankering for auction bridge. The undisguised openmouthed attention of the entire party was fixed on the homely negative personality of Mr. Cornelius Appin. Of all her guests, he was the one
who had come to Lady Blemley with the vaguest reputation. Some
one had said he was "clever," and he had got his invitation in the
moderate expectation, on the part of his hostess, that some portion at least of his cleverness would be contributed to the general
entertainment. Until tea-time that day she had been unable to discover in what direction, if any, his cleverness lay. He was neither a
wit nor a croquet champion, a hypnotic force nor a begetter of
amateur theatricals. Neither did his exterior suggest the sort of
man in whom women are willing to pardon a generous measure of
mental deficiency. He had subsided into mere Mr. Appin, and the
Cornelius seemed a piece of transparent baptismal bluff. And now
he was claiming to have launched on the world a discovery beside

which the invention of gunpowder, of the printing-press, and of steam locomotion were inconsiderable trifles. Science had made bewildering strides in many directions during recent decades, but this thing seemed to belong to the domain of miracle rather than to scientific achievement.

"And do you really ask us to believe," Sir Wilfrid was saying, "that you have discovered a means for instructing animals in the art of human speech, and that dear old Tobermory has proved your first successful pupil?"

"It is a problem at which I have worked for the last seventeen years," said Mr. Appin, "but only during the last eight or nine months have I been rewarded with glimmerings of success. Of course I have experimented with thousands of animals, but latterly only with cats, those wonderful creatures which have assimilated themselves so marvellously with our civilization while retaining all their highly developed feral instincts. Here and there among cats one comes across an outstanding superior intellect, just as one does among the ruck of human beings, and when I made the acquaintance of Tobermory a week ago I saw at once that I was in contact with a 'Beyond-cat' of extraordinary intelligence. I had gone far along the road to success in recent experiments; with Tobermory, as you call him, I have reached the goal."

Mr. Appin concluded his remarkable statement in a voice which he strove to divest of a triumphant inflection. No one said "Rats," though Clovis's lips moved in a monosyllabic contortion which probably invoked those rodents of disbelief.

"And do you mean to say," asked Miss Resker, after a slight pause, "that you have taught Tobermory to say and understand easy sentences of one syllable?"

"My dear Miss Resker," said the wonderworker patiently, "one teaches little children and savages and backward adults in that piecemeal fashion; when one has once solved the problem of making a beginning with an animal of highly developed intelligence one has no need for those halting methods. Tobermory can speak our language with perfect correctness."

This time Clovis very distinctly said, "Beyond-rats!" Sir Wilfrid was more polite, but equally sceptical.

"Hadn't we better have the cat in and judge for ourselves?" suggested Lady Blemley.

Sir Wilfrid went in search of the animal, and the company settled themselves down to the languid expectation of witnessing some more or less adroit drawing-room ventriloquism.

In a minute Sir Wilfrid was back in the room, his face white beneath its tan and his eyes dilated with excitement.

"By Gad, it's true!"

His agitation was unmistakably genuine, and his hearers started forward in a thrill of awakened interest.

Collapsing into an armchair he continued breathlessly: "I found him dozing in the smoking-room, and called out to him to come for his tea. He blinked at me in his usual way, and I said, 'Come on, Toby; don't keep us waiting;' and, by Gad! he drawled out in a most horribly natural voice that he'd come when he dashed well pleased! I nearly jumped out of my skin!"

Appin had preached to absolutely incredulous hearers; Sir Wilfrid's statement carried instant conviction. A Babel-like chorus of startled exclamation arose, amid which the scientist sat mutely enjoying the first fruit of his stupendous discovery.

In the midst of the clamour Tobermory entered the room and made his way with velvet tread and studied unconcern across to the group seated round the tea-table.

A sudden hush of awkwardness and constraint fell on the company. Somehow there seemed an element of embarrassment in addressing on equal terms a domestic cat of acknowledged dental ability.

"Will you have some milk, Tobermory?" asked Lady Blemley in a rather strained voice.

"I don't mind if I do," was the response, couched in a tone of even indifference. A shiver of suppressed excitement went through the listeners, and Lady Blemley might be excused for pouring out the saucerful of milk rather unsteadily.

"I'm afraid I've spilt a good deal of it," she said apologetically.

"After all, it's not my Axminster," was Tobermory's rejoinder.

Another silence fell on the group, and then Miss Resker, in her best district-visitor manner, asked if the human language had been difficult to learn. Tobermory looked squarely at her for a moment and then fixed his gaze serenely on the middle distance. It was obvious that boring questions lay outside his scheme of life.

"What do you think of human intelligence?" asked Mavis Pellington lamely.

"Of whose intelligence in particular?" asked Tobermory coldly.

"Oh, well, mine for instance," said Mavis, with a feeble laugh.

"You put me in an embarrassing position," said Tobermory, whose tone and attitude certainly did not suggest a shred of embarrassment. "When your inclusion in this house-party was suggested Sir Wilfrid protested that you were the most brainless woman of his acquaintance, and that there was a wide distinction between hospitality and the care of the feeble-minded. Lady Blemley replied that your lack of brain-power was the precise quality which had earned you your invitation, as you were the only person she could think of who might be idiotic enough to buy their old car. You know, the one they call 'The Envy of Sisyphus,' because it goes quite nicely up-hill if you push it."

Lady Blemley's protestations would have had greater effect if she had not casually suggested to Mavis only that morning that the car in question would be just the thing for her down at her Devonshire home.

Major Barfield plunged in heavily to effect a diversion.

"How about your carryings-on with the tortoiseshell puss up at the stables, eh?"

The moment he had said it every one realized the blunder.

"One does not usually discuss these matters in public," said Tobermory frigidly. "From a slight observation of your ways since you've been in this house I should imagine you'd find it inconvenient if I were to shift the conversation on to your own little affairs."

The panic which ensued was not confined to the Major.

"Would you like to go and see if cook has got your dinner ready?" suggested Lady Blemley hurriedly, affecting to ignore the fact that it wanted at least two hours to Tobermory's dinner-time.

"Thanks," said Tobermory, "not quite so soon after my tea. I don't want to die of indigestion."

"Cats have nine lives, you know," said Sir Wilfrid heartily.

"Possibly," answered Tobermory; "but only one liver."

"Adelaide!" said Mrs. Cornett, "do you mean to encourage that cat to go out and gossip about us in the servants' hall?"

The panic had indeed become general. A narrow ornamental balustrade ran in front of most of the bedroom windows at the Towers, and it was recalled with dismay that this had formed a favourite promenade for Tobermory at all hours, whence he could watch the pigeons—and heaven knew what else besides. If he intended to become reminiscent in his present outspoken strain the effect would be something more than disconcerting. Mrs. Cornett, who spent much time at her toilet table, and whose complexion was reputed to be of a nomadic though punctual disposition, looked as ill at ease as the Major. Miss Scrawen, who wrote fiercely sensuous poetry and led a blameless life, merely displayed irritation; if you are methodical and virtuous in private you don't necessarily want every one to know it. Bertie van Tahn, who was so depraved at seventeen that he had long ago given up trying to be any worse, turned a dull shade of gardenia white, but he did not commit the error of dashing out of the room like Odo Finsberry, a young gentleman who was understood to be reading for the Church and who was possibly disturbed at the thought of scandals he might hear concerning other people. Clovis had the presence of mind to maintain a composed exterior; privately he was calculating how long it would take to procure a box of fancy mice through the agency of the *Exchange and Mart* as a species of hush-money.

Even in a delicate situation like the present, Agnes Resker could not endure to remain too long in the background.

"Why did I ever come down here?" she asked dramatically.

Tobermory immediately accepted the opening.

"Judging by what you said to Mrs. Cornett on the croquet-lawn yesterday, you were out for food. You described the Blemleys as the dullest people to stay with that you knew, but said they were clever enough to employ a first-rate cook; otherwise they'd find it difficult to get anyone to come down a second time."

"There's not a word of truth in it! I appeal to Mrs. Cornett—" exclaimed the discomfited Agnes.

"Mrs. Cornett repeated your remark afterwards to Bertie van Tahn," continued Tobermory, "and said, 'That woman is a regular Hunger Marcher; she'd go anywhere for four square meals a day,' and Bertie van Tahn said—"

At this point the chronicle mercifully ceased. Tobermory had caught a glimpse of the big yellow Tom from the Rectory working his way through the shrubbery towards the stable wing. In a flash he had vanished through the open French window.

With the disappearance of his too brilliant pupil Cornelius Appin found himself beset by a hurricane of bitter upbraiding, anxious inquiry, and frightened entreaty. The responsibility for the situation lay with him, and he must prevent matters from becoming worse. Could Tobermory impart his dangerous gift to other cats? was the first question he had to answer. It was possible, he replied, that he might have initiated his intimate friend the stable puss into his new accomplishment, but it was unlikely that his teaching could have taken a wider range as yet.

"Then," said Mrs. Cornett, "Tobermory may be a valuable cat and a great pet; but I'm sure you'll agree, Adelaide, that both he and the stable cat must be done away with without delay."

"You don't suppose I've enjoyed the last quarter of an hour, do you?" said Lady Blemley bitterly. "My husband and I are very fond of Tobermory—at least, we were before this horrible accomplishment was infused into him; but now, of course, the only thing is to have him destroyed as soon as possible."

"We can put some strychnine in the scraps he always gets at dinner-time," said Sir Wilfrid, "and I will go and drown the stable cat myself. The coachman will be very sore at losing his pet, but

I'll say a very catching form of mange has broken out in both cats and we're afraid of it spreading to the kennels."

"But my great discovery!" expostulated Mr. Appin; "after all my years of research and experiment—"

"You can go and experiment on the shorthorns at the farm, who are under proper control," said Mrs. Cornett, "or the elephants at the Zoological Gardens. They're said to be highly intelligent, and they have this recommendation, that they don't come creeping about our bedrooms and under chairs, and so forth."

An archangel ecstatically proclaiming the Millennium, and then finding that it clashed unpardonably with Henley and would have to be indefinitely postponed, could hardly have felt more crest-fallen than Cornelius Appin at the reception of his wonderful achievement. Public opinion, however, was against him—in fact, had the general voice been consulted on the subject it is probable that a strong minority vote would have been in favour of including him in the strychnine diet.

Defective train arrangements and a nervous desire to see matters brought to a finish prevented an immediate dispersal of the party, but dinner that evening was not a social success. Sir Wilfrid had had rather a trying time with the stable cat and subsequently with the coachman. Agnes Resker ostentatiously limited her repast to a morsel of dry toast, which she bit as though it were a personal enemy; while Mavis Pellington maintained a vindictive silence throughout the meal. Lady Blemley kept up a flow of what she hoped was conversation, but her attention was fixed on the doorway. A plateful of carefully dosed fish scraps was in readiness on the sideboard, but sweets and savoury and dessert went their way, and no Tobermory appeared either in the dining-room or kitchen.

The sepulchral dinner was cheerful compared with the subsequent vigil in the smoking-room. Eating and drinking had at least supplied a distraction and cloak to the prevailing embarrassment. Bridge was out of the question in the general tension of nerves and tempers, and after Odo Finsberry had given a lugubrious rendering of "Melisande in the Wood" to a frigid audience, music was tacitly avoided. At eleven the servants went to bed, announcing that the small window in the pantry had been left open as usual for Tobermory's private use. The guests read steadily through the current batch of magazines, and fell back gradually, on the "Badminton Library" and bound volumes of *Punch*. Lady Blemley made periodic visits to the pantry, returning each time with an expression of listless depression which forestalled questioning.

At two o'clock Clovis broke the dominating silence.

"He won't turn up to-night. He's probably in the local newspaper office at the present moment, dictating the first instalment of his reminiscences. Lady What's-her-name's book won't be in it. It will be the event of the day."

Having made this contribution to the general cheerfulness, Clovis went to bed. At long intervals the various members of the house-party followed his example.

The servants taking round the early tea made a uniform announcement in reply to a uniform question. Tobermory had not returned.

Breakfast was, if anything, a more unpleasant function than dinner had been, but before its conclusion the situation was relieved. Tobermory's corpse was brought in from the shrubbery, where a gardener had just discovered it. From the bites on his throat and the yellow fur which coated his claws it was evident that he had fallen in unequal combat with the big Tom from the Rectory.

By midday most of the guests had quitted the Towers, and after lunch Lady Blemley had sufficiently recovered her spirits to write an extremely nasty letter to the Rectory about the loss of her valuable pet.

Tobermory had been Appin's one successful pupil, and he was destined to have no successor. A few weeks later an elephant in the Dresden Zoological Garden, which had shown no previous signs of irritability, broke loose and killed an Englishman who had apparently been teasing it. The victim's name was variously reported in the papers as Oppin and Eppelin, but his front name was faithfully rendered Cornelius.

"If he was trying German irregular verbs on the poor beast," said Clovis, "he deserved all he got."

1916

IN THE VALLEY OF THE SORCERESS
Sax Rohmer

I

Condor wrote to me three times before the end (said Neville, Assistant-Inspector of Antiquities, staring vaguely from his open window at a squad drilling before the Kasr-en-Nîl Barracks). He dated his letters from the camp at Deir-el-Bahari. Judging from these, success appeared to be almost within his grasp. He shared my theories, of course, respecting Queen Hatasu, and was devoting the whole of his energies to the task of clearing up the great mystery of Ancient Egypt which centres around that queen.

For him, as for me, there was a strange fascination about those defaced walls and roughly obliterated inscriptions. That the queen under whom Egyptian art came to the apogee of perfection should thus have been treated by her successors; that no perfect figure of the wise, famous, and beautiful Hatasu should have been spared to posterity; that her very cartouche should have been ruthlessly removed from every inscription upon which it appeared, presented to Condor's mind a problem only second in interest to the immortal riddle of Gîzeh.

You know my own views upon the matter? My monograph, "Hatasu, the Sorceress," embodies my opinion. In short, upon certain evidences, some adduced by Theodore Davis, some by poor Condor, and some resulting from my own inquiries, I have come to the conclusion that the source—real or imaginary—of this queen's power was an intimate acquaintance with what nowadays we term, vaguely, magic. Pursuing her studies beyond the limit

175

which is lawful, she met with a certain end, not uncommon, if the old writings are to be believed, in the case of those who penetrate too far into the realms of the Borderland.

For this reason—the practice of black magic—her statues were dishonored, and her name erased from the monuments. Now, I do not propose to enter into any discussion respecting the reality of such practices; in my monograph I have merely endeavored to show that, according to contemporary belief, the queen was a sorceress. Condor was seeking to prove the same thing; and when I took up the inquiry, it was in the hope of completing his interrupted work.

He wrote to me early in the winter of 1908, from his camp by the Rock Temple. Davis's tomb, at Bibân el-Mulûk, with its long, narrow passage, apparently had little interest for him; he was at work on the high ground behind the temple, at a point one hundred yards or so due west of the upper platform. He had an idea that he should find there the mummies of Hatasu—and another; the latter, a certain Sen-Mût, who appears in the inscriptions of the reign as an architect high in the queen's favor. The archæological points of the letter do not concern us in the least, but there was one odd little paragraph which I had cause to remember afterwards.

"A girl belonging to some Arab tribe," wrote Condor, "came racing to the camp two nights ago to claim my protection. What crime she had committed, and what punishment she feared, were far from clear; but she clung to me, trembling like a leaf, and positively refused to depart. It was a difficult situation, for a camp of fifty native excavators, and one highly respectable European enthusiast, affords no suitable quarters for an Arab girl—and a very personable Arab girl. At any rate, she is still here; I have had a sort of lean-to rigged up in a little valley east of my own tent, but it is very embarrassing."

Nearly a month passed before I heard from Condor again; then came a second letter, with the news that on the eve of a great discovery—as he believed—his entire native staff—the whole fifty—had deserted one night in a body! "Two days' work," he wrote, "would have seen the tomb opened—for I am more than ever certain that my plans are accurate. Then I woke up one morning to find every man Jack of my fellows missing! I went down into the village where a lot of them live, in a towering rage, but not one of the brutes was to be found, and their relations professed entire ignorance respecting their whereabouts. What caused me almost as much anxiety as the check in my work was the fact that Mahâra—the Arab girl—had vanished also. I am wondering if the thing has any sinister significance."

Condor finished with the statement that he was making tremendous efforts to secure a new gang. "But," said he, "I shall finish the excavation, if I have to do it with my own hands."

His third and last letter contained even stranger matters than the two preceding it. He had succeeded in borrowing a few men from the British Archæological camp in the Fáyûm. Then, just as the work was restarting, the Arab girl, Mahâra, turned up again, and entreated him to bring her down the Nile, "at least as far as Dendera. For the vengeance of her tribesmen," stated Condor, "otherwise would result not only in her own death, but in mine! At the moment of writing I am in two minds what to do. If Mahâra is to go upon this journey, I do not feel justified in sending her alone, and there is no one here who could perform the duty," etc.

I began to wonder, of course; and I had it in mind to take the train to Luxor merely in order to see this Arab maiden, who seemed to occupy so prominent a place in Condor's mind. However, Fate would have it otherwise; and the next thing I heard was that Condor had been brought into Cairo, and was at the English hospital.

He had been bitten by a cat—presumably from the neighboring village; and although the doctor at Luxor dealt with the bite at once, traveled down with him, and placed him in the hand of the Pasteur man at the hospital, he died, as you remember, in the night of his arrival, raving mad; the Pasteur treatment failed entirely.

I never saw him before the end, but they told me that his howls were horribly like those of a cat. His eyes changed in some way, too, I understand; and, with his fingers all contracted, he tried to *scratch* everyone and everything within reach.

They had to strap the poor beggar down, and even then he tore the sheets into ribbons.

Well, as soon as possible, I made the necessary arrangements to finish Condor's inquiry. I had access to his papers, plans, etc., and in the spring of the same year I took up my quarters near Deir-el-Bahari, roped off the approaches to the camp, stuck up the usual notices, and prepared to finish the excavation, which, I gathered, was in a fairly advanced state.

My first surprise came very soon after my arrival, for when, with the plan before me, I started out to find the shaft, I found it, certainly, but only with great difficulty.

It had been filled in again with sand and loose rock right to the very top!

II

ALL MY INQUIRIES availed me nothing. With what object the excavation had been thus closed I was unable to conjecture. That Condor had not reclosed it I was quite certain, for at the time of his mishap he had actually been at work at the bottom of the shaft, as inquiries from a native of Suefee, in the Fáyûm, who was his only companion at the time, had revealed.

In his eagerness to complete the inquiry, Condor, by lantern light, had been engaged upon a solitary night-shift below, and the rabid cat had apparently fallen into the pit; probably in a frenzy of fear, it had attacked Condor, after which it had escaped.

Only this one man was with him, and he, for some reason that I could not make out, had apparently been sleeping in the temple—quite a considerable distance from Condor's camp. The poor fellow's cries had aroused him, and he had met Condor running down the path and away from the shaft.

This, however, was good evidence of the existence of the shaft at the time, and as I stood contemplating the tightly packed rubble which alone marked its site, I grew more and more mystified, for this task of reclosing the cutting represented much hard labor.

Beyond perfecting my plans in one or two particulars, I did little on the day of my arrival. I had only a handful of men with me, all of whom I knew, having worked with them before, and beyond clearing Condor's shaft I did not intend to excavate further.

Hatasu's Temple presents a lively enough scene in the daytime during the winter and early spring months, with the streams of tourists constantly passing from the white causeway to Cook's Rest House on the edge of the desert. There had been a goodly number of visitors that day to the temple below, and one or two of the more curious and venturesome had scrambled up the steep path to the little plateau which was the scene of my operations. None had penetrated beyond the notice boards, however, and now, with the evening sky passing through those innumerable shades which defy palette and brush, which can only be distinguished by the trained eye, but which, from palest blue melt into exquisite pink, and by some magical combination form that deep violet which does not exist to perfection elsewhere than in the skies of Egypt, I found myself in the silence and the solitude of "the Holy Valley."

I stood at the edge of the plateau, looking out at the rosy belt which marked the course of the distant Nile, with the Arabian hills vaguely sketched beyond. The rocks stood up against that prospect as great black smudges, and what I could see of the causeway looked like a gray smear upon a drab canvas. Beneath me were the chambers of the Rock Temple, with those wall paintings depicting events in the reign of Hatasu which rank among the wonders of Egypt.

Not a sound disturbed my reverie, save a faint clatter of cooking utensils from the camp behind me—a desecration of that sacred solitude. Then a dog began to howl in the neighboring village. The dog ceased, and faintly to my ears came the note of a reed pipe. The breeze died away, and with it the piping.

I turned back to the camp, and, having partaken of a frugal supper, turned in upon my campaigner's bed, thoroughly enjoying my freedom from the routine of official life in Cairo, and looking forward to the morrow's work pleasurably.

Under such circumstances a man sleeps well; and when, in an uncanny gray half-light, which probably heralded the dawn, I awoke with a start, I knew that something of an unusual nature alone could have disturbed my slumbers.

Firstly, then, I identified this with a concerted howling of the village dogs. They seemed to have conspired to make night hideous; I have never heard such an eerie din in my life. Then it gradually began to die away, and I realized, secondly, that the howling of the dogs and my own awakening might be due to some common cause. This idea grew upon me, and as the howling subsided, a sort of disquiet possessed me, and, despite my efforts to shake it off, grew more urgent with the passing of every moment.

In short, I fancied that the thing which had alarmed or enraged the dogs was passing from the village through the Holy Valley, upward to the Temple, upward to the plateau, and was approaching *me*.

I have never experienced an identical sensation since, but I seemed to be audient of a sort of psychic patrol, which, from a remote *pianissimo*, swelled *fortissimo*, to an intimate but silent clamor, which beat in some way upon my brain, but not through the faculty of hearing, for now the night was deathly still.

Yet I was persuaded of some *approach*—of the coming of something sinister, and the suspense of waiting had become almost insupportable, so that I began to accuse my Spartan supper of having given me nightmare, when the tent-flap was suddenly raised, and, outlined against the paling blue of the sky, with a sort of reflected elfin light playing upon her face, I saw an Arab girl looking in at me!

By dint of exerting all my self-control I managed to restrain the cry and upward start which this apparition prompted. Quite still, with my fists tightly clenched, I lay and looked into the eyes which were looking into mine.

The style of literary work which it has been my lot to cultivate fails me in describing that beautiful and evil face. The features were severely classical and small, something of the Bisharîn type, with a cruel little mouth and a rounded chin, firm to hardness. In the eyes alone lay the languor of the Orient; they were exceedingly—indeed, excessively—long and narrow. The ordinary ragged, picturesque finery of a desert girl bedecked this midnight visitant, who, motionless, stood there watching me.

I once read a work by Pierre de l'Ancre, dealing with the Black Sabbaths of the Middle Ages, and now the evil beauty of this Arab face threw my memory back to those singular pages, for, perhaps owing to the reflected light which I have mentioned, although the explanation scarcely seemed adequate, those long, narrow eyes shone catlike in the gloom.

Suddenly I made up my mind. Throwing the blanket from me, I leapt to the ground, and in a flash had gripped the girl by the wrists. Confuting some lingering doubts, she proved to be substantial enough. My electric torch lay upon a box at the foot of the bed, and, stooping, I caught it up and turned its searching rays upon the face of my captive.

She fell back from me, panting like a wild creature trapped, then dropped upon her knees and began to plead—began to plead in a voice and with a manner which touched some chord of consciousness that I could swear had never spoken before, and has never spoken since.

She spoke in Arabic, of course, but the words fell from her lips as liquid music in which lay all the beauty and all the deviltry of the "Siren's Song." Fully opening her astonishing eyes, she looked up at me, and, with her free hand pressed to her bosom, told me how she had fled from an unwelcome marriage; how, an outcast and a pariah, she had hidden in the desert places for three days and three nights, sustaining life only by means of a few dates which she had brought with her, and quenching her thirst with stolen water-melons.

"I can bear it no longer, *effendim*. Another night out in the desert, with the cruel moon beating, beating, beating upon my brain, with creeping things coming out from the rocks, wriggling, wriggling, their many feet making whisperings in the sand—ah, it will kill me! And I am for ever outcast from my tribe, from my people. No tent of all the Arabs, though I fly to the gates of Damascus, is open to me, save I enter in shame, as a slave, as a plaything, as a toy. My heart"—furiously she beat upon her breast—"is

empty and desolate, *effendim*. I am meaner than the lowliest thing
that creeps upon the sand; yet the God that made that creeping
thing made me also—and you, you, who are merciful and strong,
would not crush any creature because it was weak and helpless."

I had released her wrist now, and was looking down at her in a
sort of stupor. The evil which at first I had seemed to perceive in
her was effaced, wiped out as an artist wipes out an error in his
drawing. Her dark beauty was speaking to me in a language of its
own; a strange language, yet one so intelligible that I struggled in
vain to disregard it. And her voice, her gestures, and the witch-
fire of her eyes were whipping up my blood to a fever heat of passionate sorrow—of despair. Yes, incredible as it sounds, despair!

In short, as I see it now, this siren of the wilderness was playing upon me as an accomplished musician might play upon a harp,
striking this string and that at will, and sounding each with such
full notes as they had rarely, if ever, emitted before.

Most damnable anomaly of all, I—Edward Neville, archæ-
ologist, most prosy and matter-of-fact man in Cairo, perhaps—
knew that this nomad who had burst into my tent, upon whom I
had set eyes for the first time scarce three minutes before, held me
enthralled; and yet, with her wondrous eyes upon me, I could summon up no resentment, and could offer but poor resistance.

"In the Little Oasis, *effendim*, I have a sister who will admit
me into her household, if only as a servant. There I can be safe,
there I can rest. O *Inglîsi*, at home in England you have a sister of
your own! Would you see her pursued, a hunted thing from rock to
rock, crouching for shelter in the lair of some jackal, stealing that
she might live—and flying always, never resting, her heart leaping
for fear, flying, flying, with nothing but dishonor before her?"

She shuddered and clasped my left hand in both her own convulsively, pulling it down to her bosom.

"There can be only one thing, *effendim*," she whispered. "Do
you not see the white bones bleaching in the sun?"

Throwing all my resolution into the act, I released my hand
from her clasp, and, turning aside, sat down upon the box which
served me as chair and table, too.

A thought had come to my assistance, had strengthened me in the moment of my greatest weakness; it was the thought of that Arab girl mentioned in Condor's letters. And a scheme of things, an incredible scheme, that embraced and explained some, if not all, of the horrible circumstances attendant upon his death, began to form in my brain.

Bizarre it was, stretching out beyond the realm of things natural and proper, yet I clung to it, for there, in the solitude, with this wildly beautiful creature kneeling at my feet, and with her uncanny powers of fascination yet enveloping me like a cloak, I found it not so improbable as inevitably it must have seemed at another time.

I turned my head, and through the gloom sought to look into the long eyes. As I did so they closed and appeared as two darkly luminous slits in the perfect oval of the face.

"You are an impostor!" I said in Arabic, speaking firmly and deliberately. "To Mr. Condor"—I could have sworn that she started slightly at sound of the name—"you called yourself Mahâra. I know you, and I will have nothing to do with you."

But in saying it I had to turn my head aside, for the strangest, maddest impulses were bubbling up in my brain in response to the glances of those half-shut eyes.

I reached for my coat, which lay upon the foot of the bed, and, taking out some loose money, I placed fifty piastres in the nerveless brown hand.

"That will enable you to reach the Little Oasis, if such is your desire," I said. "It is all I can do for you, and now—you must go."

The light of the dawn was growing stronger momentarily, so that I could see my visitor quite clearly. She rose to her feet, and stood before me, a straight, slim figure, sweeping me from head to foot with such a glance of passionate contempt as I had never known or suffered.

She threw back her head magnificently, dashed the money on the ground at my feet, and, turning, leaped out of the tent.

For a moment I hesitated, doubting, questioning my humanity, testing my fears; then I took a step forward, and peered out across the plateau. Not a soul was in sight. The rocks stood up gray and eerie, and beneath lay the carpet of the desert stretching un-broken to the shadows of the Nile Valley.

III

WE COMMENCED THE work of clearing the shaft at an early hour that morning. The strangest ideas were now playing in my mind, and in some way I felt myself to be in opposition to definite enmity. My excavators labored with a will, and, once we had penetrated below the first three feet or so of tightly packed stone, it became a mere matter of shoveling, for apparently the lower part of the shaft had been filled up principally with sand.

I calculated that four days' work at the outside would see the shaft clear to the base of Condor's excavation. There remained, according to his own notes, only another six feet or so; but it was solid limestone—the roof of the passage, if his plans were correct, communicating with the tomb of Hatasu.

With the approach of night, tired as I was, I felt little inclina-tion for sleep. I lay down on my bed with a small Browning pistol under the pillow, but after an hour or so of nervous listening drifted off into slumber. As on the night before, I awoke shortly before the coming of dawn.

Again the village dogs were raising a hideous outcry, and again I was keenly conscious of some ever-nearing menace. This con-sciousness grew stronger as the howling of the dogs grew fainter, and the sense of *approach* assailed me as on the previous occa-sion.

I sat up immediately with the pistol in my hand, and, gently raising the tent flap, looked out over the darksome plateau. For a long time I could perceive nothing; then, vaguely outlined against the sky, I detected something that moved above the rocky edge.

It was so indefinite in form that for a time I was unable to iden-tify it, but as it slowly rose higher and higher, two luminous eyes—obviously feline eyes, since they glittered greenly in the darkness—came into view. In character and in shape they were the eyes of a cat, but in point of size they were larger than the eyes of any cat I had ever seen. Nor were they jackal eyes. It occurred to me that some predatory beast from the Sûdan might conceivably have strayed thus far north.

The presence of such a creature would account for the nightly disturbance amongst the village dogs; and, dismissing the superstitious notions which had led me to associate the mysterious Arab girl with the phenomenon of the howling dogs, I seized upon this new idea with a sort of gladness.

Stepping boldly out of the tent, I strode in the direction of the gleaming eyes. Although my only weapon was the Browning pistol, it was a weapon of considerable power, and, moreover, I counted upon the well-known cowardice of nocturnal animals. I was not disappointed in the result.

The eyes dropped out of sight, and as I leaped to the edge of rock overhanging the temple a lithe shape went streaking off in the greyness beneath me. Its coloring appeared to be black, but this appearance may have been due to the bad light. Certainly it was no cat, was no jackal; and once, twice, thrice my Browning spat into the darkness.

Apparently I had not scored a hit, but the loud reports of the weapon aroused the men sleeping in the camp, and soon I was surrounded by a ring of inquiring faces.

But there I stood on the rock-edge, looking out across the desert in silence. Something in the long, luminous eyes, something in the sinuous, flying shape had spoken to me intimately, horribly.

Hassan es-Sugra, the headman, touched my arm, and I knew that I must offer some explanation.

"Jackals," I said shortly. And with no other word I walked back to my tent.

The night passed without further event, and in the morning we addressed ourselves to the work with such a will that I saw, to my satisfaction, that by noon of the following day the labor of clearing the loose sand would be completed.

During the preparation of the evening meal I became aware of a certain disquiet in the camp, and I noted a disinclination on the part of the native laborers to stray far from the tents. They hung together in a group, and whilst individually they seemed to avoid meeting my eye, collectively they watched me in a furtive fashion.

A gang of Moslem workmen calls for delicate handling, and I wondered if, inadvertently, I had transgressed in some way their iron-bound code of conduct. I called Hassan es-Sugra aside.

"What ails the men?" I asked him. "Have they some grievance?"

Hassan spread his palms eloquently.

"If they have," he replied, "they are secret about it, and I am not in their confidence. Shall I thrash three or four of them in order to learn the nature of this grievance?"

"No thanks all the same," I said, laughing at this characteristic proposal. "If they refuse to work to-morrow, there will be time enough for you to adopt those measures."

On this, the third night of my sojourn in the Holy Valley by the Temple of Hatasu, I slept soundly and uninterruptedly. I had been looking forward with the keenest zest to the morrow's work, which promised to bring me within sight of my goal, and when Hassan came to awaken me, I leaped out of bed immediately.

Hassan es-Sugra, having performed his duty, did not, as was his custom, retire; he stood there, a tall, angular figure, looking at me strangely.

"Well?" I said.

"There is trouble," was his simple reply. "Follow me, Neville Effendi."

Wondering greatly, I followed him across the plateau and down the slope to the excavation. There I pulled up short with a cry of amazement.

Condor's shaft was filled in to the very top, and presented, to my astonished gaze, much the same aspect that had greeted me upon my first arrival!

"The men—" I began.

Hassan es-Sugra spread wide his palms.

"Gone!" he replied. "Those Coptic dogs, those eaters of carrion, have fled in the night."

"And this"—I pointed to the little mound of broken granite and sand—"is their work?"

"So it would seem," was the reply; and Hassan sniffed his sublime contempt.

I stood looking bitterly at this destruction of my toils. The strangeness of the thing at the moment did not strike me, in my anger; I was only concerned with the outrageous impudence of the missing workmen, and if I could have laid hands upon one of them it had surely gone hard with him.

As for Hassan es-Sugra, I believe he would cheerfully have broken the necks of the entire gang. But he was a man of resource.

"It is so newly filled in," he said, "that you and I, in three days, or in four, can restore it to the state it had reached when those nameless dogs, who regularly prayed with their shoes on, those devourers of pork, began their dirty work."

His example was stimulating. *I* was not going to be beaten, either.

After a hasty breakfast, the pair of us set to work with pick and shovel and basket. We worked as those slaves must have worked whose toil was directed by the lash of the Pharaoh's overseer. My back acquired an almost permanent crook, and every muscle in my body seemed to be on fire. Not even in the midday heat did we slacken or stay our toils; and when dusk fell that night a great mound had arisen beside Condor's shaft, and we had excavated to a depth it had taken our gang double the time to reach.

When at last we threw down our tools in utter exhaustion, I held out my hand to Hassan, and wrung his brown fist enthusiastically. His eyes sparkled as he met my glance.

"Neville Effendi," he said, "you are a true Moslem!"

And only the initiated can know how high was the compliment conveyed.

That night I slept the sleep of utter weariness, yet it was not a dreamless sleep, or perhaps it was not so deep as I supposed, for blazing cat-eyes encircled me in my dreams, and a constant feline howling seemed to fill the night.

When I awoke the sun was blazing down upon the rock outside my tent, and, springing out of bed, I perceived, with amazement, that the morning was far advanced. Indeed, I could hear the distant voices of the donkey-boys and other harbingers of the coming tourists.

Why had Hassan es-Sugra not awakened me? I stepped out of the tent and called him in a loud voice. There was no reply. I ran across the plateau to the edge of the hollow.

Condor's shaft had been reclosed to the top!

Language fails me to convey the wave of anger, amazement, incredulity, which swept over me. I looked across to the deserted camp and back to my own tent; I looked down at the mound, where but a few hours before had been a pit, and seriously I began to question whether I was mad or whether madness had seized upon all who had been with me. Then, pegged down upon the heap of broken stones, I perceived, fluttering, a small piece of paper.

Dully I walked across and picked it up. Hassan, a man of some education, clearly was the writer. It was a pencil scrawl in doubtful Arabic, and, not without difficulty, I deciphered it as follows:

"Fly, Neville Effendi! This is a haunted place!"

Standing there by the mound, I tore the scrap of paper into minute fragments, bitterly casting them from me upon the ground. It was incredible; it was insane.

The man who had written that absurd message, the man who had undone his own work, had the reputation of being fearless and honorable. He had been with me before a score of times, and had quelled petty mutinies in the camp in a manner which marked him a born overseer. I could not understand; I could scarcely believe the evidence of my own senses.

What did I do?

I suppose there are some who would have abandoned the thing at once and for always, but I take it that the national traits are strong within me. I went over to the camp and prepared my own breakfast; then, shouldering pick and shovel, I went down into the valley and set to work. What ten men could not do, what two men had failed to do, one man was determined to do.

It was about half an hour after commencing my toils, and when, I suppose, the surprise and rage occasioned by the discovery had begun to wear off, that I found myself making comparisons between my own case and that of Condor. It became more and more evident to me that events—mysterious events—were repeating themselves.

The frightful happenings attendant upon Condor's death were marshaling in my mind. The sun was blazing down upon me, and distant voices could be heard in the desert stillness. I knew that the plain below was dotted with pleasure-seeking tourists, yet nervous tremors shook me. Frankly, I dreaded the coming of the night.

Well, tenacity or pugnacity conquered, and I worked on until dusk. My supper despatched, I sat down on my bed and toyed with the Browning.

I realized already that sleep, under existing conditions, was impossible. I perceived that on the morrow I must abandon my one-man enterprise, pocket my pride, in a sense, and seek new assistants, new companions.

The fact was coming home to me conclusively that a menace, real and not mythical, hung over that valley. Although, in the morning sunlight and filled with indignation, I had thought contemptuously of Hassan es-Sugra, now, in the mysterious violet dusk so conducive to calm consideration, I was forced to admit that he was at least as brave a man as I. And he had fled! What did that night hold in keeping for me?

I WILL TELL YOU what occurred, and it is the only explanation I have to give of why Condor's shaft, said to communicate with the real tomb of Hatasu, to this day remains unopened.

There, on the edge of my bed, I sat far into the night, not daring to close my eyes. But physical weariness conquered in the end, and, although I have no recollection of its coming, I must have succumbed to sleep, since I remember—can never forget—a repetition of the dream, or what I had assumed to be a dream, of the night before.

A ring of blazing green eyes surrounded me. At one point this ring was broken, and in a kind of nightmare panic I leaped at that promise of safety, and found myself outside the tent.

Lithe, slinking shapes hemmed me in—cat shapes, ghoul shapes, veritable figures of the pit. And the eyes, the shapes, although they were the eyes and shapes of cats, sometimes changed elusively, and became the wicked eyes and the sinuous, writhing shapes of women. Always the ring was incomplete, and always I retreated in the only direction by which retreat was possible. I retreated from those cat-things.

In this fashion I came at last to the shaft, and there I saw the tools which I had left at the end of my day's toil.

Looking around me, I saw also, with such a pang of horror as I cannot hope to convey to you, that the ring of green eyes was now unbroken about me.

And it was closing in.

Nameless feline creatures were crowding silently to the edge of the pit, some preparing to spring down upon me where I stood. A voice seemed to speak in my brain; it spoke of capitulation, telling me to accept defeat, lest, resisting, my fate be the fate of Condor.

Peals of shrill laughter rose upon the silence. The laughter was mine.

Filling the night with this hideous, hysterical merriment, I was working feverishly with pick and with shovel filling in the shaft.

The end? The end is that I awoke, in the morning, lying, not on my bed, but outside on the plateau, my hands torn and bleeding and every muscle in my body throbbing agonisingly. Remembering my dream—for even in that moment of awakening I thought I had dreamed—I staggered across to the valley of the excavation.

Condor's shaft was reclosed to the top.

1920

THE CATS OF ULTHAR
H. P. Lovecraft

IT IS SAID that in Ulthar, which lies beyond the river Skai, no man may kill a cat; and this I can verily believe as I gaze upon him who sitteth purring before the fire. For the cat is cryptic, and close to strange things which men cannot see. He is the soul of antique Aegyptus, and bearer of tales from forgotten cities in Meroë and Ophir. He is the kin of the jungle's lords, and heir to the secrets of hoary and sinister Africa. The Sphinx is his cousin, and he speaks her language; but he is more ancient than the Sphinx, and remembers that which she hath forgotten.

In Ulthar, before ever the burgesses forbade the killing of cats, there dwelt an old cotter and his wife who delighted to trap and slay the cats of their neighbours. Why they did this I know not; save that many hate the voice of the cat in the night, and take it ill that cats should run stealthily about yards and gardens at twilight. But whatever the reason, this old man and woman took pleasure in trapping and slaying every cat which came near to their hovel; and from some of the sounds heard after dark, many villagers fancied that the manner of slaying was exceedingly peculiar. But the villagers did not discuss such things with the old man and his wife; because of the habitual expression on the withered faces of the two, and because their cottage was so small and so darkly hidden under spreading oaks at the back of a neglected yard. In truth, much as the owners of cats hated these odd folk, they feared them more; and instead of berating them as brutal assassins, merely took care that no cherished pet or mouser should stray toward the remote

hovel under the dark trees. When through some unavoidable over-
sight a cat was missed, and sounds heard after dark, the loser would
lament impotently; or console himself by thanking Fate that it was
not one of his children who had thus vanished. For the people of
Ulthar were simple, and knew not whence it is all cats first came.

One day a caravan of strange wanderers from the South entered the narrow cobbled streets of Ulthar. Dark wanderers they
were, and unlike the other roving folk who passed through the village twice every year. In the market-place they told fortunes for
silver, and bought gay beads from the merchants. What was the
land of these wanderers none could tell; but it was seen that they
were given to strange prayers, and that they had painted on the
sides of their wagons strange figures with human bodies and the
heads of cats, hawks, rams, and lions. And the leader of the caravan wore a head-dress with two horns and a curious disc betwixt
the horns.

There was in this singular caravan a little boy with no father or
mother, but only a tiny black kitten to cherish. The plague had not
been kind to him, yet had left him this small furry thing to miti-
gate his sorrow; and when one is very young, one can find great
relief in the lively antics of a black kitten. So the boy whom the
dark people called Menes smiled more often than he wept as he
sat playing with his graceful kitten on the steps of an oddly painted
wagon.

On the third morning of the wanderers' stay in Ulthar, Menes
could not find his kitten; and as he sobbed aloud in the market-
place certain villagers told him of the old man and his wife, and of
sounds heard in the night. And when he heard these things his sobbing gave place to meditation, and finally to prayer. He stretched
out his arms toward the sun and prayed in a tongue no villager
could understand; though indeed the villagers did not try very hard
to understand, since their attention was mostly taken up by the
sky and the odd shapes the clouds were assuming. It was very peculiar, but as the little boy uttered his petition there seemed to
form overhead the shadowy, nebulous figures of exotic things; of

hybrid creatures crowned with horn-flanked discs. Nature is full of such illusions to impress the imaginative.

That night the wanderers left Ulthar, and were never seen again. And the householders were troubled when they noticed that in all the village there was not a cat to be found. From each hearth the familiar cat had vanished; cats large and small, black, grey, striped, yellow, and white. Old Kranon, the burgomaster, swore that the dark folk had taken the cats away in revenge for the killing of Menes' kitten; and cursed the caravan and the little boy. But Nith, the lean notary, declared that the old cotter and his wife were more likely persons to suspect; for their hatred of cats was notorious and increasingly bold. Still, no one durst complain to the sinister couple; even when little Atal, the innkeeper's son, vowed that he had at twilight seen all the cats of Ulthar in that accursed yard under the trees, pacing very slowly and solemnly in a circle around the cottage, two abreast, as if in performance of some unheard-of rite of beasts. The villagers did not know how much to believe from so small a boy; and though they feared that the evil pair had charmed the cats to their death, they preferred not to chide the old cotter till they met him outside his dark and repellent yard.

So Ulthar went to sleep in vain anger; and when the people awaked at dawn—behold! every cat was back at his accustomed hearth! Large and small, black, grey, striped, yellow, and white, none was missing. Very sleek and fat did the cats appear, and sonorous with purring content. The citizens talked with one another of the affair, and marvelled not a little. Old Kranon again insisted that it was the dark folk who had taken them, since cats did not return alive from the cottage of the ancient man and his wife. But all agreed on one thing: that the refusal of all the cats to eat their portions of meat or drink their saucers of milk was exceedingly curious. And for two whole days the sleek, lazy cats of Ulthar would touch no food, but only doze by the fire or in the sun.

It was fully a week before the villagers noticed that no lights were appearing at dusk in the windows of the cottage under the trees. Then the lean Nith remarked that no one had seen the old man or his wife since the night the cats were away. In another week the burgomaster decided to overcome his fears and call at the strangely silent dwelling as a matter of duty, though in so doing he was careful to take with him Shang the blacksmith and Thul the cutter of stone as witnesses. And when they had broken down the frail door they found only this: two cleanly picked human skeletons on the earthen floor, and a number of singular beetles crawling in the shadowy corners.

There was subsequently much talk among the burgesses of Ulthar. Zath, the coroner, disputed at length with Nith, the lean notary; and Kranon and Shang and Thul were overwhelmed with questions. Even little Atal, the innkeeper's son, was closely questioned and given a sweetmeat as reward. They talked of the old cotter and his wife, of the caravan of dark wanderers, of small Menes and his black kitten, of the prayer of Menes and of the sky during that prayer, of the doings of the cats on the night the caravan left, and of what was later found in the cottage under the dark trees in the repellent yard.

And in the end the burgesses passed that remarkable law which is told of by traders in Hatheg and discussed by travellers in Nir; namely, that in Ulthar no man may kill a cat.

1921

THE BLACK CAT
WILLIAM J. WINTLE

IF THERE WAS one animal that Sydney disliked more than another it was a cat. Not that he was not fond of animals in a general way—for he had a distinct affection for an aged retriever that had formerly been his—but somehow a cat seemed to arouse all that was worst in him. It always appeared to him that if he had passed through some previous stage of existence, he must have been a mouse or a bird and thus have inherited—so to speak—an instinctive dread and hatred for the enemy of his earlier days.

The presence of a cat affected him in a very curious fashion. There was first of all a kind of repulsion. The idea of the eyes of the animal being fixed on him; the thought of listening for a soundless tread; and the imagined touch of the smooth fur; all this made him shudder and shrink back. But this feeling quickly gave place to a still stranger fascination. He felt drawn to the creature that he feared—much as a bird is supposed, but quite erroneously, to be charmed by a snake. He wanted to stroke the animal and to feel its head rubbing against his hand: and yet at the same time the idea of the animal doing so filled him with a dread passing description. It was something like that morbid state in which a person finds actual physical pleasure in inflicting pain on himself. And then there was sheer undisguised fear. Pretend as he might, Sydney was in deadly fear when a cat was in the room. He had tried and tried, time and again, to overcome it; but without success. He had argued from the well-known friendliness of the domestic cat; from its notorious timidity; and from its actual inability to do any very serious harm to a strong and active man. But it was all of no use. He was afraid of cats; and it was useless to deny it.

At the same time, Sydney was no enemy to cats. He was the last man in the world to hurt one. No matter how much his slumber might be disturbed by the vocal efforts of a love-sick marauder on the roof in the small hours of the morning, he would never think of hurling a missile at the offender. The sight of a half-starved cat left behind when its owner was away in the holiday season filled him with a pity near akin to pain. He was a generous subscriber to the Home for Lost Cats. In fact, his whole attitude was inconsistent and contradictory. But there was no escape from the truth— he disliked and feared cats.

Probably this obsession was to some extent fostered by the fact that Sydney was a man of leisure. With more urgent matters to occupy his thoughts, he might have outgrown these fancies with the advance of middle age. But the possession of ample means, an inherited dislike for any kind of work calling for energy, and two or three interesting hobbies which filled up his time in an easy and soothing fashion, left him free to indulge his fancies. And fancies, when indulged, are apt to become one's masters in the end; and so it proved with Sydney.

He was engaged in writing a book on some phase of Egyptian life in the olden days, which involved considerable study of the collections in the British Museum and elsewhere, as well as much search for rare books among the antiquarian book-shops. When not out on these pursuits, he occupied an old house which like most old and rambling places of its kind was the subject of various queer stories among the gossips of the neighbourhood. Some tragedy was supposed to have happened there at some date not defined, and in consequence something was supposed to haunt the place and to do something from time to time. Among local gossips there was much value in that nebulous term "Something," for it covered a multitude of inaccurate recollections and of foggy traditions. Probably Sydney had never heard the reputation of his house, for he led a retired life and had little to do with the neighbours. But if the tales had reached his ears, he gave no sign; nor was he likely to do so. Apart from the cat obsession, he was a man of eminently balanced mind. He was about the last person to imagine things or to be influenced by any but proved facts.

The mystery which surrounded his untimely end came therefore as a great surprise to his friends; and the horror that hung over his later days was only brought to partial light by the discovery of a diary and other papers which have provided the material for this history. Much still remains obscure, and cannot now be cleared up; for the only man who could perhaps throw further light on it is no longer with us. So we have to be content with such fragmentary records as are available.

It appears that some months before the end, Sydney was at home reading in the garden, when his eyes happened to rest upon a small heap of earth that the gardener had left beside the path. There was nothing remarkable about this; but somehow the heap seemed to fascinate him. He resumed his reading, but the heap of earth was insistent in demanding his attention. He could not keep his thoughts off it, and it was hard to keep his eyes off it as well. Sydney was not the man to give way to mental dissipation of this kind, and he resolutely kept his eyes fixed on his book. But it was a struggle; and in the end he gave in. He looked again at the heap; and this time with some curiosity as to the cause of so absurd an attraction.

Apparently there was no cause; and he smiled at the absurdity of the thing. Then he started up suddenly, for he saw the reason of it. The heap of earth was exactly like a black cat! And the cat was crouching as if to spring at him. The resemblance was really absurd, for there were a couple of yellow pebbles just where the eyes should have been. For the moment, Sydney felt all the repulsion and fear that the presence of an actual cat would have caused him. Then he rose from his chair, and kicked the heap out of any resemblance to his feline aversion. He sat down again and laughed at the absurdity of the affair—and yet it somehow left a sense of disquiet and of vague fear behind. He did not altogether like it.

It must have been about a fortnight later when he was inspecting some Egyptian antiquities that had recently reached the hands

of a London dealer. Most of them were of the usual types and did
not interest him. But a few were better worth attention; and he sat
down to examine them carefully. He was specially attracted by
some ivory tablets, on which he thought he could faintly trace the
remains of handwriting. If so, this was a distinct find, for private
memoranda of this sort are very rare and should throw light on
some of the more intimate details of private life of the period, which
are not usually recorded on the monuments. Absorbed in this study,
a sense of undefined horror slowly grew upon him and he found
himself in a kind of day dream presenting many of the uncanny
qualities of nightmare. He thought himself stroking an immense
black cat which grew and grew until it assumed gigantic proportions. Its soft fur thickened around his hands and entwined itself
around his fingers like a mass of silky, living snakes; and his skin
tingled with multitudinous tiny bites from fangs which were ven-
omous; while the purring of the creature grew until it became a
very roar like that of a cataract and overwhelmed all his senses.
He was mentally drowning in a sea of impending catastrophe,
when, by an expiring effort, he wrenched himself free from the
obsession and sprang up. Then he discovered that his hand had
been mechanically stroking a small unopened animal mummy,
which proved on closer examination to be that of a cat.

The next incident that he seems to have thought worth recording happened a few nights later. He had retired to rest in his usual
health and slept soundly. But towards morning his slumbers were
disturbed by a dream that recalled the kind of nocturnal fear that
is common in childhood.

Two distant stars began to grow in size and brilliancy until he
saw that they were advancing through space towards him with incredible speed. In a few moments they must overwhelm him in a
sea of fire and flame. Onwards they came, bulging and unfolding
like great flaming flowers, growing more dazzling and blinding
at every moment; and then, just as they were upon him, they
suddenly turned two enormous cat's eyes, flaming green and yellow. He sprang up in bed with a cry, and found himself at once
wide-awake. And there on the window-sill lay a great black cat,

glowering at him with lambent yellow eyes. A moment later the cat disappeared.

But the mysterious thing of it was that the window-sill was not accessible to anything that had not wings. There was no means by which a cat could have climbed to it. Nor was there any sign of a cat in the garden below.

The date of the next thing that happened is not clear, for it does not appear to have been recorded at the time. But it would seem to have been within a few days of the curious dream. Sydney had occasion to go to a cupboard which was kept locked. It contained manuscripts and other papers of value; and the key never left his possession. To his knowledge the cupboard had not been opened for at least a month past. He now had occasion to refer to a collection of notes in connection with his favourite study. On opening the cupboard, he was at once struck by a curious odour. It was not exactly musky, but could only be described as an animal odour, slightly suggestive of that of a cat. But what at once arrested Sydney's notice and caused him extreme annoyance was the fact that the papers had been disturbed. The loose papers contained in some pigeon-holes at the back had been drawn forwards into a loose heap on the shelf. They looked for all the world like a nest, for they had been loosely arranged in a round heap with a depression in the middle. It looked as if some animal had coiled itself up to sleep there; and the size of the depression was just such as would be made by a cat.

Sydney was too much annoyed by the disturbance of his papers to be greatly impressed at the moment by their curious arrangement; but it came home to him as a shock when he began to gather the papers together and set them in order. Some of them seemed to be slightly soiled, and on closer examination he found that they were besprinkled with short black hairs like those of a cat.

About a week afterwards he returned later in the evening than usual, after attending a meeting of a scientific society to which he belonged. He was taking his latch key from his pocket to open the door when he thought that something rubbed against his leg.

Looking down, he saw nothing; but immediately afterwards he felt it again, and this time he thought he saw a black shadow beside his right foot. On looking more closely, nothing was to be seen; but as he went into the house he distinctly felt something soft brush against his leg. As he paused in the hall to remove his overcoat, he saw a faint shadow which seemed to go up the stairs. It was certainly only a shadow and nothing solid, for the light was good and he saw it clearly. But there was nothing in motion to account for the passing shadow. And the way the shadow moved was curiously suggestive of a cat.

The next notes in the book that Sydney seems to have devoted to this curious subject appear to be a series of mere coincidences: and the fact that he thought them worth recording shows only too clearly to what an extent his mind was now obsessed. He had taken the numerical value of the letters C, A, T, in the alphabet, 3, 1, and 20 respectively, and by adding them together had arrived at the total 24. He then proceeded to note the many ways in which this number had played its part in the events of his life. He was born on the 24th of the month, at a house whose number was 24 and his mother was 24 years old at the time. He was 24 years old when his father died and left him the master of a considerable fortune. That was just 24 years ago. The last time he had balanced his affairs, he found that he was worth in invested funds—apart from land and houses—just about 24 thousand pounds. At three different periods, and in different towns, he had chanced to live at houses numbered 24; and that was also the number of his present abode. Moreover the number of his ticket for the British Museum Reading Room ended with 24, and both his doctor and his solicitor were housed under that same persistent number. Several more of these coincidences had been noted by him; but they were rather far-fetched and are not worth recording here. But the memoranda conclude with the ominous question, "Will it all end on the 24th?"

Soon after these notes were written, a much more serious affair had to be placed on record. Sydney was coming downstairs one evening, when he noticed in a badly lighted corner of the staircase something that he took to be a cat. He shrank back with his natural dislike for the animal; but on looking more closely he saw that it was nothing more than a shadow cast by some carving on the stair-head. He turned away with a laugh; but, as he turned, it certainly seemed that the shadow moved! As he went down the stairs he twice stumbled in trying to save himself from what he thought was a cat in danger of being trodden upon; and a moment later he seemed to tread on something soft that gave way and threw him down. He fell heavily and shook himself badly.

On picking himself up with the aid of his servant he limped into his library, and there found that his trousers were torn from a little above the ankle. But the curious thing was that there were three parallel vertical tears—just such as might be caused by the claws of a cat. A sharp smarting led to further investigation; and he then found that there were three deep scratches on the side of his leg, exactly corresponding with the tears in the trousers.

In the margin of the page on which he recorded this accident, he has added the words, "This cat means mischief." And the whole tone of the remaining entries and of the few letters that date from this time shows only too clearly that his mental outlook was more or less tinged and obscured by gloomy forebodings.

It would seem to have been on the following day that another disturbing trifle occurred. Sydney's leg still pained him, and he spent the day on a couch with one or two favourite books. Soon after two o'clock in the afternoon, he heard a soft thud, such as might be caused by a cat leaping down from a moderate height. He looked up, and there on the window-sill crouched a black cat with gleaming eyes; and a moment later it sprang into the room. But it never reached the floor—or, if it did, it must have passed through it! He saw it spring; he saw it for the moment in mid-air; he saw it about to alight on the floor; and then—it was not there!

He would have liked to believe that it was a mere optical delusion; but against that theory stood the awkward fact that the cat in springing down from the window knocked over a flowerpot; and there lay the broken pieces in evidence of the fact.

He was now seriously scared. It was bad enough to find himself seeing things that had no objective reality; but it was far worse to be faced by happenings that were certainly real, but not to be accounted for by the ordinary laws of nature. In this case the broken flower-pot showed that if the black cat was merely what we call a ghost for lack of any more convenient term, it was a ghost that was capable of producing physical effects. If it could knock a flower-pot over, it could presumably scratch and bite—and the prospect of being attacked by a cat from some other plane of existence will hardly bear being thought of.

Certainly it seemed that Sydney had now real ground for alarm. The spectre cat—or whatever one likes to call it—was in some way gaining power and was now able to manifest its presence and hostility in more open and practical fashion. That same night saw a proof of this. Sydney dreamed that he was visiting the Zoological Gardens when a black leopard of ferocious aspect escaped from its cage and sprang upon him. He was thrown backwards to the ground and pinned down by the heavy animal. He was half crushed by its weight; its claws were at his throat; its fierce yellow eyes were staring into his face; when the horror of the thing brought the dream to a sudden end and he awoke. As consciousness returned he was aware of an actual weight on his chest; and on opening his eyes he looked straight into the depths of two lambent yellow flames set in a face of velvet black. The cat sprang off the bed and leaped through the window. But the window was closed and there was no sound of breaking glass.

Sydney did not sleep much more that night. But a further shock awaited him on rising. He found some small blood stains on his pillow; and an inspection before the looking glass showed the presence of two groups of tiny wounds on his neck. They were little more than pin-pricks; but they were arranged in two semi-circular groups, one on either side of the neck and just such as might be caused by a cat trying to grasp the neck between its two forepaws.

This was the last incident recorded in Sydney's diary; and the serious view that he took of the situation is shown by certain letters that he wrote during the day, giving final instructions to his executors and settling various details of business—evidently in view of his approaching end.

What happened in the course of the final scene of the tragedy we can only guess from the traces left behind: but there is sufficient evidence to show that the horror was an appalling one.

The housekeeper seems to have been awakened once during the night by a strange noise which she could only describe as being like an angry cat snarling; while the parlour maid, whose room was immediately above that occupied by Sydney, says that she dreamt that she heard her master scream horribly once or twice.

In the morning, Sydney did not answer when called at his usual hour; and, as the door was found to be locked, the housekeeper presently procured assistance and had it broken open. He was found crouching on the floor and leaning against the wall opposite the window. The carpet was saturated with blood; and the cause was quickly evident. The unfortunate man's throat had been torn open on either side, both jugular veins being severed. So far as could be made out, he had retired to bed and had been attacked during sleep, for the sheets were bespattered with blood. He had apparently got out of bed in his struggles to overcome the Thing that had him fast in its fearful grip. The look of horror on his distorted face was said by the witnesses to be past description.

Both window and door were fastened, and there was nothing to show how the assailant entered. But there was something to show how it left. The bloodstains on the floor recorded the footprints of a gigantic cat. They led across the floor from the corpse to the opposite wall—and there they ceased. The cat never came back; but whether it passed through the solid wall or melted into thin air, no one knows. In some mysterious way it came and went; and in passing it did this deed of horror.

It was a curious coincidence that the tragedy took place on Christmas Eve—the 24th day of the month!

1921

THE EMPTY SLEEVE
Algernon Blackwood

I

THE GILMER BROTHERS were a couple of fussy and pernickety old bachelors of a rather retiring, not to say timid, disposition. There was grey in the pointed beard of John, the elder, and if any hair had remained to William it would also certainly have been of the same shade. They had private means. Their main interest in life was the collection of violins, for which they had the instinctive *flair* of true connoisseurs. Neither John nor William, however, could play a single note. They could only pluck the open strings. The production of tone, so necessary before purchase, was done vicariously for them by another.

The only objection they had to the big building in which they occupied the roomy top floor was that Morgan, liftman and caretaker, insisted on wearing a billycock with his uniform after six o'clock in the evening, with a result disastrous to the beauty of the universe. For "Mr. Morgan," as they called him between themselves, had a round and pasty face on the top of a round and conical body. In view, however, of the man's other rare qualities—including his devotion to themselves—this objection was not serious.

He had another peculiarity that amused them. On being found fault with, he explained nothing, but merely repeated the words of the complaint.

"Water in the bath wasn't really hot this morning, Morgan!"

"Water in the bath not reely 'ot, wasn't it, sir?" Or, from William, who was something of a faddist: "My jar of sour milk came up

204

late yesterday, Morgan." "Your jar sour milk come up late, sir, yesterday?" Since, however, the statement of a complaint invariably resulted in its remedy, the brothers had learned to look for no further explanation. Next morning the bath *was* hot, the sour milk *was* "brortup" punctually. The uniform and billycock hat, though, remained an eyesore and source of oppression.

On this particular night John Gilmer, the elder, returning from a Masonic rehearsal, stepped into the lift and found Mr. Morgan with his hand ready on the iron rope.

"Fog's very thick outside," said Mr. John pleasantly; and the lift was a third of the way up before Morgan had completed his customary repetition: "Fog very thick outside, yes, sir." And Gilmer then asked casually if his brother were alone, and received the reply that Mr. Hyman had called and had not yet gone away.

Now this Mr. Hyman was a Hebrew, and, like themselves, a connoisseur in violins, but, unlike themselves, who only kept their specimens to look at, he was a skilful and exquisite player. He was the only person they ever permitted to handle their pedigree instruments, to take them from the glass cases where they reposed in silent splendour, and to draw the sound out of their wondrous painted hearts of golden varnish. The brothers loathed to see his fingers touch them, yet loved to hear their singing voices in the room, for the latter confirmed their sound judgment as collectors, and made them certain their money had been well spent. Hyman, however, made no attempt to conceal his contempt and hatred for the mere collector. The atmosphere of the room fairly pulsed with these opposing forces of silent emotion when Hyman played and the Gilmers, alternately writhing and admiring, listened. The occasions, however, were not frequent. The Hebrew only came by invitation, and both brothers made a point of being in. It was a very formal proceeding—something of a sacred rite almost.

John Gilmer, therefore, was considerably surprised by the information Morgan had supplied. For one thing, Hyman, he had understood, was away on the Continent.

"Still in-there, you say?" he repeated, after a moment's reflection.

"Still in there, Mr. John, sir." Then, concealing his surprise from the liftman, he fell back upon his usual mild habit of complaining about the billycock hat and the uniform.

"You really should try and remember, Morgan," he said, though kindly. "That hat does *not* go well with that uniform!"

Morgan's pasty countenance betrayed no vestige of expression. "'At don't go well with the yewniform, sir," he repeated, hanging up the disreputable bowler and replacing it with a gold-braided cap from the peg. "No, sir, it don't, do it?" he added cryptically, smiling at the transformation thus effected.

And the lift then halted with an abrupt jerk at the top floor. By somebody's carelessness the landing was in darkness, and, to make things worse, Morgan, clumsily pulling the iron rope, happened to knock the billycock from its peg so that his sleeve, as he stooped to catch it, struck the switch and plunged the scene in a moment's complete obscurity.

And it was then, in the act of stepping out before the light was turned on again, that John Gilmer stumbled against something that shot along the landing past the open door. First he thought it must be a child, then a man, then—an animal. Its movement was rapid yet stealthy. Starting backwards instinctively to allow it room to pass, Gilmer collided in the darkness with Morgan, and Morgan incontinently screamed. There was a moment of stupid confusion. The heavy framework of the lift shook a little, as though something had stepped into it and then as quickly jumped out again. A rushing sound followed that resembled footsteps, yet at the same time was more like gliding—someone in soft slippers or stockinged feet, greatly hurrying. Then came silence again. Morgan sprang to the landing and turned up the electric light. Mr. Gilmer, at the same moment, did likewise to the switch in the lift. Light flooded the scene. Nothing was visible.

"Dog or cat, or something, I suppose, wasn't it?" exclaimed Gilmer, following the man out and looking round with bewildered amazement upon a deserted landing. He knew quite well, even while he spoke, that the words were foolish.

"Dog or cat, yes, sir, or—something," echoed Morgan, his eyes narrowed to pin-points, then growing large, but his face stolid.

"The light should have been on." Mr. Gilmer spoke with a touch of severity. The little occurrence had curiously disturbed his equanimity. He felt annoyed, upset, uneasy.

For a perceptible pause the liftman made no reply, and his employer, looking up, saw that, besides being flustered, he was white about the jaws. His voice, when he spoke, was without its normal assurance. This time he did not merely repeat. He explained.

"The light *was* on, sir, when last *I* come up!" he said, with emphasis, obviously speaking the truth. "Only a moment ago," he added.

Mr. Gilmer, for some reason, felt disinclined to press for explanations. He decided to ignore the matter.

Then the lift plunged down again into the depths like a diving-bell into water; and John Gilmer, pausing a moment first to reflect, let himself in softly with his latchkey, and, after hanging up hat and coat in the hall, entered the big sitting-room he and his brother shared in common.

The December fog that covered London like a dirty blanket had penetrated, he saw, into the room. The objects in it were half shrouded in the familiar yellowish haze.

II

IN DRESSING-GOWN and slippers, William Gilmer, almost invisible in his armchair by the gas-stove across the room, spoke at once. Through the thick atmosphere his face gleamed, showing an extinguished pipe hanging from his lips. His tone of voice conveyed emotion, an emotion he sought to suppress, of a quality, however, not easy to define.

"Hyman's been here," he announced abruptly. "You must have met him. He's this very instant gone out."

It was quite easy to see that something had happened, for "scenes" leave disturbance behind them in the atmosphere. But

John made no immediate reference to this. He replied that he had seen no one—which was strictly true—and his brother thereupon, sitting bolt upright in the chair, turned quickly and faced him. His skin, in the foggy air, seemed paler than before.

"That's odd," he said nervously.

"What's odd?" asked John.

"That you didn't see—anything. You ought to have run into one another on the doorstep." His eyes went peering about the room. He was distinctly ill at ease. "You're positive you saw no one? Did Morgan take him down before you came? Did Morgan see him?" He asked several questions at once.

"On the contrary, Morgan told me he was still here with you. Hyman probably walked down, and didn't take the lift at all," he replied. "That accounts for neither of us seeing him." He decided to say nothing about the occurrence in the lift, for his brother's nerves, he saw plainly, were on edge.

William then stood up out of his chair, and the skin of his face changed its hue, for whereas a moment ago it was merely pale, it had now altered to a tint that lay somewhere between white and a livid grey. The man was fighting internal terror. For a moment these two brothers of middle age looked each other straight in the eye. Then John spoke:

"What's wrong, Billy?" he asked quietly. "Something's upset you. What brought Hyman in this way—unexpectedly? I thought he was still in Germany."

The brothers, affectionate and sympathetic, understood one another perfectly. They had no secrets. Yet for several minutes the younger one made no reply. It seemed difficult to choose his words apparently.

"Hyman played, I suppose—on the fiddles?" John helped him, wondering uneasily what was coming. He did not care much for the individual in question, though his talent was of such great use to them.

The other nodded in the affirmative, then plunged into rapid speech, talking under his breath as though he feared someone might overhear. Glancing over his shoulder down the foggy room, he drew his brother close.

"Hyman came," he began, "unexpectedly. He hadn't written, and I hadn't asked him. You hadn't either, I suppose?"

John shook his head.

"When I came in from the dining-room I found him in the passage. The servant was taking away the dishes, and he had let himself in while the front door was ajar. Pretty cool, wasn't it?"

"He's an original," said John, shrugging his shoulders. "And you welcomed him?" he asked.

"I asked him in, of course. He explained he had something glorious for me to hear. Silenski had played it in the afternoon, and he had bought the music since. But Silenski's 'Strad' hadn't the power—it's thin on the upper strings, you remember, unequal, patchy—and he said no instrument in the world could do it justice but our 'Joseph'—the small Guarnerius, you know, which he swears is the most perfect in the world."

"And what was it? Did he play it?" asked John, growing more uneasy as he grew more interested. With relief he glanced round and saw the matchless little instrument lying there safe and sound in its glass case near the door.

"He played it—divinely: a Zigeuner Lullaby, a fine, passionate, rushing bit of inspiration, oddly misnamed 'lullaby.' And, fancy, the fellow had memorized it already! He walked about the room on tiptoe while he played it, complaining of the light—"

"Complaining of the light?"

"Said the thing was crepuscular, and needed dusk for its full effect. I turned the lights out one by one, fill finally there was only the glow of the gas logs. He insisted. You know that way he has with him? And then he got over me in another matter: insisted on using some special strings he had brought with him, and put them on, too, himself—thicker than the A and E *we* use."

For though neither Gilmer could produce a note, it was their pride that they kept their precious instruments in perfect condition for playing, choosing the exact thickness and quality of strings that suited the temperament of each violin; and the little Guarnerius in question always "sang" best, they held, with thin strings.

"Infernal insolence," exclaimed the listening brother, wondering what was coming next. "Played it well, though, didn't he, this Lullaby thing?" he added, seeing that William hesitated. As he spoke he went nearer, sitting down close beside him in a leather chair.

"Magnificent! Pure fire of genius!" was the reply with enthusiasm, the voice at the same time dropping lower. "Staccato like a silver hammer; harmonics like flutes, clear, soft, ringing; and the tone—well, the G string was a baritone, and the upper registers creamy and mellow as a boy's voice. John," he added, "that Guarnerius is the very pick of the period and"—again he hesitated—"Hyman loves it. He'd give his soul to have it."

The more John heard, the more uncomfortable it made him. He had always disliked this gifted Hebrew, for in his secret heart he knew that he had always feared and distrusted him. Sometimes he had felt half afraid of him; the man's very forcible personality was too insistent to be pleasant. His type was of the dark and sinister kind, and he possessed a violent will that rarely failed of accomplishing its desire.

"Wish I'd heard the fellow play," he said at length, ignoring his brother's last remark, and going on to speak of the most matter-of-fact details he could think of. "Did he use the Dodd bow, or the Tourte? That Dodd I picked up last month, you know, is the most perfectly balanced I have ever—"

He stopped abruptly, for William had suddenly got upon his feet and was standing there, searching the room with his eyes. A chill ran down John's, spine as he watched him.

"What is it, Billy?" he asked sharply. "Hear anything?"

William continued to peer about him through the thick air.

"Oh, nothing, probably," he said, an odd catch in his voice; "only I keep feeling as if there was somebody listening. Do you think, perhaps"—he glanced over his shoulder— "there is someone at the door? I wish— I wish you'd have a look, John."

John obeyed, though without great eagerness. Crossing the room slowly, he opened the door, then switched on the light. The passage leading past the bathroom towards the bedrooms beyond was empty. The coats hung motionless from their pegs.

"No one, of course," he said, as he closed the door and came back to the stove. He left the light burning in the passage. It was curious the way both brothers had this impression that they were not alone, though only one of them spoke of it.

"Used the Dodd or the Tourte, Billy—which?" continued John in the most natural voice he could assume.

But at that very same instant the water started to his eyes. His brother, he saw, was close upon the thing he really had to tell. But he had stuck fast.

III

BY A GREAT effort John Gilmer composed himself and remained in his chair. With detailed elaboration he lit a cigarette, staring hard at his brother over the flaring match while he did so. There he sat in his dressing-gown and slippers by the fireplace, eyes downcast, fingers playing idly with the red tassel. The electric light cast heavy shadows across the face. In a flash then, since emotion may sometimes express itself in attitude even better than in speech, the elder brother understood that Billy was about to tell him an unutterable thing.

By instinct he moved over to his side so that the same view of the room confronted him.

"Out with it, old man," he said, with an effort to be natural. "Tell me what you saw."

Billy shuffled slowly round and the two sat side by side, facing the fog-draped chamber.

"It was like this," he began softly, "only I was standing instead of sitting, looking over to that door as you and I do now. Hyman moved to and fro in the faint glow of the gas logs against the far wall, playing that 'crepuscular' thing in his most inspired sort of way, so that the music seemed to issue from himself rather than from the shining bit of wood under his chin, when—I noticed something coming over me that was"—he hesitated, searching for words— "that wasn't *all* due to the music," he finished abruptly.

"His personality put a bit of hypnotism on you, eh?"

William shrugged his shoulders.

"The air was thickish with fog and the light was dim, cast upwards upon him from the stove," he continued. "I admit all that. But there wasn't light enough to throw shadows, you see, and—"

"Hyman looked queer?" the other helped him quickly.

Billy nodded his head without turning.

"Changed there before my very eyes"—he whispered it— "turned animal—"

"Animal?" John felt his hair rising.

"That's the only way I can put it. His face and hands and body turned otherwise than usual. I lost the sound of his feet. When the bow-hand or the fingers on the strings passed into the light, they were"—he uttered a soft, shuddering little laugh— "furry, oddly divided, the fingers massed together. And he paced stealthily. I thought every instant the fiddle would drop with a crash and he would spring at me across the room."

"My dear chap—"

"He moved with those big, lithe, striding steps one sees"—John held his breath in the little pause, listening keenly— "one sees those big brutes make in the cages when their desire is aflame for food or escape, or—or fierce, passionate desire for anything they want with their whole nature—"

"The big felines!" John whistled softly.

"And every minute getting nearer and nearer to the door, as though he meant to make a sudden rush for it and get out."

"With the violin! Of course you stopped him?"

"In the end. But for a long time, I swear to you, I found it difficult to know what to do, even to move. I couldn't get my voice for words of any kind; it was like a spell."

"It *was* a spell," suggested John firmly.

"Then, as he moved, still playing," continued the other, "he seemed to grow smaller; to shrink down below the line of the gas. I thought I should lose sight of him altogether. I turned the light up suddenly. There he was over by the door—crouching."

"Playing on his knees, you mean?"

William closed his eyes in an effort to visualize it again.

"Crouching," he repeated, at length, "close to the floor. At least, I think so. It all happened so quickly, and I felt so bewildered, it was hard to see straight. But at first I could have sworn he was half his natural size. I called to him, I think I swore at him—I forget exactly, but I know he straightened up at once and stood before me down there in the light"—he pointed across the room to the door— "eyes gleaming, face white as chalk, perspiring like midsummer, and gradually filling out, straightening up, whatever you like to call it, to his natural size and appearance again. It was the most horrid thing I've ever seen."

"As an—animal, you saw him still?"

"No; human again. Only much smaller."

"What did he say?"

Billy reflected a moment.

"Nothing that I can remember," he replied. "You see, it was all over in a few seconds. In the full light, I felt so foolish, and nonplussed at first. To see him normal again baffled me. And, before I could collect myself, he had let himself out into the passage, and I heard the front door slam. A minute later—the same second almost, it seemed—you came in. I only remember grabbing the violin and getting it back safely under the glass case. The strings were still vibrating."

The account was over. John asked no further questions. Nor did he say a single word about the lift, Morgan, or the extinguished light on the landing. There fell a longish silence between the two men; and then, while they helped themselves to a generous supply of whisky-and-soda before going to bed, John looked up and spoke:

"If you agree, Billy," he said quietly, "I think I might write and suggest to Hyman that we shall no longer have need for his services."

And Billy, acquiescing, added a sentence that expressed something of the singular dread lying but half concealed in the atmosphere of the room, if not in their minds as well:

"Putting it, however, in a way that need not offend him."

"Of course. There's no need to be rude, is there?"

Accordingly, next morning the letter was written; and John, saying nothing to his brother, took it round himself by hand to the

Hebrew's rooms near Euston. The answer he dreaded was forthcoming:

"Mr. Hyman's still away abroad," he was told. "But we're for-
warding letters; yes. Or I can give you 'is address if you'll prefer
it." The letter went, therefore, to the number in Königstrasse,
Munich, thus obtained.

Then, on his way back from the insurance company where he
went to increase the sum that protected the small Guarnerius from
loss by fire, accident, or theft, John Gilmer called at the offices of
certain musical agents and ascertained that Silenski, the violinist,
was performing at the time in Munich. It was only some days later,
though, by diligent inquiry, he made certain that at a concert on a
certain date the famous virtuoso had played a Zigeuner Lullaby of
his own composition—the very date, it turned out, on which he himself had been to the Masonic rehearsal at Mark Masons' Hall.

John, however, said nothing of these discoveries to his brother
William.

IV

IT WAS ABOUT a week later when a reply to the letter came from
Munich—a letter couched in somewhat offensive terms, though it
contained neither words nor phrases that could actually be found
fault with. Isidore Hyman was hurt and angry. On his return to
London a month or so later, he proposed to call and talk the matter over. The offensive part of the letter lay, perhaps, in his definite assumption that he could persuade the brothers to resume the
old relations. John, however, wrote a brief reply to the effect that
they had decided to buy no new fiddles; their collection being complete, there would be no occasion for them to invite his services as
a performer. This was final. No answer came, and the matter
seemed to drop. Never for one moment, though, did it leave the
consciousness of John Gilmer. Hyman had said that he would come,
and come assuredly he would. He secretly gave Morgan instructions that he and his brother for the future were always "out" when
the Hebrew presented himself.

"He must have gone back to Germany, you see, almost at once after his visit here that night," observed William—John, however, making no reply.

One night towards the middle of January the two brothers came home together from a concert in Queen's Hall, and sat up later than usual in their sitting-room discussing over their whisky and tobacco the merits of the pieces and performers. It must have been past one o'clock when they turned out the lights in the passage and retired to bed. The air was still and frosty; moonlight over the roofs—one of those sharp and dry winter nights that now seem to visit London rarely.

"Like the old-fashioned days when we were boys," remarked William, pausing a moment by the passage window and looking cut across the miles of silvery, sparkling roofs.

"Yes," added John; "the ponds freezing hard in the fields, rime on the nursery windows, and the sound of a horse's hoofs coming down the road in the distance, eh?" They smiled at the memory, then said good night, and separated. Their rooms were at opposite ends of the corridor; in between were the bathroom, dining-room, and sitting-room. It was a long, straggling flat. Half an hour later both brothers were sound asleep, the flat silent, only a dull murmur rising from the great city outside, and the moon sinking slowly to the level of the chimneys.

Perhaps two hours passed, perhaps three, when John Gilmer, sitting up in bed with a start, wide-awake and frightened, knew that someone was moving about in one of the three rooms that lay between him and his brother. He had absolutely no idea why he should have been frightened, for there was no dream or nightmare-memory that he brought over from unconsciousness, and yet he realized plainly that the fear he felt was by no means a foolish and unreasoning fear. It had a cause and a reason. Also—which made it worse—it was fully warranted. Something in his sleep, forgotten in the instant of waking, had happened that set every nerve in his body on the watch. He was positive only of two things—first, that it was the entrance of this person, moving so quietly there in the flat, that sent the chills down his spine; and, secondly, that this person was *not* his brother William.

John Gilmer was a timid man. The sight of a burglar, his eyes black-masked, suddenly confronting him in the passage, would most likely have deprived him of all power of decision—until the burglar had either shot him or escaped. But on this occasion some instinct told him that it was no burglar, and that the acute distress he experienced was not due to any message of ordinary physical fear. The thing that had gained access to his flat while he slept had first come—he felt sure of it—into his room, and had passed very close to his own bed, before going on. It had then doubtless gone to his brother's room, visiting them both stealthily to make sure they slept. And its mere passage through his room had been enough to wake him and set these drops of cold perspiration upon his skin. For it was—he felt it in every fibre of his body—something hostile.

The thought that it might at that very moment be in the room of his brother, however, brought him to his feet on the cold floor, and set him moving with all the determination he could summon towards the door. He looked cautiously down an utterly dark passage; then crept on tiptoe along it. On the wall were old-fashioned weapons that had belonged to his father; and feeling a curved, sheathless sword that had come from some Turkish campaign of years gone by, his fingers closed tightly round it, and lifted it silently from the three hooks whereon it lay. He passed the doors of the bathroom and dining-room, making instinctively for the big sitting-room where the violins were kept in their glass cases. The cold nipped him. His eyes smarted with the effort to see in the darkness. Outside the closed door he hesitated.

Putting his ear to the crack, he listened. From within came a faint sound of someone moving. The same instant there rose the sharp, delicate "ping" of a violin-string being plucked; and John Gilmer, with nerves that shook like the vibrations of that very string, opened the door wide with a fling and turned on the light at the same moment. The plucked string still echoed faintly in the air.

The sensation that met him on the threshold was the well-known one that things had been going on in the room which his unexpected arrival had that instant put a stop to. A second earlier and he would have discovered it all in the act. The atmosphere still held the feeling of rushing, silent movement with which the things had raced back to their normal, motionless positions. The immobility of the furniture was a mere attitude hurriedly assumed, and the moment his back was turned the whole business, whatever it might be, would begin again. With this presentment of the room, however—a purely imaginative one—came another, swiftly on its heels.

For one of the objects, less swift than the rest, had not quite regained its "attitude" of repose. It still moved. Below the window curtains on the right, not far from the shelf that bore the violins in their glass cases, he made it out, slowly gliding along the floor. Then, even as his eye caught it, it came to rest.

And, while the cold perspiration broke out all over him afresh, he knew that this still moving item was the cause both of his waking and of his terror. This was the disturbance whose presence he had divined in the flat without actual hearing, and whose passage through his room, while he yet slept, had touched every nerve in his body as with ice. Clutching his Turkish sword tightly, he drew back with the utmost caution against the wall and watched, for the singular impression came to him that the movement was not that of a human being crouching, but rather of something that pertained to the animal world. He remembered, flash-like, the movements of reptiles, the stealth of the larger felines, the undulating glide of great snakes. For the moment, however, it did not move, and they faced one another.

The other side of the room was but dimly lighted, and the noise he made clicking up another electric lamp brought the thing flying forward again—towards himself. At such a moment it seemed absurd to think of so small a detail, but he remembered his bare feet, and, genuinely frightened, he leaped upon a chair and swished with his sword through the air about him. From this better point of view, with the increased light to aid him, he then saw two things—first, that the glass case usually covering the Guarnerius violin had been shifted; and, secondly, that the moving object was slowly elongating itself into an upright position. Semi-erect, yet most oddly, too, like a creature on its hind legs, it was coming swiftly towards him. It was making for the door—and escape.

The confusion of ghostly fear was somehow upon him so that he was too bewildered to see clearly, but he had sufficient self-control, it seemed, to recover a certain power of action; for the moment the advancing figure was near enough for him to strike, that curved scimitar flashed and whirred about him, with such misdirected violence, however, that he not only failed to strike it even once, but at the same time lost his balance and fell forward from the chair whereon he perched—straight into it.

And then came the most curious thing of all, for as he dropped, the figure also dropped, stooped low down, crouched, dwindled amazingly in size, and rushed past him close to the ground like an animal on all fours. John Gilmer screamed, for he could no longer contain himself. Stumbling over the chair as he turned to follow, cutting and slashing wildly with his sword, he saw halfway down the darkened corridor beyond the scuttling outline of, apparently, an enormous—cat!

The door into the outer landing was somehow ajar, and the next second the beast was out, but not before the steel had fallen with a crashing blow upon the front disappearing leg, almost severing it from the body.

It was dreadful. Turning up the lights as he went, he ran after it to the outer landing. But the thing he followed was already well away, and he heard, on the floor below him, the same oddly gliding, slithering, stealthy sound, yet hurrying, that he had heard weeks before when something had passed him in the lift, and Morgan, in his terror, had likewise cried aloud.

For a time he stood there on that dark landing, listening, thinking, trembling; then turned into the flat and shut the door. In the sitting-room he carefully replaced the glass case over the treasured violin, puzzled to the point of foolishness, and strangely routed in his mind. For the violin itself, he saw, had been dragged several inches from its cushioned bed of plush.

Next morning, however, he made no allusion to the occurrence of the night. His brother apparently had not been disturbed.

V

THE ONLY THING that called for explanation—an explanation not fully forthcoming—was the curious aspect of Mr. Morgan's countenance. The fact that this individual gave notice to the owners of the building, and at the end of the month left for a new post, was, of course, known to both brothers; whereas the story he told in explanation of his face was known only to the one who questioned him about it—John. And John, for reasons best known to himself, did not pass it on to the other. Also, for reasons best known to himself, he did not cross-question the liftman about those singular marks, or report the matter to the police.

Mr. Morgan's pasty visage was badly scratched, and there were red lines running from the cheek into the neck that had the appearance of having been produced by sharp points viciously applied—claws. He had been disturbed by a noise in the hall, he said, about three in the morning. A scuffle had ensued in the darkness, but the intruder had got clear away. . . .

"A cat, or something of the kind, no doubt," suggested John Gilmer at the end of the brief recital. And Morgan replied in his usual way: "A cat, or something of the kind, Mr. John, no doubt."

All the same, he had not cared to risk a second encounter, but had departed to wear his billycock and uniform in a building less haunted.

Hyman, meanwhile, made no attempt to call and talk over his dismissal. The reason for this was only apparent, however, several months later when, quite by chance, coming along Piccadilly in an omnibus, the brothers found themselves seated opposite to a man with a thick black beard and blue glasses. William Gilmer hastily rang the bell and got out, saying something half intelligible about feeling faint. John followed him.

"Did you see who it was?" he whispered to his brother the moment they were safely on the pavement.

John nodded.

"Hyman, in spectacles. He's grown a beard, too."

"Yes, but didn't you also notice—"

"What?"

"He had an empty sleeve."

"An empty sleeve?"

"Yes," said William; "he's lost an arm."

There was a long pause before John spoke. At the door of their club the elder brother added:

"Poor devil! He'll never again play on"—then, suddenly changing the preposition— "*with* a pedigree violin!"

And that night in the flat, after William had gone to bed, he looked up a curious old volume he had once picked up on a second-hand bookstall, and read therein quaint descriptions of how the "desire-body of a violent man" may assume animal shape, operate on concrete matter even at a distance; and, further, how a wound inflicted thereon can reproduce itself upon its physical counterpart by means of the mysterious so-called phenomenon of "re-percussion."

1921

THE TIGER
A. E. COPPARD

I

THE TIGER WAS coming at last; the almost fabulous beast, the subject of so much conjecture for so many months, was at the docks twenty miles away. Yak Pedersen had gone to fetch it, and Barnabe Woolf's Menagerie was about to complete its unrivalled collection by the addition of a full-grown Indian tiger of indescribable ferocity, newly trapped in the forest and now for the first time exhibited, and so on, and so on. All of which, as it happened, was true. On the previous day Pedersen the Dane and some helpers had taken a brand new four-horse exhibition waggon, painted and carved with extremely legendary tigers lapped in blood—even the bars were gilded—to convey this unmatchable beast to its new masters. The show had had to wait a long time for a tiger, but it had got a beauty at last, a terror indeed by all accounts, though it is not to be imagined that everything recorded of it by Barnabe Woolf was truth and nothing but truth. Showmen do not work in that way.

Yak Pedersen was the tamer and menagerie manager, a tall, blonde, angular man about thirty-five, of dissolute and savage blood himself, with the very ample kind of moustache that bald men often develop; yes, bald, intemperate, lewd, and an interminable smoker of Cuban cigarettes, which seemed constantly to threaten a conflagration in that moustache. Marie the Cossack hated him, but Yak loved her with a fierce deep passion. Nobody knew why she was called Marie the Cossack. She came from Canning Town—everybody knew that, and her proper name was

221

Fascota, Mrs. Fascota, wife of Jimmy Fascota, who was the architect and carpenter and builder of the show. Jimmy was not much
to look at, so little in fact that you couldn't help wondering what it
was Marie had seen in him when she could have had the King of
Poland, as you might say, almost for the asking. But still Jimmy
was the boss ganger of the show, and even that young gentleman
in frock coat and silk hat who paraded the platform entrance to
the arena and rhodomontadoed you into it, often against your will,
by the seductive recital of the seven ghastly wonders of the world,
all certainly to be seen, to be seen inside, waiting to be seen, must
be seen, roll up—even he was subject to the commands of Jimmy
Fascota when the time came to dismantle and pack up the show,
although the transfer of his activities involved him temporarily in
a change, a horrid change, of attire and language. Marie was not a
lady, but she was not for Pedersen anyway. She swore like a fac-
tory foreman, or a young soldier, and when she got tipsy she was
full of freedoms. By the power of God she was beautiful, and by
the same gracious power she was virtuous. Her husband knew it;
he knew all about master Pedersen's passion, too, and it did not
even interest him. Marie did feats in the lion cages, whipping poor
decrepit beasts, desiccated by captivity, through a hoop or over a
stick of wood and other kindergarten disportings; but there you
are, people must live, and Marie lived that way. Pedersen was always wooing her. Sometimes he was gracious and kind, but at other
times when his failure wearied him he would be cruel and sardonic,
with a suggestive tongue whose vice would have scourged her were
it not that Marie was impervious, or too deeply inured to mind it.
She always grinned at him and fobbed him off with pleasantries,
whether he was amorous or acrid.

"God Almighty!" he would groan, "she is not good for me, this
Marie. What can I do for her? She is burning me alive and the
Skaggerack could not quench me, not all of it. The devil! What can
I do with this? Some day I shall smash her across the eyes, yes,
across the eyes."

So you see the man really loved her.

When Pedersen returned from the docks the car with its captive was dragged to a vacant place in the arena, and the wooden front panel was let down from the bars. The marvellous tiger was revealed. It sprung into a crouching attitude as the light surprised the appalling beauty of its smooth fox-coloured coat, its ebony stripes, and snowy pads and belly. The Dane, who was slightly drunk, uttered a yell and struck the bars of the cage with his whip. The tiger did not blench, but all the malice and ferocity in the world seemed to congregate in its eyes and impress with a pride and ruthless grandeur the colossal brutality of its face. It did not move its body, but its tail gradually stiffened out behind it as healthily as fire moves in the forest undergrowth, and the hair along the ridge of its back rose in fearful spikes. There was the slighted possible dimension of the lips, and it fixed its marvellous baleful gaze upon Pedersen. The show people were hushed into silence, and even Pedersen was startled. He showered a few howls and curses at the tiger, who never ceased to fix him with eyes that had something of contempt in them and something of a horrible presage. Pedersen was thrusting a sharp spike through the bars when a figure stepped from the crowd. It was an old negro, a hunchback with a white beard, dressed in a red fez cap, long tunic of buff cotton, and blue trousers. He laid both his hands on the spike and shook his head deprecatingly, smiling all the while. He said nothing, but there was nothing he could say—he was dumb.

"Let him alone. Yak; let the tiger alone. Yak!" cried Barnabe Woolf. "What is this feller?"

Pedersen with some reluctance turned from the cage and said: "He is come with the animal."

"So?" said Barnabe. "Vell, he can go. Ve do not vant any black feller."

"He cannot speak—no tongue—it is gone," Yak replied.

"No tongue! Vot, have they cut him out?"

"I should think it," said the tamer. "There was two of them, a white keeper, but that man fell off the ship one night and they do not see him any more. This chap he feed it and look after it. No

information of him, dumb you see, and a foreigner; don't understand. He have no letters, no money, no name, nowheres to go.
Dumb, you see, he has nothing, nothing but a flote. The captain
said to take him away with us. Give a job to him, he is a proposition."

"Vot is he got you say?"

"Flote." Pedersen imitated with his fingers and lips the actions
of a flute-player.

"O ya, a vlootl Vell, ve don't want no vloots now; ve feeds our
own tigers, don't ve, Yak?" And Mr. Woolf, oily but hearty—and
well he might be so for he was beautifully rotund, hair like satin,
extravagantly clothed, and rich with jewellery—surveyed first with
a contemplative grin, and then compassionately, the figure of the
old negro, who stood unsmiling with his hands crossed humbly
before him. Mr. Woolf was usually perspiring, and usually being
addressed by perspiring workmen, upon whom he bellowed orders
and such anathemas as reduced each recipient to the importance
of a potato, and gave him the aspect of a consumptive sheep. But
to-day Mr. Woolf was affable and calm. He took his cigar from his
mouth and poured a flood of rich grey air from his lips. "O ya, look
after him a day, or a couple of days." At that one of the boys began
to lead the hunchback away as if he were a horse. "Come on, Pompoon," he cried, and thenceforward the unknown negro was called
by that name.

Throughout the day the tiger was the sensation of the show,
and the record of its ferocity attached to the cage received thrilling confirmation whenever Pedersen appeared before the bars. The
sublime concentration of hatred was so intense that children
screamed, women shuddered, and even men held their breath in
awe. At the end of the day the beasts were fed. Great hacks of bloody
flesh were forked into the bottoms of the cages, the hungry victims pouncing and snarling in ecstasy. But no sooner were they
served than the front panel of each cage was swung up, and the
inmate in the seclusion of his den slaked his appetite and slept.
When the public had departed the lights were put out and the doors
of the arena closed. Outside in the darkness only its great rounded

oblong shape could be discerned, built high of painted wood, roofed with striped canvas, and adorned with flags. Beyond this match-box coliseum was a row of caravans, tents, naphtha flares, and buckets of fire on which suppers were cooking. Groups of the show people sat or lounged about, talking, cackling with laughter, and even singing. No one observed the figure of Pompoon as he passed silently on the grass. The outcast, doubly chained to his solitariness by the misfortune of dumbness and strange nationality, was hungry. He had not tasted food that day. He could not understand it any more than he could understand the speech of these people. In the end caravan, nearest the arena, he heard a woman quietly singing. He drew a shining metal flute from his breast, but stood silently until the singer ceased. Then he repeated the tune very accurately and sweetly on his flute. Marie the Cossack came to the door in her green silk tights and high black boots with gilded fringes; her black velvet doublet had plenty of gilded buttons upon it. She was a big, finely moulded woman, her dark and splendid features were burned healthily by the sun. In each of her ears two gold discs tinkled and gleamed as she moved. Pompoon opened his mouth very widely and supplicatingly; he put his hand upon his stomach and rolled his eyes so dreadfully that Mrs. Fascota sent her little daughter Sophy down to him with a basin of soup and potatoes. Sophy was partly undressed, in bare feet and red petticoat. She stood gnawing the bone of a chicken, and grinning at the black man as he swallowed and dribbled as best he could without a spoon. She cried out: "Here, he's going to eat the bloody basin and all, mum!" Her mother cheerfully ordered her to "give him those fraggiments, then!" The child did so, pausing now and again to laugh at the satisfied roll of the old man's eyes. Later on Jimmy Fascota found him a couple of sacks, and Pompoon slept upon them beneath their caravan. The last thing the old man saw was Pedersen, carrying a naphtha flare, unlocking a small door leading into the arena, and closing it with a slam after he had entered. Soon the light went out.

II

AFTER A WEEK the show shifted and Pompoon accompanied it. Mrs. Kavanagh, who looked after the birds, was, a little fortunately for him, kicked in the stomach by a mule and had to be left at an infirmary. Pompoon, who seemed to understand birds, took charge of the parakeets, love birds, and other highly coloured fowl, including the quetzal with green mossy head, pink breast, and flowing tails, and the primrose-breasted toucans with bills like a butcher's cleaver.

The show was always moving on and moving on. Putting it up and taking it down was a more entertaining affair than the exhibition itself. With Jimmy Fascota in charge, and the young man of the frock coat in an ecstasy of labour, half-clothed husky men swarmed up the rigged frameworks, dismantling poles, planks, floors, ropes, roofs, staging, tearing at bolts and bars, walking at dizzying altitudes on narrow boards, swearing at their mates, staggering under vast burdens, sweating till they looked like seals, packing and disposing incredibly of it all, furling the flags, rolling up the filthy awnings, then Right O! for a market town twenty miles away.

In the autumn the show would be due at a great gala town in the north, the supreme opportunity of the year, and by that time Mr. Woolf expected to have a startling headline about a new tiger act and the intrepid tamer. But somehow Pedersen could make no progress at all with this. Week after week went by, and the longer he left that initial entry into the cage of the tiger, notwithstanding the comforting support of firearms and hot irons, the more remote appeared the possibility of its capitulation. The tiger's hatred did not manifest itself in roars and gnashing of teeth, but by its rigid implacable pose and a slight flexion of its protruded claws. It seemed as if endowed with an imagination of blood-lust, Pedersen being the deepest conceivable excitation of this. Week after week went by and the show people became aware that Pedersen, their Pedersen, the unrivalled, the dauntless tamer, had met his match. They were proud of the beast. Some said it was Yak's bald crown that the tiger disliked, but Marie swore it was his moustache, a really remarkable piece of hirsute furniture, that he would not have parted with for a pound of gold—so he said. But whatever it was—crown, moustache, or the whole conglomerate Pedersen—the tiger remarkably loathed it and displayed his loathing, while the unfortunate tamer had no more success with it than he had ever had with Marie the Cossack, though there was at least a good humour in her treatment of him which was horribly absent from the attitude of the beast. For a long time Pedersen blamed the hunchback for it all. He tried to elicit from him by gesticulations in front of the cage the secret of the creature's enmity, but the barriers to their intercourse were too great to be overcome, and to all Pedersen's illustrative frenzies Pompoon would only shake his sad head and roll his great eyes until the Dane would cuff him away with a curse of disgust and turn to find the eyes of the tiger, the dusky, smooth-skinned tiger with bitter bars of ebony, fixed upon him with tenfold malignity. How he longed in his raging impotence to transfix the thing with a sharp spear through the cage's gilded bars, or to bore a hole into its vitals with a red-hot iron! All the traditional treatment in such cases, combined first with starvation and then with rich feeding, proved unavailing. Pedersen always had the front flap of the cage left down at night so that he might, as he thought, establish some kind of working arrangement between them by the force of propinquity. He tried to sleep on a bench just outside the cage, but the horror of the beast so penetrated him that he had to turn his back upon it. Even then the intense enmity pierced the back of his brain and forced him to seek a bench elsewhere out of range of the tiger's vision.

Meanwhile, the derision of Marie was not concealed—it was even blatant—and to the old contest of love between herself and the Dane was now added a new contest of personal courage, for it had come to be assumed, in some undeclarable fashion, that if Yak Pedersen could not tame that tiger, then Marie the Cossack would. As this situation crystallized daily the passion of Pedersen changed to jealousy and hatred. He began to regard the smiling Marie in much the same way as the tiger regarded him.

"The hell-devil! May some lightning scorch her like a toasted fish!"

But in a short while this mood was displaced by one of anxiety; he became even abject. Then, strangely enough, Marie's feelings underwent some modification. She was proud of the chance to subdue and defeat him, but it might be at a great price—too great a price for her. Addressing herself in turn to the dim understanding of Pompoon she had come to perceive that he believed the tiger to be not merely quite untamable, but full of mysterious dangers. She could not triumph over the Dane unless she ran the risk he feared to run. The risk was colossal then, and with her realization of this some pity for Yak began to exercise itself in her; after all, were they not in the same boat? But the more she sympathized the more she jeered. The thing had to be done somehow.

Meanwhile Barnabe Woolf wants that headline for the big autumn show, and a failure will mean a nasty interview with that gentleman. It may end by Barnabe kicking Yak Pedersen out of his wild beast show. Not that Mr. Woolf is so gross as to suggest that. He senses the difficulty, although his manager in his pride will not confess to any. Mr. Woolf declares that his tiger is a new tiger; Yak must watch out for him, be careful. He talks as if it were just a question of giving the cage a coat of whitewash. He never hints at contingencies; but still, there is his new untamed tiger, and there is Mr. Yak Pedersen, his wild beast tamer—at present.

III

ONE DAY THE menagerie did not open. It had finished an engagement, and Jimmy Fascota had gone off to another town to arrange the new pitch. The show folk made holiday about the camp, or flocked into the town for marketing or carousals. Mrs. Fascota was alone in her caravan, clothed in her jauntiest attire. She was preparing to go into the town when Pedersen suddenly came silently in and sat down.

"Marie," he said, after a few moments, "I give up that tiger. To me he has given a spell. It is like a mesmerize." He dropped his hands upon his knees in complete humiliation. Marie did not speak, so he asked: "What you think?"

She shrugged her shoulders, and put her brown arms akimbo. She was a grand figure so, in a cloak of black satin and a huge hat trimmed with crimson feathers.

"If *you* can't trust him," she said, "who can?"

"It is myself I am not to trust. Shameful! But that tiger will do me, yes, so I will not conquer him. It's bad, very, very bad, is it not so? Shameful, but I will not do it!" he declared excitedly.

"What's Barnabe say?"

"I do not care, Mr. Woolf can think what he can think! Damn Woolf! But for what I do think of my own self . . . Ah!" He paused for a moment, dejected beyond speech. "Yes, miserable it is, in my own heart very shameful, Marie. And what you think of me, yes, that too!"

There was a note in his voice that almost confounded her—why, the man was going to cry! In a moment she was all melting compassion and bravado.

"You leave the devil to me, Yak. What's come over you, man? God love us, I'll tiger him!"

But the Dane had gone as far as he could go. He could admit his defeat, but he could not welcome her all too ready amplification of it.

"Na, na, you are good for him, Marie, but you beware. He is not a tiger; he is beyond everything, foul—he has got a foul heart and a thousand demons in it. I would not bear to see you touch him; no, no, I would not bear it!"

"Wait till I come back this afternoon—you wait!" cried Marie, lifting her clenched fist. "So help me, I'll tiger him, you'll see!"

Pedersen suddenly awoke to her amazing attraction. He seized her in his arms. "Na, na, Marie! God above! I will not have it."

"Aw, shut up!" she commanded, impatiently, and pushing him from her she sprang down the steps and proceeded to the town alone.

She did not return in the afternoon; she did not return in the evening; she was not there when the camp closed up for the night. Sophy, alone, was quite unconcerned. Pompoon sat outside the caravan, while the flame of the last lamp was perishing weakly above his head. He now wore a coat of shag-coloured velvet. He was old and looked very wise, often shaking his head, not wearily, but as if in doubt. The flute lay glittering upon his knees and he was wiping his lips with a green silk handkerchief when barefoot Sophy in her red petticoat crept behind him, unhooked the lamp, and left him in darkness. Then he departed to an old tent the Fascotas had found for him.

When the mother returned the camp was asleep in its darkness and she was very drunk. Yak Pedersen had got her. He carried her into the arena, and bolted and barred the door.

IV

MARIE FASCOTA AWOKE next morning in broad daylight; through chinks and rents in the canvas roof of the arena the brightness was beautiful to behold. She could hear a few early risers bawling outside, while all around her the caged beasts and birds were squeaking, whistling, growling, and snarling. She was lying beside the Dane on a great bundle of straw. He was already awake when she became aware of him, watching her with amused eyes.

"Yak Pedersen! Was I drunk?" Marie asked dazedly in low husky tones, sitting up. "What's this, Yak Pedersen? Was I drunk? Have I been here all night?"

He lay with his hands behind his head, smiling in the dissolute ugliness of his abrupt yellow skull so incongruously bald, his moustache so profuse, his nostrils and ears teeming with hairs.

"Can't you speak?" cried the wretched woman. "What game do you call this? Where's my Sophy, and my Jimmy—is he back?"

Again he did not answer; he stretched out a hand to caress her. Unguarded as he was, Marie smashed down both her fists full upon his face. He lunged back blindly at her and they both struggled to their feet, his fingers clawing in her thick strands of hair as she struck at him in frenzy. Down rolled the mass and he seized it; it was her weakness, and she screamed. Marie was a rare woman—a match for most men—but the capture of her hair gave her utterly into his powerful hands. Uttering a torrent of filthy oaths, Pedersen pulled the yelling woman backwards to him and grasping her neck with both hands gave a murderous wrench and flung her to the ground. As she fell Marie's hand clutched a small cage of fortune-telling birds. She hurled this at the man, but it missed him; the cage burst against a pillar and the birds scattered in the air.

"Marie! Marie!" shouted Yak, "listen! Listen!"

Remorsefully he flung himself before the raging woman who swept at him with an axe, her hair streaming, her eyes blazing with the fire of a thousand angers.

"Drunk, was I!" she screamed at him. "That's how ye got me, Yak Pedersen? Drunk, was I!"

He warded the blow with his arm, but the shock and pain of it was so great that his own rage burst out again, and leaping at the woman he struck her a horrible blow across the eyes. She sunk to her knees and huddled there without a sound, holding her hands to her bleeding face, her loose hair covering it like a net. At the pitiful sight the Dane's grief conquered him again, and bending over her imploringly he said: "Marie, my love, Marie! Listen! It is not true! Swear me to God, good woman, it is not true, it is not possible! Swear me to God!" he raged distractedly. "Swear me to God!" Suddenly he stopped and gasped. They were in front of the tiger's cage, and Pedersen was as if transfixed by that fearful gaze. The beast stood with hatred concentrated in every bridling hair upon its hide, and in its eyes a malignity that was almost incandescent. Still as a stone, Marie observed this, and began to creep away from the Dane, stealthily, stealthily. On a sudden, with incredible agility, she sprang up the steps of the tiger's cage, tore the pin from the catch, flung open the door, and, yelling in madness, leapt in. As she did so, the cage emptied. In one moment she saw Pedersen grovelling on his knees, stupid, and the next. . . .

All the hidden beasts, stirred by instinctive knowledge of the tragedy, roared and raged. Marie's eyes and mind were opened to its horror. She plugged her fingers into her ears; screamed; but her voice was a mere wafer of sound in that pandemonium. She heard vast crashes of someone smashing in the small door of the arena, and then swooned upon the floor of the cage.

The bolts were torn from their sockets at last, the slip door swung back, and in the opening appeared Pompoon, alone, old Pompoon, with a flaming lamp and an iron spear. As he stepped forward into the gloom he saw the tiger, dragging something in its mouth, leap back into its cage.

1927

THE WERE-TIGER
Lyman Bryson

I

WHEN THE NEW soothsayer came into Ban Dong from somewhere out of the west he brought new ideas. And new ideas are always evil. Any good Moi knows that without needing an old chief to tell him so and chant the laws of the *bidouway* to prove it. Soothsayers are generally useful in discouraging innovations. They know how to throw a pioneer into a shuddering terror by hinting what will happen to him if he presumes to think and asks questions about the what or the why of something all his ancestors have done before him. But this soothsayer, this intruder who was not a Moi at all, but a Shan or a Laos tribesman probably, who came into Ban Dong as a fugitive, was full of dangerous differences.

It was Blay, the son of Tu-op, who met him at the edge of the clearing. Blay saw him standing, very tired, beside a tree trunk and thought at first his sagging body was only a heavy vine. When the stranger moved Blay made him step forward into the moonlight and be examined. He had no weapons; outside of a breech-cloth there was nothing on his body but scratches from the jungle thorns, and his ribs stuck out like the welts of heavy wounds. He begged for water and rice. Blay thought him a rather interesting capture and took him home to show to Tu-op.

The man fell twice trying to clamber up the notched bamboo into the house and threw himself at Tu-op's feet while that ancient hunter smoked and regarded him.

"I think it is a lizard, not a man," said Tu-op to his son, slyly. "He can not go but on four feet."

233

The refugee shuddered and waited. But after he had been fed three times he could stand erect, beyond a doubt, and cast a very insolent eye on these strangers who had taken him in.

The Ban Dong elders advised Tu-op to cast him into the jungle again. He was of an unknown tribe; bewitched probably, and for that reason wandering so far abroad in the forest. No good could come of keeping him. And Tu-op, for that was his habit, decided to protect the stranger because the others were against him.

Not until he was fat from eating Tu-op's rice, cooked in bamboo joints by Tu-op's lame and beautiful wife, and also from sitting from one sunset to another in the corner of the house, did Nuan, for that was the name they gave him in derision, admit he was a soothsayer.

He made this boast in answer to a repeated question as to why he was afraid of the French, the strange white men who came into the forest at times and talked weird doctrines about "protection" and "tribute" and "loyalty" and "government." He had angered the French white men, he said, by casting a spell against them.

He had thwarted them in their devilish plans for getting possession of all free lands of the people. He had stirred up a flock of spirits against them in the jungle paths so they lost their way and almost perished of thirst and fear, and had to turn back again. He had served them with admirable disasters. The Mois would not have known what he meant by such white man's words as "police" and "felony" and "opium smuggling" and others which he knew much too well; so it was sensible of him not to mention them. He was a wizard, he said, and a mighty one.

"We have one soothsayer in Ban Dong now," Tu-op commented calmly, "and that is too many."

His son, who was sitting on his heels in the corner shadow, stirred and made a noise in his throat at this but Tu-op pretended not to hear. The boy had an eye on a lissome, bronze-bodied girl who called the Ban Dong soothsayer father. Naturally his opinion in such matters would be worthless.

"If the men of Ban Dong," said the newcomer, "are not satisfied with the wizard they have now, they should get a new one. I will remain and see if they do not need me."

Tu-op laughed at this until his back hurt and his pipe went out. Blay, his son, repeated it that night to the girl's father however, and the girl's father, old Irap, who had never dreamed that his position as wizard in Ban Dong would be questioned until one of his own sons grew up, swore fearfully. He took hold of the post of his own house when Blay told him and shook it so hard in his sacred wrath that his two pigs were disturbed under the platform on which the dwelling rested and went squealing into the edge of the forest.

"Your pigs—your pigs!" cried Blay, for he was interested more in Irap's fortune than in his disposition.

"He shall be blasted and burned—I'll dry his tongue in his throat—I'll put his thumbs in a split bamboo and let the lizard spirits disembowel him!"

"Your pigs are running away, revered parent!" shouted Blay.

"My pigs go to mate with the wild boars," answered Irap loftily. "They are the pigs of a great sorcerer. And this pig of a stranger—this crocodile's filth—coming here with his tricks to take an honest man's rice out of his mouth—"

"I do not believe he has any tricks, revered parent," said Blay, trying to soothe him.

Old Irap paused. There was a fleck of foam in the corner of his betel-stained mouth where one sharpened tooth protruded like a fang, and his eyes rolled.

"Has he tricks? Does he know any medicine? We shall see. We shall see."

He turned his back on Blay, muttering savagely, and scrambled up the bamboo into his house. He must have had a great deal to talk to his daughter about that night, for, although Tu-op's son waited there for an hour, she did not so much as come to the edge of the platform.

II

THE OLD CHIEF of Ban Dong agreed, when Irap formally demanded it, that there should be a trial of strength between Irap and the stranger. The chief was worried somewhat by the presence of two soothsayers in his village. Who knew what might happen if they should get their incantations mixed? The forest spirits might be puzzled to know the wishes or the intentions of Ban Dong men, and be angry with confusions. The chief had no use for the stranger, of course, but he thought Irap could demolish him and then there would be no longer any reason for not driving him away. Even Tu-op would scarcely hold out for his guest if Irap showed him to be either an impostor or a weak magician. Tu-op was impious, but he was not a fool; he would never be friends with a beaten man.

A grand butchery of buffaloes and opening of rice-wine jugs was ordered for the next night of the full moon. The challenge to the stranger was conveyed from the house of old Irap in terms so injurious that the stranger, not having a full vocabulary of the Moi tongue, was tempted into replying in some barbarous jargon of the west, Laos perhaps. It had a sulphurous sound, and the messenger who received it shielded his face with his arm for fear it was a blistering spell.

To show his contempt for the powers of Nuan, the stranger, old Irap was willing to practice his own magic in the open clearing. He counted on his masterly control of the spirits of air and forest, light and darkness, earth and sky—a control so complete that he could challenge them all without the protection of a roof, where there was no smoke to thicken his incantations and where the buffalo heads that dripped black blood had to be hung on saplings instead of on the consecrated door posts.

The whole village of Ban Dong was there, even the woman who had once been Tu-op's wife, the real mother of the valorous Blay, in fact, who had rejected Tu-op and gone home to her mother because of his well-known impiety. She was there to see Tu-op's guest lose face forever; perhaps even Tu-op himself might get a share of the contemptuous jeering. Little Mungye and the other elephant hunters were ranked on either side of the old chef and they squatted on their heels so their women folk could see over their heads. They all made a solid fence around the magician's circle. The unholy Nuan could not escape when it was over.

To propitiate a spirit in order to have his blessing on a hunt is a simple affair; it scarcely takes the special training of a sorcerer to do that. But to summon an intimate demon out of the spirit world and compel him to manifest himself as a proof of your power is a serious business. Even Irap very seldom tried it. He owned a demon, a fearful creature who had been bestowed on him for future use by his father when Irap was a crawling infant, but for years he had not disturbed that demon's rest.

To help him with smoke and music he chose two ancients who had amateur claims to magic of their own. One kept the choking fumes pouring up from a charcoal fire by putting on green rattan slips. The other beat the long drum with his hands.

The new soothsayer sat opposite the old one, clad in a robe which he had made secretly for this night, a robe with great sleeves and loose folds around his waist. He watched the preparations with a silent supercilious air, and when the drum began to sway Irap and the crowd in a rhythmic hunching of their bare shoulders, Nuan sat straight, resisting. Tu-op, the impious, was somewhere on the edge of the spectators' circle, prowling restlessly.

Irap swayed his body at his hips, back and forth, faster and faster. With an abrupt cry he clapped his hands above his head and began to chant. He called upon his demon to come, to come up out of the fires and winds of the spirit world, to possess him and speak with the authority of irresistible power. He whirled until his hair was loosened and swung about his mumbling head. The people of Ban Dong, swaying to the drum, had their eyes fixed on him and their ears were filled with his shrill singing.

The drum stopped on a half-beat of its swift cadence. The people were stiffened. The only sound was the sputter of the fires.

Irap had thrown himself forward on his face and lay twitching for a moment, possessed of his demon. Then he lifted his head with solemn slowness. His eyes were turned upward so that only their whites showed in the dim illumination of the fire; the demon must have given him sight for he pointed a shaking arm at Nuan, the intruder.

A guttural voice, certainly not his own, came from his throat.

"There is death for Ban Dong," said the demon, through Irap's lips, "there is death in the presence of the stranger. He is vile; he has the blood of the western tribes; he plots destruction. The spirits are angry with the men of Ban Dong for feeding him. Unless he is driven out there will be death—sorrow and death!"

Irap collapsed upon his face again and a long shuddering sigh ran through the people.

Nuan only smiled.

Little Mungye and two warriors stirred and stood up from their heels, grasping their spears. The old chief, shaking his head to clear his mind of Irap's powerful spell, called for quiet.

"We have permitted a test," he said. "Let the stranger do what he can."

Nuan stood up and stepped into the center of the circle.

"Listen, O men of Ban Dong!" he cried. "There are many demons and many gods. But there is one god greater than all, greater than Nget-Ngwal of the elephants. He lives above the moon—"

Nuan pointed straight into the air, and so sharp was the command in his shrill voice that every eye in the crowd was turned toward the heavens where the round moon hung in the blackness.

"His name is Buddh'," cried Nuan, "and he is worshiped by mighty men. Watch for him; watch, for he will give a sign to his servant."

For a long time the fascinated crowd kept their gaze turned sharply upward until their eyes were tired.

"Watch his servant now!" cried Nuan, and on his wrist they saw a green feather. It was a parakeet's feather resting lightly on Nuan's brown wrist, from which he had drawn back the wide sleeve of his robe.

He began to sing in some weird language of his own, keeping his eyes not on the feather, but rolled up toward the sky. They all watched with him, expecting a portent from this god Buddh' who might possibly be a very mighty spirit in the west.

Then Nuan tossed up his arm and stood still.

There was a flash of green above his head and a green parakeet, twisting its beak and blinking at the crowd out of a canny eye, sat on his bare wrist. Out of nowhere! Grown from the feather! A murmur went through the Ban Dong people as they bent their necks, sore from staring upward, and turned their attention to the magic bird.

"A sign!" shouted Nuan. "The holy one sends a bird!" Then Nuan, the stranger, knowing he had them for the moment under his spell, did a bold and terrible thing. "The bird of the great god," he said in a low voice that made them lean forward to hear, "has the power to know the mighty beasts and men. He knows the Great Lord, the yellow beast who may not be called by his name. He knows him, the Killer, even when he lives among us as a man."

The people stirred uneasily, for even that much mention of a tiger is dangerous liberty which the yellow one who comes at night may overhear and come to punish.

"He knows the Killer even when he lives among us in the form of a man," said Nuan with an rising stridency in his voice. "He knows—he knows— Speak, O holy bird! Is there one among us?"

The bird fluttered on his wrist.

The invocation of the tiger was more horrible to the Ban Dong people than a demon who only cursed from the bloody lips of an old wizard like Irap. They shrank back from Nuan and his bird and looked at each other. Some of the women on the outer edge caught up their children stealthily and hurried away home.

"Is there one among us," yelled Nuan, "Who is a Killer but goes on two feet like a man? Betray him to us, O bird of the great spirit."

He cast the fluttering parakeet in the air. Like a green explosion it flashed across the ring. Old Irap, out in front of the squatting rows, fell over backward in astonishment when the bird fastened its talons in his hair, screaming like a devil.

The Ban Dong people ran in all directions. They fell over each other and cursed and bumped and rolled. Little Mungye knocked down a sapling that held a sacrificial head and got the bloody buffalo's flesh on the small of his back. He howled in terror and ran for his house, trampling two old women on the way.

The circle of light was empty except for Nuan standing in triumph over old Irap who writhed, fighting with the bird, and except for two others who had not run. The old chief sat in his place blanched with fright but incapable of running and deserted by the bearers of his chair. And there was Tu-op, calm and staunch, although inwardly disturbed.

Blay, Tu-op's valiant son, had fled with the first but he turned to look; when he perceived that his father was still there he crept back and took his place at his father's side, his heavy knife unslung and his bare toes dug firmly into the dirt.

Nuan laughed an unholy laugh and called to his bird. The green demon left the fallen Irap and went back to the great wizard's wrist.

"Behold, O Chief," said Nuan.

He cast the bird into the air again and it circled upward in great sweeps, straight up into the heavens. They watched it until they could see nothing more. Then a speck came floating down and the little green feather was there again on Nuan's wrist.

The great wizard came over toward Tu-op, his protector, expecting good wishes and the acknowledgment of his victory. But there was something strange in Tu-op's manner. He walked toward his chief.

"Old Irap is not a Killer," said Tu-op. "He is a man and a friend of men. He is a foolish wizard perhaps, but a man."

The chief shook his palsied head and wished in his heart that some one else were judge of the tribal laws for a day or so.

"Besides," insisted Tu-op, standing before him with respect and firmness, "Irap has lived among us for many, many seasons, and never since I was a man has the Great Lord of the forest taken a Ban Dong life. If Irap is a—a tiger—" Tu-op spoke the fearful word almost carelessly—"where has he killed?"

What Tu-op said was the truth, and since the old chief had no handy law that could be quoted in the premises, the question rested. Irap shut himself up in his house mourning his defeat, and the intruder strutted around the village and was much smiled at because every one was sick with fear of him.

III

THE NEW SOOTHSAYER had no need to be the guest of Tu-op now. He was given a house of his own, and was considering what wife he would take among the young girls in the tribe. Blay saw him one afternoon watching old Irap's daughter when she dipped water from the river. She was a gay child and was singing happily as she stood in the brown water where the sun cast reflections of tangled skeins of light on the brownness of her skin. She had a giddy red flower above her ear, woven into her black hair, and her thin wet *sampot* clung to her round limbs. Blay saw Nuan's eyes wrinkled up at her beauty, and, he added murder to his thoughts of the intruder. If he had supposed that any ordinary knife could hack the sorcerer's neck he would have ended the business with praiseworthy dispatch.

The attitude of Tu-op continued to be queerly uncertain. He protested whenever any one would listen to him that he did not believe in the least that poor old Irap was a were-tiger; in fact he did not believe that such a thing as a were-tiger existed.

"A man is a man and a beast is a beast—in this life," said Tu-op.

But he appeared still to be friends with Nuan and supported the new ideas which were brought forward by that disturbing element.

A great issue came when there was talk of an elephant drive. The auguries which had always been trusted under Irap's guidance were tried by the chief and presaged evil. Nuan laughed and said he knew by his own spells that there was a mighty hunting in the forest for Ban Dong men, if on his advice the *pakams* dared go out and try.

Tu-op, mightiest *pakam* of them all, although he had not bestrode an elephant's neck since the day of the old elephant with the twisted tail, nodded his head and agreed. Beyond any question, he thought, there was good hunting.

The matter was much discussed along the river and on the porches of an evening. Little Mungye, with regrettable disloyalty, since he had been a follower of Tu-op's, remarked that of course Tu-op would agree with the new ideas—he was *biol*, drunk, with vanity and impious recklessness. Little Mungye was making quite a speech on the subject of Tu-op when he caught sight of Blay eying him over the shoulder of a friend and he choked on his peroration.

Since Irap would not come forth to defend the ancient faiths and the new sorcerer had the *pakams* miserably worried, the chief declared that the hunt should be tried.

"Make your propitiations before Nget-Ngwal," he said helplessly, "and perhaps he will permit this new god to bless your hunting."

The night before the procession was to start off into the jungle Tu-op had a long talk with Blay.

"When you are ancient as I am," he said, "and have given over the glory of catching elephants to your son, you have many hours for thinking. I have listened to the wild talk of this Nuan—"

"He is a crocodile," said Blay, shamelessly interrupting his father.

"—and I have believed very little of what he said," Tu-op concluded, overlooking in his kindness the impoliteness of the boy. "But he comes from the west and no doubt he tells truly what men in the west believe. There are many men in the world, no doubt— not counting white men and the French. If they all hunt elephants and call on different spirits for help—"

"But do they all *catch* their elephants when they try?" demanded Blay, conscious of his own prowess.

"Hold your peace and listen, child! If they call on different gods and all the gods answer, then perhaps it is after all the skill and bravery of men that count for most in a victorious hunting."

"Ah—" Blay, whose mind was clear and simple because he was a good brave man without the poison of doubt which suffering had injected into his father's soul, breathed an acknowledgment of the skill and bravery of men. Otherwise he had no idea what his father was talking about.

"Now listen," continued Tu-op, his brown brows wrinkled terribly in the effort to think, "you must go into this hunt tomorrow and you must not come home until you have tamed a worthy elephant. That will prove that the old auguries were useless."

"It will prove also that this stranger Nuan is a better sooth-sayer than our Irap," protested Blay.

He spat a scarlet stream of betel-juice through the crack in the floor and ruminated fiercely.

"Most of all," replied Tu-op, smiling, "it will prove that my son is a *pakam* worthy of me."

"*Yu-ne Ka!*" Blay agreed. "Yes, that will be good," he lost his attempt at thinking in a bright dream of gray tuskers caught and led in triumph back to Ban Dong. "*Yu-ne Ka!*"

MOSTLY BECAUSE OF Blay's indomitable fervor and his natural cunning, the hunt went well. When they first marched out of the Ban Dong clearing, with Blay ahead on his own great hunting elephant and his rope holder clinging to their charger's rump, the *pakam* were in a mood of restless uncertainty. If there had been an unlucky incident to fix their fears they might have turned and scattered back for home, and the troublesome Nuan would have been finished then, as he deserved.

Blay kept them going and they found a wild herd four days later in the deep green forest. Blay himself rode down a fine young bull and snared him by the hind foot and tied him to a tree. That success, which made a vast noise in the forest, scared the rest of the wild herd into two days' running but it gave complete courage to the hunters. They chased the herd and got one more, a young female, and turned toward Ban Dong contented.

Within a day's journey of home, when they were beginning to feel safe and could taste already the celebrating rice-wine and roasted flesh that would greet them, they slept one night by the river.

In the middle of that night little Mungye, who was out as picket to watch the new captures, came creeping in to where the others were sleeping, so sick with terror that he went four-legged like a monkey, and whispered that two yellow eyes were looking at him from the brush.

They were all awakened and they built up the fire and sang and pounded their knives together and shouted prayers to Nget-Ngwal,

god of the elephants, forgetting of course that they were for the
time under the protection of a new god named Buddh'. They made
such a racket that the elephants could not hear anything else. What
they could not do was to change the scent of tiger on the air.

It drifted in, rank and terrible, to where the elephants huddled.
Blay's own beast, canny and well trained as he was, lifted his trunk
and trumpeted in alarm. The two new ones, tied between seasoned
females, bucked and pulled at their fastenings. Blay went in among
them and tried to soothe them. But his own beast knew there was
a strange tremble in the voice of his master and paid no attention.
They began to sway, like men in a dance. The *pakams* thought
after a long time that their noise had been effective and paused. In
the silence, when the jungle seemed for a moment to be holding
its moist breath, there was a sound—a throaty *purrrrrrrr*.

The elephants broke. Tearing the two new captures out of their
moorings, they went in a compact mass through the tangled lianas,
over young bamboos, crashing trees aside, dragging long stream-
ers of rattan behind them, plunging blindly into the darkness.

The Ban Dong *pakams* kept up their noises then and their fires
until the sun came up. Wearily they took up the pursuit, knowing
they might have to go on for days and end up empty-handed.

It had in truth been a number of years since a tiger had come
so directly across the path of Ban Dong men. Ban Dong had been
lucky. Other villages along the river, especially those farther into
the northern hills, might lose a pig or even a buffalo calf sometimes. One man in the north two years ago had lost his daughter to
the Great Lord, it was said, but gossip added that the daughter
was worthless anyway, being impudent to her parents. The tiger
was still spoken of with ceremonial respect as the Great Lord but
he had not been a present trouble to Bang Dong.

The *pakams* discussed all this as they plodded through the
damp undergrowth following the broad track of the elephants, and
they speculated as to the reason for this change of fortune. Blay
knew why it was and said so. It was the wrath of their own gods;
and surely Nget-Ngwal had reason enough to be wrathful since they
had shamed him before this stranger's spirit Buddh'.

Blay made his opinions seem more reasonable by being first to come upon his own elephant. He saw him ploughing along sullenly and called the command to halt. When the beast paused uncertain, and most of the hunters would have been afraid to approach him without some further, seductive conversation, Blay walked up and told his elephant to hold down his trunk for a stirrup. Once up there on the great square head Blay could control not only his own but the other elephants. They were all subdued soon enough, all but the two newly captured ones who never were recovered.

The disappointed hunt came back to the village. They had chosen Blay for spokesman and he went to the chief in the midst of the homecoming feast and made their accusation.

"We were deceived, O mighty judge," he said. "We were told by this false soothsayer, this Nuan, that the auguries were good for hunting. And then when we had captured two fine elephants, the finest that have ever been in the hands of Ban Dong men, we were stalked by the Great Lord at night. We were put in fear for our lives and we lost the catch. Withdraw your protection from this stranger who gives dark counsel and disturbs the gods of our tribes."

Nuan, resplendently clothed and smiling still his imperturbable contempt for enemies, waved an arm.

"Enough, son of Tu-op," he commanded. "Did you see my lord the tiger?"

"No," answered Blay with a shudder, "I smelled him and my elephant smelled him also."

Nuan smiled more widely, his wrinkled face thrust forward with a hateful leer of insolence.

"It was not a tiger," he said.

"But the smell of the Great Lord was in the air."

"It was not the Great Lord," insisted Nuan. "It was man who goes as a beast by night to make his kill."

They all crouched, ready to flee if Nuan should begin a spell. But the intruder was subtle. He asked in a sleepy voice:

"Has any man or woman of Ban Dong seen the ancient Irap while the hunt was out? Has he been seen?"

They shook their heads and nudged one another.

"I have spoken," said Nuan and left the assembly.

IV

"THERE CAN NOT be such a thing as a man who walks as a tiger," said
Tu-op to his son. Tu-op's mother, who sat in the corner of the
house, shook her ancient head and spat, missing the crack between
the bamboos in her palsied weakness.

"No," she snorted, "but there are! I have always known of them."

Tu-op's wife shook her head too, but in gentle trouble. She was
worried for the sake of Blay whom she loved as if he had been her
own instead of only her stepson.

"A man's soul may pass into the body of a tiger when he has
died, perhaps," continued Tu-op, speculating in his calm way, "and
that would be a reward for a life of bravery. But a man is a man
and a beast is a beast—in this life certainly."

Blay choked with the thing he had to utter.

"Nuan, the vile, has told Mungye and the others a tale of following tracks from the forest into the village!"

"Did any other man see them?" asked Tu-op.

"No," said Blay. "But does that make Nuan less bold? He says
that he saw them—tracks of the Great Lord—coming in from the
forest and ending by the ladder of Irap's house."

Tu-op smiled.

"You are the one who should know, my son, what tracks go in
and out from the porch of that house."

"She is like a bird that trembles in the eye of a snake," replied
Blay. "She hopes to save her father from this horrible death. And
Nuan says—from Mungye, I have these lies—that he followed the
tracks at night from the edge of the clearing to Irap's house and
they were fresh tracks, hot with the touch of the Great Lord's feet."

"And Nuan says he followed close?" Tu-op laughed. "Does even
Mungye believe that?"

"Mungye believes what he is told. And Nuan tells that he crept
up to the corner of the house post and heard the voice of Irap above

on the ladder calling to his girl to bring a bamboo torch. And while Irap's head was the head of a man, talking humanly to his child, the feet of Irap on the bamboo notch were the claws of a beast, and a striped tail swung back and forth and lashed the ground."

The old woman in the corner gave a hideous groan and fell over in a fit of terror. Even Tu-op fingered nervously the charm that hung on his breast. But he held obstinately to his doubts.

"I do not believe it," he muttered. "May the spirits of my father and my father's father stand by me, but I do not believe it."

There was a long scream of demented fear. It seemed at first that it came from within the house but, as they sat like images with contorted mouths, they realized that it was out in the village. Blay scrambled to his feet and unslung his knife and was down the ladder before his father could join him. But Tu-op went with equal boldness along the piles of house platforms where women were yelling and men were jumping down, toward the center of Ban Dong. Before the chief's house they saw a girl, one of his daughters, lying senseless on the ground. Near-by, when they searched with blazing bamboo torches, they saw the broad tracks, half-obliterated by the bloody path of a kill the Great Lord had dragged behind.

"He came over the stockade," said the chief's girl, when they had brought her back to life again. "One jump over, and he took a calf—like that!"

She tried to show how the calf had its throat torn in one paw's swing and how its body had been carried in the tiger's mouth.

Almost all of Ban Dong was there, crowded close around her. Tu-op drew Blay aside.

"Go now," he whispered, "to Irap's house and get him away into the forest. Go northward—all night. Along the river. I will do what may be done." And Blay ran.

When, led by Nuan, the *pakams* surrounded Irap's house at dawn they found only his daughter huddled by her dead fire, weeping and dumb.

V

AFTER SEVERAL DAYS, the village discovered that Blay, son of Tu-op, was missing as well as old Irap and they knew at once he had been eaten by the tiger.

"Eaten by Irap, the tiger," they said.

They were disgusted with Tu-op because he would not go through any mourning feasts for the lost Blay. His impiety was incorrigible. He did worse. He took Irap's daughter into his house where she was safe from those who said a tiger father would beget a tiger child.

And out of the jungle where Irap had buried himself the Great Lord continued to come. Once, seven nights after the chief's daughter had seen him leap the stockade, he carried off another buffalo calf. Twice his tracks were seen along the river although nothing was missing at dawn. Little Mungye, whose stories had never before been so fervently believed, said he saw him on the other side of the river, standing with his body among the vines, his head thrust out toward the town, his eyes glaring and his lips a-snarl. The expression on his face, Mungye added, was very much like the habitual expression of old Irap.

In this crisis, when the town was paralyzed, the new wizard Nuan and the old scoffer Tu-op found themselves again in agreement as to what could be done.

"Traps are as good against a man-tiger as against the tiger when he is his lordly self," said Nuan.

Tu-op smiled and said—

"Yes, certainly, if they are *good* traps."

They deferred to Tu-op's judgment about the traps. It had been so long since a tiger had included Ban Dong in his hunting grounds, that only a *pakam* with gray hair and several stiff white hairs on his chin, some one incredibly experienced, could presume to know how to go about it.

Tu-op selected the places in the forest where pits were to be dug, showed them how to build light shielding walls of *nipa* stalks and how to bait with carrion of dog.

Mungye made several impudent inquiries about these pits, suggesting that they were exactly like elephant traps except for the stink of carrion. Tu-op answered him severely. When after two days the Great Lord, or the ancient Irap, or whoever it was, leaped into one of the pits, took the bait and leaped out again, Tu-op was compelled to think harder. He deigned to consult Nuan, and the soothsayer told him of how they caught tigers in the west—with timber cages and trap doors.

It was easy. Just build a strong stockade and cover it with logs, put a ripe dead dog inside, prop the door up with a stick which the beast must knock over when he gets in to the bait, and there you are. Only what Nuan said was:

"And there you have caught Irap," and he turned away from Tu-op to leer at Irap's cringing girl. "If I had that woman," he said, "I could cure her of being a tiger's daughter. It takes a strong spell but Buddh' is great."

They built it like a rabbit trap, a few hundred paces into the jungle, and they waited while the bait got strong enough to move the nostrils of tigers in the far-off Tibet hills. They heard the beast roar once or twice and looked hopefully in their snare next morning, but nothing was there.

Tu-op came home to his house one night after moonrise. His wife was waiting patiently for him and also his mother, not so patient, but waiting because there was nothing else to do.

"Where is the girl?" he asked.

His wife, whose ways were so blameless that she seldom had need to answer his questions by scolding, sneered—

"Should I know what she does?"

Tu-op refused to sit down.

"Where is the girl?" he repeated sternly.

His mother broke forth.

"She has gone off with your mad sorcerer, of course. Hasn't he told her three times that if she will come with him he will teach her a spell that will free her from the bedevilment that has afflicted her father?"

"But does she not think of Blay—doesn't she know?"

His mother puffed out her cheeks in scorn of the simplicity of a man's thinking:

"She thinks Blay has gone and will never touch her because she is accursed. She thinks this western madman can cure her."

"But does she believe that her father is a—"

His mother laughed shrilly.

"Of course she does. Everybody does but you; and you are a great hunter but a fool!"

"Very well then," said Tu-op, shifting his knife around to have it handy on his shoulder. "I am going hunting." And he dropped down from the platform of his house to the ground silently and ran across the little moonlight space that protected him from the jungle.

VI

As soon as he got into the close pressing tangle of the brush Tu-op began to think. He had noticed that about himself: He jumped with his knife first and thought afterward, if at all. He believed that it was peculiar to his own nature and was ashamed to ask any other wise old men of the tribe whether they had ever been so foolish. Thinking did not really help much. He did not know what was going on in the jungle except that his own son was there—far away, he hoped—taking care of the unlucky Irap. Irap's daughter was there, having betrayed herself simply into the hands of the tricky Nuan. And the Great Lord himself was somewhere. Thinking helped only this much: It made Tu-op see that Nuan trusted his own powers in a reckless way. He would not otherwise have ventured into the brush even for some incantation nonsense with Irap's daughter which would put her definitely under his control.

Tu-op wished he had some such confidence in himself. He took his knife in his hand to cut the lianas out of his way and to give himself the comfort of closing his fingers tightly around it. He continued to think and decided that he was a great fool. What was he going to do to find them?

He circled warily, supposing Nuan and the girl would be within safe distance of his house, if anybody could call himself safe in the brush. He came to a little open space that he knew well. Young men came there sometimes to sing songs and hear them. But Tu-op was stern toward the memories of his youth.

The fear of the Great Lord had kept the young men of Bang Dong in that night, and if all the singing maidens of the tribe had gathered there they would have found no listeners. But over in the shadow at the edge of the moonlit grassy space he saw two figures. Tu-op rubbed his eyes to see them better. Unconsciously he reached up toward the branch of a tree and swung himself to a seat whence he could see and consider.

It was Nuan the sorcerer and Irap's daughter. The blood beat in Tu-op's temples, for he loved his son and he knew that Blay felt about this girl as he himself felt about the lame woman in their house. Now the filthy stranger was holding the girl's hands and talking to her, some spell of nonsense. Should the old fool be slain thus? Or should the girl be taken home again and Nuan told to keep away at his peril? Killing was usually better. Provided, of course, that the sorcerer would be killed with an ordinary man's good knife. Tu-op thought a strong swing would probably cut through any charm that Nuan knew.

While he considered, the girl, facing toward him, moved suddenly. He could not see why unless perhaps she had spied him hanging there in the tree. The girl cried out suddenly, wrenched her hand free as her mind was wrenched free by fright from the old man's mumbling mysteries, and she pointed straight at Tu-op. Nuan turned, and they both ran like scared deer. Tu-op would have laughed but he happened to look down. Just below him, out from the brush and into the moonlight, with a tawny shoulder higher than the tall grass, trotted a black-and-yellow beast.

The old hunter's nostrils breathed deep the rank smell of tiger. Without noticing the suspended Tu-op, trotting silently as if not deigning to hurry for his prey until the time for springing, the Great Lord went after Nuan and the girl. Tu-op's eye measured him—

longer than an elephant; longer than the longest serpent; longer than any tiger could possibly be. And he was gone.

Tu-op put both arms hard around the trunk of his tree and pressed himself close to the damp bark. It took all the strength he had to keep from falling.

TU-OP WAS AFRAID. His knees shook and his breath came in tearing gasps between his chattering teeth. But he had strength to hold on for a moment, to slide down to the ground and then to stagger along the tiger's tracks, going on straight toward a bloody, useless death.

He heard, ahead of him in the forest, a prolonged angry roar. He stopped. There was a crash, and some minutes afterward tearing sounds of a great body plunging through the brush. Every other sound in the jungle ceased, as if the whole great society of beasts and insects, worms and birds were holding their breath while the Great Lord went by.

He passed within a few yards of where Tu-op crouched but he went on. The hunter crept ahead, hoping it was Nuan that the tiger was carrying away and not the girl. But she might be struck down too. Tu-op's heart, as he pushed through the tangled vines, was heavy with the mournful sorrow that no thinking can change, the sorrow of the savage in the face of the savage forest, before the incomprehensible cruelty of the dark green world that preys on him as he struggles to prey upon it, the never-forgotten menace of sudden death.

The moonlight did not penetrate the forest depths. He felt his way ahead very slowly and the scent told him he was near the stockade trap. He came squarely up to it and rested his hand against an upright timber. On the other side a few trees had been cut away to furnish trunks for the stockade and a ray of light, greenish, uncertain, wavering, came through.

In the stockade was a sound that made Tu-op stiffen. Something stirred there. He heard a soft moaning voice and a reassuring answer. He called. Within a few steps of where he stood, inside the trap and safe, were Nuan and the girl.

"We ran and we fell against the wall of the trap and I thought of the door," said Nuan, jubilant over his cleverness. "We were inside when the tiger leaped at the timbers. I thought that if it was built to keep a tiger in it could also keep a tiger out. Has he gone, Tu-op, my friend?"

"For the present," answered the hunter thoughtfully. He did not ask any questions which might have embarrassed the girl. "When are you coming out?" he asked. "Or are you frightened enough to wait there until sun-up when it will certainly be safe?"

"I can not get out until you help with the door, my friend. It is stuck fast. The girl could creep out between the timbers; she is no thicker than a rattan vine. But I have eaten well for many years. Will you help me lift the door now?"

The hunter appeared to have a scientific interest in their adventure. He asked questions as to what the Great Lord had done when he found them inclosed and out of reach. Nuan answered that his sniffing breath had been horribly close, that he had seemed interested in all the inhabitants of the inclosure, making no snobbish difference between the living human animals and the dead dog.

"Pfui!" said Nuan, "the bait has a mighty smell."

The sorcerer's spirits were high in rebound from his few moments of despair.

"Let us out now, Tu-op," he commanded. "We can go safely home from here, because the beast knew finally that this was a dangerous place for him. He stopped sniffing, snarled at us, and ran away. Let us out."

"Let me see if Irap's daughter really can creep between the timbers," suggested the maker of the trap. "I want to know if perhaps a very young tiger could escape from the place if once we got him in."

The girl had not spoken. She rose to her feet, trembling still with her fright, but trusting Tu-op. Her lissome body, slender as a child's, went easily between the posts.

"And you see that I can not follow," said Nuan, squeezing himself into a narrow interval. "Let me out, Tu-op."

Tu-op smiled in the darkness.

"It would not be safe for you," he answered. "I can take the girl to my house. You can wait until daylight."

"But I will not stay here with this dead dog all night," protested the sorcerer.

"What is a little carrion to a great master of the spirits and the ghosts?" Tu-op's question came floating back out of the jungle. He was already on his way with the girl to the village.

VII

BEFORE DAWN Tu-op was at the door of the house of the old chief.

"In the night I heard the Great Lord roar," he said.

"We heard him also," answered the chief, rubbing his rheumy eyes and teetering and supported by two of his sons on the edge of his bamboo porch, while Tu-op looked up at him respectfully from below.

"I believe we have him in our stockade trap."

The chief blinked and gave orders. Behind him a drum began to sound and a conch of buffalo horn to bray. Out of all the houses in Ban Dong the men and boys came tumbling with their knives ready and their long spears in their fists. They pressed around the hunter at the chief's porch and demanded a reason for the alarm. The chief waited solemnly until they were all there.

"To the stockade trap!" he cried. "We have caught the tiger!"

With the chief in his chair at their head and Tu-op at the chief's side, they went down the length of the village where the brown river glittered in the morning sun. They plunged into the forest where the damp vines clung to their shoulders and whipped across their faces. They sang and thwacked their drums and pounded metal gongs and shouted like a great army on the march. As they came close to the little clearing around the trap they spread out to surround it. Spears were set in readiness. The chief gave a high shrill command and they rushed in.

As they broke out of the brush and saw the trap, their shouts died on their lips. They stopped. There was Nuan the sorcerer, gibbering at them angrily.

The chief came up with Tu-op.

"What I heard in the forest last night," said Tu-op at the chief's ear in a voice of awe, "was certainly the Great Lord himself, and what I see now in the trap is Nuan, the sorcerer. But look there, O mighty judge."

He pointed to a tiger's footprint, fresh on the wet ground.

The old chief scowled at the tracks, puzzled and distressed.

"It might be good to ask Nuan again," whispered Tu-op, "if there are men who go as we do by day but kill as tigers in the night-time."

Nuan was trying to explain, chattering feverishly in his dismay at their suspicious silence.

"Tu-op knows that I came in here to escape the Great Lord," he wheezed. "Ask Tu-op."

But the *pakam* only looked worried and said he had heard a tiger in the brush. It was different to be sure just what had happened, of course, but it was Nuan himself who had said that men could change themselves into Killers.

So the men of Ban Dong circled around Nuan in the cage, their long spears leveled at him, and Nuan shrieked that it was all a lie, that he was not a tiger, that no man had ever been a tiger, that he was a man like themselves. He denied his witchcraft and his great god Buddh' but none of that helped him at all. With superstitious tremors, thinking he might at any moment begin to change into a striped beast and snarl at them, the Ban Dong hunters came in and put their long spears between the timbers and pierced his body in a hundred places.

The strange part of it was that after Nuan's death the tiger did not come again.

A MONTH AFTER, when old Irap was brought back into Ban Dong by Blay and the bethrothal of Irap's daughter to Blay was celebrated expensively, the boy boasted to his father—

"There are not many men who have killed the Great Lord alone in the forest but I killed one, and—"

"Hush," muttered Tu-op. "Never speak of that again."

"But my fame as a great *pakam?*"

"When you killed that tiger you killed what might have been a grave question for this tribe, for your father and for old Irap," answered Tu-op. "Enjoy your luck and your pride inside your own house. Is fame better than a quiet fire and peace with your woman? I have never thought so."

1929

THE LEOPARD WOMAN
Edith Ross

When I was engaged to Leonardo, I remember one of my friends said to me: "Marta, you have everything. You—why, you are a darling of the gods. But be careful—for when one has too much, the gods are apt to become jealous. Don't be too triumphant, too happy, or you may live to be sorry."

I laughed. Such foolishness! Who could help being happy with a man like my Leon for a lover? I looked back on the time before I had met him, and wondered how I had managed to live through all the years before I knew he was in this world.

He had not been in America very long before we met and fell in love. He was the representative of the Gianella Silk Importers, whose headquarters were in Naples. They sent him to New York to take charge of their American office, and it was there that I met him. I knew very little about him, beyond the fact that he was a descendant of an excellent old Italian family; that both of his parents had died while he was a little boy; and that he had been raised by an older sister named Fiametta.

There were moments during our acquaintance when he was overcome by an unaccountable depression. He would sit, chin on hands, a look of sadness and worry resting like a shadow of despair on his dark, beautiful face. But he refused to acknowledge any such feeling and laughed my questions away. Why, what was there to feel depressed or sad about? Should not a man be happy—with the loveliest girl in the world for his promised bride?

"Leon," I asked once, "will we ever go to Italy to live?"

He shook his head and his eyes were shadowy and somber as
he answered.

"No!" he said. "A thousand times, no! If I can only stay here in
America—here where I have at last found freedom—then, indeed,
I will be happy. Italy? I love Italy! But never—never do I go there
again!"

"But why?" I asked, puzzled. "If you love Italy, why do you not
plan to return there some day? Why are you so sure you will never
want to go back?"

He shook his head. "That I may not tell you, Marta," he said
slowly. "All that is important about me and about my family, you
already know. Listen, dear heart—little white dove—listen! There
is only one member of my family left in Italy. That is Fiametta, my
sister. She is all of fifteen years older than I am, and she loves me.
When I was a wee baby, she took me. She has given her life to my
service—willingly, generously—because she loved me. And, for her
kindness, I love her, too. But very jealously she loves!"

"'But I will love her, too, Leon," I said. "Surely, if she loves you,
she will want you to be happy. And if she comes to America, we
will make her welcome and give her so much love between us, that
she will have no room for any jealousy."

Leon spoke slowly.

"Pray!" he said—"pray every night, for both our sakes, that
Fiametta stay in Italy! You do not know—you are not the type to
know a love that can be both strong and cruel."

"Leon, you frighten me," I said. "Why, what could she do?"

But Leon refused to talk of it any longer. With his lightning
change of mood, he was again the carefree lover, ardent and im-
pulsive.

"See, little white dove! I love you! You love me! Forget the
Fiametta! Think of me—or perhaps I grow jealous, too! You like
that, yes? Smile, now, and forget to be frightened. See—I kiss you—
again—again—"

And that continued to be his way of ending my questions. I dare
say I was too much in love to be really very sane in those days—or
to pursue a topic which I saw annoyed and worried him.

When we were married, Leon cabled the news to Fiametta. It was her first intimation of our love affair. No doubt, it was a shock to her.

We were married in June. For our honeymoon month Leon had extravagantly leased a beautiful house in the hills. It had been built by an artist and was his home, but he was willing to let it for the summer, while he was abroad. It was situated on the top of a little rise called Misty Hill. The plan had been dictated by the fancy of the owner, and the house had grown to a lovely though somewhat fantastic completion. From a distance it seemed a tiny fairy castle, with softly tinted towers and arches. Surrounding it was a garden of roses, so that every stray breeze was laden with summer sweetness. Surely an ideal place for a honeymoon.

Even its name was in keeping with its fanciful beauty. "Waning Moon!" Just the name it should have had, I thought, the first time I heard it. Little did I imagine how hideous a thing that name and that setting was to become for me!

Leon and I had lovely rooms on the second floor. But had I been alone, I know I should have chosen the tower room for my own. It was reached by a little circular staircase, opening out of the second-story corridor. Situated high over the rest of the house, it seemed a dream room—something lifted from some old medieval story or poem. In such a room Elaine might have guarded the shield of Lancelot.

Octagonal in shape—and windowless—it was lighted by a huge skylight of tinted glass that threw an ever-shifting pattern of jeweled color across the gloss of the black, mirror-like floor. The walls were hung with dull scarlet-and-silver tapestries that fell in straight, still folds to the floor. There were only a few pieces of furniture—an old carved chest, two high-backed, massive chairs; an old, time-dimmed mirror; a huge, silver-draped bed. Altogether, a most fascinating and unusual room. The few hours when Leon was absent, I went up there to read and dream.

But for some reason it did not appeal to Leon. He drew a sharp breath, the first time he glimpsed it. Then I heard him give a half-stifled exclamation.

"Why, what is it, Leon?" I asked.

He turned to me with a queer, twisted smile.

"Nothing to worry you, little dove," he said, "but—I have seen a room like this one, before. It—it reminds me—that perhaps I have bought my happiness with a price. Perhaps I have been a fool to dream, Marta! Come away from this place! It is not good! Lock the door, and stay away from this room!"

"Why, Leon, I think you are being foolish," I exclaimed. "This is the loveliest room in the whole house! Nothing could be more beautiful! Nothing!"

"You are right, Marta," he answered softly; "nothing could be more beautiful—or more sinister. If I had known that the house held such a room, we would have gone to some other place."

"No other place could be as beautiful as Waning Moon," I said.

"Waning Moon!" he repeated musingly. "Waning Moon! If I had not been a fool, perhaps that name in itself would have held a message for me."

I stared at him in perplexity. And he, seeing my doubt and distress, laughed, shrugged his shoulders and, catching at my hand, drew me back down the stairs and out into the rose garden.

THERE FOLLOWED DREAM days and nights of exquisite, almost heart-breaking loveliness. Honeymoon. Roses and June and blue-skyed noondays. Radiant, silver-flooded nights of moonlight and velvet warmth. A week and a half of heaven on earth!

And then—the cablegram from Italy. A black omen.

It was from Fiametta, announcing that she had sailed—that she would be with us in America—with us here, at Waning Moon, in a week's time! Leon read the cable and the blood drained from his face, leaving it a queer, greenish hue under the olive tint of his skin. He stood for a minute with the flimsy yellow sheet crumpled in his hand. His eyes, fixed unseeingly on me, had the hunted, hopeless look of a trapped animal. I was disappointed—upset—that she could not at least have waited until the end of our honeymoon. It was unfair, unkind of her, to intrude so abruptly. With a whole lifetime before her, surely she could have given us a few short weeks! Did she begrudge us our ecstasies? A premonitory shudder shook my heart.

"Oh, Leon—so soon?" I pleaded.

But Leon did not heed my words. He was staring straight ahead, and on his face was the incredulous, dazed look of a waking sleep-walker.

"I should have known," he half whispered. "I should have known! But I loved you so, little white dove! Surely love can protect its own from any harm! I had no right—no right to marry you. But I—fool that I was—I dared to dream—"

"Leon!" I was terrified and clung to him, questioning. "Leon, what is it? You are afraid? Why, you talk as if you were! What is it? Why do you act in this strange way? What is wrong?"

My lover looked down at me. He gave me a little smile, forced, unnatural. But he put his arm around me and drew me close against him. Then he took from his pocket a little ebony cross, attached to a tiny silver chain.

"I'm afraid I have never been a very religious man, Marta," he said soberly, "but take this cross. It is the symbol of the greatest thing in the world—Christianity! That is the shining weapon which can hold at bay those powers of darkness that would encroach on this earth. You will wear it for me? For Leon?"

He clasped the chain around my neck and dropped the little cross inside my dress over my heart. But when I would have questioned him more, he turned my face up and looked deep into my eyes.

"It is best that you be in ignorance, Marta," he said gently, "so do not ask me questions. I know that you suspect something, of course—that you are curious and alarmed. But not knowing—that is your best protection now. This much you have a right to verify. It is true that I fear Fiametta. Oh, not for my own sake! She would die, rather than that any harm should come to me. But for yours! Her love for me may he a very terrible gift. I feel now that I did wrong to marry you—but I have no excuse except my love for you."

"I think you are being too excited about it all," I said, making a grasp at my practical commonsense. "I won't ask you any more questions if you don't want me to, of course. But if you are afraid that your sister will not like me—that she will try to hurt me—if that is what is worrying you, don't let it any more. For I'm perfectly able to take care of myself. There isn't a thing in the world she could do, if she wanted to. But Leon, I'm going to make her like me so much that she won't even think of being jealous. And I'm going to like her, too. So there!"

But Leon shook his head doubtfully.

"I hope you may," he said. "Yes, there is a chance that she may love you, too. Oh, little white dove, who could keep from loving you? You are so sweet—so sweet! And if she should love you, therein lies your protection."

"I hope she will—I know she will," I answered. "But, Leon, we have a week left—alone. Let us be happy now, together, and when she comes, we'll treat her in the loveliest way we know. Everything will work out all right. Leon, don't look so worried, so unhappy, dear heart! There's nothing to be upset about! We're worrying over something that can't happen. Come down to the little lily-pond with me and bring your book, and you shall read and I'll sew and we'll pretend we've been married for—oh—ages!"

The next week flew on gossamer wings. Leon had occasional moods when he struggled with the old depression, and I knew it was induced by the expected arrival of his sister. But, on the whole, he seemed fairly confident and I did not ask questions. Privately, I must tell you, I regarded it all as more or less ridiculous. I even derived a tiny secret amusement from the idea that a jealous older sister could so train and rule a small boy, that, when grown, he would still dread her presence and authority. I formed a mental picture of Fiametta: middle-aged, staid, perhaps—horror of horrors—even stout.

ON THE DAY she was to arrive, Leon went to meet her. I stood at the gate of the garden and waved to him as he raced down the road at the usual breakneck speed he affected in our little roadster. And after he was out of sight, I turned back again to the midsummer riot of the flowers. Then, suddenly, for no reason, I was overcome by a sense of desolation and unhappiness.

Premonition is an odd thing. I stood in the midst of the great sunny garden and I shuddered as though a winter wind had chilled me to the marrow. The sunlight looked bleached and devoid of its gold, like the bleak, dreary light of late winter afternoon.

I turned from the garden and went slowly into the house. Something whispered to me that our happiness at Waning Moon was a thing of the past—an idyll that had ended.

I was upstairs when Fiametta and Leon returned. I had arranged the lovely tower room for Fiametta, hoping that she might find in it the same charm and beauty that had appealed to me. When I had told Leon of my choice, at the same time voicing a protest against his foolish prejudice, he had looked at me oddly.

"Yes, it should please her," he had said—"or at least keep her from feeling homesick. You will not find Fiametta showing what you call my prejudice. For the room is almost a duplicate of one in which she dwelt when we lived together in Florence so many years ago."

I hurried down to the library. They were there, Leon standing near the door, Fiametta by the huge table in the center of the room. I stopped at the threshold, looking at the black-draped, darkly veiled figure of the woman. My lover turned and caught at my hand, drawing me forward; his voice was full of a sort of forced gaiety and welcome.

"Little white dove—Marta—see, here is Fiametta! Fiametta, you will surely love my wife? Oh, if you love me, you must love Marta!"

The somber figure advanced toward me and threw back the floating folds of the veil. I drew a deep breath of amazement; Leon should have told me! For Fiametta was beautiful—radiantly beautiful!

She was tall, slender, graceful, with a lovely, heart-shaped face and the reddest lips that I had ever seen. A lovely mouth but a cruel one. But it was her eyes that fascinated me. Golden, gem-like eyes. I got the impression that in the night they would glow green, like a black cat's eyes.

"So this is—your little white dove," she said in a voice of languid music—"your Marta! Child, since you have married my Leon, I must welcome you in my own fashion. Will you kiss me, Marta?"

She leaned toward me and I caught a whiff of a perfume, exquisite, faint, yet with a disagreeable undertone that repulsed me. Her face was close—close—to mine! Then her great golden eyes blazed into mine and I could have cried aloud at the flaming hatred that suddenly dilated them. It was as if inadvertently I had opened the door into a glowing furnace. I half uttered an exclamation and stumbled back. But Leon intervened. He caught my arm, supporting me.

"Be careful, Marta. You will fall," he said. "Come now. Show Fiametta her room. She must be very tired. See—it is only an hour until dinner. Then we will all meet again—to talk, to get acquainted. But first, rest—"

Fiametta shrugged her slim shoulders. From the table she lifted a curious little black casket and prepared to follow me. But Leon stepped between her and the door. His gesture was one of authority.

"Leave the casket," he said bluntly. Fiametta turned on him, her eyes opening wide in surprise.

"Leave it!" she repeated, as if wonderingly. "But, Leon, I dare not. It is my jewel box."

"I will put it in the safe for you. Leave it here."

Leon's voice was harsh and commanding. Fiametta started to speak, then changed her mind and handed the box to him with a slight, indulgent smile playing about her beautiful lips.

"As you will," she said quietly, and followed me into the passage.

I tripped over something on the threshold—and it moved under my foot! I gave a startled half cry as it rose and faced me in the dim light of the hall. A little old woman—preposterously old! Hideous toothless, with rheumy eyes but half visible between the dried and shriveled folds of skin. She seemed more like a mummy than a human being.

As I stared amazed, Fiametta spoke to the creature in rapid, fluent Italian.

Then she turned to me. "I am sorry you were startled. She is my old nurse. I had intended to leave her at home, but she grieved so much that I brought her. Do not fear; she will not trouble you. She is with me constantly. She even sleeps beside my bed."

"I am glad you brought her if it will make either you or her more happy," I said slowly. And I led the way on up the stairs.

But I was not glad. I was afraid, with a childish, foolish fear of the poor, witchlike creature. A feeling illogical but too strong to yield to reason.

The hag-like creature seemed agile despite her apparent immense age and slipped along behind us soundlessly.

At the door of the tower chamber Fiametta drew a sudden breath. Her eyes, when she turned to me, were luminous.

"Marta." she said, "did Leonardo prepare this room for me?"

"No," I answered, "but he said it was almost a duplicate of one in which you once lived."

I thought it better to say nothing of Leon's dislike and fear of the room. Fiametta looked slowly about her. Her nostrils dilated and her eyes widened as she gazed.

"It is—ideal," she said softly.

She laid a hand caressingly on my shoulder. Then, as if the contact were too much for her self-control, her hand tightened relentlessly. Her face was again close to mine—again I gazed into the seething hatred and jealousy that inflamed the molten depths of those uncanny golden eyes.

Her voice was the hiss of an angry cat. "So—Marta—'my little white dove,' is it? And did you never hear that to a leopardess a dove is coveted prey? Leon—my Leon! And you! *You!* His 'little white dove'!"

The old woman plucked at Fiametta's skirt and burst into feverish, hurried speech. Fiametta hesitated, then slowly released me.

"I am sorry," she said, and her voice was again softly musical. "Oh, Marta, I am so sorry! But bear with me, child, bear with me! He was mine—mine alone—for so long a time! Leon says that in time I will come to love you as well as I love him. Will you not teach me how? Will you not love enough that I shall learn, Marta?"

Her voice was so coaxing, so luring, that I responded in spite of myself with a faint smile.

"I wish you wouldn't be jealous, please," I said, "for Leon still loves you, even though he loves me, too. Rest now, and at dinner we will all be together. That is an hour from now."

I WENT ON to my room after I left her. Somehow I did not care to face Leon just then. I was beginning to understand why he felt that he had taken a risk in marrying me. I was unhappy, stirred, apprehensive. But after a brief rest and a bath I felt more nearly mistress of myself and went on down to the library.

Leon was already dressed, standing by the window, gazing somberly out into the twilight. He turned as I entered—turned and regarded me soberly, questioningly. He held a paper in his hand.

"Marta," he said, "I have just gotten a message from Carver—and there is another meeting in the city. I must go—it is absolutely necessary! There is nothing else to do. I shall start immediately after dinner, and I will be back here by midnight. Tresquil sails a week earlier than was expected and our plans must be accommodated to his. If it were anything else—oh, I'm sorry, Marta! It's bad to leave you alone on this first evening with Fiametta, I know. But surely—if I am back by midnight—Marta, have you your little cross?"

I drew it out silently and held it before his eyes. He nodded and I dropped it back inside my dress again.

He would have said more, but Fiametta was at the door—her queer, oversweet perfume enveloped us—she was in the room with us. Her costume of filmy, transparent black emphasized the charm of her scarlet lips and brilliant, gem-like eyes. She moved with the lithe noiselessness of a cat.

There was little of ease in the meal to which we sat down. Difficult, manufactured talk. Long, awkward pauses. Leon was absent-minded and worried. His brow was dark and though he stirred himself to courteous conversation with Fiametta, both she and I could see that it was with effort. Outwardly Fiametta seemed not to mind. She remained gracious, pleasant. But inwardly, I am sure,

Leonardo's attitude must have hurt her, and she probably imputed it to me and my influence. Which was fuel added to the searing flame of her jealous hatred.

Leon was to start for town immediately at the close of the meal. The little roadster had been brought round and stood waiting on the drive before the house. Before he left, Leon took me in his arms and held me close, lover-fashion.

"Good-by, Marta," he said—"only for a few hours, though. I will be back with you by midnight. Kiss me!"

He gave Fiametta a grave salute on one cheek—a gesture probably taught him in babyhood by his sister. It was so little-boyish and stiff that I could have smiled. But Fiametta did not smile. Her eyes were dark and her face sober.

We both walked out onto the terrace with him. It was a dark, starry night.

"No moonlight for you to go," I said, "but plenty of light for your return. The moon will be up by then."

"It is the season of the waning moon," Fiametta said.

She said nothing more till Leon was gone; then, as we turned back to the lighted room, she added with a slow, mirthless smile:

"Tonight is the third night past the third night of the waning moon—the second third. Until the moon is full, it is for lovers. But after that it changes. You will see that I am right."

The first part of the evening passed in a commonplace enough fashion. Fiametta made every effort to be friendly. She was apparently trying hard to overcome her feeling of bitterness toward me and I tried my best to like her and make her like me. But we had no common meeting ground. Leon, whom we both loved and who should have been a bond between us, was the cause of our bitter antagonism. So the noble effort we made was more or less a failure.

WE SEPARATED EARLY, to go to our rooms, Fiametta saying that she was still very tired.

After I had watched her climbing the stairs toward the tower chamber, I went into my own room and sat down on the broad window-seat. The cushions were soft and I sank back with a little sigh of fatigue. Then I started violently. Something moved in the shadows beyond the ring of light about the dressing-table!

Startled, I sprang to my feet, my heart leaping wildly.

It was the old woman, Fiametta's nurse!

She was crouching over the waste-basket, which stood in one corner, and was apparently searching among the few trifles thrown there. She rose when she knew that I saw her, and made an incredibly swift dart for the door. Indeed, she was gone before I more than realized her presence—before I could glimpse what it was that she had taken from the basket. But I could see that she held something tightly clutched in one skinny, monkey-like talon.

It worried me a little as I sat there. But there was nothing in the basket of importance. Why should she search it? What could she want? Some torn sheets of notepaper, a powder box, a few strands of my hair, twisted into a little ring, after I had taken them from my brush. All equally worthless.

Soothed by the utter loveliness of the warm, star-jeweled night that rested over the sleeping summer lanes and gardens, I must have dozed at last, half reclining on the window-seat.

It was late when I woke, with a sudden strong feeling that I was being most urgently called. Still sleep-dazed, I sprang to my feet. Leon! Surely it was time that he had returned!

But I was still alone in the room. He had not come.

The little chamber was in shadow. The lamp on the dressing-table had been extinguished. Outside, the moon had risen. But not the cheerful golden lantern that lovers know. A great, leering, lop-sided moon that cast an ashen, bleached light over a world that seemed to be waiting in a sort of breathless pause. I shivered involuntarily.

Then suddenly, without any volition of my own, I took a step toward the door. It was as if I were walking in a dream. In a panic, I tried to stop. I could not will myself to stand still. I fought frantically for the control of my own body. But I still continued to advance deliberately toward the door. My forehead was bathed in icy perspiration. I laid my hand on the knob, turned it, flung open the door into the corridor. I tried to call out, to scream. No sound came from between my lips. It was ghastly. Terror leaped to life in my heart.

Slowly, draggingly, I walked down the hall. Pulling back, fighting desperately, I must yet have looked like a woman walking calmly, quietly along. I went toward the stairs that led up into the tower chamber.

Then, at the sight before me, my voice returned in a sudden shrill cry of fright. On the lowest step of the winding stair crouched a great, black, emerald-eyed leopardess! The weird, unholy moonlight revealed it plainly—showed the tiny ears laid flat and angry against the satiny head, the threatening, snarling muzzle, the savage lashing of the long tail against the ebony sides. A vicious snarling came from those fiercely lifted lips.

And yet I could not stop! The power drew me irresistibly toward it—toward certain death!

But in spite of its menace and rage the great beast retreated before my advance, flashing noiselessly up the stairs. On each step it would stop to whirl in swift fury, threatening; then it would leap soundlessly on velvet feet in front of me.

I followed, struggling hopelessly with the invisible bond which dragged me so surely upward. Up, up, until I at last stood within the portal of the tower chamber.

And then I saw that there had been changes. Fiametta, clad in a straight black garment through which her flesh showed rose and snow, was seated in the huge carved chair. Before her on a table was a tiny iron brazier, in which glowed a hot red heart of fire and from which rose a thin spiral of blue smoke. On the floor, enclosing the chair and the table, a great triangle had been inscribed in broad, white lines. Touching it at one point was another and larger triangle. It was the old figure used by all the sorcerers down through the ages to protect themselves from those dark powers which they summoned—though I did not know that at the time. And surrounding these two triangles was still another mark, outlining an enormous pentagon.

The room was lighted only by the glow of the brazier and the pale moonlight that fell dimly through the colored skylight. But it was sufficient to show these things—and the old woman, huddled on the floor beside Fiametta's chair—and the black leopardess, crouched low just outside the pentagon, green eyes luminous in the dusk!

Fiametta looked at me and smiled—a smile that changed her face into a mask of dark, malevolent triumph.

"So!" she said softly, tauntingly. "Leon has not yet returned to protect his little white dove. No, there is no one here! No one but Fiametta! Even though now she needs him as she never has before, he has not come. To Fiametta he leaves the 'little white dove'!"

She threw back her head and laughed, a hateful, screaming sound that tore at my heart. I shook with an uncontrollable tremor at its sound. Though I did not yet understand fully, already I knew enough to be certain of my doom—to see, all too late, the reason for Leon's doubt and mental agony.

"It is not that he does not love you, little dove," she mocked, "though soon—very soon—there will be only Fiametta for him to love again. Fool! To think that I would give him up! But tonight he is delayed. In spite of all his caution, all his goodness, he is not so clever, my Leonardo. He did not think—he did not know—this is the third night after the third night of the waning moon! Else he would not have left you alone for a second. So easy it was for me to do! So easy! Under such a moon and on such a night I may do my will unhindered!"

She paused to laugh again and the shrill cackling laugh of the old crone by her side broke and died with hers. She drew toward her an object on the table—the ebony box. From it she lifted a miniature image of the leopard at her feet and set it beside the brazier. The great animal on the outer rim of the pentagon rose and snarled menacingly, its eyes a blazing green. It rose and prowled swiftly up and down the chalked line, as at the bars of a cage. But it reached no clutching paw over that dead-line, for all its thwarted fury.

"So much neither you nor Leon could know or dream," she went on, her voice soft and singing, "though Leon—I think sometimes he suspects. There was that boy at Cavalli—and the sister. Leon, he wondered at the time what became of them! So suddenly they went! But no—he does not know! Tonight, 'little white dove,' you suffer for the times you have made me suffer. Tonight you pay a long score—a long score of agony and tearing pain and loss. No, never shall anyone take from me my more-than-life—my Leon. Did I not say to you—the dove is the prey of the leopardess? Did I not tell you?"

And again she laughed. She stooped and scooped from the casket a handful of some powdery stuff and threw it on the fire of the brazier. It leaped upward, flaming high, filling the room with a moving green light, scarlet-shot. I smelled the odor of the same perfume that Fiametta had worn, increased a thousandfold, overpowering in its deathly, cloying sweetness. The black leopardess seemed incited to frenzy by the action. It raced and turned ceaselessly, frantically, along the chalked line, and its snarl rose to a screaming fury. Fiametta, glancing at its sinister, flashing litheness, laughed softly. She looked across at me.

"See!" And she picked up something from the table. "See—this is your hair! The old nurse—oh, she helps her Fiametta! Hair—strands thrown carelessly away. Did you not know, fool, that each single hair would give me power over you! Power to slay—to annihilate you—consume you utterly, body and soul! Look, now! Watch, while you yet may."

She held one hair to the blaze. Instantly, released from its invisible leash, the great leopardess swerved from the line along which it ran and sprang in a great leap toward me. I saw its open, slavering jaws; its green eyes blazed down into mine.

I screamed, a feeble, futile sound.

But in mid-air the beast whirled and came down heavily in a jarring fall upon the floor. It sprang up, maddened, to dash insanely toward the edge of the great pentagon beyond whose bounds it might not pass. Fiametta shrieked aloud with shrill laughter.

Half fainting with terror, my heart pounding furiously, I caught at the back of the great chair.

Then Fiametta screamed her message above the snarling clamor of the great beast.

"Not yet, not yet," she cried. "Just death—that is too easy! First, we torture you—then you die. That is best, yes! See, then!"

Again she threw a hair into the green blaze. Again the black leopardess leaped, only to fall back thwarted. But this time the great claws raked me lightly in passing. Blood sprang out on my shoulder—trickled warmly down my arm—stained my sleeve with a dark blot.

The old hag joined her cracked cackle of mirth to Fiametta's laugh. Again and again the leopardess sprang—never quite close enough to attain its desire.

But at last Fiametta seemed to tire of even this royal sport.

"This time," she screamed, "this time—we shall end the 'little white dove.' This leap—it shall be the last! Think now of Leon, white dove, for never again—never again on this earth—or any other—will you meet—"

She did not finish. She picked up the little ring of hair and dropped it into the blaze. The light flared high with an explosive sound. The leopardess leaped in a great arc toward me as though released from its leash, and as it sprang—I remembered the little cross. I jerked it forth, held it up.

"Leon—Leon," I wailed, my voice a despairing prayer.

But before the little cross the black beast swerved aside—fell to the floor—lay there, groveling, snarling. Fiametta sprang up, enraged, uncomprehending.

And as she rose, I heard feet—frantic fear-sped feet—racing up the twisting stair!

"Leon, Leon!" I cried again.

And he answered me!

"I am coming—I am coming—" And then he stood beside me in the room! His clothes were torn and his breath came in the gasps of a spent runner—but out of his gray face his eyes glowed, courageous, unafraid. He spoke, and through his catching breath his voice was a frenzy of rage and fury.

"Fiametta—for God's sake—are you mad—insane—to do murder—to kill—"

He was holding me close in the curve of one steel-muscled arm, he faced his sister like a lion at bay, his face dark with horror, loathing—yes, with hate. He was quivering with rage and excitement.

Fiametta's eyes, full of wild unbelief, were fixed on him. Her face was set in lines of incredulity and amazement. Then, as she comprehended that he was really there in the room—as his presence became real to her and she sensed his white-hot hate and horror—it changed. I saw the despairing expression of one who has staked his all on a turn of the wheel—and lost. Her words were a wail.

"Leon—Leon—I love you! I could not bear to give you up! Mine—mine—you are mine! Leon—I will keep you always!"

Across the blazing brazier, in the weird light of the tower chamber, the two faced each other, forgetful of all else. Two stripped souls, looking at each other, longing, yet separated by the fires of hell itself. He spoke slowly, with awful scorn.

"Keep me—by destroying the one most precious to me, the woman I love! Oh, yes I have known—maybe for years—that you still practiced the black art—that you consorted with unclean things! But—you were my sister! I never dreamed—I could not know—that you were a fiend! A murderess! But never again—never again—do you—"

He sprang forward, carrying me with him—inside that whitely outlined pentagon! Fiametta retreated before him—backed against the table—her eyes fixed on his face.

Swifter than thought, he snatched the black carved casket. He dashed it twice against the table edge, shattering it into fragments, scattering the contents over all the room!

In that instant it was as if a great gale was loosed in the tower chamber. A rising fury of sound, a yelling clamor—the rush of sinister, sweeping wings—of lashing, angered winds, unleashed and racing down from the outer darknesses of space! Outside the line of the pentagon it raged and rose, to beat in deafening, insane waves of sound. And the green, scarlet-shot air was filled with vaguely seen shapes, all swirling in furious motion. Scaly wings, dark, enormous, bat-like. Clawing talons—diabolic, staring eyes—faces, figures, too hideous to record. All caught in that mad, surging hurricane of sound and motion that rocked the tower chamber!

An odor, indescribably vile, as though from the opening door of a long-sealed charnel-house, reeked through the room. My mind reeled with shock and terror but I was unable to lose consciousness in that screaming uproar—that unclean pandemonium of sound.

I heard Fiametta shriek, "Leon—Leon—what have you done—"

I saw the toothless crone spring erect, gesturing violently—saw that she was swaying, falling—falling across the line—outside the protecting mark of the pentagon! She was *gone*—gone before she was halfway to the floor—consumed utterly—sucked up to destruction by that maelstrom that swept in such mad circling around us. *Gone!*

And the uproar rose another tone in the screaming scale of its anger.

Now no longer did the line of the pentagon absolutely restrain them. Closer and closer they pressed; second by second they became more daring. Ever the circle lessened. From the maze, snatching skeleton hands, gnashing fangs, vicious claws reached out, striking at us ever more boldly.

The fetid air stunk of decay. I lay in shuddering collapse against Leon's shoulder. Fiametta crouched back against the table, gazing with anguished, terror-stretched eyes into the midst of the madhouse chaos of elementals.

I saw a hand—long, ashen-white—grab at her shoulder. And then—the leopardess! Right from the center of the obscurity she made her lightning-like leap, across Leon and myself!

Fiametta! The demon, unleashed at last, had turned on its mistress!

They crashed to the ground together, and even above that hellish clamor I caught her desperate scream of agony and despair. Shrinking, sickened, I hid my eyes.

But Leon dragged the little cross from about my neck and held it aloft. He shouted words that I could not hear in the hideous din that surrounded us. Holding the tiny symbol of love and sacrifice above us, he lifted me with one arm and plunged outside the pentagon into the commotion.

The floor of the tower chamber was covered with an obscene slime and he slipped and almost fell. The hellish pack, balked of its victims, rose to even wilder clamor. But Leon, shouting his invocation, bore me safely, strongly. I felt the fanning of mighty wings, but we were not touched.

Half stifled by the stench, dazed, semiconscious but safe, Leon carried me across the tower chamber and on down the stairs. The black-paneled door slammed shut behind us. Swiftly he raced along the hall, down the broad front stairs and out through the open door—out into the midst of peace and silence and sleeping, fragrant flowers.

In the little rose arbor at the end of the garden he dropped onto a stone seat and held me close, cradled in his arms. Silence! Sweet, pure air! A hushed, dew-drenched midsummer night!

Incredible that such things should be, after the mad hell of the tower chamber. Unbelievable that we should live! A tiny fountain in the center of the arbor splashed and fell in its marble bowl with a soft, prattling music. A katydid shrilled at the grass-roots. A lacework of moon-shadows lay on the floor of the little court.

Leon drew a long, quivering sigh. We rested speechless until the first exhaustion was past. Then Leon stirred. He lifted the little cross to his lips. He looked down into my face.

"I did not know—I did not know! Little white dove, can you ever forgive me? I so nearly failed you—so nearly lost you! If through all my life I love—I serve—can you forgive?"

We left Waning Moon that night. And I have never seen it since. But Leon told me later that the tower chamber was a scene of utter destruction and that the mutilated, torn bodies of Fiametta and the old nurse were found by searchers, half-buried in the slime and wreckage.

I never knew what steps Leon took to secure secrecy in the affair. But I know the consul of his country, after a long conference with Leon, bent all his efforts toward aiding him. And only a very few people in this world today know anything of that night of horror and death at Waning Moon.

Once, when I gathered courage to ask, Leon told me of the boyhood chum and his sister—the boy whom he loved so dearly, and who, with his sister, had disappeared so completely and so mysteriously. After all these years of doubt their fate was at last known. I wept at the pity of the little story—the tragedy of the two whose only offense was that they had loved Leon too dearly and that he had returned their love.

1932

TIGER
Bassett Morgan

Sitting on the porch of his bungalow, Harden watched the copper-colored moon creep stealthily from the black waters of the Malacca and tried to fight down the feeling that he would have done better to sell his plantation than pit his courage and wits against the mysterious forces that baffle a white man in the Sumatra highlands. That morning his native workers had deserted the fields of young rubber trees and sugar cane, leaving only a few Chinese coolies and his three house-boys who explained that an alarm of tiger had frightened the natives.

From the river village the beating of drums came to Harden, incessant and annoying as the throb of pain. Djac, his number-one boy, came to the porch and asked for an advance of wages to buy jimats, which are love-charms, or talismans against evil. Harden shook his head, which was a mistake.

"You've got one wife," he said. "Love-charms are a silly superstition. Is your old wife willing for you to marry again?"

Djac's manner was cringing, but his black eyes glittered. He explained that he wanted to buy a dancing girl from the temple and her price would take all his wages. Undoubtedly his old wife was jealous, for she belonged to a headhunting tribe of Dyaks and she had made gifts and said prayers in the temple to cure Djac of his desire for the girl. But her youth and comeliness were gone, and the girl was beautiful. Of a truth, Djac needed jimats.

Harden was generous with wages, but he was new to Sumatra and had all a white man's scorn of superstition. He left Djac in a sullen mood with his refusal, and went for a stroll down the path to the road between a double wall of flame-trees and hibiscus in heavy bloom. The shadows on the moon's face were not unlike the eyes and muzzle of a tawny tiger-head, and he was glad when the disk sailed high and changed to silver.

COMING BACK TO the porch he neglected to catch the door. Pajama-clad, his toes thrust in grass sandals, he lighted a cigar and lay back in his chair conscious of the maddening buzz and drone of insects beating against the copper-wire porch screens. Then something cold and horrible touched his bare foot. At the same moment came Djac's whisper, soft as the flower-scented wind:

"Don't move, Tuan."

Paralyzed by fear, Harden held his body rigid while a seemingly endless length of cobra slid over his instep toward the door. There came the thud of a weapon, a lashing and grating disturbance on the matting and Djac's yelp of triumph. Sitting on his own feet in the chair Harden saw Djac behead the cobra with a kriss and toss its still writhing body into the jungle grass beyond the flower hedge. A minute later he thrust a glass of brandy into Harden's hand. His whispered warning had saved Harden's life.

"Thanks, Djac," he said. "You get the money for jimats."

"To-morrow, I will kill the cobra's mate," said Djac. "There is a cousin of my old wife who is a priest at the temple, and he has great power," he added, sighing like a man with great odds against him. "But the girl is like the flower of the Tjindanwan-matahara, Tuan."

"But what took you, a Mohammedan, to this native temple to see the girl?" asked Harden.

"I did not go," protested Djac. "She danced out there in the star light, Tuan, and charmed me so that my liver is fire for her. It was your own good fortune to be sleeping, or who knows. . . ."

Harden snorted his disdain of native women and charms, yet he wondered about the affair, whether it had anything to do with the desertion of his field workers. Cromley who wanted to buy his plantation had warned him to step warily on native mysteries.

NEXT MORNING DJAC built a crude stage on stilts above the jungle grass, and under a sheltering palm thatch he sat, piping tunes on a bamboo whistle. Harden, fuming inwardly over his neglected trees and cane, returned to the bungalow and writhed at the irritating monotony of Djac's weird tunes.

Yet the following morning a seven-foot length of cobra with its head smashed to a pulp lay near the house. Harden was generous in rewarding Djac, and the small brown man departed to visit his old wife and go about the business of bringing his girl bride to the hut near the river. Sonar, the second boy fingered a jimat hanging about his neck as he watched Djac depart.

"Evil will come," he assured Harden earnestly. "The priests can do anything. And My Lord prowled in the night near this house, though he never came before." Harden remembered that he had been warned never to speak of a tiger by its name, but to refer to it as "My Lord," lest the beast hear and take vengeance for the disrespect. He fought a growing sense of evil until Djac returned that night with bad news.

His old wife had disappeared. There was the trail of crushed jungle grass where My Lord had crouched to drink his fill of blood, then dragged its prey to a hidden lair. They also found the blood-stained sarong of his old wife.

In spite of the tropic heat, Harden shivered. The cobras had been bad enough. A man-eating tiger was far more dangerous.

"Then we had better go tiger-hunting," he said emphatically.

SHRIEKS OF PROTEST came from the three house-boys who gathered to hear Djac's story, and they now chattered excitedly in native lingo and broken English. Harden listened and began to understand that this particular tiger must not be killed. Having devoured Djac's wife it had become a family tomb, subject to veneration, worship and dedicatory gifts. If Djac failed to observe the reverence due this receptacle of his wife's mortal remains, he would be haunted in this life and damned in the next incarnation. He groveled in fear as he talked, bumping his head on the matting, moaning that his old wife had laid a terrible curse on him.

But was he to blame that the girl, whose name was Senyap, had danced for him in the starlight until he could not live without her? True, he had given her his old wife's bracelets, at which his wife wept and raged. But only a woman possessed of a devil would deliberately feed herself to a tiger because of jealousy. He would have to kow-tow all his life to this feline tomb to gain forgiveness of the lady in the tiger who took this means of suicide and vengeance.

Everyone knew it is the worst of evils for a relative to commit suicide, for the spirit of the departed haunts the place where his or her body lies. My Lord, the tiger, was not only sacred as a tomb, but he was ghost-haunted until vengeance was accomplished.

"This tiger—" began Harden, bringing howls of anguish from the three natives at the direct mention of the beast. He cursed and gave in to their fears. "My Lord," he began again, disgusted with his own helplessness, "has tasted human flesh and will be dangerous. If he is not killed he must be captured. Djac, gather your relatives and trap the beast. Otherwise I will shoot My Lord."

From that instant Harden felt a queer sense of loss, as if he had capitulated and sold his soul to some demon. The never-ending throb of tom-toms in the village was carried on a gust of wind, rippling in his flesh like the purring of a great cat. Now again he felt that he ought to dispose of his plantation.

DJAC DEPARTED TO gather his people and make a tiger-trap on the river trail where there had been pad-marks in the soft ooze. All signs pointed to an old beast. Young tigers are seldom man-eaters. Also, it was the mating season when tigers in their prime are not flesh-greedy. Harden gave his servants a brief holiday for the hunt and went himself to the river where he saw the long stockade of bamboo lashed together, ending in a corral with a dead-fall gate weighted by a teak log.

In a natural cave in the hillside, Djac was building a cage-front of formidable bars. He beaded it with clean grass, decorated it with flowers and placed bowls of food as votive offerings. The native drums pounded incessantly. Harden went from the cave to where a second stout cage stood on a carabao cart near the corral.

Beyond the trap-gate a carabao calf was tethered as bait, bawling piteously, and adding to Harden's dislike of the whole business. The natives were feasting and working magic, and his fields were still deserted, except for the faithful Chinese

In his house that night Harden tried to forget the tiger and avoided the sight of the yellow moon peering above the darkly brooding sea, but he could not shut out the purring throb of drums which got under his skin and behind his eyes, rippling in his flesh.

NEXT MORNING WHEN Djac returned to report no luck in tiger-trapping Harden lost patience. It was lonely hill country, with natives unfriendly to white men and under the domination of temple priests and their tricky superstitions. But he had the courage to tell Djac sternly that unless the tiger was trapped that night he would go gunning for it, and Djac shuddered in fear at the threat.

"My Lord now sees with the eyes of my old wife who was a woman of wisdom, Tuan. She will not be lured by the carabao calf. But there is one thing she desires above all else, and that she must have."

There was a resignation in the man's voice which alarmed Harden. Unable to shake off the feeling of impending trouble he went to the river in the evening and saw a dangerously excited group of natives near the hut where Djac had brought his bride-to-be.

Above the jabbering and clamor rose the high shrill scream of a woman, and Harden stalked to the hut and demanded an explanation of that cry of fear. He learned that, despairing of taking the tiger by other means, Djac had hoisted the girl, who was the cause of all the trouble, high in a nearby tree to attract the tiger.

Harden's gorge rose at the idea of baiting the tiger-trap with a woman. He marched through the crowd of natives, a commanding figure in his fresh white ducks and pith helmet, and talked to Djac as he never before talked to a native. His commands were met with sullen defiance from Djac and the other natives. Excitement exploded into rage and Harden found himself the vortex of an angry mob gesticulating with their wicked-looking waved krisses.

The Dyak relatives of the dead woman were in a nasty rage, and Harden knew his two revolvers could not hold that mob in check even if he wanted to attempt a shot that would be a signal for slaughter.

Controlling his voice and rising alarm, he argued and commanded in vain, then resorted to the only way he could think of to protect the woman in the tree from a possible attack of the tiger. He yelled that he would share her night vigil, and, after a lengthy argument with Djac as interpreter, the crowd agreed. But they made it very plain that if Harden killed the beast its spirit would have company in death.

Although the death of the old wife was one of many such tragedies in a land infested with tigers, crocodiles, orang-outangs and cobras, the affair struck Harden as being out of all proportion to its significance. Alone in the village of semi-naked brown men, Harden saw blood-lust in their eyes, heard murderous threats in their jabbering, and, like flame in dry grass, the excitement swirled until it required courage of a ruddy order to face them and demand to be bodyguard for the young girl in the tree.

WHEN THE CHATTERING died to mutterings Harden walked through the village until he came to the tree. Already the bamboo stockade was in shadow, and the carabao calf in the corral wailed with hunger and fear. Once up the tree Harden found the least uncomfortable perch near a small figure swathed in white and lashed to a seat in a limb crotch. She sobbed pitifully and strained at her bonds. His blood boiled with the indignity of making a marriage chattel of the girl and using her as tiger bait. Yet, at sight of the menacing horde below, staring up and chattering, their betel-stained mouths suggestive of cannibal feasts, Harden could only control his rage and wait.

They vanished, and night fell with tropic swiftness. The insect noise grew louder and the calf bawled monotonously. Harden wondered if a tiger that ignored carabao calf was now hungry enough to be tempted by the scent of a human being. The woman near him had ceased sobbing. He caught the gleam of starlight on her metal anklets and bracelets and heard the tinkle of bangles. Then she spoke:

"Tuan, you will kill the ghost-tiger," she said, pleadingly.

In his halting Malay, Harden explained that he had given his word not to shoot the tiger, but once it was trapped she need not fear it again.

"Kill it, Tuan," she begged, "or it will live to haunt you."

It would not haunt him, he protested, because he did not believe in ghost-tigers. He talked for some time, quietly persuading her that the worst to be feared was an attack by the beast. Yet his reasoning did not shake off his own uncanny chill, or the tensity that puckered his flesh as he awaited what the night might bring.

IN THE TREE the darkness was profound, but just as the moon-rim rose above the far-away black sea, the calf ceased bawling and the insect clamor died away. There was a quiet rustling as little monkeys scampered off. Then came deep, thick silence in which Harden felt something like the purring of muted drums that came nearer, set time to his rapid pulse, tingled on his skin. He stared below with his scalp prickling as if some indefinable presence were approaching.

The revolver in his hand came to full cock! Then, as if the tiger had heard the metallic click, it streaked into the open and turned its green, shining eyes towards the tree. He saw the black muzzle and white fangs, the venerable look of a white beard and magnificent stripes on the amber hide. Its tail lashed the grass with a silky hiss, and there came the frightened whimper of the calf.

The girl's hands clutched at him, and, sharing her terror, Harden slipped an arm about her as the beast prowled below, gliding about the tree and trap, evidently confused by two different scents of prey. Harden felt cold sweat trickling inside his shirt until the tiger moved away, sniffed about the trap-mouth, then shot, like a streak of gold, in a splendid leap on the whimpering calf. There was a shrill bleat, the crash of a teak log, the vicious snarling of the tiger. The bamboo creaked at its angry lunges against the walls, but the natives came running from cover and bowled their joy around the trap.

Cutting the girl's lashings, Harden lowered her to the ground and, as he followed, she was running toward the river hut.

DRUNK WITH TRIUMPH and native liquor Djac lorded it among his fellows, but Harden did not wait to see them prod the tiger into the cage on the carabao cart backed to the trap-gate. Returning to his house he slept through the noisy celebration at the river which continued through the next day. By evening he felt that enough time had been wasted on Djac's affairs, and seeing the torches of the river town flaring through night darkness he strapped on his guns and strolled down to interview Djac.

The early night was dark and the light of a solitary torch against the hill took him to the cave. On the clean straw, behind the cage bars of its den, he saw a splendid tiger. Its golden eyes followed every moment of Djac who squatted on his heels, chattering prayers and incantations, touching his head to earth at intervals, worshipping his family tomb. Fresh flowers draped the cage bars. Inside were fresh offerings of meat and rice. And after watching at a distance Djac's fervent petitions, Harden told the man it was time to get back to his work.

But Djac came to him with a rambling tale of more trouble. The dancing girl he had bought refused to worship at the tiger shrine and they could not begin the wedding until she showed proper veneration for his old wife's tomb, especially since her spirit dwelt in such a terrible home as this body of My Lord. He could not mate with a woman who refused to placate the "berhauntu." Instead of showing proper grief, the girl danced for joy. She outraged Djac beyond all reason. He could not beat into submission a woman not yet his wife. Perhaps the Tuan would talk to her, for she was loud in her praise of his master who had been with her in the tree.

"Bring her to the house," said Harden. "I'll try to talk sense to her. And you get back to work. Anything, for peace!"

HARDEN RETURNED TO his house with Djac and the girl. He finished dinner, after which Djac went to say more prayers to the tiger and left him alone with the woman. She had been sitting motionless in her white wrappings, with bowed head, until Harden spoke. Then she rose, dropped her white garment and stood like a bird of gorgeous plumage in the glow of lamp-light. Her jacket and trousers were kingfisher green. There were scarlet pompons on her red slippers. The teeth shone white between lips like a bitten pomegranate. Jeweled butterflies quivered in hair of dusky silk, slightly curly, and, by the rose-tinted amber of her skin Harden knew she was hybrid. Coquetry and allure shone in her eyes. She swayed on her feet like a flower in the wind.

"Why do you refuse to obey Djac?" he began, sternly.

Dimples stirred the warm gold of her cheeks.

"I am not yet a wife," she said.

"But a woman should obey her man," he protested.

"How should you know who have no woman in your house?" she asked with pretty impertinence.

Harden laughed. Instantly her feet twinkled nearer. She knelt with her pretty head on one side like a pert bird, the butterfly ornaments twittering, her young breasts straining the silk of her jacket. Harden tried to scowl, but he was thinking how wasted this child was on Djac.

As if she knew his thoughts she swayed forward touching her forehead to his foot. Harden caught and lifted her to her feet, but she suddenly slipped to his knee and curled like a gorgeous doll in his arm, red lips parted expectantly, her eyes like pools of dark fire, her whole body an invitation.

For a moment he allowed the girl to clutch at the woman-hunger of loneliness in the Sumatra hills, then his face grew stern. She read his face like print and slipped from his arms. Then, crooning a wordless, tuneless song, she danced.

IT WAS AS IF humming birds were released to quiver like living jewels, as if fountains played brightly and butterflies flashed as bits of wind-blown silk. Her feet slipped from the sandals and with her arms she wove a story of passionate appeal. Never had he seen such fire veiled in sensuous gestures. His stern scowl melted, and through lowered eyelids he watched until she sank on the matting at his feet.

"My dancing pleases the Tuan?" she entreated.

"It is very pretty, Senyap," he admitted cautiously, then reached for a cigarette. Like a flash she caught the match from his fingers, struck a light and held the flame in her cupped hands. He caught the fragrance of her perfumed body, saw the opal moons on her fingernails.

When he lay back inhaling smoke, she again danced, circling about the white garment which lay in a heap of silk gauze on the floor.

Suddenly she snatched it up, and, from a small basket he had not noticed before, two cobras glided, coiling their lengths on the matting. They lifted their swaying heads as she danced between them, twinkling, glittering as she sang, in so perilous a dance that Harden sat gripped by admiration and fear, a clutch that held him rigid as Senyap spun faster in the maddening whirl of the terrible death dance of the temple. Harden had heard of it. He heard of dread rites in which the dancing girls file out slowly leaving one alone as the bride of the awful hamadryad god that lay hidden in a golden urn above the altars.

WATCHING THE DANCE, fascinated by the swaying, hypnotic glitter of the cobras, Harden felt as if the walls of his house receded and left him motionless, trapped in a vast gloom of which the lamp was the altar fire, and this girl a priestess of evil rites that chained his will and lured his senses. With hair rising on his scalp and sweat starting on his palms, he found himself powerless to move or speak as she bent slowly backwards until the flat of her hands and feet rested on the floor and made of her body a living arch of flesh.

The silk jacket fell open. Her breasts were smoothly molded and gold-tipped with coral. And, as if trained to that lure, the cobras swung aloft and glided over her motionless, rigid body that shone like pale metal, then disappeared into the basket.

Still Harden stared, leaning forward in his chair, waiting, waiting, hearing the slow thud of his own heart, seeing the girl sway upright and begin a deliberate padding dance with her feet, keeping time to the pulse of his veins. Her pale arms writhed like white snakes, she moved with the grace of a cat, holding his gaze until he could have screeched at her. Yet no sound came from his parted lips, nor could he move foot or finger. He knew he was caught in a hypnosis, yet he was conscious of some dread thing to come and his inability to avert it. He knew he should have crashed a fist at this glittering creature trained by temple priests.

He was conscious, then, of the menace that had by devious ways sought contact with his life. Serpent lure and tiger ferocity breathed about her, and there came from her parted lips the strange purring sound of a tiger.

The sudden stab of memory cracked a little of that spell she cast. She leaped, but his hands met her as her white teeth grazed the skin of his throat. He caught her wrists as she screamed an inhuman, feline cry that started a rustling in the basket on the floor. Free of the trance gripping his will, Harden snatched at his revolver as he held the girl in one arm. Two shots rang out, and two cobras, with smashed heads, twisted in death frenzy on the matting. Then, as if a spell had been broken for her also, Senyap lay limp on his arm. He swung her to his shoulder and turned to the door, only to face Djac who had returned in time to see Harden catch her in his arms and start toward his bedroom.

FOR A MOMENT Djac stared, then turned on his heel and ran. Harden touched his fingers to his throat where her teeth had struck and felt them sticky with a few drops of blood. He dropped the girl and ran for permanganate, daubing the tiny wounds thickly.

Sonar heaved the reptiles from the porch and began to scrub the blood from the matting as Harden returned. The girl crouched in a corner of the couch, sobbing.

"Tuan, Tuan. You saved us both from the curse of My Lord," she said, and Harden stared. She seemed so pretty, so soft and helpless now, that he could not believe her teeth had drawn blood in that savage lunge at his throat. His mind was chaos as he went near the couch and she clung to him, quivering in perfumed warmth, her arms about his neck. Then he felt her body stiffen, and at the window he saw the face of Djac and his flattened brown nose against the wire gauze. The face vanished as Harden called him.

"Tuan, keep me here in your house. If you send me away, I die. Djac will think I am your woman."

"You had better be taken to the temple where you belong," said Harden.

"Tuan, Tuan, they will make me the bride of the serpent god! I have disobeyed."

"Disobeyed what?" he demanded, catching her wrists, forcing her arms from his neck, pressing her back on the couch cushions.

"Tuan, Tuan," she sobbed in hysterical fear. "It was commanded, and I was forced to obey. I have failed, and I shall be given to the hamadryad god of the temple."

Sonar had darted away with his task only half done, as if he feared to breathe air of this small temptress. Harden had not the heart to turn her into the night alone with Djac nursing the belief that she had given her charms to his master, so he carried her to the guest room and closed the door.

All that night he expected trouble, nor could he sleep for thinking of the strange hypnosis of that dance of death and the tigerlike leap of the self-hypnotized dancing girl who had been sent from the temple, trained in some wickedness that concerned himself. The dark and devious ways of priestcraft were inscrutable to a white man. Some mystery pressed close, but he assured himself he need only keep his wits and will working to shake off the clutch of evil that undermined a white man's morale.

MORNING DAWNED. The silver and pink mists of the valley disappeared, and the hot sun shot out of the distant sea. There was an ominous peace over the house, and Sonar's disapproval was tangible when he reported that Djac had not returned. In high dudgeon Harden started for the village to tell Djac to take his bride away from the bungalow and get down to work, or he would get another boy. But he did not find Djac, and the natives whom he tried to question ran from him, muttering incantations.

Thinking Djac was feeding the tiger, Harden went to its rock den and peered inside. For a moment he saw nothing. Then, as his eyes became accustomed to tree-shadowed gloom after the sun-glare, his breath caught. The grass was stained with evidences of a gory meal. The cage door was open and the tiger was gone!

Striking a match Harden held it until the flame nipped his fingers. He was not mistaken. The horrid remains of a man lying on the grass was Djac!

An exceedingly frightened white man ran through the hot sun to his own house and dropped in a porch chair, spent with heat and fear. Senyap was among the cushions of his day-couch, eating fruit, and the sight of her made him furious. She was the cause of this tragedy, the death of Djac's wife and Djac. She had dared bring her cobras and temple tricks to his house for some fell purpose. Yet he dared not send her away now to the cruel vengeance of Djac's relatives, and it was worse than folly to keep her there. She had half confessed that she was sent from the temple for no good. She enticed Djac by dancing for him in the starlight and encompassed his death. When Harden told her about it, she preserved a callous calm, then said childishly and simply:

"He was only a servant, Tuan. I had to come to you."

"Why did you have to come to me?" he demanded. "Who sent you?"

"The god, Tuan. But I have failed his command. I will be an outcast, except to become the bride of the god."

HARDEN GREW COLD inside. Dimly he saw the wickedness of priest-craft dispatching this pretty messenger of death to charm him with her dance until he should have been helpless in her hands. Then the cobras! Well, he had robbed her of the cobras, and now he dared not send her away. He himself felt insecure and was afraid to leave the house. He could not eat, and at night he sat on the porch until the moon rose.

Then the girl who had sat all afternoon on the couch with her slender hands in her lap, motionless as a small Buddha, glided to the porch and curled at his feet on the mat regarding him with unwinking dark eyes. Harden dozed. He was wakened by the faint tinkling of her bangles and whisper of her voice. Small brown fingers touched his wrist. One hand pointed to the dark jungle grass, and, as Harden turned his head, he saw two twin green flames— the eyes of a beast staring at him. Tiger!

Those eyes moved up and down, across and back. The girl threw herself between his knees, clutching at his arms. Breaking her grasp, he went into the house for his gun. He was firmly resolved to kill the tiger menace once and for all time. But when he came to the porch the tiger was gone.

He slept badly, troubled by fearful dreams. As he shaved in the morning a gray-faced Sonar came with news that the ghost-tiger had killed a woman and her two children in a hut along the river, and terror stalked the land. Harden screwed his courage to visit the village to gather natives for a tiger hunt, but they not only refused to listen, they threatened him with death if he harmed the ghost-tiger which was now the tomb of both Djac and his wife. His life was in double jeopardy. Djac had seen the girl in his arms, and laid on his house the curse of suicide: his ghost would take vengeance on Harden.

With a naked rabble at his heels he went to the river hut where the sleeping victims had been struck down with merciful swiftness. Preparations for a funeral were in progress, always a precarious time, because of the consumption of liquor which inflamed the natives to murderous mood and the honor of winning a reward after death by slaying an unbeliever like Harden.

THAT NIGHT DRUMS made the darkness hideous. Senyap sat at his feet on the porch, her eyes turned to the jungle. Her sudden cry whipped him to his feet and again he saw the twin green flames of tiger eyes!

Snatching the gun beside his chair he fired twice, aiming between those glowing orbs. But they only moved nearer! Both shots had gone wild. Harden stared at the round clean bullet holes in the wire gauze where mosquitoes streamed inside. A second cry from Senyap turned his head. The tiger was on its hind legs, swaying to and fro, taller than a man, swaying and stepping in a cumbersome and uncouth dance. Harden was horrified as he stared at the grotesque spectacle.

"Tuan, Tuan, the Death Dance!" moaned Senyap, hiding her face.

His skin prickled as he took a second aim and fired, then cursed the gun. The tiger dance went on until it grew into a slow, undulating cat walk. Harden was breathless as he watched the tiger's grinning muzzle, his gleaming fangs, his lolling tongue. Senyap writhed in a frenzy of fear on the floor.

"Djac and his old wife have come for me, Tuan," moaned Senyap.

He carried her into the house, shut and locked the door, lighted lamps and turned on the gramophone, then called for whiskey. All night the spectral beast haunted him. At dawn he told Sonar to reenforce the windows with wooden bars. The house was now a cage with the humans trapped within it, while the beast stalked at large outside. Harden laughed, but his laughter sounded queer. He drank heavily, and the third boy wound the gramophone all day. He commanded Senyap to dance—anything to drive out the memory of the golden beast.

To satisfy his reckless mood the girl became, in turns, bird and butterfly, and the room glittered and twinkled with her radiance. Drinking many pegs of brandy, Harden forgot the racial barrier between them. He caught her from her dance to his arms and lowered his head until their lips met.

A WILD SCREECH of beast rage jerked him from that kiss. With the girl clinging to him, he turned to the window and saw the swishing tail and green eyes of the tiger. He tore the small fingers from his arms, feeling as merciless and brutal as the tiger and told Sonar to lock the girl in the bedroom. Her screams maddened him, and the night was one of terror.

In the darkness he heard the tiger snarling and purring at his windows. At times he heard it scraping the wire grating with its paws, and he smelled the fetid breath of the big cat. Gun in hand, he prowled all night shooting at beast eyes from every window. Drink and fear shook his hands, yet he felt cold sober except for those hot spurts of terror at the base of his brain. The shots sped harmlessly into the darkness. Finally he dropped into a chair with the gun across his knees and fell into a drunken sleep from which he wakened, unrefreshed, to the hot day.

He assured himself the affair was the result of loneliness and inaction, a touch of tropic fever, a disordered liver. But Sonar reported that even the Chinese had gone from his fields, and that there had been another tragedy in the night, an old man and an unbeliever who refused to make obeisance to the ghost-tiger.

"Tuan," added Sonar, his face a greenish hue with fright. "The number-three boy has gone to visit a sick mother. I also crave permission to visit my grandmother who lies at death's door. I have shown respect to the 'berhauntu,' My Lord, Tuan. Nevertheless it will not leave your house until this dancing woman is gone, nor will your gun kill it!"

Harden snarled a curse. Then, as Sonar left the house on winged feet, the laughter of the white man held a note of incipient madness. The servants were gone and he had to get his own meals or go hungry. When he went to the larder it was to find only the spoiled remains of yesterday's food, and he knew that Sonar had been refused when he went to buy food from the village and for that reason had deserted.

He had to have food, and there was his car, seldom used because of the almost impassable hill roads made only for carabao carts. He might go deeper into the highlands and buy food from natives not affected by this mysterious curse laid upon him. But, as he left the bungalow, there came the tinkling of a bell, and he saw the patch of blazing yellow of a priest's robe, under an umbrella shielding him from the sun. The sight of it halted Harden. The girl crept to his side crooning songs, but his face was averted and he cursed her in words she could not fail to understand.

UP THE PATH between the flame trees came the poongie, black eyes gleaming wickedly below his shaven head, holding out his begging bowl for alms. Harden laughed and spat in the dust.

The girl crouched at his feet whispering hoarsely:

"The priest who laid the curse, Tuan. The tiger-lord."

Harden remembered that Djac's old wife had a relative who was a temple priest. The robe of the poongie was tiger-yellow. His shaven head, the long narrow eyes and lips stained with betel looked bloody, carnivorous and cruel. He paid no attention to Harden's commands and curses as he stared through the screen, glaring at the girl who threw an arm up to shield her eyes. Harden caught the tiger-stench, heard the whirring prayer-wheel like the purring of a great cat as the girl's fingers curved like claws. Her eyes were glassy and flecks of foam gathered on her lips from which came a snarling, mewing sound, horrible to hear, answering in some beast way the uncouth sounds from the poongie's mouth.

The screen door was fastened. Harden caught up the girl who fought at him and he carried her, struggling and hissing like a wild cat to the kitchen, where he sloshed water over her. At the touch of water her body stiffened as in a convulsion, then went limp, and she slipped to the floor. But a noise on the porch took Harden to the living room with his flesh crawling and cold with fear. He knew now that the crisis of the mystery was at hand and dreaded the swift falling tropic darkness which swooped over the hills as the sun set. In the gloom of vines and trees about the bungalow he felt a presence that stilled the insect clamor and his own heartbeats. The little monkeys that played in the trees fled whimpering far away. Somehow he must keep this poongie from the girl whom his glance hypnotized into an unspeakable creature.

HE STARED INTO the porch and the breath caught in his throat. From a hole torn in the heavy wire netting advanced a tigerish yellow shape with eyes like dark coals, yellow fangs showing from lips drawn back in a snarl. It glided toward him in a grotesque and growing form that was no longer human. Fascinated by terror, Harden watched the eyes change from black fire to glowing green that came nearer, holding him spellbound and helpless. Taller grew the shape of the creature until above him towered a tiger head with quivering red tongue drooling, purring so loudly that the sound shut out the moaning of the girl in the next room.

Slowly the beast thing was stalking him and Harden backed towards the wall with one hand groping. His fingers touched the barrel of his gun standing against the door frame and the touch of metal seemed to release a catch in his numbed brain. He caught up and swung the gun, firing against that advancing terror. The shot crashed and brought a screech of animal fury, a lunging shape tearing through the screens, vanishing in the darkness. Through the tiger stench, Harden was grateful for the honest smell of gun powder.

THEN IN THE silence he heard the girl sobbing, splashing water, and saw her bathing her amber body. She wrapped herself in white and knelt touching her head to the floor. He was staring into the night from windows and doors when she came on dragging feet. Then he remembered the significance of bathing to these Orientals and that white is their mourning color. He wheeled and caught her in one arm.

"Twice have I disobeyed when I should have killed you, Tuan. It is the curse of Djac's old wife whom you took into your house where he lived like a fighting cock and made her jealous. Because I loved instead of killing you, I die out there in the grass, not honored as is the bride of the hamadryad god, but tiger-meat!"

He held her close to his breast with one arm, his other hand clutching the gun.

"Why is this curse laid on my house?" he cried.

"I have said Djac's old wife wanted him to live in her river hut. She asked her relative, the tiger-lord, to lay a curse, and I was sent to dance for you, and the cobras would have killed you. But you slept and Djac saw me dance, and desired me. Thus it was the old wife entered the tiger to haunt you and me. And a curse is laid on me because I could not kill you, Tuan."

His mouth touched her lips lightly. She was merely the trained tool of a demoniac temple priest, and her heart had betrayed her master's training. Then looking toward the window he saw in the starlight the twin green eyes of the tiger. It stood on its hind legs, dancing. At it glided nearer his flesh again rippled with the evil purring of that beast. His scalp crawled and his legs were limp.

THE GIRL SLIPPED from his arm. He tried to catch her, tried to call her name, but he was powerless to move or speak. She glided to the door, down the steps, and Harden saw the great beast pad-padding nearer, lifting its head in a roar of triumph. Then, like a blow came a memory of Senyap dancing for him, all glitter and color, parted red lips near his own, her body curled on his chair.

The gun falling from his nerveless fingers was caught up. He braced it against the window frame as the girl baited and dropped on her knees before the terrible ghost-tiger in the jungle grass. Harden's fingers jerked again and again. In that room the shots were deafening. From the darkness came a scream of rage, a thresh-ing of the grass, a pitiful cry from the girl: "Tuan, Tuan!"

Clubbing the gun, he rushed to where she crouched and snatched her to his shoulder. Then, as the old moon with its bro-ken edge peered above the sea, the girl laughed softly and slipped her arm about his neck, spreading her fingers between which blood trickled from the tiger's claw marks that would scar her flesh for all time.

"They will not have me at the temple now, Tuan," she said, "for the brides of the god must be unblemished by birthmark, scar, or the caress of a man!"

But Harden was staring down a something dead in the grass. There was the shaven head of the tiger-lord. There were his cruel features and lips stained as if they sucked blood, and on the yel-low robe lay bars of black that were shadows of jungle grass and light of the old moon. But now he was conscious of Senyap, speak-ing softly to him.

"You could not kill the tiger, Tuan. But when he changes his shape for the body of a priest he may be killed," said the girl, cling-ing happily to his neck. "But you did not kill the tiger so the work-ers will return to your fields, and the young trees and cane will thrive."

Harden made a generous gift to the temple for the accident to the poongie. Sonar and the number-three boy returned next morning and his fields were busy with workers. Senyap danced and filled the room with jeweled butterflies and birds, but Harden's eyes lingered on the claw marks of a tiger striped down her arm, the visible brand of a mystery still incomprehensible to a white man, even one who survives the tiger curse.

1937

FANGS OF VENGEANCE
NATHAN HINDIN (ROBERT BLOCH)

CAPTAIN ZAROFF WAS not his real name. But then, of course, it did not happen at Stellar Brothers Circus, either. Both appellations are fictitious, though the facts—more the pity—are all too true. I know, for I was there to see the drama unfold; a drama of death and blood-stained vengeance, set against the glittering background of circus make-believe.

The affair occurred, fortunately, in winter quarters. That is the only reason it was fortunate enough to escape press notice. Despite its sensational aspects, I am very thankful that we were able to hush the whole thing up. It is not good for the common herd to know too much, and there are certain terrible questions in connection with it that are extremely difficult to answer. All that has ever leaked out is that Captain Zaroff met death in the big cage during a rehearsal of his act, and that his animals were shot in a vain effort to save him. Concerning the Ubangis, the press was informed that due to disagreements over salary, they severed their connection with the show.

There was something wrong from the very start that winter. We had had a bad season, and the old man decided that innovations were in order. Culper sent out an agent for the Ubangi troupe—six duck-billed and exceedingly ugly savages, only a year removed from their native jungles. But the old man didn't stop there, either. He decided to go back to wild animal acts—a policy we had discarded some eight years previous. He argued that the public wants excitement—the cracking of whips, the snarling of sullen cats, the roaring of restless lions.

Now for some unknown reason, the majority of the larger shows have abandoned the cat acts within the last ten years. The result is that good animal-trainers are mighty hard to find. Practically the only ones available are Europeans, and they're scarce enough. So the old man counted himself lucky when a German agency sent him Captain Zaroff.

He arrived early in January. I wasn't there at the time, but he was described as very distant, and very foreign. He had his own quarters, and special cages for the nine leopards in his troupe. He even insisted on keeping his personal assistant to clean the wagons and feed the animals. These affectations of exclusiveness, coupled with his extremely reserved manner, did not win him any friends. He, on his own part, seemed unmindful of the circus people; eating alone, sleeping in his own private wagon on the winter grounds, and devoting all his time and attention to his act.

There were many vague and conflicting rumors floating around concerning the man. For one thing, there were speculations as to his age and nationality. It was said that he was just back from Africa, and that he was breaking in these jungle leopards for the new act. Another version of the story represented him as being driven from the Continent in disgrace, following a scandal over a woman. By the time I returned to headquarters, the whole show was engaged in wild speculation. I disregarded it all.

Then I saw him work. It was the first time, and only the old man and I were present in the barn-like hippodrome which held the great steel cage. Zaroff had promised the old man something distinctively different. He got it.

PICTURE TO YOURSELF a vast wooden arena, with white, bare walls that reflect hideously all the glare of a hundred overhead lights. In the center, a steel cage. Two assistants stand beside it, tense and alert. Occasionally, they finger nervously with their guns—guns that are not loaded with blanks. The boss and I sat on chairs placed near the door, our eyes glued on the runway. The old man chewed viciously on the stub of his cigar. The atmosphere was charged with the static electricity of fearful expectation.

There are no bands playing in the winter quarters, no happy, cheering crowds. No clowns perform their antic drolleries to ease the tension with a laugh. Working with newly broken jungle beasts is by no means the same safe routine as a developed act. The real danger does not strike after the spectacular routine is perfected— it comes before, during the long, slow hours of winter training. It was with this thought in our minds that we waited in that silent, empty barn; waited, and worried.

Suddenly the silence was broken by a moan. From the wooden runway on the other side of the steel cage came the soft and purposeful padding of velvet feet—and the scrape of razored claws. Short, guttural coughs echoed in the air. At the same time our nostrils were filled with a warm, fetid odor of jungle musk—the wild-beast smell that makes the short hairs rise on the nape of one's neck. More coughs—amplified to a menacing roar in the vast silence of that looming atmosphere. They were coming!

Down the runway stalked a tawny shape—the spotted, sinister shape of a giant African leopard; graceful as a serpent and beautiful as death. Green eyes roved restlessly over the arena with an emerald glare. Yellow fangs parted, revealing a long, slavering tongue. The beast slunk stiff-legged around the arena, then turned to us with a roar. I suddenly realized that I was bathed in perspiration.

Another yellow body catapulted into the cage. Like a streak of amber lightning it leapt to the bars and clawed madly at the steel. Suddenly it subsided, and sank to the sawdust in a spasm of insanely hysterical laughter. A third spotted devil entered, suavely. Like an overgrown cat it purred, mincing its way as it made a circuit of the cage. Feline-like, it rolled over on its mottled back, exposing a sleek belly beneath which muscles played like bands of pliable steel. The other two animals growled deeper still. Then, like a golden avalanche, a horde of fanged furies raced down the runway—six snarling demons charged into the arena, and hell broke loose. In a moment the steel enclosure became a maelstrom of yellow shapes, tearing with frenzied talons at the iron barriers, and howling in fiendish chorus to the skies. There was death in their claws, hatred in their foam-flecked jowls, and blood-lust in their feral eyes. Beasts of the jungle, awaiting the coming of man.

They did not wait for long. Into the hippodrome stalked Captain Zaroff. A tall, thin, commanding figure of a man, his was the walk of a conqueror. Beneath his gorgeously-epauletted red coat I sensed the strength of supple sinews; the resiliency of his walk betrayed a perfection of muscular control. His face was immobile, but his eyes held a faint tinge of amusement. Slightly graying black hair worn in pompadour style, and a tiny waxed mustache—by these signs alone did he betray his foreign birth.

With a brief nod to the old man, he motioned the two assistants to unbar the cage. I gasped. For Zaroff had no chair! All he carried in his hand was a whip—to face nine ravening wild beasts, mad with animal excitement!

Clang. Steel grated on steel. The cage door was open. Quickly, Zaroff stepped inside—into that maelstrom of bared fangs, raking claws, and supple bodies crouched to kill. A roar of animal ferocity greeted his appearance. I gasped. Zaroff, weaponless in that vast cage with a jungle act! Every trainer carries both gun and chair during the breaking in of a new cat routine. With the points of the chair outthrust before him he can ward off the sudden charge of a nervous beast. The animal, confused by the underside of the chair presented before him, usually bruises his nose and paws on the four projecting legs. For many years this protection, slim as it is, has saved dozens of trainers' lives. But Zaroff had no chair. Nor was there a gun at his hip. Alone, he faced them—a sneer on his face and a whip in his hand; man's eternal defiance of the brute.

For an instant he stood there just inside the cage, while ten feet away jungle eyes roved restlessly, jungle bodies flexed stealthily, jungle throats roared fearsomely. Suddenly, a leopard detached itself from the rest and began, ever so slowly, to edge its way forward on its belly. It was the big cat that had entered first. Zaroff watched it, his face flushed. To all intents and purposes the beast's body appeared relaxed, but it was slinking forward nevertheless, and its yellow tail lashed in fury.

WITHOUT WARNING, the leopard sprang. Into the air it soared, straight for Zaroff's shoulders; red maw glistening, ferocious claws outspread to rend, and tear, kill and destroy. Swift as the attack was, Zaroff had anticipated it. His hand shot out, loosing the thongs of the whip. The lash hissed like a serpent as it wriggled through the air. The heavy, weighted end curled smoothly around the spotted murderer, imprisoning the tawny neck and jerking the feline's body to the ground, where it lay choking and gasping for several moments. The other cats, meanwhile, had retreated to the other side of the cage. Zaroff, drenched and panting, turned his head to us—and smiled!

Then began the most amazing animal routine in circus history. While the old man and I trembled and the assistants gasped in awe, Zaroff, with only a whip in his hand, put those animals through paces so amazing that they pass the bounds of credibility. The beasts did everything but fly. Balancing, juggling, jumping, group-posing—everything in the regular wild-animal show repertoire was used and improved on. At the sound of Zaroff's whip every cat was in its place. Despite snarls, growls, and obvious attempts to bullet the trainer from their perches, the creatures obeyed him perfectly. It was a great act—and I sighed with relief when it was finished.

The old man waxed enthusiastic. Surely Captain Zaroff would make show history! How he ever got new cats intelligent enough to build a routine like that was a mystery. Zaroff should be more careful, though. It was a bad business, going into the cage with only a whip.

After we left the hippodrome I went over to the front office for a quiet smoke. Somehow I couldn't agree with the old man. The act was good, no doubt, but there were some queer things to be explained.

To begin with, I know enough about the big cage to realize that no trainer could do what Zaroff had done when his animals hated him. An act is built very slowly, one animal at a time; for the tamer must instill trust and respect into the minds of his performers. Learning the tricks is a task founded on affection for the teacher.

Yet the leopards hated Zaroff—hated and feared him!

Then, too—Zaroff knew that they were dangerous and un-friendly. Even a well-trained leopard is never tame, as a lion or a bear can be. And despite that knowledge, the captain was foolish enough not to use a chair.

Surely there was some mystery here. New African leopards, and a foreign trainer who dislikes strangers. Private cages for the beasts, and a special attendant. A wonderful act, beautifully per-formed by raw beasts who are openly antagonistic to their trainer.

I recalled some of the rumors floating around the lots concern-ing Zaroff and his cats. Something about queer adventures in Af-rica. Oh, well, it was all nonsense—the man was merely a skilful trainer. But even a skilful trainer cannot make his animals work so intelligently. The whole thing was very strange. I decided to keep an eye on the man and wait for something to turn up. I didn't have to wait very long.

THREE DAYS LATER the Ubangis arrived. They had been signed for the act in New York, and were shipped south under the personal supervision of Culper himself. To me they proved a woeful disap-pointment. Six small, timid-looking blacks; three male and three female—their only exotic feature was the widely publicized lip de-formity that gave them mouths projecting almost a foot from their faces. Even this barbaric feature looked sadly incongruous, since all six wore American clothes. Imagine a Harlem flapper with lips a foot long and eight inches wide and you will get some picture of what I saw.

But the old man was pleased. The Ubangis must have special quarters. Was their interpreter here? He trusted that none of them had suffered overmuch on the journey. He hoped they would find the accommodations sufficiently comfortable. In the face of all this effusiveness, the blacks remained nervously silent. Without a word they suffered themselves to be led off to their sleeping-quarters.

During the next few days the Ubangis kept us busy. Not only did we have our hands full trying to explain their part in the performance through an interpreter, but we also had to contend with a really profound ignorance. They obviously knew the meaning of money—dollars meant francs, and francs meant luxury back on the Ivory Coast. That was why they had signed up. But as to the meaning of their duties, they were completely in the dark. Personally, I was not able to work up any enthusiasm over the whole venture. The poor savages were unhappy, the old man was unhappy, and the prospects of box-office draw were uncertain. But the old man had to touch off the fireworks.

He decided to stage one of the preliminary rehearsals, and arrange for the Ubangis to attend. There they could actually see a circus, and perhaps their part would be easier to understand thereafter. I was not pleased with the idea, but it was carried out. The six blacks occupied one of the observation booths, and the show went on.

At first everything went smoothly enough. Even the savage can appreciate the instinctive appeal of clown humor, and realize the agility of the aerial performers. They beamed like carefree children and jabbered constantly among themselves.

I was waiting for Zaroff. I knew that for the past few days he had been rehearsing at great length, and was eager to observe the changes or improvements in his act. The rest of the show waited, too. They had never seen him work, and the rumors had only whetted their curiosity.

The act went on. For fifteen minutes all eyes were glued on that steel cage. Zaroff outdid himself that day. His whip forever cracking, he put the carnivores through their paces in a way to keep everyone's attention riveted to the arena.

At last, when the coughing, snarling leopards had bounded back down the runway into their cages, the boss and I turned to the Ubangis to get their reaction.

It was not slow in coming. The entire troupe were excitedly haranguing one another in their box. At length they approached us, headed by their interpreter.

Hesitatingly, he announced that the troupe would not play in the show; that it resigned. Nor would he give any further explanation, save that the Ubangis did not care for Captain Zaroff and his act.

The boss fumed, swore, threatened, entreated, and pleaded. It did not avail. The savages left the following day.

But before they departed I went around and had a talk with their interpreter myself. Somehow I sensed a mystery behind their reasons for departure, and I questioned the man very closely. At last he abandoned his reserve and told me the details as he had overheard them.

Briefly, the Ubangis did not like Zaroff's act, but their aversion did not have a natural cause. They were going because they thought Zaroff himself was a. witchdoctor; because they had heard him *talk to his animals.*

Naturally I was inclined to scoff at this statement. But then I began to remember certain details. Zaroff lived alone, took care of his animals alone. He had his own cages, his own assistant keeper. He avoided company, and spent most of his time with the beasts. It was quite possible that he did talk to his leopards.

But when I told the interpreter, he laughed. The Ubangis knew of such men, and feared them. Zaroff was a wizard, for they could see that he talked to the animals and they answered him! They had seen Zaroff growl in the cage as if he himself were a beast, and they saw the leopards answer his commands. The man was an evil shaman.

That was the substance of the Ubangis complaint, as I got it from the interpreter. I left him a puzzled man. There was something hidden away in my brain that was beginning to bother me as it tried to edge into consciousness. Something about leopards.

THE NEXT DAY brought a train of events which further puzzled me. I was walking through the menagerie quarters when the affair began. It was midafternoon, and the place was deserted, for the entire troupe was over in the arena for regular rehearsals. I rounded the horseshoe bend where the regular cages stood, and passed by the partitioned section. Here Zaroff's leopards were quartered.

Behind the canvas which screened the cages from the rest I caught a glimpse of booted feet. That would be Zaroff himself, feeding the beasts. Low moans and bestial laughter drifted over the canvas walls.

Then all at once I heard a sudden roar, louder than the rest, and a terrible clang of bars. Zaroff's voice rose in an angry curse, and it was answered by a terrible growl. Suddenly a streak of spotted lightning leapt through the side of the canvas, which shredded before saber claws. One of the leopards had escaped.

It landed on its feet and stood crouching there not a dozen feet before me; a great, tawny monster with flaming fury in its evil eyes. Slaver dripped from its wrinkled, furry snout as it glared at me with unmistakable menace. Its back stiffened, and I broke out into a cold sweat as the fanged horror edged toward me, tensing to spring. Quivering with fright I watched it, unable to move, or even breathe. Its feline gaze held me hypnotically rigid; for I knew that I was staring at the face of Death. The leopard gathered itself for a leap.

Crack! The sound of Zaroff's whip broke the tension. The tall figure stepped into view from behind the canvas, blazing fury in his face. At the sound of his master's approach the sullen carnivore turned. With a snarl it gazed up into the captain's face, but its body was still crouched and ready to hurtle in attack.

Then I heard with my own ears that which my mind told me could never be. I heard Zaroff talk to his leopard!

Low barks and growls issued from his throat. The voice of a beast came from human lips. And the leopard answered! Cringing, it fawningly approached its trainer, growling in return. And its growls and cries held a note that was dreadfully, unmistakably *human!*

It was hideous to hear a beast murmuring like a man and a man roaring like a beast. I trembled afresh as Zaroff, with cries of animal rage, brought his whip down over the leopard's shoulders; brought it down with full force again and again until the poor creature's dappled hide was streaked with crimson stains. And all the while it kept whining, purring, pleading in monstrously human tones, while Zaroff screamed like a great cat.

With never a look or word for me, he drove the leopard to its quarters. From behind the canvas I heard the bars grate into their place once more, and then Zaroff reappeared.

This time he was not alone. There was a woman with him—a beautiful woman.

She was tall and slim, like a Grecian Diana, with a body of ivory and hair like ebony. Jade-green eyes dominated her aquiline face, contrasted oddly with her vivid red-lipped mouth and tiny white teeth. She wore a regal velvet dress which stood out incongruously amidst the sawdust atmosphere surrounding her.

I prided myself on knowing the entire personnel of our show, but I had never seen the woman before.

Zaroff, after apologizing to me for the disturbance, introduced her as his wife, Camille. The woman bowed graciously, but remained silent, eyeing her husband with restrained anger. I was speechless.

I had never known that Zaroff was married. I was just beginning to realize that there were a lot of things about him that I didn't know; a lot of things requiring considerable explanation. The scene I had just witnessed, for example, He was explaining about that now.

With elaborate ostentation he again apologized for the accident. The beast had escaped as he was feeding it. He was very sorry, and he would see that it did not occur again. He would be extremely pleased if I would refrain from reporting the affair to the management; it would unnecessarily upset people, he explained.

Here the woman broke in.

"He's lying, *M'sieu*. It will happen again, I know. You must report it; it happened in Europe, and a little boy was killed. He did nothing to prevent it, *M'sieu*, even when it began to—feed. You must make him stop beating them—it frightens me. Please, tell them and make them stop him. Please!"

Zaroff's countenance, as he listened to this recital, turned red with rage. He raised his whip—the long, cruel whip, still red from the lashing of the leopard—and brought it down on the woman's back with full force. She screamed, once.

Then he seized her, and without a backward glance, bore her behind the canvas.

I stood stunned at the rapidity of events, then stumbled off to my own quarters. I wanted to be alone and think.

Zaroff—a foreigner whom nobody knew; a man who beat his leopards and his wife. Zaroff—the most brilliant trainer I had ever seen; hated and feared by his animals, yet obeyed. Zaroff—the man who talked to his cats like a beast, while they answered with the cries of men; Zaroff, whom the Ubangi savages denounced as a witchdoctor and wizard. Who was this man? What was he? Why was he so furtive and unfriendly? What was he doing to his wife that made her hate and fear him as much as the leopards did?

Before the show opened that year I must find out. And Camille Zaroff, I decided, was the woman who could and would tell me.

SHOW BUSINESS OCCUPIED my time heavily for the next few days, but the mystery of Zaroff still occupied my thoughts. Somehow, I was beginning to hate the man. I disliked his cruel, unsmiling features, his reticent, almost disdainful manner, and his pompous, arrogant walk. I did not care for the way he treated his feline charges, and I did not wonder that his wife was afraid.

His wife—there was another angle. When I saw her she had been afraid, but I could see that she wanted to speak. Perhaps that was why Zaroff had kept her away from the rest of the show-people. Maybe she was his prisoner, because of what she knew. He had beaten her with the whip. . . .

He beat her often. Several nights later, as I went through the menagerie quarters on my way to the main office, I saw a light behind the canvas partition where Zaroff's tent stood. I am not by nature or inclination an eavesdropper, but no one could ignore the shouts that came from the other side. The voices were audible throughout the deserted menagerie, and I recognized the guttural tones of Zaroff blending with the thrilling, husky speech of his wife, Camille.

"I will tell them all," she was saying. "I can't stand it any longer, do you hear? Knowing what I know, and seeing what I see. Unless you stop this dreadful business, I will tell them all."

A cynical laugh, almost gloating in its sardonic cadence. That would be Zaroff.

"Oh, no you won't, my dear. I have been gentle with you in the past—too gentle. But if you persist in making these—ah—demonstrations, I can take harsher measures."

"I'm not afraid of you any more. Tomorrow I shall go to him who is the head of this show and tell him the truth. You will no longer keep me caged up here like one of your beasts."

Again that mocking cackle of laughter from the man.

"So—I, shall no longer cage you as I do my beasts, eh? We shall see. You know about my leopards, and what happened on the Guinea Coast, eh? Well—how would you like it if I were to—"

The voice trailed off here into a loathsome whisper, then culminated again in peal after peal of demoniacal mirth.

"No!" the woman screamed. "You dare not do that. I will go now—do you hear me?—now! I'll tell them all! Oh!"

There was a low moan, and then the hateful sound of a striking whip. Again and again I heard the hiss of a lash.

Clenching my hands in a frenzy of fury, I bit my lips to keep from crying aloud and rushing into that tent. I wanted to tear the whip from that unnatural monster and flog him. Red anger surged and poured into my brain, but something held me back.

There was more to this than a domestic quarrel. That woman, with her half-heard hints of secret things, was being mistreated for a purpose. It would do no good to accost Zaroff himself for an explanation and it would be worse than useless to precipitate a scene before the entire company. No, diplomacy urged me to wait. Tomorrow I would seek an opportunity to speak to Camille Zaroff alone. She would gladly talk then. Perhaps things could be straightened out.

Meanwhile, the show went into its final rehearsal in two days, and Zaroff was a good animal-trainer. I decided to bide my time, and left the tent. But that night I dreamed of a man, a leopard, and a whip. And the dream was far from pleasant. . . .

The next day brought with it an entirely unexpected surprise. At nine o'clock a man walked into my office and casually took a seat. Looking up, I gazed into the impassive face of Captain Zaroff.

I was astonished. The man had never come to me before; he habitually kept away from the rest of the company. Concealing both my surprise and distaste, I asked him his business.

"I am bringing in a new animal for my act," he said, calmly.

For a moment I was too startled to speak. The final dress rehearsal only two days away, and he was going to work a new cat! It was unheard of. I told him so. Besides, what did he need a new leopard for?

"Do not worry," he assured. "It is already broken in; I—I had it shipped here this morning. And it is not a leopard—it is a black panther."

A black panther! That *was* a novelty. A trifle mollified, I told him that he would have to take the matter up with the boss.

"I will rehearse tomorrow afternoon," he agreed, suavely. "Would you care to come over and look at the animal?"

TOGETHER WE WALKED across the lot and entered the menagerie. There were ten cages behind the canvas partition now. In nine were the leopards; the other held the new beast. We approached the bars.

There is nothing more beautiful than a black panther. Sleek, sinuous grace is personified in its ebony body, and aristocratic poise blazes forth from its jade eyes. Its nervous pace is regal; it is a picture of dignified beauty even when enraged. Consequently I expected much of Zaroff's acquisition. But I was to be disappointed.

The animal crouched behind the bars, its body limply lolling on the floor of the cage. Its exquisite black coat was disheveled, and on its back I detected the marks of the whip. Had Zaroff already begun his usual practices? The animal's eyes were lusterless; they gazed on me with a sort of dazed, numb expression in their depths. It whined, piteously, and once again I was shocked at the almost human tones in the throat of a jungle beast. When Zaroff approached closer, the panther cringed, and crawled away from the bars.

"Is it sick?" I inquired.

Zaroff smiled. "No, my friend. Perhaps the journey has tired it—the change, shall we say? It will be all right."

The great black cat whined dolefully. It kept staring at me with those amber eyes—staring and staring, as if it were humanly aware of my presence. With a slight shudder, I turned away. In order to make conversation, I casually asked after the health of Zaroff's wife.

A queer look came into the man's face.

"She—she has gone away," he said. But his stolid features were averted. "She has been nervous and ill of late, so I thought it would be best if she went for a rest instead of going out with the show. We had an argument last night, and she took the train this morning."

The man is lying. Accuse him.

The words ate their way into my brain.

He may have beaten her to death.

But such thoughts were mad. My eyes searched wildly for something on which to rest; something to divert my thoughts. I looked at the leopard cages. The cats were all curled up somnolently near the bars, as if they had just eaten. As if they were sated with food, rather.

Maybe he fed her to the leopards.

Was I really going insane?

She was going to tell a secret. I heard him threaten her with something, and he spoke of leopards before she screamed.

Why not? No one would ever know.

My mind rocked with chaotic confusion. The woman was gone; as we passed the living-quarters I saw that the tent was empty and I knew he never allowed her to wander free. What had become of her?

Zaroff watched me with an enigmatic smile. Did he suspect?

"I will see you at rehearsal tomorrow," he said. "Good day."

I stumbled out into the menagerie. As I passed the last cage the panther raised its head and moaned.

I OFTEN WONDER how I got through the rest of that day. The morbid suspicions that preyed on my mind had come to a harrowing climax. I kept thinking of Zaroff, and the queer rumors I had heard about the man. His leopards were queer, his act was queer, his whole history was shrouded in a cloak of nebulous dread. His wife knew, and she had disappeared. I must find out the truth.

But perhaps I was wrong. Imagination, once unleashed, can distort facts immeasurably. Possibly his wife had left. True, he had beaten her, but they do such things on the Continent. The leopards were queerly trained, but Zaroff was an eccentric man. Was I unduly suspicious?

These two conflicting trains of thought ran riot through my brain. The afternoon was a dream. I performed my routine functions automatically, but I could not forget. I neglected to inform the boss that Captain Zaroff had a new black panther, and I said nothing about the rehearsal on the following day.

That night was the beginning of the end.

What impelled me I cannot say, but I felt that I must learn the truth. So at midnight I rose from my restless cot and staggered off to Zaroff's quarters. The lot was black and deserted, save for the looming shadows that lurked and capered in the corners beneath a leering yellow moon.

There was a light in Zaroff's tent when I entered. How I meant to excuse myself or what I intended to say I did not know. But Zaroff took the situation into his own hands.

He was quite drunk. There was a bottle on the table before him, and another on the floor. He sat there sprawled back so that he resembled a seated corpse in the dim light, and his face was equally pale. He had discarded his uniform, but the ever-present whip still rested on the ground beside him.

"Sit down, my friend," he mumbled. His foreign accent became more noticeable under the influence of liquor.

I seated myself beside him and haltingly began to talk. But his libations had made him loquacious, and he interrupted.

I cannot say to this day what got him started, or whether he was too drunk to understand, but he told me plenty.

Somehow he launched out on the story of his career during the war. He had, it seems, been an officer in the "Belgische Congo." Later, he had become an animal trader in Senegal, and served as guide to several expeditions on the Sierra Leone coast.

I let him ramble, occasionally prompting him to refill his glass. Sooner or later, I believed, something would slip out. It did.

As the shadows about us deepened, his voice became lower and more confidential. He was speaking of the blacks now—the furtive, sinister blacks of Sierra Leone, who practiced voodoo and obeah rites in the hidden swamps. He told me of the witchdoctors who invoked the Crocodile God to the beat of jungle drums; spoke of the snake-gods of secret, inner Africa. And he whispered of the Leopard-men.

I had heard of them before—the human leopards of Sierra Leone, whose cult was dedicated to the beasts of the forest. They were said to be vampires, possessing the power of anthropomorphism; that is, they could, by means of secret spells, become leopards themselves. This they were reputed to do, at certain times. As leopards they lay in wait for their enemies and destroyed them, or else invoked their rites to transform their foes into animals. I had read newspaper stories about the British police and their futile efforts to stamp out the dreaded clan.

Zaroff, mumbling incoherently, told me of these things again; spoke of how he himself had been initiated into the Leopard Cult one night beneath the waning autumn moon that gloats over Africa when the devil drums boom in nighted swamps. He told me of the spells he had learned from the shriveled arch-priests, and of the powers he could invoke by chants and rituals.

"Remember the legend of Circe?" he whispered, and his eyes were alight with unnatural flame. "Man into beast. Man into beast."

Abruptly he recovered himself once more, and changed the subject. By now he was so drunk that his voice slurred unintelligibly as he droned on. All I could catch were occasional phrases, but that was enough.

"I decided to show the fools a real act . . . knew the proper spells . . . rest was easy . . . nobody suspected. . . . Came to Europe with me. . . . Wish to God I'd never met and married that slut . . . spying on me at night . . . found out . . . spoiled the act . . . that damned child. . . . They wanted blood . . . scandal. . . . Looked all right here, but those Ubangis knew . . . her stubbornness . . . had to do it . . . was the only way. . . ."

As his voice droned on, his body slid flaccidly to the floor. I left, but I had not found the satisfaction I sought. Instead, my heart was filled with a greater and more hideous unease.

The man's drunken tales had disturbed me. Of course all that rot about Leopard-men was childish, but still I felt afraid. There were those who believed it, and some of his furtive hints had smacked of the truth. Funny, what liquor will do to a man. But I could not dismiss the incident so easily. There was a strange and terrible mystery here.

As I stalked off to my quarters I saw the blazing eyes of the black panther staring silently at me in the darkness. A crazy thought assailed me—perhaps it knew the truth! With a shaky smile I turned away.

OF COURSE I SHOULD have reported all this to the boss. A drunken trainer who abuses his animals is never to be tolerated in a show. But something held me back. I would at least wait until the final rehearsal the following afternoon. Zaroff would work the new panther then, and there would be a showdown.

There was a showdown, but not the kind I expected.

I can see it now, in my mind's eye—that bare arena, with the great steel cage in the center. The boss and I were sitting in the box, just as we had sat that first day. The clown number had just ended, and now four men took their places about the grim, barred barrier.

Zaroff swaggered into view. Despite his debauchery of the previous evening he was as cool and erect as ever. As he entered the little green-grilled door, his hand clenched tightly about the butt of his whip.

The runway into the arena jerked into place between the bars. The wooden gates opened.

Claws and fangs clicking, growls and coughs rumbling, tongues lolling and tails lashing, the leopards entered. Tawny bodies and green eyes, red throats and white teeth.

Nine leopards, and then—the panther.

The leopards had raced in, roaring their defiance. The panther sidled down the runway with stealthy tread. It uttered no sound, but entered the arena like a silent black shadow.

Zaroff cracked his whip. But today the leopards did not move. Instead, they held their places, a note of menace rumbling low in their great throats. They gave the curious impression that they were waiting for something. Zaroff, cracked his whip again, impatiently.

The black panther padded over to the group of giant cats, then turned and stared at Zaroff.

Captain Zaroff stared back. There was a strange look on his face; he actually appeared to be nervous. He cracked his whip again, and swore. The growling in the leopards' throats rose in a thundering crescendo, but they did not move. The panther lashed its tail and continued to stare hypnotically at the tamer with evil, lambent eyes.

Sweat broke out on Zaroff's brow. I could have sworn that I saw a look of positive hate on that black beast's face as it gazed at the man. The trainers, guns ready, moved closer to the bars outside. They sensed something. Why didn't the man do something?

The leopards roared louder. They were grouped behind the panther now, and the panther, step by step, was slowly inching forward. Its tail shot erect, but it never took its eyes from Zaroff's tormented white face.

Suddenly, with a shriek of almost human fury, the black body of the beast rose in the air and sprang for Zaroff's neck. The leopards closed in, and the man went down beneath the fangs of ten jungle cats. There were shrieks from crimson-dabbled lips, then all sound was blotted out, as the four trainers shot blindly, pumping lead into that knot of blazing yellow bodies, shooting and shooting and shooting.

THE END CAME quickly, and only dead bodies remained about the mangled ruins of the thing that had once been Captain Zaroff.

Nobody ever speaks of that scene any more, but the tragedy itself was not the greatest horror. For I found the truth in Zaroff's private papers, and learned those things that had been hidden.

Now I know why Zaroff left Africa, and what he had really learned about the Cult of the Leopard-men. I know now why he boasted that he was going to have the greatest animal act in the world, and why he took such unusual precautions to guard and care for the beasts himself. I know how he was able to train them so well, and why the Ubangis thought he was talking to the creatures.

And I know just how his wife went away, too, and what she would have tried to tell the boss. It's not pleasant knowledge—those things in the papers and diaries of the dead trainer.

But it is infinitely more endurable than the memory of that last terrible sight—that dreadful glimpse of what lay in the arena when Zaroff, the leopards and the panther died. I can never forget that, because it is the final proof of all I dreaded to believe.

Captain Zaroff's chewed and lacerated form lay in a great pool of blood. Around him were the bodies of what the men with the guns had slain—nine bodies, not of leopards, but of negro men. Negro Leopard-men, from Africa.

And the tenth—the dreadful thing that was tearing at Zaroff's throat; the new black panther with the human eyes—*was his wife, Camille!*

1938

TOEAN MATJAN
Vennette Herron

At a dinner given by the British consul in Batavia I first met the Lady Violette Adair; but one way or another we met rather often after that and became friends, until finally she asked me to visit her. The house which she had had built out there—one in which to hide herself away for months on end alone with her writing and painting—was a quaint affair of mixed *billiek* and stucco; an enormous round studio, with its upper wall a ring of skylight windows under the eaves, hung with thick mustard-gold and mauve curtains, which could be drawn to shut out either sun or moon when desired, and no windows below; with a half-circle of small rooms, like monks' cells, at the back—and entered by a door stolen from a temple in Bali. The odor was of intricately carven teak, covered with an incredible detail of tiny symbolic figures, at which many Europeans would probably have sniggered or blushed, but which made a perfect frame for the strangely blond and mask-like, more Scandinavian than British beauty of the Lady Violette. And the threshold of the door was a solid block of hand-hewn wood nearly a foot square, forming the central and topmost step of a little bridge of stairs, which led up to and then down, into the studio, the floor of which was sunken a couple of feet below the level of the ground outside. A fascinating house, with a personality as exotic as that of its mistress, which is saying a great deal. And in it also there was the white cat.

"What a gorgeous animal, Violette!" For we had become fast friends before ever she invited me there.

"Yes, isn't it?"

But still she did not tell me its story—not until several weeks later indeed, only a few evenings before I was to leave. Then, however, she did. Not that I asked it of her even then, much as I would have liked to, but it was one of those portentous happenings which one simply has to relate to someone, sometime. And the hour was ripe, and I was there; wherefore, thanks be to Allah, I heard it. We were sitting side by side upon the threshold of the temple door, just at twilight, smoking lazily and watching the sunset behind the distant Tangomann Prahoe, sensing the exquisite melancholy of the rose-gray dusk, of the long lines of black-winged flying-foxes flapping westward into infinity; out of one cave, then into another, with a flash across space between—symbol of sad yet seaching little egos born to die, while life itself goes on for ever.

"What would you think," propounded Lady Violette suddenly, "if you saw a tiger pass across the lawn right now? I did, one night— a little later than this, just after the moon had risen. I was sitting here alone just as we are now when all at once I heard a piteous bleat from the goat-pens, and a great clamor of frightened fowls, And then I saw the tiger, with a kid in its mouth. He was padding along rather slowly, not even looking at the house, as though knowing that nothing would harm him, and content with his kill, enjoying the night."

"Weren't you frightened? What did you do, Violette?"

"I dashed inside, and came back with the short, double-barreled shotgun which I always keep loaded for jungle emergencies; and he was still in sight—right over there by those trees." She pointed. "But just as I raised the gun to my shoulder, suddenly he stopped stock-still and looked at me. And—I never saw anything quite so magnificent! Tawny-striped, enormous, royal—'fearful symmetry' indeed! With great golden-green moon-eyes, wise, flaming, wild and sad. With blood dripping from his jowls—with in every line of him that marvelous feline pride which makes a few creatures appear above all pettiness, above all little common things, no matter what they may do. And without trying to escape, it just stood there staring. I don't know what it saw in *me*, but *I* saw beauty incarnate, and some awful unnamable cosmic tragedy. It was speaking with its soul—in words, just as you and I speak; and suffering as no human being can suffer because in words it could not speak. The natives believe, you know, that the souls of their great hero ancestors and likewise those of some of the lesser gods are locked up in tiger bodies. They will never kill one of the beasts themselves, if they can help it; and if they meet one in the jungle, instead they kneel and pray to it. And they'll all swear that, if one does that, the tiger will pass on without harming anyone."

"But what did *you* do?" I asked my hostess, intensely curious to know, and thinking to myself that the tiger might well have seen in her—in her mystic golden egg-shell fairness, in the fey blue eyes beneath the thread-thin dark arcs which were her brows, in the mask-like oval of her face—very much what she'd seen in it. Both were greater even than their super-finished shells. And both were part of a pitiful personal transciency, terribly and rebelliously aware of all around and just outside of themselves a mocking, jibing, ruthlessly ruminating, living eternity—Garoeda or the Sphinx—knowing it there; yet never quite able to break into and become a part of it.

"I?" replied the Lady Violette Adair. "What *could* I do after that? I lowered my gun and salaamed to him. '*Toean matjan besar*—great Lord Tiger,' I said, 'go home in peace. You are too beautiful to kill. But don't steal any more of my live-stock, please'."

"And then?"

"Then he did a strange thing. He opened his mouth and let the dead kid fall onto the grass; his lips curled in a tiger-smile, showing off his great white fangs, and he gave a little low rumbling roar. Then he was gone, like a streak of bright light—not daylight, but light of enchantment—burning its way beneath the trees, leaving behind him a ripple and swish of dew-drenched foliage, like a phosphorescent wake, for a second; then nothingness—a kind of soundless blank, which had not been there before he passed."

"And did you ever see him again?"

HER FACE WAS DREAMING, inscrutable, with its lips slightly parted and queerly quirked at the corners, like the mask of a *serimpe*—one of the Javanese dancers of the Soesoehoenan's court. "That very same night once again I heard him. After I'd gone to bed, suddenly, upon the roof above my room there came a soft heavy thud and the grate of a slithering tile. Then a long soft, savagely tender purring, which went on and on."

"And still you weren't afraid?"

The Lady Violette smiled. "I fell asleep listening to it," she said, "and knew that I was protected."

"And is that the end of the story?"

She shook her head. "Oh no—only the beginning. The next morning Ati—my head-boy, as you know—brought me the kid, with his face gone almost white with excitement. 'Look, *nonja!*' he said. 'It was killed by a tiger—there are marks of its teeth on the body, and also its footprints, gigantic ones, in the dust of the compound. Something out of the ordinary indeed must have happened to cause it to drop its prey; but probably it will return. What does the *nonja* want us to do? Shall we set a trap for it? For if it has once killed—'

"But I hastened to reassure him. 'Don't worry, Ati. I talked to the tiger myself; even as your old men and *doekoens* talk, knowing the truth, even I, in so much of their knowledge and ways. And the tiger answered me. It said that it would attack nothing here again, that no one belonging to me need be afraid; and of its own accord it left the kid to show that it would keep its word.'"

"And the boy believed you?"

"Of course." My hostess shrugged, a trifle impatiently.

"And did it ever come back after that?"

The Lady Violette hesitated, then went on: "The natives believe also, you know, that the tiger can change its shape at will—like the werewolf—like all of the animals which are half-gods. Be that as it may, several days after that first appearance, as I was sitting at breakfast one morning in the studio, I looked up and beheld in the doorway, backed by a sheet of gold sun, an enormous white cat."

I started. *"Matjan Ketjil?"*

She nodded. "The same. Thoroughbred and dainty, with a great plume of a tail—like something out of fairyland. And its eyes—have you noticed them? In miniature they are twin replicas of those of the tiger. Without scruple, yet so fastidious, so aloof. And flooding in all around him was the scent of sun-bruised marigolds."

"I know." As indeed I did—that peculiar pungence which seemed to contain in it the very essence of Java mornings. "And then?"

"I held out my hand and called to it—in high Malay, suited to its rank. 'Enter, cat; dost want to be friends? Welcome to my house.' Then I told Ati to fetch a saucer of cream and offer it to him; but when the boy approached, the animal arched its back and spat. Then I ordered Ati to set the cream upon the table opposite me and to draw up a chair as though for a guest; and I myself salaamed to the cat and again held out my hand. 'Wilt do me the honor of sharing my meal, *Matjan Ketjil*—little tiger?' I invited. And at that my visitor walked over, with the tip of its coral tongue and the grace of a courtier kissed my fingers, then sprang onto the chair and with a comically polite little mew commenced to lap up the cream.

"And after breakfast," continued my friend, "it followed me all about the studio, until finally I placed a big velvet pillow for it beside my work-chair and sat down at my writing-table. Then *Matjan Ketjil*—for of course already that was his name—arranged himself upon the cushion and remained there, unblinking, unstirring, sometimes purring, sometimes seeming to sleep, occasionally looking up at me. And then—"

"Well?"

"My dear, I scarcely know how to tell you—it was the queerest thing! Of course everything in the East speaks to me; but between us two there was pure communication. I was not conscious of hearing sentences of an audible voice at all; but simply all kinds of fantastic ideas beyond any that I had ever known flowed in and out of me—and I understood the East and the cosmos as never before, and wrote as I had never thought to write. And I felt strangely young and well, too. It was fascinating and exhilarating, a kind of enchantment. I wrote on and on. Some day very likely you will read some of it; but much of it will never be published until after I am dead. And since then the cat comes every day, as you yourself have seen. And toward dusk, as you will have noted too, he leaves and goes into the jungle."

I looked at my friend. Her eyes were shining stars, her lashes were infinitesimal glittering bronze-gold wires curving up to meet her brows; her mouth was a scarlet hibiscus blooming against a pale bamboo wall. Many men had paused to look at her; but it was often said that, except for the impersonal courtesy and consideration which was a part of her breeding, she never looked back at them; but confined her gaze instead to statues and shrines, to masks and animals, to occult lore, to the things which gave to the innermost core of her a thrill and to nothing else. Very ancient was the ego of the Lady Violette, although her so strangely perfect body was still so young. "Your cat is a magic creature—even without knowing what you've just recounted, and even though he will never let me stroke him," I said.

"He'll never let anyone touch him but me," Violette answered. "But likewise he will never harm you." Then she added slowly: "And neither would the tiger. Should you ever chance to see him, although I doubt if you will—but should you, you need not be afraid."

"You mean that the tiger too still sometimes returns?" I was not precisely afraid; but I peered across at the compound, from out of which seeped every now and again the comforting night sounds of sleepy goats and fowls, the stamp of Violette's riding-horse, or the whining wail of a Malay love-song—peered with the sort of horrified unable-not-to feeling with which one regards a mangling accident in a street.

"Sometimes he purrs on my roof at night—he's not apt to while you're here; but should you ever hear him, be calm—you have nothing to fear."

"You are a strange woman, Violette! But thank you for telling me."

"That's not quite all, either," she said. "And the rest may sound to you pretty terrible. But stark beauty is that, isn't it? Do you want to hear it?"

"Of course," I responded, wondering what could be more, if there were any inner truth in it at all, than what she'd already told me.

"Did you ever know Haviland Nesbit? He was rather the rage in London at one time. Just after—yes, that one. Then you know how handsome he was. But perhaps you don't know that he came out here last year—just wandering, as he so often did—and hunted me up, with a letter from my aunt, Lady Leila Carruthers. Yes, I thought you must have. Well—" She paused, then went on musingly: "Men as a rule do not attract me—I suppose you know that too; but more than any other Haviland Nesbit did. There *was* something about him which made me feel more—more as I suppose most other women feel; and I've never cared a damn for conventions, of course—so I asked him to stop awhile up here. And he did. But still we were only friends—although he would have liked, of course—"

"And was that *after* the episode of the tiger—and the white cat?" I interrupted, too interested to consider whether or not I was being rude.

My hostess laughed. "Of course! I forgot that *you* couldn't just know," she said—kindly, but as though there were a way in which I might have known without asking. "But after the first day of his visit, *Matjan Ketjil* walked out, and did not return until after Haviland was—was gone." For an instant her face was inhuman in its cold, clear, dreaming beauty.

"Yes?" I ventured, to egg her on.

"I MISSED MY—my companion, of course; yet the days were complete and full. Until—until after some weeks like that, there finally arrived a night when I too thought that there might, after all, be something in—in that something which usually is between a man and a woman shut up alone together. A night when I called myself a fool for at least not trying and learning. A night when at last—standing down there in the moonlight, just outside the temple door; Haviland Nesbit put his arms about me—and I let him. And we kissed. And just at that moment, although neither of us had heard even a rustle before, there came a spring from the roof, and somehow I was knocked to one side; while Haviland—not even much mauled, but dead of a broken neck before he could so much as cry out—lay in a crumpled heap at my feet. And then I saw the tiger, without a backward look, like a fierce yellow river, flowing off through the jungle."

"Violette!" I shuddered, and glanced involuntarily up toward the eaves beneath which we were sitting.

At which my hostess laughed again—a little, low, pearly gurgle, soulless and bell-like—fairy laughter. "And still you need not be afraid," she repeated gently. "For he knows now that I will not experiment again."

"But what did you do—about Haviland? For no one at home has ever heard what became of him—have they?"

"You see how I trust you, having made you my friend," she answered. "No, no one knows—nor will, till I too am dead. But then, if you should happen to be still alive, you may tell, if you like. But no, I didn't tell then. My aunt would have hated it so—all the talk; and there seemed no reason to. I called Ati, and we buried him over there, under that lovely tree, half purple flowers on one side and orange berries on the other. I don't know where he would rather lie for that last long rest—do you? But I was furious then too—furious! If *Matjan* had come back then in any shape—especially in his big tiger body—"

"Violette, you don't mean that you actually believe—"

"It's no matter. You may think what you like, but if the tiger had returned. . . . However, he didn't—not then; and neither did the white cat. Not for several days. But then one morning I locked up and there he was, standing in the door again, with the sun a bright blob behind him. And I took down a kris from the wall, the one which hangs always above my desk, and I walked toward him—meaning to put an end to it all, of course—remembering poor Haviland, who had hardly earned the fate which befell him. But then—but then *Matjan Ketjil* didn't run away, you see; instead just stood and looked at me. And I knew myself better by then—so what would you? I am not as other women. This *is* my life. And although

I am fond of you, my dear, very—and one or two others—still I am always a little lonely, except when I am alone. And he *was* too beautiful to kill. So—so after a moment I hung the kris back on the wall again. And that's all."

For a breath we both sat silent. Then over our shoulders came the voice of Ati. "*Nonja, makan* is served." And we rose and went in.

AFTER DINNER, over our coffee and liqueurs, there was a little more talk—fragmentary, but satisfying—mostly about the East. But I felt unusually tired and so excused myself early and withdrew to my cubicle—so perfect in its appointments, but so austere and cell-like. Then hastily I prepared for bed, but weary as I was, found that I could not sleep. And presently I heard a soft thud and a slithering tile, not quite above my room, but somewhere not far away upon the roof of the house. And I sprang from bed and stood on tiptoe to look out through my single window—a very high one, protected by stout steel bars. From there I could catch a glimpse of the lawn, backed by a black wall of jungle. The clearing was a bowl of moonlight, white and clean and lonely, with no movement in it at first. Then I saw my hostess walk across the open space in her trailing white dinner-gown, with a cigarette, glowing like a fire-fly, in her hand. Like some rare white tropical bird, stately and cold and lovely, she paced back and forth, slowly, superbly. And then—then I saw melt out of the shadows, like a thicker shadow forming, a sinuous, splendid shape, tawny-striped and fearful. And suddenly there was a tiger walking beside the woman. Two creatures of another world they seemed, one no more royal than the other, both lofty, lord-like, stately, pacing up and down in the witchlight, in a weird contentment of untellable communion. And God, how beautiful they were! I stared until my teeth chattered, then crept back to bed, feeling myself very small and child-like and earthy.

And the next morning the white cat came as always, and lapped its cream, sitting solemnly upon a chair placed for it between my hostess and me. And I saw that its eyes were two slit-gashed moons, solemn and wise, sad and inscrutable—and big—bigger than it. And later it lay upon its cushion, while Violette as usual, even when I was there, sat at her desk for a little, writing—with the sun-scent of marigolds all about them—concentrated in them. And I knew that in all that she wrote there would be the swirling, spiraling, leering, heart-scorching, twisted, other-world thoughts which had once gotten themselves engraved upon all of the temple doors out there—thoughts like the carvings upon the door which guarded the house I was in. The sun on the fur of the cat was blinding—the hair of my friend was virgin gold. They were sun and snow on a mountain—they were all that most of us are not. . . .

Two days later I came away. And now Violette Adair is dead of a fever, and lies buried—not beside Haviland Nesbit, but by her own request, just beneath the ground, very shallowly, in the center of the lawn before her own house, where her bones may be blessed and bleached for ever by the sun and the moon and the rains of Java. And no one goes near or disturbs her; for it is said by the natives that night and day a tiger, or its ghost, patrols her grave.

Whether that last is true or not, I do not know; but I do know what I saw. . . . And now that she is gone, as she said I might, I give you her story.

1940

SPOTTED SATAN
Otis Adelbert Kline and E. Hoffmann Price

I

HARRISON STEELE'S BROAD shoulders and rugged features usually got two glances from women: the first being one of approval, the second a query. They could never quite decide whether his tanned face was handsome, or merely interesting. But the Eurasian telephone operator in the outer office of the Irrawaddy Teak Company upset the routine. Her black and faintly slanted eyes were saying, "Too bad!"

Then she caught Steele's pleasant gray glance, shook her sleek head, and brightened. He might have a chance in the jungle, after all, though none of the others had survived.

"Mr. Powell will see you at once," she said.

A Chinese clerk in white led the way down the hall and to Eldon Powell's spacious office. The room was paneled in teak, and the broad desk was made of that noble wood, dark, heavy, enduring. The big Englishman liked the solidity of the teak taken from the company's forests, but for the moment, Powell did not like Burma. Steele could see that at a glance.

"You lost little time packing. Awfully good of you to take it all so seriously. I rather feared you'd not be interested in anything as common as leopards."

"Why not?" Steele's smile became an amiable grin, and his face no longer seemed to have been hewn from knotty oak. He optimistically dragged his chair into what he thought was the spot where the lazily swaying *punkahs* (fans) stirred the humid air. "When a

326

leopard gets you worried, that's news. But it was a lot cooler in Penang!"

"Beastly climate," Powell deplored. He did not waste any effort in mopping his ruddy face. Rangoon was steaming. "Now, this business of a reward for shooting the brute. I know jolly well you're not interested in that. We've offered the native *shikaris* a thousand rupees, and no takers. Er . . . not anymore, I mean. They used to flock in but—"

"Got the wind up, eh?"

Powell nodded. "Can't say that I blame them. So the directors authorized me to offer you five times that much." He made an apologetic gesture. "No offense, old man. But the only way to make a thing look important to you American chaps is to—ah—put a cash appraisal on it, so to speak."

Steele smiled wryly. "Now, what's the catch? Leopards aren't sport, ordinarily. But with the cash appraisal you British chaps put on everything, I knew this must be a two-fisted beast or you'd not be so extravagant."

Powell threw up his hands. "I say, now. You're ribbing me, eh?"

"I guess we're even," Steele chuckled. "What's the score?"

Powell stroked his straw-colored mustache. "None of the white hunters who went after the leopard had much luck. Two disappeared entirely. Another—really a promising chap—all we found of him was a belt buckle and a few other inedible bits. Quite too bad. I had to get in touch with poor Henderson's relatives and explain just why we couldn't ship the remains home."

"That would be awkward, telling them there just wasn't anything to ship," Steele agreed. "But I won't embarrass you. First, I may drill the brute, and second, I have no relatives—though there's an oversized Afghan who follows me around like a nurse-maid. Achmet will be a good gun-bearer."

During all this exchange of grim pleasantries, Steele was thinking of the pretty Eurasian girl's obvious concern and sympathy. He would have paid little attention to Powell, who was always inclined to pessimism. A servant brought in whisky and soda. Steele selected a cheroot, and watched Powell spend a few moments at indoor mustache chewing.

Finally the big Englishman squirmed in his chair, coughed, and looked very uncomfortable. "Ah—er—I say, Steele, I've not told you all of it. It makes me no end of an ass, but I simply must tell you. The natives at our teak camp in the Chin Hills insist the leopard isn't a leopard except at night. During the day he's supposed to be a man or a demon or a *nat*."

"Huh?" Steele straightened. "What's that?"

"Now, see here, old chap. I don't believe that blasted rot. But if you don't kill the beggar pretty soon, our coolies will desert to the last man, and we won't get any logs down to the creek beds in time for the freshets. *That's* why there's a reward, you know. Important hunter gunning for thousands of rupees. Good for the native morale. Then you get him, and everything is peaceful and happy."

"And dear old Irrawaddy Teak pays dividends—provided I hunt down the spotted satan?"

"Exactly. And you'll go, of course?" Powell leaned forward in his chair. "I'd appreciate it, no end. As a personal favor."

"The devil wears spots by night." Steele frowned. Asia has her share of the inexplicable, but men sometimes pull the strings. "I've heard of such things. But I've also heard of jugglery by unscrupulous competitors. Tricks to demoralize laborers."

Powell had considered that angle. "I said as much to Kirby—he's our camp superintendent—but he assures me it's not that simple."

"Kirby—" Steele slowly pronounced the name. It suggested something unpleasant, but he did not quite know how to justify this feeling. "He's reliable, of course? Old employee, I mean?"

"Not old, no, but well recommended. A bit odd, but what teak-logger isn't! He's all broken up by the furor."

THE FOLLOWING MORNING, Steel and his Afghan servant set out by rail for Mandalay, and thence for Monywa. There they boarded a wheezing stern-wheeler, the *Shillong*, and headed up the river. At

Hlai-bin-doung they disembarked. The remainder of the trip would be a day's march through jungle trails.

The headman of Hlai-bin-doung escorted Steele and Achmet to the *dâk bungalow* (inn) which the Government maintained for travelers. It stood on stilts which raised it from the steaming ground; a weather-beaten and uninviting house with a corrugated iron roof and a veranda canopied with similar material.

The long shadows of ruined pagodas marched across the compound which inclosed the bungalow. A Buddhist monk in the nearby monastery was beating a wooden bell; the hollow notes were mournful, and they blotted out the chatter of the village, which was a few hundred yards away. Other monks intoned a ritual in Pali, the sacred language. Someone, centuries ago, had acquired merit by endowing this monastery, and thus men with shaven heads and yellow robes praised the Buddha Gautama, quite as though the jungle had not remorselessly engulfed what once had been cleared ground.

Steele could not understand the chanting, but it made him shiver. Where slayers lurked in every thicket, where villages were surrounded by thorny hedges to keep out murderous *dacoits*, these monks praised the Buddha who had forsaken a throne to bring peace to all living things. All slaying was evil, and hunters were the most accursed of men: and this thought lived in a land where each ate until he was eaten.

The voices and the bells shook Steele. If monks could stay here and sing of peace to all living things, then anything was possible. Incredible Burma began speaking to him, and he was uneasy. This was not quite like sitting in Eldon Powell's office and saying that a leopard was a leopard; in the jungle, a man might become a spotted satan. . . .

When the sun dipped over the jungle and reddened the tops of crumbling pagodas, Achmet combed his hennaed beard and faced toward Mekka for evening prayer. "*El hamdulilah i rab' il alameen!*" the big Afghan rumbled. "*Malik i yaum id-deen!*"

It was good to hear a man's deep voice call on One God, where every tree was guarded by a demon, and where many gods haunted every mountain. "Praise be to Allah, Lord of the Two Worlds! King of the Day of Judgment. . . ."

The sound was aggressive, deep-chested, confident: it fought the insidious cry of wooden bells. Gaudily dressed natives gathered at the open gate of Steele's compound. Averaging but a few inches over five feet, they marveled at the Afghan's height and his hooked nose and fierce eyes; though his henna-dyed beard was the greatest wonder.

They could no more understand his guttural speech than he could their sing-song Burmese; but Steele caught enough of their chatter to know that the news of his mission had preceded him. The natives were certain that in spite of the size of master and man, the leopard demon would dispose of them as readily as he had the other *shikaris* (native hunters).

ACHMET'S PRAYERS WERE scarcely completed when the crowd parted to admit Panbyu, the headman's daughter. Balanced on her head was a wicker tray which contained half a dozen bowls of food. There was rice, chicken, curry, and small dried fish whose high fragrance convinced Steele that the Burmese must be immune to ptomaine poisoning.

She wore a scarlet jacket with purple sleeves. Her pink skirt was slit up the side so that despite her mincing, pigeon-toed gait, her legs were exposed well past the knee. "*Billahi*," said Achmet, eyeing the smiling girl, "these chattering apes have pretty women."

Neither could understand the other, but Steele caught the exchange, and Panbyu's smile and the flash of her oblique eyes. He was certain that Achmet would not need an interpreter.

The tall Afghan wolfed his rice. He grinned broadly when he heard the sounds from the village. Musicians were tuning up their instruments. Panbyu said that a festival was about to start, and that the honored visitors were welcome.

"*Sahib*," Achmet began, when Steele translated the girl's remark, "it would be well if I mingled with the villagers. By Allah, I might learn some secrets about the Satan-leopard. With your honor's permission—"

The girl smiled, and came nearer, to get the empty dishes. Steele said to his servant, "Go ahead, but don't get into any fights."

That Achmet could not understand a word of Burmese did not for a moment make his request seem illogical to him. He was a master at devising reasons for following his stubborn fancies.

The villagers had little confidence in the hunters. Thus there was ample reason for music and dancing and the impromptu clowning of a *pwé* (celebration). The festival was not in honor of Steele; his arrival had been merely an excuse for celebrating. Had he not been there, the full moon would have been ample reason.

And knowing that Burmese peculiarity, Steele lit a cheroot, and watched Achmet crossing the compound, to follow Panbyu.

And then night invaded the clearing. The chilly breeze stirred the bamboos to ghostly, inarticulate speech. A jackal howled from afar, and owls hooted from the jungle over which towered the spires of long-ruined pagodas. Laughter and strangely syncopated music filtered from the toddy palms and tamarinds and mangoes that half concealed the village. The *dâk bungalow* had become a dark island in a deceptive sea of moonlight. It was incredibly isolated. Some trick of the wind, perhaps, made the festive cacophony of the *pwé* as though it came from another world.

Steele was no longer conscious of the soporific drumbeats and xylophone notes; nevertheless he felt the incessant impact, and began to feel the concentration of the disturbing, vague whispers that had centered on him ever since he had entered Eldon Powell's office in Rangoon.

Steele kicked the dying fire, shivered in the penetrating chill, and told himself that he had listened to too many whispers concerning Thagyâ Min, King of Tawadeintha—the land of demons, *nats* who haunted every stream, every grove and forest, lurking by night to slip up on unwary Burmese. From afar he heard the excruciating *creak-creak* of a cart-wheel. The ungreased axle did not betoken laziness on the part of the driver; it was a studied effort to frighten away night-roving *nats* that contribute to terror of darkness.

He began to sense that the *pwé* itself was more than festivity: it was to discourage with light and noise and a concentration of humans the *nats* who must have followed Steele to the village.

The demon subjects of Thagyâ Min would have a hearty interest in anyone setting out to kill the ghost leopard of Kokogon.

"To hell with this!" he finally muttered, shaking off oppressive, errant fancies. Instead of heaping more fuel on the fire, Steele sought the warmth of his blankets. The wind, sifting up between the cracks in the floor, was peculiarly penetrating—as penetrating as the insidious, scarcely heard rhythm that filtered from the *zariba** (thornbush fence) that surrounded the village. A dizzying procession of Burmese girls statuesquely postured before Steele's closed eyes. They were now pacing and gesturing to demon music from the court of Thagyâ Min, and the hollow notes of cunningly tuned pieces of hardwood, vibrant under dancing mallets, whispered to the ears of sleep.

A touch of fever . . . too many of those dried, reeking fish that no white man should eat . . . or trying to keep pace with Achmet's demolition of a heap of curry as tall as a pagoda . . . but finally the trenchant chill ceased lancing the blankets, and it no longer seemed cold in the *dâk bungalow.*

It was now very warm and pleasant. Yet, though Steele was asleep, he was nevertheless aware of the moon-flooded clearing, and the gable-roofed monastery in the eastern wing of which sat the Buddha Gautama. Oddly enough, the walls of the bungalow did not keep Steele from perceiving the three-roofed *pyathat* beneath which the Buddha sat in the posture he had prescribed for meditation.

One acquires merit through meditation. But it was much more spectacular to acquire merit by building pagodas. The ruined pagodas at the jungle's edge were the ghosts of merit forgotten save by the lords of Karma.

The clearing was dominated by the shadow of pious work, and the Buddha Gautama could scarcely help being pleased. His face was still obscured, although Steele could now perceive the gilded bulk that loomed in the darkness of the *hpaya kyaung.* It no longer seemed odd to Steele that he could be aware of so many things at once.

And then a jarring thought intruded: something was urging him to open his eyes, which was absurd, since with his present clarity of vision the position of his eyelids was immaterial. Steele became intensely annoyed. It was Achmet who was urging him to open his eyes. Achmet, full of intoxicating *kaungye*, would be boisterous as well as bawdy. . . .

It was Steele's instinct that saved him: an indefinable shred of perception that had not been submerged by the glamour of the *nat*-infested night. Even before he opened his eyes or ceased to resent the disturbing summons, he flung himself clear of blankets and cot. In the darkness he saw a flashing streak of frosty silver, and a blotch of shadow that moved with it. He felt the rake of steel, the passing contact of a wiry body, heard the roaring voice of Achmet, and the Afghan's feet pounding from the veranda to Steele's room.

Steele's foot lashed out as he hit the floor. There was a gasp of exhaled breath. The broad blade of a *kukri* savagely probed the gloom. Steele's fist warded off the descending wrist—but before he could seize the wiry assassin, Achmet had cleared the threshold.

A wrathful yell—a crash—the splintering of wood—the tinkle of steel—a cry of dismay that ended in a gurgling groan—and Achmet, cursing in polished Pushtu, struck a match.

The intruder was dead: a wiry, grizzled Burmese with straggling wisps of gray beard. His brown skin was intricately tattooed, and his body gleamed from freshly applied palm oil. He was nude save for a breech-clout.

Steele assured Achmet that the fellow must be a *dacoit* (robber). The Afghan respectfully agreed: but Steele knew that his comrade at arms had a private and dissenting opinion.

II

"OUT WITH IT, Achmet!" Steele finally demanded. "What makes you think he's not a *dacoit?*"

"*Billahi!* Since when does a *dacoit* sit in the darkness making music while his fellow seeks you with a knife? Nay, by Allah, that was not the music of the *pwé* which you heard—that was devil music. The *pwé* has been over these several hours—I? *Wallah*, I was otherwise engaged—I had no thought—by Allah, it is a disgrace to my beard that this thing should have happened, but by your head, I had no thought—"

"Say no more about it," chuckled Steele. "After all, there was doubtless certain unfinished business which required your attention after the *pwé*, but then what?"

"As my lord suggested, when that was done which was to be done, I returned and heard, and I liked not that sound which came from the shadows. So I smote the musician, and then I saw another—*Wallah*, I will here and now kill that son of a noseless mother!"

The Afghan's pious intent, however, was wasted. Neither musician nor instrument was lying where both had dropped.

"Get Maung Hkin—the headman of the village," said Steele. "At once."

The Afghan stalked cursing into the moonlight. He knew no Burmese—other than what he might have learned from Panbyu—but there was no doubt that he would arouse the entire village and thus, perforce, the headman as well. Steele had learned to put much trust in Afghan directness.

And within a very few minutes Maung Hkin entered the compound, followed by half the inhabitants of Hlai-bin-doung. They were trotting to keep up with Achmet's leg-stretching strides.

"May pigs befoul my grave if I destroy not all of this village!" growled Achmet as he stalked across the compound. "*Wallah*, I have here the father of all these apes! Shall I slay him now?"

Steele, however, was willing enough to dispense with further slayings; and he mustered up enough of the tricky Burmese language to make it clear to the headman that there had been odd doings in the *dâk bungalow*. But one glance at the deceased was sufficient for Maung Hkin.

"This man," he explained, "is an apprentice wizard. Behold—he is tattooed with *inns* to protect: him against knives, bullets, poison, and lightning. Fortunately he wore no *inn* to protect him against a broken neck and a crushed skull.

"And as for that music: that was a charm to keep you from awakening. It seems that you were taken for a rival wizard. Or perhaps he wanted your head to use in preparing a spell. But it is most likely that he is a servant of the demon leopard, sent to protect the devouring *nat* against your skill."

That was the headman's story. He seemed to believe it, and it was obvious that nothing could change it. It was quite irrational, and thus entirely in keeping with the beliefs of devil-haunted Burma, where Indian, Mongolian, and indigenous fiends do their best to oppress the inhabitants of the mountains and forests. But Maung Hkin had one constructive hint: "Let no one know the hour of your birth. And there is a certain but dangerous way of defending yourself against *sohns*. Go up the Chindwin to Kalay-Thoung-Toht—the-Small-Town-at-the-Top-of-the-Sandbank. The inhabitants are supernaturally gifted. Appeal to the king of wizards who lives there. He will summon the *sohn* who is working against you, demand an explanation, and if he can show no just cause, he will be punished.

"But it is only fair to warn you that many bewitched people who have made that pilgrimage have disappeared."

"Thanks," acknowledged Steele. "But as long as wizards' heads are readily broken I don't think we'll bother to go to Kalay-Thoung-Toht."

In less than an hour breakfast would be served, the elephants loaded, and the ponies saddled in preparation for the last lap of the trip to the teak camp at the head of the Kyouk-mee-Choung. Steele sat down and drew up a brief report to be sent to Eldon Powell in Rangoon. He outlined the circumstances, and concluded:

"*Your were-leopard has human allies. I am inclined to think that the depredations of the beast are directly designed to interfere with your floating teak logs down in the coming freshets. I suggest that you investigate your neighboring competitors while Achmet and I put a crimp into the local guild of wizards.*"

STEELE AND ACHMET cleared the compound at sunrise; but it was not until fourteen hours later that they reached their destination at the teak camp of the Irrawaddy Company. The corporation bungalow was in a grassy plain. Near it were storehouses, stables, and a cluster of huts for the native woodmen; and beyond was the expanse of dense forest, towering teak interspersed with pyingado, padauk, and other unreserved or "jungle" woods not subject to Government regulation.

The *kansammah* (headman), Saya-myo, emerged to receive Steele and Achmet. Kirby, the camp manager, was out in the forest, hunting the man-eating leopard. And while Saya-myo set about preparing supper, Steele made a round of the camp, watching the unloading of the baggage and the grooming of the shaggy Shan ponies. The day's work was done; the elephants had been fed. Some were bathing in the creek nearby, others were crashing through the underbrush, foraging to supplement their evening meal.

The camp, Steele observed, had been demoralized by the leopard's raids. The loggers and mahouts squatted about their fires, furtively eyeing the darkness beyond; and while Steele could scarcely understand their low, sing-song conversation, scattering phrases told him of the fear that lurked. There was talk of *inns*, and amulets to ward off the destructive night demon; and there was more talk of desertion, and certain mutterings about a sacred grove. . . .

Kirby, it was obvious, was in charge of a simmering nightmare.

Supper was more than adequate, despite can-opener cookery. The camp commissary was well stocked, and the cook was competent; yet Kirby, oppressed by the inroads of the marauder, had at the first sign of dusk plunged alone into the forest, ignoring the meal that awaited him.

"He won't last very long at that rate," Steele reflected. "One white man, surrounded by superstitious natives, and for months out of contact with civilization—no damn wonder it gets his goat."

Ten o'clock, and still no sign of Kirby.

"Achmet," Steele finally said, "grab yourself some sleep. I'll wait until midnight, and then wake you for the next watch."

"No, by Allah! Last night my face was blackened. If there are any wandering wizards tonight—"

The Afghan loosened the pistol in his holster, and shifted the Khorassan tulwar whose silver hilt gleamed from his belt.

"Without doubt," he continued, "Kirby *Sahib* has been eaten by this *shaitan*-leopard. Do you therefore sleep, while I stand guard."

And seeing that Achmet would stubbornly insist upon redeeming himself for the previous night's distraction, Steele let him stand guard.

STEELE'S SLEEP WAS SOUND, but it was violently interrupted. An agonized yell brought him to his feet at a bound. Then savage growls, and a howling panic from the woodcutters' huts. Steele seized his loaded rifle. "God, by the very God, by the One True God!" roared Achmet as Steele followed him, clearing the veranda at a bound. "Hear the accursed beast!"

As he caught up with Achmet, Steele thrust a flashlight into the Afghan's hand.

"Pick him out while I plug him!"

They crossed the clearing in a matter of seconds. The savage snarling of the marauder, and the gurgling, strangled cries of the victim guided them. Achmet turned the beam of the flashlight toward the sound and the phosphorescent eyes that gleamed in the gloom.

"In the great name of Allah I take refuge from Shaytan the Stoned!" exclaimed Achmet as the tongue of light picked the eater and the eaten. "The grandfather of leopards!"

The white glare confirmed the Afghan's words; but for the jet-black spots that dotted the sleek, tawny hide, Steele would have thought that it was a tiger that growled and bared fangs like ivory scimitars. Its jaws dripped red, and its tail lashed in slow, menacing cadence as its muscles rippled beneath its silky hide. But more striking than its feline savagery and unusual size was the wrath and menace that it radiated. Steele felt the fury of the creature as though it emanated waves of tangible force.

The chilly breeze was laden with the feline odor of the beast—like the odor of a lion's den, but more intense.

Grandfather of leopards—in a flickering instant, Steele's impressions confirmed the Afghan's incredulous ejaculation. The mangled woodcutter still twitched, but he no longer groaned.

It was an easy shot, and the beast seemed dazzled by the blistering glare of the flashlight. Steele's rifle flashed into line. The fluent, long-practiced gesture ended in a spurt of flame, a gust of nitrous fumes, and the ear-shattering blast of cordite. A streak of orange velvet—a wrathful, almost human yell—and before Steele could shift his line of fire, there was a scarcely perceptible rustling in the farther shadows.

The leopard was gone. He had seemingly timed the contraction of Steele's trigger finger, and flung himself aside as the front sight of the express rifle registered between his glowing eyes.

"Damn!" growled Steele; and Achmet muttered unmentionable things in Pushtu as he saw something he had never seen before: Steele *Sahib* missing an easy shot.

"But you must at least have wounded him," the Afghan insisted. Steele shook his head.

"Can't tell. So much blood spattered about. Fact is, I'm sure I didn't. I'd swear the —— evaporated just as I poured it to him."

"And now," was Achmet's optimistic prediction, "since we have interrupted his feeding, he will go out and hunt down Kirby *Sahib*—if he has not already done so."

Very likely, Steele reflected, if Kirby was not dead, or fatally wounded, he must be lost. No one in his right mind would be bushwhacking from sunset until well after midnight.

"But if Kirby has had much of this to contend with," Steele added, listening to the panicky chatter of the surviving woodcutters, "he can't be in his right mind. By Heaven, if I can't shoot any better than that I'm going to get a bayonet and charge the next time I see that spotted ——!"

And Achmet Nadir Khan of the Durani clan was somberly muttering to himself, "*To the Lord of the Daybreak I betake me for refuge against Satan the Damned, and against the evils of creation, and against the envy of the envier when he envieth, and against the wiles of women who murmur and blow on knots. . . .*"

III

ACHMET, DESPITE HIS mutterings, insisted on standing the remainder of the watch; but he built a fire just in front of the veranda steps, and walked his post with curved tulwar drawn and ready to strike. And Steele, despite the tragedy that had taken place, borrowed the fatalistic attitude of the Burmese woodcutters who had composed themselves with the cheery thought that since the demon leopard had drunk blood he would not return until the following night.

"By Heaven," was Steele's last waking thought, "I couldn't miss that beast at that range and in that light. Something's cockeyed."

But the fault could certainly not have been with Steele's ammunition. The unexpended cartridge in his rifle was sound in every respect, and the vigorous recoil of the shot he had fired precluded the possibility of its having been a blank. Nevertheless, he was convinced that human skullduggery was allied with the monstrous leopard. The attack by the apprentice wizard at Hlai-bin-doung was ample proof of that; although this time there had been no disturbed sleep nor music from the halls of the King of Demon-Land to bemaze Steele's wits. Aside from the size and unheard-of ferocity of the beast, there had been nothing out of the ordinary except his having missed an easy shot.

And a man suddenly roused from slumber could have a lingering kink in his trigger finger.

The stirring about of the mahouts, and the loggers preparing *chota hazri*, woke Steele before the dawn was even gray. Achmet shook the dew from his red beard, sheathed his curved tulwar, and muttered a devout *"al hamdu lilahi."*

And then the Afghan made uncommonly careful ablution in preparation for the sunrise prayer. But that prayer was delayed by the arrival of a white man from the fringe of the jungle. Achmet hailed Steele; and as the newcomer stalked across the grassy clearing, they knew that he must be Kirby, the manager. There would be no other white man attached to the camp.

Achmet's eyes flashed toward Steele's; and then they both regarded the haggard, bedraggled man in shorts. Even in that wan, gray light he was unusual. There was no doubt that he was a white man: his skin, tanned as only that of a Nordic can be, and the high bridge of his nose, and the unprominent cheek-bones, testified to his race. Yet his hazel-flecked eyes were slanted like those of a Tartar or Mongol. His mustaches, sandy-colored and bristling, jutted straight out on both sides instead of being upturned at the ends, or decently drooping, or close cropped.

His eyes widened and assumed an odd expression that Steele found disturbing and unpleasant.

"I'm Harrison Steele—from Rangoon office," Steele greeted. "I fancy Powell wrote you I'd be up to give you a lift on this leopard mess?"

"Don Kirby," was the acknowledgment. "Managing this damned madhouse, and I'm mighty glad you arrived."

The perturbed, haggard look left his face as he spoke, and his voice was amiable enough; but Steele, without knowing why, was glad that Kirby did not extend his hand. And then Steele wanted to give Achmet a sound booting: the burly Afghan was eyeing Kirby from head to foot and muttering in a hoarse whisper that carried like a cavalry bugle, "*Astaghfir 'ullah min-ash-saytan. . . .*"

"There are times," was Steele's unspoken thought, "for betaking one's self for refuge against Satan, but that red-bearded ruffian shows the damn'dest judgment in picking them."

He wondered if Kirby understood Arabic, and catching the sudden shift of the slanting, topaz eyes, Steele remarked, "Achmet's had a tough night of it—he thinks the place is bewitched because I missed letting moonlight through our friend the leopard."

"So you missed him too?"

Steele could not quite decide whether that one carried an edge or not. It might be Kirby's natural tone.

"Right enough," replied Steele. "The brute turned tail and vanished like Satan in a puff of smoke—but not until another poor devil of a woodcutter was hopelessly mangled."

And then, for a man who for months has had no occasion to use English, Kirby was uncommonly fluent. His blasphemous wrath was impressive. Finally he concluded, "And I was bushwhacking all night long, getting torn to ribbons. I figured the brute might come down to the *jeel* to drink—that's a couple of miles to the east—and I'd get a crack at him."

THAT WAS SOUND ENOUGH. The great cats do usually drink; *after they have dined*. Kirby apparently had assumed that the leopard would not miss his nightly fare. Steele noted the mud that had copiously bespattered Kirby, and concluded that it had been rough going along the banks of the marshy *jeel*.

"Taking a long chance, aren't you, going it single-handed?"

Kirby shrugged, spat disgustedly, and said, "If this keeps up, I'll not have a logger left, and I won't be able to get any from the village. The freshets are almost here, and so far we've not taken out enough logs to notice. There'll be a new manager here to handle the problem if I don't put a stop to this." Then he hailed the *kan-sammah*, ordered breakfast, and stepped to his room in the corporation bungalow to clean up after his night's fruitless chase.

"Achmet," demanded Steele as the Afghan approached, "what the hell were you driving at with your '*astaghfir 'ullah*' and so forth a few minutes ago?"

"There is evil in this camp, *Sahib*," grumbled the Afghan. "And this Kirby *Sahib* is the forgotten of Allah. By Allah, in his eyes I saw the eyes of that *shaitan*-leopard, and for a moment I was going to cut him down with my tulwar. But instead, I spoke as you heard, and I was no longer afraid."

"Since when," reproved Steele, "is one of the Durani clan afraid of anything?"

"Since when," came the crackling retort, "has a *sahib* the eyes of a leopard, and the curved nails of one? Do you now understand why he did not offer to grasp your hand as is the custom among these infidel dogs, saving your honor's presence? It was that you would not note that his nails curve more than any man's should."

And before Steele could think of a convincing answer, Achmet was stalking toward the huts of the woodcutters.

Steele joined Kirby at breakfast. The *kansammah*, serving the meal, walked as though he were treading on eggs. Despite his efforts to disguise his furtive moves, it was obvious that he was avoiding any unnecessary approach to Kirby. The fellow's manner had with the appearance of his chief changed from fatalistic resignation to wire-edged apprehension.

Kirby minced with his meal, grimaced wryly, cursed each dish in succession, then said, "This thing is getting under my skin. And the devil of it is, I dare not make a truthful report."

In response to Steele's trenchant glance, Kirby significantly tapped his forehead.

"I don't think I'm balmy yet, but I dare say I soon shall be. But if I told all that I know, Powell would order me to Rangoon and before I could say three words he'd have me in the booby-hatch— on the evidence of my own report."

Kirby was oppressively serious. And while Steele had been unable to conjure up the last trace of cordiality—beyond decent politeness—he was heartily sorry for the manager. The poor devil was in a blue funk; but his tacit admission that his reason was beginning to waver was a hopeful indication. If the man were mad, he would be the last to question his own sanity.

"The hell you say?" Steele's exclamation carried a distinct query. Kirby's hazel eyes were disturbingly unwavering for several seconds, but he ignored the hint. Steele then persisted, "Don't write it, then. While I can scarcely demand your confidence, I'm in a way entitled to it. You needn't worry about my quoting you. I won't. And if I did—well, who'd believe me?"

Kirby nodded, declined a cigarette, and finally said, "Last year, just before the freshets, we had an unusual tangle of logs and little time, as usual, to get them to the creek. The roundabout road my predecessor had built seemed insufferably stupid, so I laid out a new route for the elephants.

"I jolly well had a mutiny on my hands, but I fairly booted the woodcutters into clearing a direct approach that skirted the village, just over the hill. That road, it seemed, passed directly through a sacred grove, or some such rot—and there was no end of muttering about the *nats*—"

Kirby gritted his teeth, snarled a compound oath, and continued, "And the long and short of it is they claim that this leopard is a devil sent to avenge my—our—violating the home of the forest *nats*—the blasted unspeakable country is filthy with *nats!* The natives count 'em off by the million—offer sacrifices to them—shiver when they think of 'em—and by the Lord, I'm getting that way myself!

"Damn it, Steele—I'm convinced this devil leopard is a *nat!*—that it's hounding me to death, killing my men—but can I report that story to Powell? Can I?"

Steele stroked his chin and exhaled a jet of smoke. He could not offer Kirby any assurance. You can't assure a grown white man against the wrath of wizards and evil spirits. And regardless of what alienists might say, Kirby was painfully sane. He elaborated on the apparent chain of cause and effect, and concluded, "Irrespective of my personal sanity, there is a leopard, and the camp is demoralized, and if I ask Powell to shift operations to the eastern sector, I'll have to offer him some reason other than that this one is devil haunted.

"The only thing I can tell him is that I'm not competent to handle these woodcutters. Just one whimper about native wizards, and—"

"Correct," agreed Steele. "But just between the two of us—how about giving me the address of this wizard?"

Kirby eyed him suspiciously. He seemed on the point of answering but instead, he abruptly rose and said, "I'm placing an elephant and a mahout at your disposal. Also come *shikaris*, though they'll no more beat the brush than they'll fly. After all, Powell sent you to hunt a leopard, not a wizard. And I'm not so sure that I appreciate your trying to humor my whims."

And that, Steele perceived, put an end to any chance of getting Kirby's confidence. His only resource was to look for the spoor of the killer: which should not be difficult, as it was improbable that there was more than one beast of such unusual size in the district.

One thought, however, gnawed at Steele's mind. The demon leopard had human allies, and native wizards were involved—unless the headman of Hlai-bin-doung had been fabricating to deflect suspicion from his villagers. Yet he could as well, and much more logically, have asserted that the man Achmet had brained was a *dacoit*.

"Just a few more kinks like that," muttered Steele, "and I'll join Achmet's *astaghfir 'ullah* chorus! I'll be as screwy as Kirby."

IV

STEELE SOON LEARNED that tracking the demon leopard was a thankless job. Neither he nor Achmet could pick up the beast's trail; and while a native *shikari* would undoubtedly find some mark that survived the milling of many feet about the place where the leopard had last struck, none could be bribed or browbeaten into the attempt. And as the result of their futile efforts, Steele and Achmet patrolled the logging-camp by night, hoping to catch the marauder as he made a raid. But again they reckoned without taking into account the diabolical cunning of the leopard; the beast avoided the huts of the woodcutters and, instead, struck at the neighboring village.

His victims were a native girl, and a mahout *en route* to the camp.

And then woodcutters began disappearing without a trace. No sign of struggle, no blood, no mangled remains indicated by the low-flying scavenger birds collecting about the scene of a slaying.

"They're deserting," said Kirby, alternating between inertia and high-pitched wrath. "By the Lord, Steele, you've not a chance. Neither have I—but I'll hunt the beast myself until one of us is accounted for."

And thus, at sunset, Kirby would slip into the forest for a night of bushwhacking as Steele and Achmet began their vigil at camp.

The manager had scarcely reached the edge of the forest when Saya-myo, the *kansammah*, accosted Steele. The fellow was obviously perturbed, and seemed to be mustering up his courage for some desperate step, but his remarks were scattered and irrelevant.

"Sound off," encouraged Steele. "What's on your mind, Saya-myo? Has that Afghan ruffian of mine been monopolizing all the ladies of the village?"

That, however, was not the trouble. It was something much more serious. And it in no wise concerned Achmet. Saya-myo glanced over one shoulder, then the other, and fingered the nine-jeweled amulet that hung from his neck. The amulet business had enjoyed a boom at the expense of teak logging.

"It is Kirby *Sahib*," the Burmese finally said. "He is the leopard. At night the man disappears, and he becomes a beast. He—"

"Shaytan rip him open! I suspected as much!" boomed the voice of Achmet, as his red beard heralded his advance around the corner of the bungalow. "Es-Steele *Sahib*, I will kill this man. There be only these Burmese apes, who will dare not tell what I have done."

"Shut up, you jackass!" snapped Steele. "Allah gave you much valor and no brains. Who ever heard of a man becoming a leopard by night?"

Steele had heard all too much of such things, but this was no occasion to admit it.

"*Wallah*," grumbled the Afghan, "that at least is better than having neither brains nor valor. If that *shaitan*-leopard had killed even one of my kinsmen, I would have slit him crosswise as soon as he took back the shape of a man.

"Is it not plain as your nose that this man Kirby is the slayer? Does he not always walk by night? Is he ever seen near a slaying? Is he ever attacked by night by any beast? And mark you this: I found no footprints of a leopard near the body of the woodcutter who was killed before our eyes, but there were marks left by the boots of an infidel—"

"My own boots," interrupted Steele. "Before you could get a good look, there had been so much trampling about that all heel marks looked alike."

"The Red Beard is right," interposed Saya-myo. "And we are all dead men if he does not kill Kirby. If we stay, we die. If we run, he will hunt us down and kill us."

THE THREE-CORNERED debate was interrupted by a scarcely perceptible rustling at the edge of the clearing. Steele whirled, rifle at the ready. But it was no beast of prey that stepped from black shadow into light of the waning moon. It was Don Kirby, and the feral gleam of his eyes showed that he had heard more than enough.

"I think, Steele," was his ironic remark, "that your red-bearded wild man is nearly as bad as the Burmese. Now if you think you can keep that Afghan within the limits of the clearing, I'll risk resuming the hunt. As you say, he has more nerve than brains, and unless you restrain him, he would venture into the bush to track me down."

"God, by God, by the One True God!" growled Achmet, "verily, I would not risk meeting you in the forest by night! But saving my lord's presence, I would throttle you at sunrise when you resume the form of a man."

Kirby shook his head, eyed Steele, then said, "You begin to see what a madhouse this has become. And you, Saya-myo, what manner of talk was this you made?"

Kirby's voice was low, but vibrant. The *kansammah's* brown face had become ghastly with fright. He licked his lips, made a false start at speech, then ran howling into the forest.

"The fool's going to the temple to get some more charms," explained Kirby.

"Temple?" queried Steele. "That's a bit odd, up here in the hills. Or is it that monastery up over the hill, and beyond the village?"

Kirby shook his head.

"Not a monastery. Ruined temple. Something like those square heaps in Pagân—you might have seen them on the way up."

"Didn't cross the river," replied Steele. "But speaking of temples—is that the nest of wizards that's put the jinx on this camp?"

"Suppose you figure that out," was Kirby's somber challenge. "I'm fairly addle-brained from guessing. And in the meanwhile, I'm taking a jaunt out to the *jeel* again. I saw his footprints there, last night."

So saying, Kirby turned toward the clearing. Steele frowned as he watched his lithe, cat-like tread.

"How that guy supervises a logging-camp and stalks game every night is something to think about," he muttered. "It's a blistering cinch he can't turn into a leopard at night, but Saya-myo's mortally afraid of him. Somebody's going to get hurt. And it's not a leopard that'll put period-quotes to Kirby."

Steele hailed Achmet.

"Thou blustering oaf," he said in Pushtu, "keep a sharp eye on this camp. I am walking by the *jeel* myself."

"By Allah, *Sahib*—it is death!" warned the Afghan. "Wait until morning to slay him."

"If I see him turn into a leopard," compromised Steele, "then will we kill him as you say. Not until then."

Steele headed for the path that led through the forest to the adjoining village, but he checked his stride at the stockade that had just been built around the huts of the native foresters and hailed his mahout in a low voice.

The mahout was a fellow of indeterminate race, and named Jang. Jang's mother had doubtless bestowed the name on him in memory of some wandering Gurka. At all events, his resemblance to the Nepalese mountaineers was striking.

"Shall I get my brother?" wondered Jang, referring to his elephant. "I hear his *kalouk* over there."

"No. Hunting that *pukka shaytan* (out-and-out evil spirit) from a howdah," said Steele, "is like trying to spear porpoises from a battleship. Bring your *kukri* and we will walk by moonlight—near the *jeel*."

Jang swallowed his aversion to walking, and in a moment reappeared with the short, heavy-bladed Kurka knife which served every purpose, from paring radishes to clipping the nose from an unfaithful wife. And as they plunged into the forest, Steele whispered, "I have changed my mind about the *jeel*. Lead the way to the village, and especially toward that temple."

Jang's teeth flashed in the moonlight. The sooner the *sahib* showed some sense and made magic, the sooner the marauder would cease his depredations.

Steele's suspicions concerning Kirby were far more grave than he had dared to admit to the hot-headed Afghan or the morose woodcutters. Reviling Achmet's somber mutterings was no more than a move to put a damper on the Afghan's tendency to solve all difficulties by sudden violence; and while Steele was convinced that something was startlingly wrong with Kirby, he dared not make any admissions that might lead to the camp manager's summary and secret assassination.

Leopards can be trained to hunt. And Kirby's alternation of frankness and reticence hinted that he knew more than he admitted. It was conceivable that some enemy of the teak company was using a trained leopard of unusual size to demoralize the camp, and that Kirby dared not reveal his knowledge or suspicion. And Steele's real mission that night was to overtake Saya-myo, the *kansammah* whose fear of Kirby had driven him in a panic toward the temple beyond the village.

JANG BORE A straight course among the teak trunks, with his *kukri* deftly chopping the underbrush that blocked his advance. And save for such interruptions, their progress was swift and silent. Presently, as they cleared the first range of hills, Steele saw the fires of the Burmese village flickering among the vegetation and huts within the *zariba* that enclosed it.

They descended the slope, crossed a clearing, skirted a small paddy field; and in a cleft that ran cross-wise of the range, Steele saw the squarish, quasi-pyramidal bulk of the temple.

"There is a shrine of Thagyâ Min, King of Demons, *sahib*," said Jang. "Give him gifts and perhaps he will recall his servant."

"Maybe," countered Steele with a wry grimace, "that's why Thagyâ Min sent him in the first place!"

And then Steele perceived a moving blot in the darkness ahead. It had charged from the shadows cast by the further side of the village stockade. Someone was heading for the ruined temple.

"Cut over, Jang," whispered Steele. "But don't let him know we're following him."

He had only Kirby's word for Saya-myo's destination, and in the darkness it was impossible to decide whether or not it was the *kansammah* who had slipped from the village to go to the temple;

but whoever it was, it would be worth investigation. Eavesdropping would be more informative than any possible questioning of the frightened natives whose panic would inevitably intensify their distrust of any white man associated with Kirby.

As Jang beat a swift, silent course, the solitary pilgrim broke from shadow and into a moonlight clearing. It was Saya-myo, hurrying as though the devil pursued. Whether his object was a charm or counsel, it must be potent indeed to induce him to leave the *zariba.*

"Steady, there," cautioned Steele, as Jang pushed forward.

Jang halted. And then the moon patch exploded in a blaze of action. In an instant it became a contest between feline swiftness and the speed of a man whose moves short-circuited reason and perception. A snarling streak of spotted ferocity catapulted from the farther shadows. Saya-myo yelled, instinctively threw up a warding, futile arm; but the flying mass of whipcord sinews, raking claws and ivory fangs bore him to the ground as Steele's rifle-blast shook the clearing. He knew that he would miss; no marksman could possibly hit that inhumanly swift streak of tawny doom. He bounded forward, heard the savage snarl, the half-stifled yell of the *kansammah,* and leveled his rifle as his leap gave him a line of fire quite clear of the leopard's victim.

Another tearing, crackling blast of cordite; the whine of a ricochet bullet, and then a second shot. They were closely spaced as blows of a riveting hammer. Only then did Steele realize that he had again missed a perfect target. The beast should have been torn in half by the expanding bullets aimed just in the back of his shoulder.

Steele ejected the spent shells and with trembling fingers thrust fresh ones into the breech. Saya-myo was thrashing and yelling. The leopard's head shifted from his victim, and his feral eyes blazed like monstrous topazes as he snarled and spat at Steele.

Smack-smack!

The leopard's head should be a tangle of shattered bone and brains. But as the concussion of Steele's rifle died, the leopard blurred in fluent flash of motion. One long, soaring leap, and it plunged into a thicket, and disappeared. Steele and Jang pulled Saya-myo to his feet. He was pawed, and bleeding, but his throat had not been torn.

"Can't find him by daylight, and can't hit him by moonlight!" Steele wrathfully growled.

"But you did hit him!" yelled Jang, thrusting the wounded *kansammah* aside. "Look at the blood—"

"Saya-myo's."

"No, *sahib!* Yonder—see the splash?"

Jang was right. The splashes were small, but unmistakably beyond where the *kansammah's* wounds had reddened the ground. Steele, however, shared neither Saya-myo's fear of the leopard's vengeance, nor Jang's triumph and confidence. Instead of scratching the beast, the expanding slugs should have torn it to a tangled heap of bones and fur. As he fired, Steele had "spotted" his shots, and knew that at the instant of concussion, his rifle had been aimed on the leopard's shoulder. When a trained marksman cannot call his shots, something is entirely out of gear.

"Let's see the priest," was Steele's next remark.

Saya-myo led the way. Tapers were flickering in one of the four shrines of the temple. The priest listened to the story of the encounter. His comment was brief.

"This beast is Kirby *Sahib*. He is a leopard by night. His very name—*Kirba*—in the Kanarese language means leopard. You cannot kill him unless you learn from the King of Wizards what weapon can hurt him."

"Kalay-Thoung-Toht?" queried Steele.

"Yes. The-Small-Town-at-the-Top-of-the-Sandbank. And if you still doubt that this Kirby is a leopard, consider that he knew Saya-myo's destination, and followed him—even as you did. It is plain."

V

"By Allah, *sahib!*" boomed a deep voice from the doorway. "That man speaks sense."

Achmet was at the threshold, nodding and stroking his red beard.

"I told you to stay and watch the camp," reproved Steele.

"*Wallah*, seeing that thou wert gone, there was nothing to watch, except these ape men. And I heard the sound of firing."

There was no arguing with the Afghan. True to type, he masked his breath of discipline by appealing to Steele's appreciation of loyalty. The worst of it was that Achmet had heard the old priest's ideas on Kirby. Something had to be done to keep the Afghan from setting out at once to hunt Kirby; but before Steele could find words, his attention was distracted by the wailing of pipes and the mutter of drums from within the temple. And Steele had unpleasant memories of eery music by moonlight.

"What's that?" he demanded of the priest. Then he recognized the three-eight time of Indian music, utterly different from the tempo and five-note scale of Burmese musicians.

"A company of *nautch* (East Indian professional dancing) girls on their way to the Shan states," he replied. His gesture invited him to witness the rehearsal; and Steele, though in no mood for *nautch* dances, decided it would be good policy to humor the old fellow.

They followed him to the inner courtyard, where the strolling players were performing.

"By Allah, *sahib!*" declared the Afghan, as he eyed the slender, golden brown bodies swaying in the moonlit court, "these be finer game than those village girls."

Achmet was true to form.

"Nilofal and Nur Mahal," commented the priest. "Kashmiri dancing-girls. Perhaps my lord would be interested in a—ah, one might say, a private performance, at the bungalow."

Steele gave him the Burmese equivalent of "hell, no!"

Achmet, however, had been thinking rapidly.

"*Sahib*," he interposed, "those lovely girls are in great peril from the *shaitan*-leopard. And those dogs from Hindustan"—his contemptuous gesture indicated the musicians—"would make no move to protect them. Nor the old priest either. They should be at camp where I could stand guard."

"Get out," ordered Steele.

"Or let me stay here and watch the temple for this excellent old priest," persisted the Afghan.

But Steele this time had a ready weapon: "While you were whispering sweet nothings to that Burmese girl, an assassin came near, knifing me."

"*Billah!* My face is still blackened," the Afghan penitently admitted; but as he followed Steele, he cast covetous glances at Nilofal and Nur Mahal. Then he sighed and resigned himself to his master's uncommon whims.

As they headed back toward the teak camp, Steele noted the Afghan's thoughtful face, and wondered whether he was thinking of the King of Wizards or the unprotected Kashmiri girls.

"Kashmiri wins by a length," was his verdict as he seated himself at the table in his room.

He composed a letter to Powell, giving him a complete report. The situation was becoming tense, and Steele wanted further information as to Kirby. A skilful trainer of hunting-leopards, introduced into the camp by a rival teak company, and aided by native wizards, could completely demoralize the organization.

"Which is a damn sight more reasonable than *shaitan*-leopards," concluded Steele, as he added his signature to the letter that was to go to Rangoon in the morning. And Achmet, now more than ever determined to kill Kirby, would be just the man to act as runner. The following morning, however, Steele saw that his strategy had failed. Achmet was gone; and shortly after breakfast, Steele learned the cause of his desertion. One of the *mahouts* finally told him that the Afghan had set out on foot to seek the King of Wizards, determined to settle things, once for all.

WHEN STEELE'S WRATH subsided, he philosophically decided that an Afghan is an Afghan, and sent a woodcutter with the message to Powell.

That afternoon brought a second upset, though one that was more welcome. Powell himself, riding a shaggy Shan pony, came ambling into camp.

"Your first letter set me thinking," he explained. "Your being nearly knifed at the Burmese village convinced me that the forest devils had human allies. So I looked up Kirby's references, and found out that they were faked. He was on the payroll of the Kokogon Teak Company until I put him in charge here—which entirely contradicts his story about working in the Pahang gold belt.

"And our friend Kirby will be dismissed at once. I'll manage this camp myself until a new man can come from Rangoon. In the meanwhile, you can be killing the leopard."

"Flattering as hell, Powell—unless the natives happen to be right about Kirby."

Powell eyed him narrowly, shook his bead, and twisted his drooping, straw-colored mustache.

"The first thing I know, Steele, you'll be following Achmet to the village of the King of Wizards."

"Anyhow," countered Steele, "don't fire Kirby. Let's look into this a bit further."

They argued it back and forth for half an hour, but finally Steele's counsel prevailed. He maintained that dismissing Kirby would at the best be begging the question, and that the only way to restore order in the camp was to kill the *shaitan*-leopard.

For a week there were no depredations. The morale of the camp improved, and when Kirby realized that Powell had not come to dismiss him, relations between the three white men were less strained. Yet for all his assurance that Steele had not been undermining him, Kirby was far from cordial toward the American. Steele often caught the camp manager fixedly regarding him with a strange, appraising stare. He wondered whether Kirby still feared that he would report to Powell their conversation the evening of the American's arrival at camp.

"I'm beginning to think," observed Powell one evening after dinner, "that you must have seriously wounded the beast the last time you encountered it, and it crawled away to die."

Steele shook his head. "I think the natives have been so scared that they're keeping under cover, so it can't grab any of them. I know I had my rifle lined right at it, but I'm just as sure that I didn't touch the beast. My guess is that as soon as the natives become careless again, we'll hear plenty."

"Maybe," was Kirby's ironic comment, "it waylaid your Afghan playmate and died of indigestion."

Powell saw the wrathful flash in Steele's eyes, and tried to change the subject.

"You know, we really ought to see a performance by those *nautch* dancers before they go north," he remarked. "I hear they're uncommonly talented."

As he spoke, Powell's glance included the American and Kirby.

"Thanks, but I'm going out to do a bit of bushwhacking tonight," Kirby answered. "It's about time for the beast to show up again."

They watched Kirby shoulder his rifle and set out on foot toward the *jeel*.

"By Heaven," muttered Powell, "I don't half blame the natives for feeling funny about Kirby. Quite aside from the expression of his face, did you ever see anyone that reminded you more of a cat? Just look at that stride—he even moves like one."

"Suppose," countered Steele, as he struck light to a cigar, "that *you* take a jaunt to the village of wizards."

And when Steele's cigar was down to its final inch, they sent a *mahout* to tell the old priest that they would presently be on hand to witness a performance.

"By Allah, *sahib*," rumbled a deep voice at the doorway, "now that I have returned, I will guard you and the manager *sahib* on the way to the temple."

Achmet, tattered, bedraggled, but triumphant, had returned. He wore his silver-hafted Khorassan tulwar; but as he spoke, he patted the butt of his service revolver. Before Steele could demand an accounting, the Afghan grinned amiably and explained, "As your honor doubtless knows, I went to see the King of Wizards, and got a charm to protect me against leopard *shaitans*. Furthermore, my revolver is loaded with silver bullets. And for good measure I have engraved on each one: *'I betake me to the Lord of the Daybreak for refuge against Shaitan, and against the evils of the night when it darkeneth'*."

Steele, putting little trust in the hundred and thirteenth chapter of the Koran, even if engraved on a bullet, reached for his express rifle as he and Powell set out for the temple. But when they were only a little more than halfway to their destination, Steele knew that they would witness no performance that night. From the half-ruined heap came an agonized cry that was abruptly cut short. Then a confusion of yells, savage growls, and the wailing of a woman. And as they dashed toward the temple, Steel saw a monstrous leopard bounding from the terrace. It had seized one of the dancing-girls, and was dragging her into the jungle. He halted, fired a crackling volley at a streak of golden brown that was scarcely perceptible in the light of the waning moon; but it was a perilous shot as likely to kill the victim as the beast. There was a savage snarling, thrashing in the brush, then a blur of tawny, silken hide.

"You got him!" shouted Powell, as he followed.

"Then it's blind luck," panted Steele, as he approached the spot where the abandoned victim lay moaning. "I barely caught a flash of him."

The Kashmiri girl, mangled by the beast's fangs, was beyond help. But as Steele knelt beside the pitiful remnant of loveliness, he heard a yell, and a rattle of pistol fire; then a crackling in the underbrush, and a wrathful rasping volley of oaths. Steele leaped forward, rifle in hand. Powell and Achmet were at his heels. A dozen strides brought them through the thicket and into a small clearing. They saw Kirby emerging from its farther edge, pistol drawn in hand and stretching his long legs toward them. He was utterly out of breath, and it was not until they reached the body of the Kashmiri girl that he was able to explain.

"I was coming from the *jeel*, and I heard a shot. The first thing I knew the beast was on me, running as if the devil was after it. Knocked me end for end, but went on. It seemed as anxious to get away as I was, but I fired as it cleared me."

During Kirby's narrative, Achmet's sharp eyes covered him from head to foot. Kirby's shoulder was bleeding.

"*Billahi, sahib*," he whispered to Steele. "Verily, he is the *shaitan*-leopard. Look where your shot grazed him!"

"Shut up, you idiot," Steele growled; "that's a slash, not a bullet crease."

But he began pondering when the natives, mustering up enough courage to leave the temple, approached the group gathered about the body of the Kashmiri girl. One of them carried a spear, and its tip was dripping with blood. Someone, cornered and desperate, had struck at the marauder as he bounded out with his prey. And a lance-head would make a slash in passing!

VI

STEELE AND ACHMET carried the remains of the Kashmiri girl back to the temple. There he learned that Nur Mahal, the other *nautch* dancer, had been badly clawed while trying to save her sister.

"*Sahib*," said the girl, whose dark eyes now blazed with wrath, "we were twins, born only an hour apart, and our destinies are closely interlaced. The beast will therefore return for me. There is no help for it, but before the evil stars of my horoscope reach the House of Death I will devise vengeance."

"What do you mean?" he demanded. Although Nur Mahal's argument was fairly sound astrology, it meant little to Steele; but she might suggest some device that had not thus far occurred to the hunters. The valley of Kashmir is infested with leopards, and the natives are unusually skilful in disposing of the beasts.

"It was ordained that the demon leopard would kill my sister," declared Nur Mahal, "and likewise, that he must kill me, since we were born so little apart. Therefore, he will seek me; and you may watch, and thus kill him. My fate is certain; so let me bait a trap, instead of using a young goat, as is the custom."

As she spoke, Nur Mahal's eyes shifted toward Kirby, who stood at the fringe of the crowd. Steele saw their eyes clash, and sensed the antagonism between the two. The girl was firmly convinced that Kirby was a leopard in human form; and he, in his turn, was wrathful because of the girl's unspoken accusation, and the muttering among the natives as they edged away from him.

"That's entirely too wild, Nur Mahal," countered Steele. "You're pretty badly scratched, and you'd better come to camp and get yourself doctored up a bit."

If infection set in, Nur Mahal's dire forebodings would be fulfilled without another attack by the leopard. The Kashmiri girl was being carried on by her nerve. Even as he spoke, she wavered on her feet. Steele caught her as she collapsed.

"You are right," asserted the old priest. "Take her, lest she die of those clawings."

His suggestion was eagerly echoed by the natives. Nur Mahal's saying that her destiny was linked with that of her dead sister and that of the demon leopard made them eager to get her as far from them as possible.

They devised a rude litter. Powell and Achmet carried her to camp.

During the discussion, Kirby had wrathfully left the temple.

"My Heaven, Steele," muttered Powell, as they headed across the clearing, "it's all perfect rot, but Kirby has to leave here at once, or I won't have a logger or mahout left in camp."

"Better wait a while," temporized Steele. "This girl is in bad shape, but I think I can pull her through. That will prove that her astrology was all wrong, which will encourage the natives."

Powell conceded Steele's argument. Halfway across the clearing, they saw Jang running toward them.

"*Sahiban*," he began, "you must not bring the girl to camp. The news has spread. All the woodcutters will leave at once. They are certain that she will draw an attack from the demon leopard."

Steele cursed heartily.

"What'll we do with her?" demanded Powell. "Jang is right. I didn't think of that."

"Build a shelter here near the edge of the clearing," suggested Achmet, "and I will run to camp and get the medicines and bandages for Steele *Sahib* to apply. I will help him guard this woman." Then he added, "Until Allah permits the *shaitan* leopard to eat her."

"Jang," demanded Steele as Achmet bounded across the clearing, "who the devil started this, anyhow?"

"Kirby *Sahib* heard the woodcutters' mutterings," answered Jang. "But as for me, I think that he gave them the thought, so that the girl would not be placed in a bungalow where he could not get her when he takes the shape of a leopard."

"You're crazy," growled Steele. "How can a man become a beast?"

"This is no true leopard," Jang stubbornly persisted. "In my native country there were many of them, but they were only nuisances, not a danger. We hunt them on foot—with a turban cloth wrapped around the left arm, to ward off their claws, while we take a kukri and slice them in half when they attack. Verily, this must be a demon, to be hunting men in such an unnatural manner."

That left Steele no argument. This beast was different from the vicious pests of Kashmir and Nepal.

While awaiting Achmet's return, Jang set to work with his kukri, chopping down bamboos and saplings to construct a shelter for the injured girl and her guardian. And presently Nur Mahal received first aid.

DESPITE STEELE'S EFFORTS, infection set in. For three days and nights he was at his wits' end, trying to use his sketchy medical knowledge to save the Kashmiri girl. When she was not delirious, she stared at the matting wall of her shelter, fatalistically resigned to the beast's return.

Powell was in a high-grade funk. "If she dies, we're jolly well blown up. The camp depends on your proving that a first-aid kit can beat this devil leopard, even if a rifle can't."

Steele somberly shook his head. "She'd pull through if she weren't sold on the idea that her number is up. So she has absolutely no resistance, no will to hang on. For all the good it's done, my taking care of her, I might as well have been out bushwhacking. Better, perhaps. If I nailed the leopard, she'd be on her feet in an hour."

"*Sahib*," Achmet cut in, "if Nur Mahal dies, I will then and there kill Kirby, or may Allah do as much to me, and more."

The burly Afghan meant exactly what he said. He was not blus-tering. He squatted on the ground, grimly fingering the hilt of his blade. That in no way lightened Steele's problem. Powell said, "You can't have that chap running around executing wizards. He's off his chump. I'm referring to Achmet, you understand. No doubt Kirby's a bit of a scoundrel, offering me forged credentials, but we can't have him butchered."

"Now, don't get tough with Achmet," Steele answered impa-tiently. "Not that I approve of his ideas any more than you do. But it wasn't so many years ago that fellows as smart as you are were burning witches—right in your home territory."

"Don't be absurd!" Powell snapped. "Couple of centuries ago, at least."

"Did you ever hear of the *Malleus Maleficarum?*" Steele persisted.

"No, and I'm sure I'd not want to. Who were they?"

"It was a book of instructions for detecting wizards, witches, and the like. Written in 1485—"

"Oh—of course. *Hammer of Evildoers.*" Powell had unraveled the title. "Beastly stuff, Latin. Strike me dead, but I could do with such a hammer in this camp. What about the blasted book? Filthy superstition, for an educated person."

Steele rubbed his chin. He eyed the restless girl, the Afghan who crouched like a beast ready to spring, and the harassed man-ager. "Powell," he went on finally, "there is something filthy in this jungle, but I'm not so sure it's superstition. The authors of the *Malleus Maleficarum—*"

"Collaboration, eh?" Powell was gnawing his mustaches.

"Right. Two priests. Iacobus Sprenger and Heinrich Kramer. I remember hearing quite a bit of one of their chapters quoted. About human beings that could assume animal forms—"

"By Jove!" Powell snapped to his feet. He choked, blinked. "Now you give me this blighted rot! I sent you out here to kill a leopard, not explain him. I—I—why—"

"What I meant was," Steele cut in, "that you mustn't be too impatient with Achmet—when people of our own race had similar notions, not so long ago, as history goes. Suppose you trot along and get some sleep, old fellow."

He took Powell's elbow, and edged him toward the door. At the threshold, he added in a whisper, "And keep an eye on Kirby. Don't tell him Achmet is making threats, but persuade him to quit his prowling around. It'd be awkward if this red-bearded ruffian did go off his chump!"

"Beastly awkward," Powell muttered as he stalked from the hut.

The tall Afghan moved from the foot of Nur Mahal's cot and toward the door.

"*Sahib*," he said, "now that these sons of wild pigs are gone, I will tell thee something. Be of good cheer. As long as you watch here, I also watch, and I shall slay no one as long as you are busy attending to her wounds as you once did mine."

Steele sighed. He was considerably relieved. "That's fine, Achmet."

"Later, there will be enough time to do that which is to be done," the Afghan explained.

VII

ANOTHER DEVIL-HAUNTED Burmese night, when every furtive stirring and twittering outside the hut frayed Steele's nerves. He was still watching beside the *nautch* girl's cot. A kerosene flare cast a flickering yellowish light on her immobile features. Every other resource having failed, Steele had administered opiates to blot out Nur Mahal's delirium.

Fear, rather than fever induced by infection, was the danger. If he could keep her from worrying herself to death, her natural vitality would have a chance. Her sister's fate, much more than her own injuries, held Nur Mahal's life in the balance.

Steele was nodding from weariness. He had been guarding a secret from Powell, and most of all from Achmet, who still squatted in the doorway. Only the haggard American had gotten a close look at Nur Mahal. He was no longer entirely certain that leopard claws and fangs had caused her wounds. The other victim, beyond any help, had been turned over to those who laid out the dead; the *nautch* girl was the first one to receive close scrutiny.

Steele had long since forgotten the difference between being asleep and awake. Nur Mahal, unevenly divided between terror and opium, was beginning to make him wonder what difference there was between life and death. And thinking of those curious wounds had ended by making him doubt whether more than a hair divided man and beast.

He cursed that treacherous memory which had exhumed the sense if not the exact words of Iacobus Sprenger and Heinrich Kramer. His first verdict on the opinions of the two German priests had been, "Wretched superstition!" Bit by bit he modified that to, "Logical, but impossible." And now he not only admitted the logic, but failed to deny the possibility.

Burma had been getting under his skin. The uncounted millions of malignant *nats*, the sorcerers who peopled the forest, the tattooed symbols the natives wore to counteract the oppression of Thagyâ-Min, Lord of Demon-Land: these things became increasingly real to Steele during his long vigil beside Nur Mahal. He told himself that oft-repeated suggestions were poisoning his mind. Then he asked himself, "But what suggested these things to the natives?"

The answer was remorseless enough: Burma and her breathing soil.

He started, jerked violently, and sat upright. Nur Mahal was stirring. As the opiate wore off, she murmured uneasily. Her thin hands, almost transparent in the light, rose in a clawing gesture. He could not understand what she said; he was not even sure that it was in Hindustani.

Steele fumbled for a cigarette. He had none. He glanced toward the door. The big Afghan no longer crouched at the entrance.

"Achmet!" He listened, heard no stirring outside, nor any reply. He raised his voice. "Achmet!"

The Afghan was beyond earshot, or he would have answered. His revolver lay on a packing-case near the door. It was loaded with the hand-cast silver bullets. He had apparently left his master a charmed weapon to take the place of the rifle which had so consistently failed.

And there was another inference: Achmet's pent-up wrath and fear had sent him out to settle Kirby.

The camp was beyond hailing distance. Steele could not abandon his patient for long enough to get in touch with Powell. He was trembling, not from any ordinary fear, but from a premonition. He began to feel that this eery drama was marching to a climax; that one careless move would undo all his work. But it would be almost as bad, if Achmet ran amuck and cut Kirby to pieces. Stolid, plodding British law would show the loyal fellow no consideration.

Steele reached for his rifle. He stepped out into the chilly mists of the jungle. The moon was clearing the treetops that fringed the clearing. The night had become a whirl of silver glamour and deception. No small animals made any disturbance, nor did any birds cry out or twitter. Strangely, the murmuring forest had become a tomb tenanted by a haggard man, and a girl who wavered between life and death.

Steele raised the heavy weapon to his shoulder. He fired one barrel, and as the clearing's farther side threw back the blast, he cut loose with the second charge. That would arouse Powell and the whole camp, and interfere with Achmet's plans.

The spare cartridges were on the improvised table, near Nur Mahal's cot. This was hardly more than three strides, but Steele had no chance to reload. The matting wall of the hut parted, and the spotted slayer entered. The beast flowed through the breach, and into the room.

For an instant they faced each other. The leopard snarled, and its tail lashed slowly. Its silken hide rippled, and its phosphorescent eyes radiated malevolence beyond that of any animal. From long experience with hunters, the beast knew that the rifle was empty; thus it was no longer necessary to wait for the watcher to doze. The only problem now was to take the choice of victims.

Steele was far heavier than the undersized Burmese the brute had carried away, or the frail *nautch* girl. In that instant of appraisal, he sensed what the leopard's choice would be. As the great cat whirled toward the cot, Steele snatched Achmet's revolver. He had to move too fast for any chance of aim.

The blast shook the flimsy shelter. Steele moved as in a nightmare in which time had ceased. Only split seconds had passed since he emptied the express rifle. Powell and his men would scarcely be on the way. It would all be over before they arrived.

The leopard wheeled from Nur Mahal. Any other of its kind would have fled, since a way of retreat was open; but Satan in a spotted coat had come to Kokogon, and Steele's blazing weapon had not yet left his hip when the beast lunged. This would be hand to hand. Whether or not he riddled the beast, the long fangs and raking claws would finish him.

He flung himself aside and thrust out the heavy revolver to ward off the attack. If that first leap missed, he had a chance.

The leopard shouldered Steele off balance, just as he jerked another shot. The barrel burst, half blinding him with flecks of burning powder. Achmet's hand-loaded cartridges had kicked back, leaving the gunner stunned and unarmed, the useless butt and warped breech mechanism in his bleeding hand.

The leopard, missing its victim, flashed in a silken arc through the doorway. Steele did not see it land and whirl, ready to close in again. He had snatched the rifle and was bounding toward the cartridges on the little table. Whether his trembling hands could shove them into the breech in time was an open question.

Then he heard a yell. Still fumbling with the shells, Steele sidestepped, facing the doorway. The crouching leopard's leap was checked before it fairly began. An arc of frosty metal blazed in the moonglow, and something dark dropped from the tree near the hut. It masked some of the beast's body.

There was a terrific snarling, a man's guttural voice, and the rise and fall of a blade. Achmet, dropping from overhead, had struck with his tulwar. As he hacked, he cried above the *chunk* of steel biting flesh, "I split him from end to end, *sahib!* Yea, the slayer and spoiler is slain!"

A huddle of fur twitched in a spreading pool of blood. Steele was dazed and trembling. In the distance, he heard shouting: Powell, and the chatter of natives aroused by the firing.

"Your silver bullets nearly finished me! The next time you load any cartridges, don't ram the slugs too tight. Not with smokeless powder, you big ape. That's a different matter from the kind you fellows use back home. But what were you doing up in that tree?"

The Afghan wiped his tulwar on his baggy trousers. "I hid there, *sahib*, knowing that you would presently call me. And when I did not answer, you would begin shouting 'damn,' after the fashion of the infidels, saving your honor's presence. Then the *shaitan*-leopard would know you were alone, and when he attacked—"

"Nice," said Steele, "except that he slipped from the rear, and nearly finished me before you got into action. But it worked, and—"

Then he saw Achmet's change of expression. His glance followed the Afghan's gesture. "Look—*ya chahar yar!* O Four Companions of the Holy Prophet! The demon leopard is becoming a man!"

STEELE STOOD THERE and watched it happen. He could not speak. He could only stare. The blood-splashed tawny body was becoming tenuous and misty. He could almost see through it. Its shape was altering, as though a figure of sea foam were slowly collapsing. When the dissolution was complete, he would know what was dark and solid beneath that thinning phantom shape.

Shrubbery crashed, torches flared. Powell and a dozen natives came on the run. "I say, what's all the shooting?" Then he saw Steele's face and Achmet's gesture, and the thing that lay on the red ground. Powell licked his lips and stuttered. "By Jove! The leopard. But it's collapsing. Like a blasted omelette, if you know what I mean."

Achmet was saying, "I betake me to the Lord of the Daybreak for refuge against Satan the Stoned! It is not a leopard, but a man!"

He was right. Kirby, slashed and stabbed, was now plain. He groaned and twisted. His lips were curled back in a snarl that showed his white teeth. Some incredible vitality still kept him alive. But the illusion of tawny fur and spots still persisted. That was what sickened Steele; he did not know whether this was a beast to be put out of its misery, or a human being who should get the last vain assistance which his own kind could render.

"Kirby!" Powell muttered, wiping the sweat from his forehead.

A snarl. A shudder. The phosphorescent eyes glazed. And as a match flame winking out, the last trace of illusion faded. The natives fled, screeching, now that their suspicions were confirmed. Dead or alive, a wizard is a fearsome thing. Achmet would have done the same, but if the *sahibs* could stand fast, so could he. But he muttered.

Finally Powell said, "Ghastly! Simply can't believe it, but there it was. Glad I saw it happen. If you'd told me this, I'd have been forced to conclude your man Achmet had made good his threat. That you were—ah—lying to save his hide."

Steele nodded and said nothing. Powell had to have reasons; what had happened upset all his convictions. He demanded, "How do you account for it? Why couldn't anyone kill it until now? Speak up, man! Blast it, you were telling me something about a chap named Sprenger, and another one, Kramer—here, the other night."

"So I was. Kirby himself dropped a hint the first day I arrived, though he probably wasn't aware of it. He told me that last season he aroused antagonism among some of the native wizards by felling a sacred tree which blocked a runway leading from the forest to the creek.

"But no one will ever know just how the wizards put a curse on Kirby, to make him prowl around at night and become a leopard."

"Curse!" Powell had to deny himself any admissions that would confirm what he had seen. "A leopard's body and bones can't become those of a man, and then change back again."

Steele smiled and made a helpless gesture, "Possibly not. What I mean is that what we saw was not actually leopard form. We saw

Kirby, and his beast-personality was uppermost, so strongly that
its impact made us for the moment visualize a leopard. Those
priests, Iacobus Sprenger and Heinrich Kramer, as I was on the
verge of telling you the other night, suggested that the transformation of human to animal is only apparent, because of a spell
laid upon the eyes of all beholders."

"Ah—you mean, this poor devil's obsession was so strong that
we joined him in believing? Like a bally hypnotist's suggestion?"

"That's as close to it as we can ever come," Steele answered.
"And it likewise hints at the reason for my rotten shooting. A lot of
it doubtless was nerves, the uncanniness of everything shaking me
in spite of myself. Then again, Kirby might not have been on all
fours. But with the leopard image so deeply burned into me, I
thought I saw a crouching beast, and fired accordingly. So I drove
the bullets between his knees, for instance."

Powell frowned, nodded, and muttered something about hypnotism. Having a definition put him more at ease. Then he looked
up and demanded, "But this Afghan chap? Very successful."

"When he dropped from the tree, milling that tulwar, he covered more ground than any number of bullets. Regardless of posture or illusion, Kirby could not avoid being slashed. And Kirby, I
think, could not have been conscious of what he did by night. The
poor devil was the most bewildered and harassed of us all, when
he shook off the leopard obsession and became himself."

Powell tugged at his mustaches. "Those blasted Burmese wizards!" he muttered, uneasily.

Then he said, "Nice work, old chap. I mean, your man Achmet
seems to have qualified for the reward. Frightfully embarrassing,
putting it that way, but he was swinging the tulwar, you know."

Steele sighed. "I'm glad I didn't win. With the way it turned
out, I couldn't accept it. Perhaps Kirby did have some underhanded
reason for offering you forged credentials, but God knows, he didn't
plan to become anything like that."

They turned to tell the tall Afghan that he had earned more
rupees than any of his clan had seen in generations; but Achmet

was no longer standing by. He was in the hut, kneeling beside the *nautch* girl.

"*El hamdulilahi!*" he was muttering. "Praise be to Allah, the fever is gone and Satan the Stoned has flown away."

She was still unconscious, but he would be there when the opiate lost its hold.

Powell said to Steele, "Lucky beggar, that chap. Seems as though he'll be collecting a double reward."

COACHWHIP PUBLICATIONS

COACHWHIPBOOKS.COM

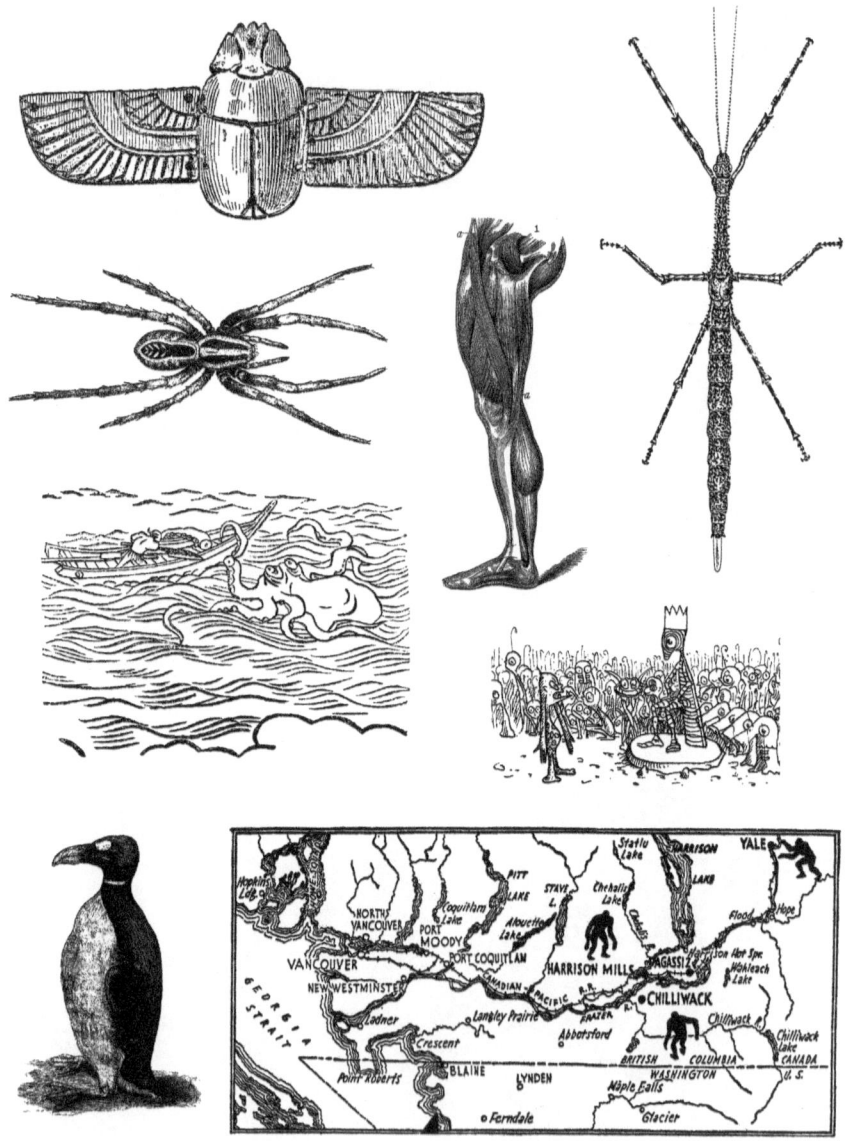

Wulf: Tales of Wolves and Werewolves

ISBN 1-61646-056-3

COACHWHIP PUBLICATIONS

ALSO AVAILABLE

Shadows Gothic and Grotesque

ISBN 1-61646-059-8

COACHWHIP PUBLICATIONS

ALSO AVAILABLE

Ancient Haunts

ISBN 1-61646-005-9